GREEN MOUNTAIN HEARTS

The Complete Trilogy

CAMERON D GARRIEPY

For anyone who believes
—even a little bit—
in magic.

GREEN MOUNTAIN HEARTS

Ambitious Heart

BOOK ONE

Chapter One

____

There were few things Marnie Burnham loved more than a bluebird day in January, when a fresh flurry sugared the week-old slush and the late afternoon sun gilded the frosted mountains that stood sentry over the village of Blueberry Hill.

The second Thursday of January in 2002 was going to the top of her list. Not only were the makings of a storybook sunset assembling over the far distant Adirondacks, but she'd spent the cloudless day on the slopes with her dad, testing out the new Burton demo board he'd gotten in at the pro shop, and tonight... Tonight, after a hundred years, the lease on the Blueberry Hill Grange Hall expired, and per town ordinance, the board of selectmen could re-designate the property for public use.

Marnie Burnham had a plan.

She dodged a patch of ice, tightening her grip on the sheaf of paperwork tucked under her arm. Her iBook was fully charged, ready to plug into the projection system she'd borrowed from the Thornton College tech library. If she was using a bedsheet as a display, well, Truman Bixby and the rest of the board would just have to excuse her lack of professional presentation equipment.

Her phone rang, and Marnie stopped to perch on the bench

outside Karly's Klips while she took the call. The name on the display brought a smile to her face.

"Sam!" Marnie tucked the phone between her cheek and sat on the file folders to keep them from blowing away. "I got your email earlier. How was the first day of subbing? Those kids don't know how lucky they are."

"I'm the lucky one." Samantha Ellis was her oldest friend. Oldest and farthest away. Sam was at Tulane getting a masters in education, and in Marnie's opinion, not seeing nearly enough live jazz. "The kids are great, my graduate program is great, and I'm volunteering through a charitable foundation sponsored by the Lacroix family, which is kind of a big deal."

"You know what else is a big deal?" Marnie grinned, winding up for a well-used inside joke.

"Live music in New Orleans," Sam said with a sigh. "I know. I promise. Maybe I'll ask Craig to go with me."

"Did you just bury a man-lede on the second Thursday of January in 2002?" Marnie resisted the urge to shriek. Selectman Bixby was a block away headed for the town offices. "I wish you could be here tonight to watch me convince that bunch of fossils to give the one-woman Blueberry Hill Farmer's Market Committee the Grange Hall...right before I grill you about *Craig*."

"I'm sure you won't forget to do that as soon as it's over," Sam said. "And I wish I could be there, too. Now go set up your magic. I love you, crazy lady."

Marnie was about to hang up the call when a shiny mid-size pickup with New York plates growled to a stop outside Video Visions and more than six well-filled-out feet of Viking-meets-surfer dropped down from the driver's side.

"I'm going, but before I do, let me say that a Toyota Tacoma just parked outside Jim Dix's video store like he owned the place, and I'm thinking about including myself as a rider on the contract, if you know what I mean."

Sam's laugh was loud enough through the phone that the surfer Viking turned in Marnie's direction, catching her in the act of checking him out. His face was in shadow, but she got the impression of a strong profile, and holy hell, he wore glasses. Seriously sexy frames and a low, not-too-long ponytail of dirty blond hair; a body built for pillaging dressed in a crisp button down and wool pants that fit like they'd been tailored.

Who was this guy and what on earth was he doing in Blueberry Hill, Vermont?

"Helloooooo? Marnie," Sam said, maybe for the second or third time. "I'm hanging up. I love you. Good luck!"

"Thanks, Sam. Talk soon!" Marnie flipped her phone shut and shoved it toward the bottom of her bag, sucking in a lungful of cold air to clear her head. She had a room of selectmen and townsfolk to wow.

What Marnie lacked in resources, she more than made up for in passion and forward thinking. Her mother's homemade soaps and cleaning products flew out of the baskets and bins in the refurbished pop-up trailer she towed around to county fairs all summer. Local folks knocked on the Burnhams' back door, and the general store over in Catmint Gap sold out weekly. The Beasleys' honey was legendary as far south as the Deerfield Fair, and any number of veggie patches and chicken coops around town traded and sold goods between neighbors in their foothills hamlet.

All across the state, farmers markets were cropping up and expanding like wild mushrooms. Blueberry Hill was near a major ski area, a good-sized college town, and the Appalachian trail, and there were a bunch of local farms, orchards, and crafters around who could anchor a diverse market. The kind of market that could support a micro-economy if it ran year-round, and where better to run year round than in the Blueberry Hill Grange Hall, a wide open indoor space that would belong to the town as of midnight.

"Marnie!"

Marnie spun around to find her mother rushing down the sidewalk, a cloud of scarves and graying curls floating around her face like a corona in the sunset.

"Hey, Mama Llama, you ready?"

"I slipped into the town meeting room earlier this afternoon and worked a little charm for favorable outcomes, I have samples in a basket to leave near the door and some notes for my testimonial–" Daphne Potter caught Marnie's brewing interruption and cut her off. "No love potions in the shampoo, promise, and I won't even bring up that I'm your mother. Did you wear your sapphires?"

Marnie sighed and touched the sapphire chip earrings her parents gave her for her sixteenth birthday. "Because they're the nicest ones I have, Mom."

"They're lucky." Her mother *tsk*'d. "You have magic in your blood, Marnie. All the Potter women have it. You shouldn't knock it 'til you try it."

"I'm a Burnham, Mom."

Her mother muttered something about the patriarchy as she drifted past her on a bergamot scented cloud, patting Marnie's cheek as she passed.

It took twenty minutes to hang up the white sheet, find a suitable place to set up the projector and get her iBook connected. She tested her PowerPoint slideshow, went through her notes, and fidgeted with her dress's hem. The straight sheath style with the short–but not too short–skirt was the most adult thing she owned, bought for job interviews after college a few years before. She'd debated showing up in her usual uniform of thrift store flannel, bootcut jeans, and Bean boots, but she wanted the board to take her seriously.

It was an eternity waiting through the shuffling of seats, the reading of minutes, and the discussion of a minor change to the dog licensing bylaws. Finally, Truman Bixby announced the matter of the Grange Hall lease.

"The terms of the Pinckney estate stipulate that we must hear proposals for the use of the hall prior to the close of the hundred-year Grange Hall lease period. The town will then choose, at the discretion of the board of selectmen, which proposal to grant the next lease period to and for how long. If no feasible proposal is offered, the land reverts to the town to dispose of as it sees fit."

Tom Crawford hefted his portly frame out of his chair and

announced the Blueberry Hill Farmer's Market Committee. Marnie ignored the smattering of laughter from the assembled crowd as she walked to the front of the room.

"Good evening, Selectman Bixby, Selectman Crawford, the assembled board, friends, neighbors." She paused to snatch a breath and squeeze her fingers together to quell her anxiety. "I'm fairly certain I know everyone here, but I'll introduce myself anyway." Her gaze fell on the Viking surfer from New York, as if on cue. He sat in the third row, his hair gilded by the terrible overhead lighting in the meeting room, his expression carefully neutral. He did have a strong profile, but a gentle mouth, with laugh lines, or maybe too-much-time in-the-sun lines. "I'm Marnie Burnham, founder of the Blueberry Hill Farmer's Market Committee, and I propose the Grange Hall be turned into a year-round open market for regional crafters, farmers, and artisans to create a local micro-economy that serves both community interests and tourism demands. If you'll all indulge me, I've prepared a short presentation."

As she spoke the jittery nerves melted away. The technology actually behaved, and the presentation went off without a hitch. Even her mother, with her hippie folk magic vibe, managed to stay on message, and people around town did love the soaps.

"Thank you all for your time. I hope you'll consider this proposal to enrich our community in spirit and in commerce."

She took her seat, and let her hands and feet shake the way they'd wanted to for the last twenty minutes.

Arlene Levesque stood, prim and formal as she'd been twenty years before when she'd taught Marnie's Kindergarten class. "The number of proposals submitted in advance was a matter of public record. We had planned to hear three tonight, but the two remaining have withdrawn, citing financial reasons." Arlene's brow creased slightly as she surveyed the room. "If there is anyone in the audience this evening with a proposal to add, we will hear it now, otherwise I think I speak for the board when I say Marnie Burnham's passion for the marketplace certainly grants her at least a short term lease to try the idea out."

Marnie's heart flipped over in her chest and she bit her lip to keep from letting her joy get the better of her volume control. There was no way anyone in the room would take this away from her. Not now.

"Excuse me, Madame Selectman, members of the board." The Viking surfer stood, tugging at his cuffs and clearing his throat. "My name is Micah Reynolds, representing Simmons-Doyle Development of Albany. My firm is prepared to buy the property outright at 110% of market value for the development of a boutique micro-hotel property, should the board decide not to grant a lease."

Marnie's pulse slowed and the floor seemed to fall away beneath her, even as she straightened her spine and stared the handsome stranger down for the second time that day. This time, she didn't see a long-legged, seafaring god. The man who'd just offered the town a fortune in exchange for her dream resembled nothing so much as a flint-eyed marauder.

Chapter Two

As Blueberry Hill's town meeting erupted around him, Micah Reynolds lowered himself into his folding chair with a sigh. His knees bumped the seat in front of him, and his shoulders took up too much space, which didn't matter, since the people on either side of him were standing now, shouting at the board of selectmen seated at the front of the room.

The older woman cleared her throat and spoke, settling the room with a quiet authority Micah admired. "That will be all. This is unexpected, and unprecedented."

"It's bullshit," a voice proclaimed from the back.

"Language, Theodore," the woman said. "The board will need time to review this offer's validity under the terms of the Pinckney estate's bequest, as well as its potential merits. We'll reconvene in a week's time." A buzz of conversation started to build up around him again, but she raised an eyebrow in Micah's direction and spoke over the din without shouting. "I assume you will be available for consultation, should we have questions between now and then, Mr. Reynolds?"

"Yes, Ma'am," Micah said, though he was sure she couldn't actually hear him over the noise.

She nodded, proving him wrong, and resumed her seat to confer with her colleagues. The meeting, whether intentionally or not, was over, and Micah seized the opportunity, using his size to part the crowd and make his way out to the street. There was at least one muffled curse in his direction, and a covert shoulder shove or two along the way; Micah breathed a sigh of relief when he reached the sidewalk.

Darkness had fallen while the meeting was in progress. Edging into the shadows, Micah relaxed against the corner of the town hall to take in the view, recalling the night sky's familiar patterns from his years at nearby Thornton College. He'd been looking forward to this trip ever since the partners had assigned him this property. He hadn't been back to Vermont in the three years since he'd graduated, and he'd been hoping to wrap things up quickly, get in some snowboarding, maybe play tourist a bit before it was back to Albany with a signed contract to hand to the architects and project managers.

The double doors opened behind him, spilling out townsfolk whose voices dropped when they caught sight of him. He fidgeted with his coat and gloves, wishing he'd grabbed a hat. He'd stumbled into a hornets' nest, that much was clear. The beautiful–and young, she had to be close to his age–Farmer's Market Committee chairwoman was a factor that hadn't come up in his research on the property.

It was a unique situation. Originally built in 1898 by Boston philanthropist Oscar Pinckney on a parcel of land he owned in the center of Blueberry Hill, the Grange Hall was technically a private property, held in a trust managed by the town. Pinckney opened it to public use, and left it to the Blueberry Hill chapter of the National Grange of the Order of Patrons of Husbandry in his will as a one hundred year lease, which would revert to the town upon its termination.

What Pinckney and the Grange never considered was that the Grange chapter wouldn't survive the twentieth century, that Blueberry Hill's population would shrink, that agriculture would change. The building had been vacant for nearly a decade, maintained against the merciless nature of New England's climate as best the trust could manage, but otherwise falling to neglect.

Fading like a beautiful old woman, overlooked by passersby.

Clusters of locals formed and dispersed along the block, carrying snatches of opinions on the night air, none of them pleasant. The farmer's market wasn't their champion, he realized. It was her. The passionate committee of one.

If he hadn't been in Blueberry Hill to broker a real estate deal that effectively shut her proposal down, he'd have supported the farmer's market concept. It was sound business, and the way Marnie Whoever-She-Was looked presenting a PowerPoint on a bed sheet in a little black dress and shiny blonde hair in a messy twist, talking about local apiaries and dairy concerns would stay with him long after he'd driven down the mountain to his hotel outside of Rutland.

"It won't work, you know."

Micah dropped his gaze from the stars and met blazing fury.

"I'll find a way to stop this." Marnie Whoever-She-Was stood, far too close for comfort, barely five-five in her now snow-booted feet, her low-heeled shoes dangling from one hand while the other waved to encompass the entire town center. "You can't just waltz in here with a million dollars or whatever and destroy a town for fun and profit."

Her eyes weren't green or brown, but a fascinating pale shade somewhere between. Her rage was stunning. And justified. But he was only the messenger, and suddenly weary of the dirty looks cast his way from all sides.

"Actually, it happens all the time," he said, pushing up from the wall and tugging at the cuffs of his coat. "My firm handles a hundred of these transactions a year. I've done my homework, Ms..."

"Burnham. Marnie Burnham." She stumbled a little on her own name, a sure sign, in Micah's experience, that he had the upper hand.

"Ms. Burnham." He fished the keys to his truck out of his coat pocket and slipped past her, determined not to notice the hurt creeping in near the edges of her anger. "The cash influx and the resulting tourist dollars, never mind the jobs the project will bring to the area, far outweigh an unproven experiment in communal agriculture. I suspect your board of selectmen already knows that, but it's kind of them to humor the hometown girl."

He refused to look back. It was bad enough he'd spoken to Marnie Burnham like that. What was worse was the instinct to run back and beg her forgiveness.

____

"Then, he just walks away, tossing his keys in his hand like it's a done deal." Marnie smeared a thick layer of cream cheese on an everything bagel and chased an ibuprofen with a slurp of coffee so light and sweet it was basically over-caffeinated milk.

"Shit, Marn." Stu King, above whose eponymous diner Marnie lived, topped off the milk in her mug, followed by a splash of coffee. He nudged the sugar shaker her way as he swung around to tack up an order and put up a fresh pot of coffee. "I know folks give you a hard time, but some kid from outta town stealing your thunder like that ain't right."

Marnie poured a sizable waterfall of sugar into her mug, then took a bite of her bagel. Three days earlier, Stu told her over the same breakfast order that folks just weren't going to shop in the Grange Hall for fancy cheese when you could get Cracker Barrel down at the Grand Union for half the price. Cabot if your snotty sister-in-law Libby from Connecticut was coming for Thanksgiving.

Just the same, Stu's words echoed the toasts and encouragements to which she'd drowned her maelstrom of feelings the night before over at the Tipsy Catamount. She winced, recalling the bar napkin with a rather lurid likeness of Micah Reynolds of Albany penned on it that ended up pinned to the dartboard behind several aggressive games. None of which she won.

Maybe Micah Reynolds had done his homework. Maybe he knew something she didn't about the laws. Maybe he had a fat checkbook at his disposal. But he'd done more for her cause in one brief statement to the board than she could have managed in a year of door-to-door canvassing and hours of stupid PowerPoints.

He'd given Blueberry Hill a common enemy.

She finished her bagel and downed her coffee, determined not to let the Grange Hall situation ruin a perfectly good day.

Twenty minutes later, she was exceeding the speed limit around the last hairpin turn that dropped into the Singing Bowl Ski Area parking lot. She parked her Jeep 4x4 near the lodge and dropped the keys in the cupholder. Good luck to the thief who tried to take it. The clutch was delicate, to say the least.

Her dad was hours ahead of her, bustling around the rental shop, setting up the day's pre-ordered rental gear. He raised a hand and grinned in greeting.

"Heard you had a night, sweetheart."

Marnie dropped her duffel behind the counter. "Something like that. Am I in or out today?"

"Out. Lucky duck," her dad said. "Assignments are up."

The whiteboard behind the rental counter told her she had three private lessons, two on skis and one on a board, which meant tips–and another chance to take that Burton for a few runs. Tips, a sweet ride, and a soft, overcast day, though she'd smelled snow on the air in the parking lot. Might just be enough to forget Micah Reynolds for a few hours.

"I'm going to suit up and grab some coffee before the family lesson."

"Marnie?"

"Yeah, Dad?"

"I'm proud of what you're trying to do with the Grange. No matter what happens."

Tears prickled in the bridge of her nose. "Me too, Dad. See you later."

By the time she'd taught her lessons, including an impromptu lunch with the family from South Carolina at the snack bar on Flycatcher Summit, and stowed the borrowed board back in the ski shop lock-up, her dad had gone home for the day and the snow she'd smelled in the morning was falling softly.

There was a note for her on her staff locker that read, "Call your mother."

The phone in her dad's office was somewhat private. Marnie grabbed the worn backpack that served as purse, briefcase, and gym bag most days and closed herself in.

"Marnie!" her mom sounded out of breath. "Where are you?"

"At work. Where else would I be?"

"Arlene Levesque called here looking for you when you didn't answer at your apartment. They want to meet with you and that young man from Albany."

"Okay..." Marnie wedged the phone between her chin and shoulder and applied a quick layer of deodorant with her shirt half up on one side. "When?"

She switched sides to her mother's exasperated shriek.

"What, Mama Pajama? I didn't catch that?"

"I said, 'In a half hour.'"

"Oh, shit," Marnie dropped the stick of Secret into the backpack. "Why didn't you say? At Town Hall? I can be there in twenty minutes."

"Not without driving like a bat out of heck, you can't, young lady. There's a charm on your Jeep, but it's not going to keep you safe if the whole thing goes off the ravine on the way through Catmint Gap."

"Twenty-five. Gotta go, Mom."

Even on her snow tires, she did drive like a bat out of *heck*, parking the Jeep in her spot behind King's Diner with a minute to spare. She was four minutes late to the board's meeting by the time she mushed across the common and burst through the meeting room doors.

"Sorry I'm late. I was working today down at Singing Bowl, I didn't get the message until five and the roads are starting to get a little messy."

Unlike the previous evening's formal proceedings, this meeting was just the board and her opposition gathered around the long folding table the board typically sat behind. All eyes were on Marnie as she hurried toward the only empty seat. The one Micah Reynolds stood and pulled out for her, as if he were a gentleman, instead of a heartless raider.

Chapter Four

Micah wasn't sure what he'd expected to see when Marnie Burnham pushed through the double doors to Blueberry Hill's town hall meeting room, but a wind-burned winter goddess wasn't it.

The polished, sheath-dress-wearing, small town glamour girl was gone, replaced by a ski lodge siren in a flannel button down and down vest. Her athletic stride was encased in snowboard pants, and slush clung to a sturdy pair of L.L. Bean winter boots.

Marnie's hair was braided in matched pigtails under a knit hat bearing the Singing Bowl Ski Staff insignia. He'd skied nearly every mountain in the state over four years, but Singing Bowl gave Thornton College students a generous pass discount, so he'd spent a lot of free afternoons learning moguls on Flycatcher's Flight or taking lazy-turn cruises down Twilight Notch Road.

She snatched the folding chair from him and scootched it closer to Arlene Leveque's seat. "So," she said, looking around the table, skipping over him as though he weren't there. "What's going on?"

He wasn't proud of what was about to happen here.

Selectman Bixby tapped a stack of papers and clipped them together. He cleared his throat. "Marnie, we asked you both here because there's been a development with the Grange Hall."

At the word development, Micah watched Marnie's spine stiffen. She sensed everything was about to go wrong.

"Mr. Bixby, I–"

"Let him finish, *Miss* Burnham," a younger woman, maybe ten years older than Micah, snapped. Micah couldn't see Marnie's silent reply, but he read the answer to whatever Marnie hadn't said aloud in the other woman's face.

"We had a call from Mr. Reynold's partners in Albany this morning. It seems they had some additional information they neglected to share in their initial proposal." Bixby narrowed his eyes a touch at this, and Micah felt the weight of it. It was a cheap maneuver. "Simmon-Doyle claims the Pinckney bequest is invalid due to a prior claim of ownership, and they have a descendant of that owner living in Ohio who's willing to sell to them if a court decides in their favor."

"That's bullshit, Mr. Bixby."

"Language, Marnie," Arlene Levesque whispered, laying a hand on Marnie's arm.

Truman Bixby turned on Micah. "It's a difficult position, Mr. Reynolds, as I'm sure you can appreciate. Blueberry Hill is a small, working class town. We don't have the resources to mount a massive legal case to protect the Grange Hall, from developers *or* bluffers, and your firm knows it. Our safest bet from a purely dollars-and-cents standpoint is to sell to you and wash our hands of the whole thing, but I'll tell you, son, that leaves a bad taste in my mouth."

Marnie Burnham shot up from her folding chair so fast it fell backwards with a bang and a clatter. "Give me a shot. I'll do the research." She wheeled on him next. "This isn't over. You can't just have it, no matter how many sneaky little surprises you've got rolled up your sleeves. Please, Mr. Bixby, Mrs. Levesque. Mr. Crawford." Marnie turned to the sour-faced thirty-something who'd scolded her. "Tina. Please. Give me a chance to try."

Some of the others might have shot her down, but Arlene Levesque stood up and took command of the table. "Seven days, Marnie. Come back and tell us what you've discovered."

Micah wanted to applaud, but there was no way she'd take it as anything but snide. He was utterly smitten by this woman, and it was literally his job to smash her hopes at every turn.

He got to his feet as unnoticeably as possible and shrugged on his coat. "If you'll excuse me. Selectman Bixby, you know where to reach me."

He exited the town hall into a proper snow storm. The gentle, steady snow that had fallen since later afternoon now whirled and danced on gusts of mountain wind, piling up against cars and buildings.

It was going to be a long, slow drive down to Rutland.

He turned the engine over to warm the truck up and was met with nothing, not even the telltale clicks and whirs of common engine failures.

"What the hell?"

Micah popped the hood and got out of the truck. He wasn't sure why. He was no mechanic, but it seemed the thing to do under the circumstances.

He stared at the unresponsive guts of the Tacoma for a long moment before the town hall doors opened again and Marnie Burnham stormed out. She stopped short when she saw him, helpless under the hood of his truck while the snow crusted his eyelashes and frosted his shoulders.

She cocked her hip and framed him with her fingers. "I call this one, 'Poetic Justice.'"

"Funny." He slammed the hood. "Hell of a night for the truck not to start. I don't suppose you'd tell me where I could find a phone?"

"If we were friends, I'd let you use my cell phone." She took a few steps closer to him and grinned—though the glint in her chameleon eyes said otherwise—seemingly unaffected by the swirling snow. "But it wouldn't work anyway, since the signal's dicey to begin with up here, never mind in a storm. I don't recommend the Tipsy Catamount, but if you've got a quarter, there's a payphone at King's Diner."

"I've got change in the truck."

"Then you're all set, aren't you?" She stuck her hands, cozy in a pair of wool mittens, in the pockets of her vest, and spun on her boot heels.

"Marnie." She paused mid-spin. "I'm sorry, for all of this. I just thought I was coming up here to present a proposal to buy an old building from a quirky town. I didn't know about your Farmer's Market."

She appraised him, the storm appearing to slow down and bend around her as she looked him over and found him lacking. "Sure. Whatever. Stu closes soon. You better go make your phone call."

Micah waited at the mercy of the storm until Marnie made her way safely down the street and into the very bar she'd warned him away from before heading in the direction of the corner lunch-style diner with the flashing neon *OPEN* sign in its frosted and fogged window.

The place smelled predictably of hot griddle and stale coffee, but as promised, there was a payphone by the door. It wasn't until his quarter was in hand that Micah realized it was six o'clock on a Friday and even if Shawn still worked at Thornton Auto, he'd probably been off the clock for a few hours now.

He dropped the coin into the phone and opened his wallet for his hotel key card. He'd call the Holiday Inn and find out if he had any options.

Five minutes later it was clear he had precious few options. He hung up the phone and grabbed the end stool, reluctantly asking for a mug of past-due coffee from a tired waitress named Nikki.

"You need sugar?"

He stirred listlessly. "Lots."

"I hate to ask," she said, sliding the sugar shaker his way, "but we're closing in a few, and I need to close the register." She tore a receipt off her pad and slipped it down next to his mug.

"No problem. Hey–" Micah laid down a five from his wallet to cover the coffee and get more change for a tip and the phone

"Yeah?"

"Is there a B&B in town or anything? My truck broke down and I'm supposed to be staying down in Rutland tonight. I don't know anyone in town, and..."

"Oh, hon." Nikki scooped up his five dollar bill. "That sucks. There's a couple of small places, mostly outside of town, though, and I don't know how you'd get there even if there was room. You know, I've got a comfy couch. I might be willing to take in a pretty stray."

Shit. Not part of his game plan at all.

"You ought to toss him out on his gorgeous behind," said a voice from behind him.

Micah spun on his stool to find the soap maker who'd spoken at the town meeting. She was shorter than average, with a cloud of gray-threaded pale brown hair, and a hippie fashion aesthetic that reminded him of his favorite college history professor. She smelled like a summer forest, even in the middle of a greasy spoon.

"I think you're right about that, ma'am." He offered her his hand. "Micah Reynolds."

"Daphne Potter. And I know who you are, and why Nikki there ought to leave your rear end in a snow drift."

"You're the soap maker. I remember you from the meeting." She had a firm handshake for a small woman.

"My husband–that's him over there–and I..." She waved at a booth, and a tall, lanky bald man waved back at them. "We're awful eavesdroppers and we can't just leave you stranded in the middle of a storm. We live about a mile out of town on Old Quarry View Road. We've got a loft over my workshop with its own entrance and a private bath. You're welcome to it if you don't mind riding out there with Max and me."

Nikki returned with his change. He left a full price tip on his untouched coffee and decided that this week couldn't get any weirder, and if it got worse, it probably wasn't going to be with an aging hippie couple and their homestead soap factory.

"I'd be grateful, Ms. Potter."

"It's Daphne, Micah." She cocked her head like a bird and gazed at the air around him intently for a moment. "You've got a better aura than your actions suggest. Otherwise, I might have left you in a snow-bank, too. C'mon. Let's get you settled before we have to shovel out the Subaru."

As he grabbed his coat and followed Daphne and Max out of King's Diner, Micah was already questioning his decision.

Chapter Five
————————

Marnie wasn't really in the mood for the Tipsy Catamount for a second night in a row, but she'd needed to make a strong exit. A well-nursed hard cider and a few pool games later, she'd made her point and settled her tab.

She took a meandering route back to her apartment over the diner, meaning to clear a little of the snow off the Jeep and flip up the wipers to save herself some time in the morning, but the snow had stopped and it was still early. The clouds were moving off, leaving behind a clear, moonless sky and a soft, silent village under at least eight or nine inches of snow since afternoon.

She grabbed the shovel she kept behind the seats in the winter and burned off the cider buzz digging out around the Jeep's tires, accepting a pat on the back from her morning self, who could take a little time over breakfast before a day spent researching how to run Micah Reynolds out of town, preferably on the end of something pointy.

On her way around the corner to her apartment, Kurt Blake flagged her down from the cab of his plow.

"Hey, Marnie."

"Hey. K.B.. Good night for business."

"Yeah, well," Kurt leaned out of the cab of the truck. "I've been seeing Jen Miller some, and I'd rather be seeing more tonight than out moving snow, but it pays the bills, you know?"

Marnie did know, but she really didn't want to hear about it. "Sure."

"Anyways, I noticed your folks over at Stu's place a while ago when I was in for a refill." He showed her his Thermos. "They were getting into the Subaru with that asshole from the meeting. Heading out toward your folks' place. Seemed weird to me, but you know how your mom is."

Marnie narrowed her eyes. "How *exactly* is my mom, K.B.?"

Kurt pulled his head and shoulder back inside the truck. "Hey, hey. Nothing like that. Just she's kinda, well, anyway, I thought you'd want to know, seeing as how he's looking to mess up your fancy market plans."

"Right. Sure. Yeah. Thanks." What the *heck* was Micah Reynolds doing with her parents?

"Jesus, Marnie. Ease up. See you 'round." Kurt put the plow truck in gear and moved along.

Her cell phone was as useless as she'd told Micah it would be. She took the stairs to her apartment two at a time and breathlessly dialed her parents' number, forgetting that her mother hated the phone ringing "late," and turned the ringer off on the kitchen phone–the only one she ever turned on at all–after dinner.

Out the window, she caught sight of Kurt's plow making a final pass of the downtown before heading out in the general direction of the farmhouse Jen Miller shared with a couple of girls they'd gone to school with.

The way Marnie saw it, she had two choices: stay up all night stewing, or drive out Old Quarry View Road and find out for herself.

Chapter Six

The loft was, as promised, in possession of a separate entrance and a private bathroom, but it took Micah nearly an hour to get there once the Subaru pulled in at 972 Old Quarry View Road. Daphne Potter insisted on feeding him leftover chicken stew first, then packing him a basket of toiletries–sage and cedar scented, very manly, he was assured–for the shower.

Max let him use the phone to leave a message for Shawn, or whoever might be able to come tow the Tacoma down to Thornton for repairs in the morning, after which Daphne met him with tea and brownies.

He was halfway up the exterior stairs to the loft over the barn when a pair of headlights cut through the dark. Micah put a hand out to shade his eyes.

Without cutting the engine, the driver opened the door, and Marnie Burnham emerged from the light. "What the hell are you doing at my parents' house?"

He took a step backwards and up. "Your parents what?"

"House." She advanced on him. "Where they live."

"Wait."

"No." She kept coming.

Micah backed up the stairs, fumbling for the doorknob.

"It's not enough for you to march into our town meeting like you own the place already, then double down with that shady invalid bequest story. Now you've scammed my parents into taking care of you?"

She was relentless. Gorgeous and passionate, but relentless. And maybe crazy. "Listen. It's freezing, and you're engine's still running. Can we talk about this inside?"

She muttered something under her breath and clomped back to the Jeep to yank the keys from the ignition.

Micah turned the doorknob and felt for a light switch. Unlike the cozy country feel of the main house, the loft was uncluttered and modern. Marnie stomped up the stairs behind him and pushed past him into the loft, toeing off her boots and making herself at home.

She sat down heavily on a low-profile sofa and put her wool sock feet up on the coffee table. "So?"

Micah paced the length of the room. The view from the large picture window was almost surreal. Even without moonlight, the snow was bright on the yard, glimmering unblemished from the forest around the property. "Did you grow up here?"

"Of course." She shifted to lean over the back of the sofa. "Why? Don't change the subject."

"Isn't your last name Burnham? Daphne said hers was Potter, and–"

Marnie laughed. It was a bitter laugh, but not unkind. "And she didn't even mention at the meeting that she was my mom. She kept her maiden name. My dad's last name is Burnham, but I bet she never let him get a word in edgewise."

"I went to the diner. They were there. They insisted."

"Sit," Marnie said. "You're too tall."

Micah settled gingerly on the arm of a nearby chair. It had been a long day. He'd spent the bulk of it in his hotel room arguing against the firm pushing the less honest part of their agenda, but Marnie didn't need to know that. He'd lost that argument with the partners, and his job wouldn't be worth the stock his business cards were printed on if he didn't see his share of the project through.

He desperately wanted a hot shower with some of Daphne Potter's soap and a decent night's sleep.

He'd have settled for a world where he and Marnie weren't enemies and this conservation would end with the two of them naked and somewhere more private than in front of the picture window in her parents' spare loft–though if she kept looking at him the way she was, he'd concede the picture window.

He was saved from his wayward thoughts by Daphne Potter, who walked right in–she did own the place–bearing a tray filled with bottled hard cider, a plate of muffins, and a vase of rust-colored blossoms with long, deep green stems and leaves. She blew a kiss to her daughter and set the tray down on the peninsula that formed the kitchenette.

"Hi, sweetie. Dad saw your Jeep. We figured you two had some talking to do. Snacks always help. Snacks and alstroemeria. Don't stay up too late." She was gone again before Micah could thank her.

"Whose side is she on?" Marnie was watching the space her mother had previously occupied with baffled intensity.

Micah took the opportunity to stand again. The arm of the chair was the wrong place for his long legs. He grabbed the two bottles of cider and brought one back to Marnie before returning to the view out the window.

"It's really beautiful up here."

"It is beautiful," Marnie said, standing to open the bottle and toss the cap expertly into the trash can. "It's also my home. And it's dying. Most of the people I grew up with left. The ones that are left are struggling. The median age is rising, and businesses are closing." She sat back down, resting her elbows on her knees and dangling the bottle. "I'm trying to find a way to make our community better, to make it a place people want to settle in. What you're doing will just kill it."

"Bullshit." He took a long drink to avoid yelling at her. "The hotel would bring in jobs, bring in tourists. Put Blueberry Hill on the map, make you part of the ski area's ecosystem."

"Sure," Marnie countered. "For a few years, until Singing Bowl trends out, like all the little places do. We're not Killington or Stowe. Once the next new thing comes along, the hotel will fail–"

"It won't–"

"It might take ten years to run all the way into the ground, but it will fail." She sipped off the bottle, her expression grim and serious. "And the jobs will dry up. The businesses and the housing that popped up around it will die with it, except this time people will have come here for work and they'll be stuck in mortgages they can't afford, and there will be empty houses and devalued land. And you'll be long gone, probably a partner drafting contracts or golfing or whatever you people do, married to some Jennifer with two and half kids or whatever, and I literally can't imagine where I'll be, because there won't be anything for me here, and this is the only place I've ever wanted to call home."

She'd prowled the room like a big cat while she talked, holding him in place with her eyes and the apocalyptic future she laid at his feet.

"Why are you telling me this?"

She stopped, shaking her head. "Honestly? I don't know. It's not like I'm going to change your mind."

"What if you had? Changed my mind?" He'd *lost* his goddamn mind, but there was something witchy in her amber eyes. Or he was really, really drunk on a single hard cider.

"That's a dick move, even for you." Those eyes flashed and she closed the remaining distance between them. "Get me talking, get my guard down, then tell me you're going to change your mind and take it all back. *Right*. Then I back down, and BOOM. Your firm takes the Grange, and I lose. Nice try."

She barely stood taller than his shoulder in her sock feet. She had to tilt her chin to look him in the eyes up close. He smelled snow and wool in her hair, and the deeper woodsier scent of her skin. It made him dizzy.

"I mean it," he said. "I don't want any of that to happen. I just came to do my job. I didn't even know this place existed until last month, even though I lived in Thornton for four years."

"You're a Thornton College alum?" Marnie stepped back.

"That's why I got assigned to handle the contract. The partners thought I 'had a knowledge of the area.'"

"When did you graduate?"

"Ninety-eight. Why?"

Marnie laughed the bitter laugh again. "Did you ski Singing Bowl while you were a student?"

"Yeah. Of course. It was the best deal going, on top of being a lot of fun. Why?"

"A lot of this town works for the mountain, one way or the other, and you've never even heard of us. Hell, I probably checked your lift ticket once or twice and you and your buddies Kip, Trip, and Skip didn't even notice me."

"Hey, easy." She cut a little too close to the truth for comfort. "I didn't know anyone named Kip or Skip."

Miraculously, the truth pierced her armor. Marnie started to laugh. She held out her bottle for him to hold. Marnie laughing reminded Micah of sunlight through stained glass. The glass was objectively beautiful on its own, but when the light struck it, it became something luminous and otherworldly.

He waited while her laughter ran its course. When she had her breath again, she took the cider bottle back.

"Sorry. It was that or throw something, but you're funny." She drained the bottle and walked back to the peninsula to put it on the tray. "Viking marauders aren't supposed to be funny."

"Viking marauders?" Had she really just said that?

"Shit." Marnie turned around, cheeks flaming. "I said that out loud. Well, just look at you." She waved her hands at him. "You're too tall and you have more shoulders than is fair, and I'm pretty sure Thor is looking for his hair..."

Her praise, awkwardly flung at him as it was, stoked the fire her nearness kindled in him.

"I have three days off," he said, deliberately not acknowledging her compliments. "I'll help you look for information, if you promise not to rat me out. I'll come back to the table when it's time and pretend I don't know anything about it and you'll win and my firm will think I've done everything I can."

Marnie narrowed her eyes at him. "What's the catch?"

You, he wanted to say. *I get to be close to you. Torture myself with daydreams about us together. Try to make you laugh like that again. Get you to kiss me instead of insulting me.*

"No catch." He took advantage of his longer stride and crossed the room to take her hand. "I meant what I said back in town. I'm sorry about all of this. If I can help, I will. I just don't want to lose my job over it."

Marnie stared at their hands, then at his face. He liked the way her fingers felt twined with his, the way their bodies brushed when she leaned back to look up at him. Her lips parted, and if he leaned in, he could be kissing her.

"I'm turning into a lightweight," she said, taking her hand back. "Because I am definitely drunk. Or crazy. I'll take your help, I'll keep your dirty secret for the fun of sticking it to the corporate pirates who want to spoil my town, and I'll even win gracefully."

She gave him a little mock curtsy and Micah was fairly certain he was more than half in love with her.

"I'm sure you will."

"I'm going to crash at Daphne and Max's," Marnie said, yawning broadly. "Get some sleep, Viking. We've got a lot of work ahead of us."

Chapter Seven

Marnie woke to the smell of coffee and bacon, which was normal, since she lived over a diner. The lavender and lemon scented sheets, however, were not normal, nor was the unchecked sunlight pouring over her bed.

When her father started singing Creedence Clearwater Revival songs offstage in an off-key baritone, the previous evening came roaring back to her.

What the *heck* had been in those ciders?

She scrounged around in her childhood closet for abandoned clothes before heading downstairs to find her mother collecting dirty kitchen towels while her father cooked–and rocked out over a cast iron skillet.

"Morning, Mama Drama."

"Morning, sweetie. Why don't you go over to the barn and wake Micah for breakfast. Your father says he can ski today on a guest pass if you're going to be busy." Her mother took a basket of laundry down the basement stairs.

"Maybe he doesn't ski," Marnie said, knowing full well she was wrong about Micah and sneaking some bacon from the plate at her father's elbow. "He's got to get his truck fixed, and I'm sure there are a million reasons he should scram. Not the least of which being he is really not welcome here."

She'd had two drinks over a couple of hours and decided to join forces with the enemy to save the Grange Hall. There had to be something she was missing. Trouble was, her gut said there wasn't.

"That's no way to treat a guest, Marnie," her father said. "Go offer him some food. If he's going to be stuck here while they fix the truck, the least we can do is be kind."

"Dad, he's trying to undo the last year of my life." Maybe, if she remembered their conversation correctly, and the deliciously hungry look in his eyes just before she'd ducked away, that wasn't strictly true, but her parents didn't need to know that just yet.

"He's here for business that happens to be at odds with your goals, my girl. Maybe if we show him what a nice place Blueberry Hill is, he'll see that Simmons-Doyle's proposed plan is all wrong and take it off the table."

Marnie poured herself a mug of coffee. "Maybe Mrs. Levesque will take up pole dancing at the Tipsy Cat on Wednesdays, too."

Her mother reappeared, empty handed and shocked, but also amused, if the sparkle in her eye was any indicator. "Marnie!"

Her father only shook his head. "Go on over to the barn and ask Micah if he'd like to join us for breakfast."

Marnie complied, shoving her feet into her boots and jogging across the driveway and up the stairs. She rapped twice and let herself in, pleased somehow that the city boy hadn't locked the door. "Micah?"

She'd made a rambling comment about Thor the night before, but the joke dried up on her tongue. The bathroom door opened and the Norse god himself emerged, one of her mother's colorfully woven Turkish bath towels wrapped around his hips. The effect was devastating. His wet hair was still shedding droplets down his shoulders and into the fine gold hair on his chest and *holy cats*, he could probably bench press her.

There are things I'd rather do with those muscles...

"Whoa, hey." His hand went to the gather of the towel. "I didn't hear you come in."

Marnie could barely hear herself think over her own heartbeat. "Sorry. My parents are making breakfast. Come on over if you're hungry. When you're dressed, of course."

She was staring, and it was obvious.

The corner of his mouth lifted. "It's a little cold to drop in for breakfast in a towel, even if it is the nicest towel I've ever used."

"Mom spent a few years in Istanbul. She brought a bunch home. Before I was born." She tore her eyes away from the sunlight tangling with the lingering dampness on his skin. He'd used her mother's sage and cedar soap; Marnie could smell it across the room. A decent number of men she knew used it, but this was the first time she'd ever wondered what it would taste like. "I'll see you at the house."

Chapter Eight

By the time Marnie dropped him off outside Thornton Auto Body, Micah wasn't entirely sure which way was up. Breakfast with Daphne and Max and their beautiful, complicated daughter was delicious and ridiculous. Max had offered to take him skiing for the day. Daphne wanted to draw up his astrological chart, and right up until Marnie insisted on driving him to Thornton to talk to Shawn, who not only still worked at the garage, but had sent a tow truck up early on a Saturday to collect the Tacoma, she'd treated him like dirt on her insulated boots.

Marnie drove her Jeep exactly the way Micah predicted she would. Just this side of reckless, enjoying every moment, pointing out local points of interest on the roads through town. Once they cleared Blueberry Hill's town line, she slipped the clutch into fifth gear and opened the engine like it was a European performance car, cranking up a live Phish show on her tape deck.

Micah watched the winding road rush by, accompanied by a stream on one side and the steep incline of the mountain on the other. The roads were clear, the asphalt dark and wet, but the sun was out and the snow pack was already compressing as it thawed.

"Sorry about the little show in the kitchen," Marnie said, "but if you want this to stay any kind of secret, my mother is not a great ally. Her greatest triumph in that department might be not revealing to you that I was her daughter."

He gathered his hair back in a tail and wrapped a hair tie around before pulling his hat over his head. "That was an unintentional secret, right?"

"Exactly." Marnie's gaze flicked away from the road to give him a lopsided grin. "I want to start in the county records, which are archived at the Thornton Public Library. I'll drop you off at the garage. You can meet me there when you're done."

"I was thinking about dropping by the history department at the college," Micah said. "I took a class on Ethan Allen and Benedict Arnold during January term one year. My professor was really into local history. I bet she's got something to say about Oscar Pinckney. Maybe it'll help. I can find you after. Maybe we can grab lunch?"

"Sounds good."

"It's a date–"

They spoke over one another. He hadn't meant *date*, had he? He'd said it, though, and no one knew them in Thornton.

They pulled in at Thornton Auto Body, and Micah had no choice but to get out of the Jeep and wish her good luck on her research. Watching her drive away, he decided it would be a good idea to call in for his messages. He needed to ground himself a little.

Too much time around Marnie Burnham was actually intoxicating.

Shawn hadn't had a chance to get under the hood of the pickup, but promised to call his hotel in Rutland when he had an update. Micah set off on foot for the Thornton College campus, about a mile away on a ridge west of downtown Thornton. He started in the library, where he used his old student ID to access a phone and call his office phone to retrieve his voicemails from the office.

His boss wanted to know if the Blueberry Hill "thing" was settled, and there were calls about two other deals he was involved in that he'd need to give some attention to when he was back in Albany next week.

On his way to the History Department offices, he chewed on that reality. He'd been in Vermont for less than forty-eight hours and everything was upside-down and sideways. He was going to need to figure out where he was sleeping until the truck got fixed, and if he was being honest, he didn't want to go back to Rutland alone when he and Marnie were done today.

He wanted to go back to Blueberry Hill with her. He wanted to light a fire in the wood stove in the loft, settle into the sofa, and coax her into his arms.

This was insane.

Professor Case was in her office, which was lucky, given that it was January term. She was happy to see a former student, and happier still to tell him everything she knew about Oscar Pinckney, which unfortunately focused more on his relationship to Thornton and its railway-heiress benefactress, Faye Bartram. She did say that her research had uncovered some uncomfortable truths about his dealings with the local populations, including some unscrupulous land grabs and exploitative contracts.

His heart sank. He knew the legal team at Simmons-Doyle were generally pretty thorough. Chances were, this tactic was above-board, even if the way they were using it was completely shitty. Marnie wasn't going to be happy.

Marnie was alone in the reading room at the Thornton Public library, surrounded by a set of massive record ledgers that looked far too new to be the ones they needed. He waved and raised a silent brow at her reading material.

"Copies," she said, her library voice pitched low and soft. It shivered up his spine like a caress. He was pathetic. "These are county land transactions from 1875-1907. So far, I haven't found anything that even mentions Blueberry Hill."

"Let's get lunch. I'll fill you in on my chat with Professor Case. Maybe we can figure out where to look from there."

Marnie asked the librarian to hold her materials for an hour. They got a table at a sandwich shop in the old millworks, and he told her what he'd learned.

"It's so weird that I can't find anything. Blueberry Hill is definitely part of the county, there were settlers there before the Civil War. I double checked with the librarian before I started." She puffed a stray curl away from her eyes. "Hey, so what's going on with your truck?"

He repeated Shawn's lack of answer.

Marnie opened a bag of chips and offered it to him without meeting his eyes. "I'm sure you can stay another night in the loft if you need to."

"Should I call your parents and ask?"

Marnie finally looked at him, a flush on her cheeks. "I'm making an executive decision. I'll even drive you back."

That seemed like flirting

"How can I thank you?" He was flirting back. He couldn't help it. She was such a temptation. Today she looked like a college student herself, hair in a messy bun, worn Johnson State College tee hugging her body, and jeans with flannel lining rolled up over her snow boots.

Their lunch order was called, and Marnie jumped up to go get it. Micah cursed himself for being too obvious.

They were nearly done with their sandwiches when a Thornton Student paused at their table. "I didn't mean to eavesdrop, but you said something about Blueberry Hill being part of this county but not in the records. You know, it used to be called Doddstown, and the town line was closer to the village center. And the whole north side was part of Catmint Gap until the 1890s. Oscar Pinckney bought the village parcel and renamed it because his mistress liked to pick blueberries in the woods near Gooseneck Creek."

Marnie nearly choked on her sandwich.

"How do you know all that?" Micah asked.

"Thesis research," the kid said. "Hope it helps. I gotta go."

"Thanks," Marnie called. She turned to Micah with wide eyes. "I grew up there and never knew that. So we need to go back to those transactions and look for Doddstown."

"So we do," Micah said. And he would go wherever she asked until he had to go back to New York.

Chapter Nine

Marnie parked the car outside her parents barn under a quilt of night-dark clouds. The student tip had paid off. They'd celebrated the discovery of a bill of sale–drawn up between one Emory Dodd of Doddstown, Vermont, and Oscar Pinckney of Boston, Massachusetts for a parcel of 200 acres of hillside and farmland–by driving down to Rutland to check Micah out of his Holiday Inn and bring his things back to the loft until Tuesday, when Shawn would have the truck fixed.

On Monday, she could bring the research to the board of selectmen and it would all be over. Micah could go home, and she could get started building the Blueberry Hill Farmer's Market.

Micah climbed out of the Jeep and grabbed his bag. In the cold light of the barn's exterior flood lamps, his features were stern, but a day with him had shown Marnie where to look for the softness.

"Do you want to come up?"

She played it cool, but her heart hammered behind her ribs. "Let me say hello to the parentals first."

The lights were on in the kitchen, but the only parental affection that greeted her was a note in her mother's looping handwriting that read, "Pottery show in Waitsfield. Leftover roast chicken in the fridge. Cider in the workshop cooler. You two kids have fun. Love, Us"

She hadn't actually told her mother either one of them was returning to the house on Old Quarry View. Marnie didn't literally believe her mother's tales of family magic, but her mother did see right through people sometimes.

Marnie left the food, planning to ask Micah if he was hungry. She took the steps two at a time, and pushed the door open to find him on the other side of it, hands braced on the door jamb.

"Micah. I–"

The kiss was sudden, but her body had been waiting for it almost since the moment she'd laid eyes on him two days before. His touch was gentle, but his lips plundered. Marnie wrapped her arms around his shoulders and stretched up to meet him, matching the kiss until they both came up for air.

A quiet laugh rumbled low in his chest, sexy as hell. "We're letting the heat out," he said, and drew her inside.

Marnie pulled the door closed behind her, unsure of what to do with her limbs in the empty space where Micah had been. "Daphne and Max took off for the evening, but they left food."

"Do you know what I've been thinking about all day?"

The look in Micah's eyes gave Marnie a few clues.

"The wood stove." He crossed the room and crouched in front of the old cast iron stove in the corner. It opened with a reluctant creak, then Micah was loading firewood inside and pulling a long match out of the basket on the hearth.

"The wood stove?"

The flame flickered and caught. He adjusted the levers for the flu and set the screen across the open door. When he turned around, there was fresh firelight in his hair and a predatory gleam in his expression that sent a thrill along Marnie's skin.

"The wood stove, you, that sofa." Three long strides and he was right there, a touch away. "I can't get you out of my head. One kiss isn't nearly enough, Marnie."

On that they could agree. "So, I'll just leave the leftovers in the kitchen for now..."

He laughed, wrapping his arms around her waist and resting his cheek against her temple. His laughter gave way to a delicate exploration. His lips traced her hairline while his hands caressed the topography of her ribcage and hips. A deep coil of tension began to unwind even as desire raced through her blood like lightning.

He whispered a path of kisses along the underside of her jaw before claiming her lips again. Unlike the impulsive kiss in the doorway, this was a careful seduction. Micah took his time. Where she sighed, his touch lingered. When her lips parted in invitation, he sampled, letting her lead him.

Time stretched as they moved together, peeling away their outerwear and collapsing together on the couch. Recalling the view from that morning, Marnie slipped her hands under the hem of his tee shirt, smiling to herself when his stomach muscles tightened at her touch. She skimmed her palms over his nipples and nipped his lower lip when he sucked in a breath.

His hands found their way to the waistband of her jeans, and the lovely ache of lust between her thighs leveled up. She wrestled him out of his button-down and tee; he helped her shimmy out of her jeans and fleece.

Rationally, Marnie knew it was just hormones. It had been a while, and sure, she was certainly capable of the basics on her own. But *damn*, his skin felt good.

When she shivered, he pulled an afghan over them and held her closer against his big, warm body. Her heart whispered, *just hormones?*

She straddled him, letting the afghan fall away, leaning down to kiss him. His hands came up inside her tank top and when his fingers brushed her nipples she rocked against him with a breathy sound she didn't even recognize as her own voice.

He tugged the fabric aside to kiss the curve of one breast while caressing the other through her top. Marnie arched into his touch, letting him take her weight when his teeth scraped the sensitive tips of her breasts and stars burst at the corners of her vision.

The hard length of him was anchored between her thighs. He

wanted her; she knew it as surely as she knew she wanted him, but she hesitated. There was something tender and unhurried about how he handled her, something inexplicably sexy about the barriers of his unbuttoned, rumpled khakis and her underwear and the fragile newness of their bond.

His clever hands abandoned her breasts to gently unwrap her hair tie. He threaded his fingers through her unruly mop of not-quite-curls, massaging her neck and combing out the braids. "Your hair is gorgeous," he whispered, before scraping his teeth over her earlobe.

Marnie traced a stray lock of his Viking surfer hair that clung to the golden scruff on his jaw. "I like yours better."

She lost track of how long they made out on the couch, half dressed and tangled under the blanket, but her stomach complained, reminding them both that they'd skipped a meal in favor of one another.

Micah rolled them over, tucking her into the sofa before grabbing his cable knit sweater from where it lay discarded on the coffee table and pulling it over his head.

"I'll go over to the house for the food."

"You can't miss it," she called as he slipped out the door.

For a moment, she snuggled in the cozy hollow made by their bodies, but his absence left a void for cool clarity to creep in. This was crazy. She sat up, tugged the afghan around her shoulders and combed through her hair.

He wasn't gone long enough for the mood to escape completely, though. He'd piled the leftovers in the roasting pan and hauled the whole damn chicken across the yard, complete with a stop for a couple of bottled ciders from her mother's stash in the workshop.

"It's cold out there," he said, setting his loot on the floor by the stove. "Come over here and eat."

Marnie dragged the blanket with her to the spot on the rug near the hearth where Micah was unpacking containers of her mom's garlic and olive oil roasted potatoes and chunks of fennel that had cooked in the pan with the chicken. There was bread, too. Whatever ability her mother possessed, Marnie blessed it and tore off the heel of the bread to drag through the chicken juices.

Micah opened the bottles and handed her one. He was more fastidious, searching out cutlery from the kitchenette and carving off slices of the bird.

She watched him covertly while they ate, delighted by the contrasts of his warrior physique and gentle manners.

"Are you from Albany originally?" she asked.

"New Jersey. My folks are still there, in the Tudor-style house a mile from my dad's country club where I grew up." He stuck a fork in the fennel and tasted. "This is fantastic. My sister lives in the same town. My brother lives in Colorado."

Once she'd cracked him open, his stories poured out. They talked by the fire as the first sliver of new moon rose over the loft. Her stories wove into his, and she found herself wishing that Sam were here to meet him, to tell her if it was really possible to feel this connected to someone after so little time.

Sam was far away in New Orleans, and there was someone called Craig there with her.

As they'd traded histories by the fire, Micah had gathered her into his arms again, twisting one of her wayward half-curls between his fingers and punctuating their conversation with languid kisses.

Marnie wasn't sure when she'd drifted into sleep, but the sun woke her, streaming in through the picture window. Her toes were freezing and her shoulders were stiff, but she didn't dare break the dreamy cocoon they'd made there on the floor until Micah stirred next to her.

He pushed his hair out of his face, kissed her and said, "Let's go skiing today."

She blinked, wondering briefly if she'd missed good morning, but it didn't really matter. The sun was up, the skies were clear, and she had another day off.

Ignoring the very real possibility she had absolute dragon breath, she kissed him back, then poked him in the sternum. "I snowboard. I'll teach you."

Chapter Ten

When Micah woke on Monday morning, Marnie was once again asleep half on top of him, but this time they were in the bed. He stretched, gently extricating himself from her sleep-heavy limbs. A glance at the clock told him Marnie's alarm would go off any minute.

She had to be at Singing Bowl early to open the lodge, and Micah planned to do some more research on Doddstown, and be back to pick her up after work.

She wanted to call a meeting with the selectmen that evening to present them with the evidence. He knew she was only thrilled to have her shot at the Grange Hall and her farmer's market vision, but the truth was, once that business was concluded and his truck was repaired, his life was several hours away in Albany.

Without the intimacy of being co-conspirators, without the almost magical quality of Max and Daphne's loft, would they feel the same?

He didn't know. Not when the time they had together was winding down at an alarming rate. Instead, he replayed their conversation from the night before. She'd pushed him hard all day, getting him fitted for a rental snowboard and taking him through her typical lesson plan–though admittedly with more breaks to make out with the instructor on the chairlift than he hoped she was used to.

He didn't know if he'd ever ride a lift again without remembering the way the wind tasted on Marnie Burnham's lips.

They'd stopped at her apartment over the diner so she could shower and change. He'd entertained filthy fantasies of joining her in the cheap, cramped fiberglass enclosure and answering his body's more impatient questions.

As if she'd paged through his NC-17 thoughts, she'd leaned back against her bathroom door and said, "I just want you to know that there's a big part of me that wants to drag you in here with me and get us both very clean and more than a little dirty."

He groaned. She was killing him.

"But that would complicate something good, and you have to go back to Albany tomorrow." She turned the knob and slipped into the bathroom, peeking back around the door with a saucy grin. "Consolation prize, Viking: call in a pizza from Zorba's and I'll definitely let you get to third."

The old-fashioned alarm clock on the dresser rattled and rang. He swung his legs out of the bed and shut it off. Marnie propped herself up on her elbows and squinted at the clock face. "I'll call in sick. We can do something fun before I meet with the board."

"You can't call in sick. Everyone you work with and half the town saw us together yesterday," he said, crawling into the bed and pulling the quilt up around them. "But I'm sure I can find at least a few places I haven't kissed you before you have to go."

She stretched, pressing her body to his, from toes to lips. "I dare you."

Her camisole had ridden up in her sleep, revealing the flat expanse of her belly and the tantalizing curve of one breast. Micah decided he would start there.

She lent him the Jeep for the day in exchange for a ride to work, and Micah took off for Thornton, hoping to use the college library again to connect with his office. He dropped in at Thornton Auto Body just as Shawn was bringing his truck out of the bay.

"I was just about to call you," Shawn said.

Micah didn't like the look on his mechanic's face. "What's up?"

"I had a couple of repairs come in on Saturday. Had to bump yours to the end of the day, so I didn't get under the hood until this morning." He looked back over his shoulder at the truck. "I feel shitty about it man. I could've had this back to you an hour after you dropped it off. Someone has a pretty sick sense of humor."

"What do you mean?" The truck didn't look like it had been mistreated.

"There were signs your hood was jimmied, and someone yanked a bunch of your spark plug leads and put them back wrong. It's mean, but no real harm done. Looks like a breakdown. Not your fault you're not a car guy, man. You wouldn't have known to check."

"And whoever did it was banking on that." Micah didn't like the gut-punched feeling stealing over him.

"I hate to even charge you for it," Shawn said.

"Don't worry about that," Micah replied, trying his best to keep his tone light. "I'm in town on business. I can actually expense some of the repairs, since it happened where I was for a meeting on Friday night."

"I appreciate that, man." Shawn tossed him the keys. "I did put a quart of oil in there and check your fluids. You should be good to go. I'll have Benny write up an invoice and we'll get you back on the road."

Friday night, while he'd been inside the Town Hall with Marnie and the board, some local asshole—or assholes—had fucked with his engine to make him look like an idiot. And what local girl had strutted off to the town watering hole, warning him to stay away, just after taunting him about *poetic justice*?

Jesus. They'd spent the weekend together. She'd gotten her goons all riled up, then what? Set them loose and played dumb when they struck. Had her way with him all weekend. Gotten him to betray his company and help her sink the deal. Christ, he'd thought it was his idea.

Shawn emerged from the office with a carbon paper slip and a manual credit card imprinter. Another day Micah would have laughed at the outdated technology.

"Shawn, what would it cost me to have a couple of your guys run this Jeep up to Singing Bowl and leave the keys at the staff lounge, so I can get on the road right away?"

Chapter Eleven

Marnie's shift ended at three. She'd worked lift lines all day and her fingers were freezing. She cruised through the staff lounge for coffee and to wait for Micah to pick her up, but her dad cut her off at the entrance.

"What happened with Micah?"

Marnie's heart flipped over in her chest. "What do you mean?"

"Your Jeep is in the lot, and Carol at the Snack Shack said some guy in a mechanic's jumper dropped it off a few hours ago with instructions to make sure you got the keys." Her dad fished her keyring out of his parka pocket. "Carol saw me at lunch and gave them to me. They said you were working the line on Dark Side of the Moon."

"I was." She took the keychain, and unease skittered down her spine. She stared at her keys, as though they carried a message she couldn't read. "He's fine, but I don't understand this."

"You had a little of your mother going there just now," her dad said, motioning at her face. "But then again, Grandma Potter took one look at me the day I walked into her bookstore and said, 'Took you long enough, Maxwell.'"

Marnie usually shared an eye-roll with her dad over her parents' meet-cute, involving her maternal grandmother's perpetually struggling bookstore-slash-wiccan-supply-store and the newly arrived retail manager at Singing Bowl Ski Area who was just looking for a map book for his car, but with the keys silently jangling in her palm and Micah inexplicably not there to pick her up, her thoughts were spinning.

"I'm going to go, Dad. Love you."

Charm or no charm on the Jeep, Marnie took the mountain road back to Blueberry Hill as fast as she dared. Her apartment was cold and empty, but the answering machine light was blinking.

"Hey Marn, it's Sam. I tried your cell, but it's going straight to voicemail and the box is full, so...Anyway, I had a weird feeling like you might need to talk. I'm at work until four my time, but I'll be home all night. Call me, okay?"

Maybe she and her best friend were switched at birth: Sam was far witchier than she was.

Marnie contemplated picking up the phone and pouring her heart out, but she was supposed to meet with Mrs. Levesque and Mr. Bixby to present her findings at five and the folder with their research in it was at the loft...

Shit.

The folder. She'd just left it there, trusting as a lamb.

A shower would have to wait. The old guard had met with her in her mountain gear before, they could do it again.

The mile drive to her parents' place took no more than five minutes under normal circumstances, but normal circumstances didn't account for a modular home transport convoy crawling out Old Quarry View. Marnie pounded the steering wheel and swung the Jeep around. She could loop around downtown, take the Catmint Gap Road and cut through Old Man Strickland's hunting camp. The Jeep could handle his overbuilt ATV trails, and she'd end up in her parents' back forty.

It wouldn't take any longer than sitting still behind three wide-load flatbeds full of some pre-fab monstrosity.

Or it wouldn't have if Steve Carney weren't out shining his brand new Sheriffs badge on Catmint Gap Road. He let her off with a warning, but the pull-over for speeding cost her time.

"So much for your charms, Mama Bahama," Marnie muttered as she turned up the Strickland's camp lane.

Even with the ridiculous slow downs, she'd still made it back before her dad, but her mother was–if the smell of lye was any indication–in her workshop in the barn. Marnie killed the engine and tiptoed up the stairs to the loft.

She'd fully expected the plain manilla folder to be gone, or empty, but it was exactly where they'd left it on Saturday afternoon when they'd returned triumphant from the Thornton library. Marnie thumbed through the papers, but the copies were all there. The register page where the transaction was recorded, the handwritten bill of sale–surprising given Oscar Pinckney's history as a tycoon of sorts, but Dodd *had* been a hill country farmer.

It was all there. The proof she needed to repudiate Simmons-Doyle's claims that the land was never Pinckney's to build on or bequeath. So why had Micah left? And without a word?

She swallowed hard against the threat of tears and checked the clock on the microwave. *Screw him.* Time to go get the Grange Hall back for her farmer's market.

Chapter Twelve

Micah shared an office with another junior associate at Simmons-Doyle. They'd always gotten along fine, but by the time he'd stormed south on the Northway, the day was more than half over, and he wasn't in the mood for small talk.

He'd come to his senses somewhere around Saratoga Springs, pulling over at the next rest stop to call Marnie and make some excuse for bailing on her. He rehearsed it for a few miles, but no amount of practice made it sound any less lame, and there was no way he was going to admit he'd thought she'd deliberately ordered the sabotage. Not for a moment.

Once more, he'd found himself at a payphone with no one to call. He and Marnie had fallen into their weekend out of time without any of the usual courtships. He didn't have her number. Or her parents' number, or her address over the diner–though that he could get once he was back in Albany.

Banging the receiver into the cradle, he'd turned back for the truck.

Carter was working on a strip mall in Schenectady, and wanted his feedback. There were emails and messages, and his boss wanted a word about a potential main street rehab project over the border in Pittsfield.

When Micah finally grabbed a moment to call the operator for the Potter-Burnham's home, he realized Marnie was already sitting down with the Blueberry Hill board of selectmen.

What would she think of him?

"Give 'em hell, Marnie," he whispered.

"Hey, Reynolds?" Carter swung into their office, RedBull in hand. "We're heading to Maloney's in fifteen. Janelle's working tonight. You in?"

He was seriously considering driving back to Blueberry Hill, but the smart decision would be a good night's sleep in his own bed before he tracked Marnie down to plead his case.

"Go on. I'll catch up."

Carter raised his can in salute. "Don't stay too long. Vic's got his eye on her."

Micah nodded, but he knew he wouldn't follow his colleagues. He picked up the phone and dialed directory assistance to get Marnie's number.

When Marnie's voice answered at her apartment, he almost jumped the gun. There was laughter in her recorded message. He missed her acutely.

"Hey, it's Marnie. I'm probably out having more fun than you. Leave a message. I'll call you back if you tell me how."

He took a deep breath and waited for the tone.

Chapter Thirteen

Truman Bixby perched his glasses on the tip of his nose and re-read the last of Marnie's papers. Marnie sat forward on her folding chair, unable to stop tapping her heel on the floor.

Arlene Levesque closed her leather folio. "Truman, this is more than I expected. In essence, Pinckney bought the village as we know it, and it's likely the Doddstown name fell out of use around the same time. Our formal incorporation is relatively new, almost the beginning of World War I, so it never occurred to me to look beyond that for clues. I can't imagine this Albany developer would have any such insight."

"So you think they were bluffing to strong-arm us?" Mr. Bixby took off his glasses, folded them, and tucked them in his jacket pocket.

"I think we need to see Mr...." Mrs. Levesque opened her folio to check Micah's name.

"Reynolds," Marnie said.

"Yes, Reynolds. We need him back here to discuss some of the details in this file." Mrs. Levesque closed the folio again. "Excellent work, Marnie. I'm impressed."

Marnie flushed. Mrs. Levesque was her first teacher; she couldn't help feeling proud.

"Thank you. I just want what's best for Blueberry Hill."

"We've heard quite a lot about your interpretation of what's best, Miss Burnham," Truman Bixby remarked.

"Truman." Mrs. Levesque barely raised her voice. She stood. "Marnie, we appreciate the work you did, and will consider it carefully, along with the rest of the board. I don't think any of us wants to do business with a company that would stoop so low, regardless of the short-term outcome."

"Thank you both." Marnie rose and said polite goodnights before escaping into the cold stillness outside.

The stillness didn't last long. Kurt Blake's pickup rumbled into downtown, and Jen Miller spilled out of the cab. The seat flipped forward and Jen's roommate Nikki crawled out. Kurt came around the other side with Will Dryer in tow.

Kurt slowed when he saw her, and Marnie recalled she'd been a little edgy on Friday night when she'd seen him outside her apartment.

"Hey, K.B., Jen," she said. They'd all grown up within a grade or two of one another. There were worse people to celebrate reclaiming a piece of their hometown with, and Micah's disappearance ached. "Hi, Nikki. Long time, no see, Will."

"Marnie!" Will ran over and scooped her up in a long hug. "I hoped you'd still be around."

"I might roam, but I'll always come back here," she said, as he set her down. "How's Montana?"

"Far away, but I love the ranch, and I'm playing some hockey, so..." Will shrugged. He shoved his hands in his pockets and glanced at a spot over her shoulder. "How's Sam?"

"Getting her Masters. Subbing in a private school." Marnie hooked her arm through Will's and fell into step behind K.B., Jen, and Nikki, in the general direction of the Tipsy Catamount. She wouldn't mention that Sam was casually dropping the name Craig these days, just like she wouldn't mention to Sam that Will had been back in town. Too complicated. "Buy me a beer, and I'll catch you up."

"K.B. says you're turning the whole town upside down lately."

It felt good to have a friend by her side. "Buy a second round, and I'll tell you the whole story."

Will stopped, searching for something in Marnie's face. "Folks talk, Marn. Pretty sure the whole story might take more than two."

Chapter Fourteen

When Marnie didn't call right back, Micah packed up a few files from the office and drove to his Jay Street apartment. His studio apartment felt cramped and stuffy after Daphne and Max's airy loft, and lonely without Marnie's easy laughter.

He called in a Thai food order and booted up his computer. Blueberry Hill's Grange Hall was a small project, relatively speaking. He had market research to do on a major acquisition proposal, and the partners were making noises about promotions. He knew Blueberry Hill was going to fall through; it was in his best interests to have the Pittsfield ducks in a row.

He'd left his company cell number on Marnie's machine. The phone was with him in Vermont, but the cell signals were awful in the mountains, so he'd barely turned it on in days. Regretting not leaving his land line number, as well, Micah set the phone on his desk and tried not to let thoughts of her distract him from getting to work.

A few false starts in that direction led him to Daphne's rudimentary website, which listed her products and where to buy them, as well as a link to her LiveJournal, which detailed her adventures in homespun magic. Micah clicked around on Singing Bowl's website, hoping to catch a photo of Marnie, but she eluded him.

When he searched for the Blueberry Hill Farmer's Market Committee, he hit pay dirt. There she was, with her mother at their booth at a local market. There were photos of local farmers, beekeepers, potters, and bakers. It was a well laid out site, if bare bones.

He clicked the *News* tab, and read her proposal. She'd uploaded images of her PowerPoint slides. A punch of longing hit him in the chest, and he fought the urge once again to get in the truck and drive back to Vermont right then and there.

Instead, he closed the browser window and started over again, this time determined to stay on track with his work.

Page after page of real estate transactions and market research clicked away as he made notes on a legal pad. His food was delivered and eaten in a haze, and Blueberry Hill faded into the background. Micah worked himself to the brink of falling asleep on his keyboard, and crashed on his comforter, fully dressed.

His cell phone woke him. The persistent ringtone was disorienting after a few days of silence, and he fumbled for the phone too long to catch the call. He scrolled to his missed call, heart in his throat, hoping it was Marnie.

Instead, there was a message from Barney MacMillan, his boss at Simmons-Doyle, calling to tell him he was being sent to Syracuse with a team that was going to close on a pair of shopping malls the firm was going to acquire and rebrand.

"I want you on this team for the experience, Reynolds. Pack a bag and be at the office for nine. Our shuttle pick-up is at ten and I want you to go over the details with the team."

Only a week before, Micah would have been thrilled to be picked for a trip like this. It was a tacit tap for a promotion. Now he looked at his day planner and realized that he'd be gone for the final meeting of the Blueberry Hill board of selectmen. Hopefully, Marnie had already convinced them, and the meeting would only be a formality, but he'd hoped to be there.

He'd wanted to see the triumph on her face.

He'd wanted to celebrate with her afterward.

He'd wanted her.

Instead, he'd been the village laughingstock, and hadn't trusted Marnie enough to ask questions before he let his pride get behind the wheel.

Micah turned on the coffee maker and started the shower. Barney would notice if he didn't shave before he left for the office.

Marnie woke up in someone else's bed with a jackhammer inside her skull, wearing someone else's boxers and a UVM tee shirt. The sheets smelled clean, and the room was familiar, but she couldn't quite place it.

She sat up too quickly and the walls lurched, along with her stomach. Her clothes from the day before were carefully folded over the back of a hideous green paisley armchair near the door.

Will's room. What the?

Clutching the wall and the ugly chair, Marnie managed to get herself into the rest of her clothes. She hadn't been upstairs in the Dryers' house since middle school, and they'd definitely redecorated since she and Will had built a motorized, scale model of the solar system for seventh grade science class. The awful chair had been in the living room back then. Had her head not been in the process of detaching from her neck, she'd have laughed at it ending up in Will's room.

The bathroom, if she remembered correctly, was down the hall on the right.

A cold water splash and some found toothpaste on her finger helped. She scrounged up some ibuprofen and picked through a nasty knot in her hair while she took stock of the previous night's events.

They'd gone to the Tipsy Catamount. Will bought a few rounds for everyone, and a few more for her. She'd poured out the whole sorry story of Micah and the Grange Hall while K.B. showed off his questionable darts skills for Jen and Nikki who–*oh, shit*–was pouting because she was supposed to be their fourth with Will.

Nikki got all up in her face about whoring around with the guy from Albany then trying to get with Will the minute he was gone, and she'd taken a swing at Nikki. It mostly missed, but she'd clipped Nikki's cheek and Jen had hustled her friend out of the bar, shooting Marnie dark looks.

K.B., pissed that he'd lost out on a chance to impress Jen, had started yelling at her about loyalty, after all, hadn't he and the guys...

Marnie groaned, pressing her head against the cool tiled wall to steady her tossing stomach. K.B. had said, "And after me and the guys rearranged that asshole's leads so his truck wouldn't start. Bet the prick felt pretty stupid when he realized he'd been had by a bunch of country boys. Seems you could be at least a little grateful, Marn. After all the stuff you said about him last week after the town meeting, we thought you'd appreciate us making his life suck for a few days."

Practically a soliloquy from K.B., and all the information she needed to fill in the missing pieces of the puzzle that was Micah's swift and silent departure. He'd gone into Thornton in her Jeep, stopped to check on the Tacoma, found out what happened, and assumed she'd known about it.

She gripped the sink and started down her gray, bleary reflection in the Dryers' upstair's bathroom. Well, the *heck* with him.

"Marnie, you in there?" Will knocked on the door as he spoke.

"Yeah. Hang on," she said.

Will's nose wrinkled at the sight of her. "You look like crap."

"Thanks, old friend. And after I defended your honor last night."

"So, you remember punching Nikki Desrosiers and telling her you'd never sleep with your best friend's first crush?" Will's mouth smiled, but his eyes were sad.

"It all came back to me while I was facing down my transgressions in the bathroom." She sniffed her armpit—not the worst, anyway. "Tell me I undressed myself, at least?"

"You did. I tossed you some clothes and slept on the pull-out sofa downstairs."

"You're a gentleman, Will Dryer, and don't you ever let anyone tell you different."

"If I do, you'll punch them." Will squeezed her shoulder. "You were in pretty rough shape. I didn't want to leave you alone. I'm sorry about that guy Micah."

"Yeah, well, it gets worse," Marnie said. "I was just too drunk to put it all together last night."

"My mom's making pancakes. Come downstairs and get some food, and we'll figure it out."

Chapter Sixteen

Carter was already in the office when Micah arrived. He was on the phone and elbows-deep in paperwork. Micah's arrival was met with visible relief.

"Do you have five minutes to bring me up to speed on Blueberry Hill? I have to go up there today and wrap that up, then I'm headed to White Plains tomorrow to scope out a site for the same hotel chain." Carter pushed a hand through his already artfully mussed hair. "More driving than I'm psyched about, but since *somebody* got tapped for the Syracuse trip..."

Micah stopped halfway to his desk. "What do you mean, you're going to Blueberry Hill today? The meeting isn't until Thursday."

"Barney wants to get moving on it. He called someone up there this morning. Boxley? Bexton?"

"Bixby," Micah said.

"Him." Carter leaned back in his chair. "They said they'd be happy to have everything settled today, so I'm up. You gonna give me a hand or not? Is this Farmer's Market thing a real problem or just some nuisance chick with a half-baked claim?"

Micah took a deep breath. Carter had no idea. "Easy, man. I don't think you need to spend a lot of time worrying about it. Just go up there and meet with them. The situation is pretty cut and dried."

Carter stuffed the paperwork into his messenger bag briefcase. "Then I ought to be able to fax over a contract like anywhere else in the civilized world."

Micah smiled. "They're not a fax-it kind of town."

"Just my luck." Carter shrugged on his suit jacket and grabbed his coat. "Please tell me there's a decent place to grab some food before I hit the road after."

"King's Diner's okay. Stay out of the Tipsy Catamount, though."

Carter gave him a sideways glance and a shrug. A moment later the elevator opened with a ding and Carter was on his way to Vermont. Micah didn't envy his officemate the reception he'd get from the board, but he was glad Marnie had won.

He hoped she'd be there to crow a little over the victory. Would she turn up in her black dress and heels with her waves and curls pinned back, or would she cruise in dressed for the mountain? Jeans and flannel? Like snapshots, he flipped through his memories of the last couple of days. She'd taken up residence in his heart almost overnight; it was only too easy to picture the way her lashes fell on her cheeks while she slept, the way her lips parted when he touched her the way she liked.

What the hell was he doing in Albany when she was in Blueberry Hill? And why was he letting Carter go in his place?

Micah looked at his watch. Not yet nine. Barney wasn't expecting him for another ten minutes.

Chapter Seventeen

Marnie unlocked her apartment feeling significantly better. Mrs. Dryer's pancakes, strong coffee, and Will's steady friendship did wonders for her mood.

Her answering machine was blinking again. Maybe Sam's freaky intuition was tuned to Will's presence in town.

Marnie hit play and opened the fridge. A trip to the grocery store in Brandon was more or less critical. She wasn't on the schedule at the mountain, so today would have to be errands. When Micah's voice filled her space she almost dropped the jar of maraschino cherries in her hand. When he stumbled over his own voice, she laughed.

"Hey Marnie, It's Micah…obviously. I hate answering machines. I owe you an apology and an explanation. I shouldn't have taken off without talking to you first, and I'm sorry. Please call my office if you get this right away, or you can call my cell–"

He left a string of numbers but Marnie wasn't hearing them. She was crouching in front of her refrigerator, clutching a jar of sundae toppers and trying not to cry. He was such a dork. Such a big, hunky, Viking raider dork.

And she was so very pissed at him.

A second message followed from Arlene Levesque. The board

was planning to meet with the young man from Simmons-Doyle at noon to reject their proposal, and did Marnie want to be there? Marnie put the jar back in the fridge and closed the door. Her former Kindergarten teacher was a rare bird to make Micah drive all the way back up here to turn him down. She hadn't thought she had that much outright support, but perhaps the questionable tactics brought out the board's–or Arlene's in particular–vengeful side.

Did she want to be there?

Hell yes, she did. Looking fine and extracting the apology as painfully as possible. Groveling would be acceptable. And then she wanted to drag him back here, to her space and have her way with him without all the complications and doubts between them, assuming he was up for it.

Her closet was full of denim, flannel and band tees, but other than the black sheath and a little black skirt, she didn't have a ton of dressing up clothes. She was about to call her mother and beg for something from the vintage wonderland that was the cedar closet when she found a garment bag at the back of the rack. Puzzled, she unzipped it. Inside was a gray wool pencil skirt and a white blouse. A green silk scarf hung around the blouse's collar.

"Sam, you magnificent creature," Marnie said to the empty room. Sam had worn the outfit for a job interview at the high school in Vergennes right before accepting her spot at Tulane. She'd spilled coffee on the drive back and taken the clothes at the cleaners in Thornton. Marnie had picked them up months later when Sam remembered they were still there, and promptly forgot they were in her closet, awaiting a visit home from their owner.

She didn't have exactly the right shoes, but her dressy winter boots were at least warm and weather appropriate, and she'd had enough time to deep condition her mane and play with the flat iron Sam had given her for Christmas the year before.

She sailed into the town hall in her sexy librarian get up with her straight, smooth waterfall of hair, fully prepared to make Micah Reynolds weep.

Instead, a suit with over-moussed bedhead, who didn't stand

when she walked in, gave her a wolfish once-over and crossed his arms over his chest like he owned the negotiating table.

Marnie's stride hitched, but she recovered and sat down, greeting the board before turning to the newcomer.

"Marnie Burnham, Blueberry Hill Farmer's Market Committee."

A hint of something nasty curved the corners of the suit's expression. "Carter Pugliesi, Simmons-Doyle. I'll be taking over for Mr. Reynolds on this project. He's no longer with the firm."

Marnie's pulse skipped; blood rushed in her ears. Micah had worried about his job when he'd agreed to help her, but she hadn't really taken him seriously. She kept her reply as neutral as possible. "I'm sorry to hear that."

"I'm sure you are," Carter said.

Selectman Bixby cleared his throat. "Thank you for coming all the way up here on short notice, Mr. Pugliesi. I am aware these things are more often done using more modern methods, but this town is still somewhat removed from those conveniences in many ways."

"I understand, sir," Carter said. Marnie didn't like his tone.

"I don't think you do," Mr. Bixby replied. The older man stood, taking his glasses off and facing the younger man down across the table. "We are choosing to give a year's lease to the Farmer's Market with a conditional five-year extension if the project meets certain benchmarks. During that time, we will be exploring historical protections and trust options for the building to protect it from future predatory actions like yours."

"Yes!" Marnie jumped in her chair, unable to contain her glee, but worry for Micah tempered it.

At the same time, Carter pushed his chair back and snatched up his briefcase. "I drove almost two-and-a-half hours after nearly being assaulted by a colleague over this damned case, and now you're telling me no?"

"Watch your language, young man," Mrs. Levesque said mildly. "And it would appear so. Your purchase offer was generous enough, but this board resents the attempt to strong-arm the town with false claims of fraudulent stewardship of the land and building. Your firm may have done its homework, but I'm afraid you didn't research carefully enough to pass."

A beet-red flush rose up the back of Carter's neck. His mouth worked around words he didn't–or couldn't–say for a moment before he simply turned and walked away.

"Wait!" Marnie called, stopping Carter's flight.

He didn't turn. "What?"

"What do you mean, you were nearly assaulted by a colleague?"

The sneer on Carter's face when he spun around made Marnie step back. "Maybe you should ask him, since you and *Mister Reynolds* are so close."

He turned on his heel again and strode out of the room, letting the heavy steel door bang closed behind him.

"Excuse me," Marnie addressed the board. "Thank you so much for the opportunity you're giving me, but I have something incredibly important I need to take care of."

Arlene Levesque smiled. "Go on, Marnie. And bring him back with you, if you can. He's a good boy."

She found her mother in the barn, over a steaming kettle of soap. "Mama Iguana, I screwed up."

Her mother looked up from stirring, smiling through her safety goggles. "His address is on my notepad by the workshop phone."

"Mom?" A shiver ran down Marnie's spine. "How?"

"It's hardly witchcraft, Marnie," her mother scolded, returning to the stirring. "I went into town this morning for some of Stu's doughnuts for your father, and Jan Desrosiers' daughter was in the diner congratulating herself for blowing the whistle on 'that jerk from Albany.' Her mom adjusted the temperature on her burner. "She hadn't noticed me, and went on to say some very unpleasant things about both Micah and you. I take it you two had an argument over something recently?"

"Micah and I?" Marnie's head was reeling. *What was going on?*

"No, sweetheart. You and the Desrosiers girl. Why else would she be so proud of having ruined Micah's life and taught you a lesson?" Her mother pointed to the phone. "I might have had a good feeling about the boy, but that doesn't mean I didn't pick his pocket for a little information when we brought him back here last week. I thought it might come in handy."

When her mom shrugged, Marnie started to laugh. She still wasn't sure exactly what had happened, and how it had ended with Micah picking a fight with that slimy co-worker of his, but Marnie had plans to get to the bottom of all of it.

"Mom, maybe you really do have magic in your gene pool. Can you call Dad and tell him I'm going to have to call in sick tomorrow? I'm going to Albany as soon as I make a phone call."

"Already did, and it's your gene pool, too, Marnie."

Chapter Eighteen

Micah had been walking for two hours.

The day, despite his best efforts, wasn't over yet, and he still couldn't get his head around how he'd ended up unemployed and aimlessly wandering Albany's Capitol Hill in near freezing temperatures as the sun sank.

He'd taken the stairs, chasing Carter to the parking garage, intent on swapping assignments. There weren't any plane tickets purchased, since the Albany-Syracuse flight was chartered, so it shouldn't have been hard to switch. Certainly, he was passing up a chance at fast-tracking his career, but his gut was telling him to get back to Marnie—to Blueberry Hill.

Barney's secretary caught up with him two floors below, breathless and bearing an urgent message that Micah was wanted in the partner's office immediately. Micah had blown her off, asking for ten minutes to stop Carter from leaving and offer him a seat at the Syracuse table.

He'd found Carter in the garage, on the brink of leaving. At first, his officemate was thrilled with the idea of switching, but suspicion nudged past elation when Micah seemed genuinely relieved not to be going to Syracuse.

Suspicion and envy turned into a shouting match that set Micah's already raw nerves on edge. Even he had to admit that when Barney found them, he was crowding Carter. It didn't look great. Barney was furious, and the situation with Carter didn't help. Some woman from Blueberry Hill, Vermont, had called him full of tales of Micah *fraternizing* with the chair of the Farmer's Market Committee. A *concerned citizen*, with the village's *best interests* at heart, wondering if there was some kind of *conflict of interest.*

The next thing Micah knew he was boxing up his office under the watchful eye of a security guard, and he was accompanied home by an HR rep who confiscated his company cell phone and work materials and checked his personal computer.

Feeling stir-crazy, Micah had left his apartment on foot, walking until his dress shoes pinched his feet and he couldn't feel the tip of his nose. Just as he rounded the corner of his block and fished his keys out of his coat pocket, a blond woman in a gray skirt and a down jacket stood up on the front stoop of his building. Her long, straight blonde hair reflected the last of the dwindling sunlight. He wondered if she was locked out and waiting for another resident to let her in.

She peered down the sidewalk at him, and as he approached, she jumped down from the stairs. Instead of the sensible business shoes or boots he'd grown accustomed to seeing on women around the office, she wore snow boots over tights and she was grinning at him over the jacket's popped collar.

"Marnie? How?"

She didn't say a word at first, only launched herself at him. He caught her, holding tight, wondering at yet another version of this woman who'd bewitched him. She squeezed hard before letting him go.

"I'm so sorry about Nikki Desrosiers—"

"What did you do to your hair?"

"My hair? What happened with that Carter creep?"

"Who is Nikki what? How did you find me?"

They talked over one another, impatient to get to the answers they needed, but Micah didn't really care about Marnie's hair. "Come inside. You've got to be freezing. Where are you parked?"

"The garage four blocks away." She stuck her hands in her armpits. "And yes. I am."

They took the elevator in slightly awkward silence, and Marnie followed him down the hall to his door. His studio, affordable and sufficient for his long work hours and bachelor life, suddenly seemed cramped and shabby.

Marnie peeled off her coat and shucked her boots, blowing on her fingers and dropping her bag by his coat tree. She wasted no time.

"My mother picked your pocket the night she brought you back to her house. She copied down all your license information and tucked it away in case you turned out to be an axe murderer or a legitimate corporate raider."

Micah started to reply, but Marnie held up a hand to stop him.

"She has a good feeling about you, so she says. She also says we're descended from actual Salem witches who fled the trials, so you decide how deep the crazy goes in my family. Nicole Marie Desrosiers is a former classmate of mine who's pissed because I ran into an old friend last night and he preferred my company to hers." Marnie paused and her eyes grew shadowed. "She's the reason you lost your job. I'm so sorry."

Micah hung his coat up. "I'll find another one. She's not making any trouble for you, is she?"

Marnie shrugged. "My mom'll put a hex on her or whatever if she does."

"Marnie, I," Micah began, needing to clear the air. He'd set all of this in motion by leaving; he needed to start fixing it. "I know you didn't have anything to do with my truck."

"Maybe not directly." She sat on the edge of his bed like she'd been doing it forever, and Micah began to hope. "But I definitely got some intoxicated good ol' boys riled up."

He itched to go to her, but he stayed near the door, determined not to overplay his hand. "I let my pride ruin what should have been a great day, what should have been more time with you. I was an idiot."

Marnie laughed. "You did, but you said that already. And I went out and got drunk with an old friend and missed your calls. I decided to be pissed off instead of trying to get a hold of you sooner."

He stepped closer as the hope unfurled. "I wish I'd been there to see them turn Carter down."

A wide smile lit Marnie's face. "It was awesome. I thought he was going to explode, and then he said you almost assaulted him about something, and that's how I heard you got fired."

"I had a long day at the office before I got escorted out at nine-thirty this morning, but I didn't even come close to assault. Sounds like he didn't make a great impression on the board."

"He's a creep." Marnie shuddered.

"Maybe I should have decked him."

"Down, Viking," Marnie said, and the air in the room shifted. She stood up, and Micah gave in to the need to be close to her. "I missed you."

"Me, too." His voice broke, and he wasn't even bothered by it. Her white button-down shirt was unbuttoned enough to reveal a lace trimmed camisole. A lock of her hair was tangled in one of the shirt buttons, brushing at the lace inside the placket. Micah reached out to untangle it, gently smoothing it between his fingers.

"I used a flat iron." Marnie looked up at him, her eyes sparkling. "When Mrs. L. said *the young man from Simmons-Doyle* was meeting them, I assumed it was you. You don't own the market on pride, Mr. Reynolds."

"This was to impress me?" He tucked the hair behind her ear, letting his fingers brush down the side of her neck, loving the way she leaned into his touch.

"More to make you want me so badly you'd regret ever leaving," Marnie said, her eyes drifting closed as he stroked his fingertips along the line of her open blouse.

"You exist," he whispered, finally drawing her close. "That's enough to make me regret ever leaving."

Marnie stretched up on her toes, bringing her mouth achingly close to his, and whispered back, "Maybe I am a witch after all."

When she kissed him, Micah was sure of it. She wound her fingers in the hair at the nape of his neck, bringing every nerve in his body to attention when her nails grazed the skin there. She rolled her hips against his in response, humming in appreciation.

Micah groaned.

"Marnie?"

She kissed him again. "Yes."

"Maybe we should go get something to eat? Get some air?"

She smoothed her hands down his chest and over his stomach, letting them linger at his hips. "I'm not hungry."

He was starving for more or her, and it was absolute agony, but less than forty-eight hours before, they'd held back, afraid to spoil something fragile and new. Until she said differently, those were the rules.

"And there are things I want more." She reached for his belt buckle and he almost lost himself right then and there. "I even came prepared."

"Oh, my god," he murmured, distracting himself from the delicious torture of her fingers undoing his khakis by memorizing the shape of her face by kiss. He stepped out of the pants where they fell, and Marnie stepped back, bumping backwards into the edge of his bed.

He caught her hand to steady her, then pressed her palm to the center of his chest where his heart hammered under his skin. "I want them, too. I just want you to be sure."

She wrapped her free hand around his wrist and steered him around before giving him a little shove so he toppled back onto his bed. A sly smile dawned on her face, and Micah knew without a doubt that Daphne Potter's daughter had some kind of magic in her blood.

Marnie undid a blouse button. "I want to be with you, Micah."

She reached behind her back and unzipped the skirt, shimmying a little to slide it over her hips. It puddled on the floor on top of his discarded khakis. The button-down shirt's hem skimmed her tights-clad hips. He found it unreasonably sexy.

She undid two more buttons. "I want to spend hours learning how you like to be touched, and," she unbuttoned the last two buttons and dropped the shirt. Her camisole hugged her rib cage and belly. He'd seen more of her body the two nights they'd spend together in Vermont, but this was different. She was offering him everything now, and it humbled him. She hooked her thumbs under the waistband of the tights and drew them off. "I want to wake up tangled in you so we can do it all again in the morning."

She lifted the camisole over her head and dropped it. Words dried up on his tongue save two. "Come here."

She crawled into the bed with him, straddling his hips. He shuddered at the closeness of her warm, wet heat. She leaned over him, sliding her body along his, and he reached for her.

The slow seduction went up flames. He opened the clasp of her bra, feasting on the soft curves and puckered flesh of her breasts. She drugged him with long, breathless kisses and hands that found their way inside his boxers, stroking the length of him, pushing fabric aside to press his hardness against her slick, hot core. She rocked like that, sliding their bodies together, the added friction of their underthings unspeakably erotic. Micah lost himself in the taste of her skin, finding just the right touch of hands and lips to make her cry out and offer her breasts to him, begging wordlessly for more while she moved over him, driving them both towards the edge.

Micah stilled when Marnie's thighs quivered over his and she rocked hard against him, biting her lip and opening her eyes to lock their gazes. "Hold that thought."

Her voice was as ragged as his breathing. He rolled to one side to watch her cross the room to where she'd dropped her backpack near the door. Looking back, she caught him staring and wiggled her ass. She rummaged around in the bag, pulling out a small makeup bag. Halfway back to the bed, she tossed him the makeup bag and–so quickly he almost missed the constellation of freckles on her left hip bone, she whipped off her underwear and pounced on him.

"Prepared," she said, nodding at the bag and reaching for the waistband of his boxers.

He lifted his hips to let her strip him, and then sat up. He looped an arm around her and rolled them over, resting on his elbows over her. She twirled the ends of his hair around her fingers.

Micah touched his forehead to Marnie's, fighting a grin when he saw a wide array of condoms and lube spilling out of her makeup bag on the duvet cover. "I would very much like to make love to you right about now."

Marnie laughed and wrapped her legs around his hips and pulled him down to her. "I would like very much like that, too."

Chapter Nineteen

Marnie's rumbling stomach woke them both sometime before dawn. She padded naked to Micah's refrigerator. In the cold glow of the fridge light she discovered that her Viking needed a supply run.

"You have leftover Thai noodles, beer, and orange juice in here. Seriously? I'm pretty sure Joey and Chandler have a better stocked fridge."

"Check the freezer," Micah muttered. "There might be bagels or something."

No bagels, but she found Eggo waffles in the freezer, and put them in the toaster, returning to the bed with waffles wrapped in paper towels.

"Post-sex waffles are pretty good," she said, sitting cross-legged and wrapping his quilt around herself.

Micah rubbed his eyes and took a waffle. "Okay fine, you're right, but no crumbs, please."

Marnie brushed a few crumbs off the sheets and shot Micah a sideways look. "I don't know what your plans are, but I don't have to go back to Vermont until tonight."

Micah ran a hand up her thigh, his fingers questing.

"That's definitely on my list. Along with some other pairings." She folded the paper towel and snuggled into his waiting arms. "And we should talk about what happens when we're not in bed."

Micah yawned, which made her yawn.

"Maybe when we're not in bed," Marnie conceded; her eyes were drifting closed again.

They slept in, waking well after nine, and Micah took her on a tour of his neighborhood that ended with a late breakfast. Marnie wondered, as they walked, if he remembered their moonlit conversation the night before, until he brought it up over coffee cups.

"I'd like to spend some time in Blueberry Hill."

Her hand shook just a little. "Yeah?"

"Only if you think it would be okay," he said. "I can sublet my studio for a little while, find a place to stay up there. Try it out." Micah reached for her hand. He'd barely gone two minutes since they woke without a casual touch–a brushing of hands, a spontaneous kiss. She wanted to get used to it. "Get to know you better without all the complications."

She could see it clearly. And she knew, without a doubt that her mother was already prepping the loft for a long-term tenant.

"I'd need to find a job, but I think I need a whole new direction, so for now, whatever comes along will work. I know it sounds impulsive and crazy, but–"

"I love impulsive and crazy," Marnie said. *I think I might love* you. "How soon could you make it happen?"

Their server delivered their breakfasts, and after she left, Micah leaned over his plate and lowered his voice. "It's unconventional foreplay, but want to get naked later and help me list my apartment for rent?"

Marnie laughed. "You're on, Viking. Now eat up. You're going to need your strength."

Unbound Heart

BOOK TWO

Prologue

BLUEBERRY HILL, SUMMER 1994

Despite the boning that dug into her ribs and constricted her lungs, Samantha Ellis segued easily from the Electric Slide into more Eighties footwork she'd picked up watching John Hughes movies with her aunt. She might be the youngest–and the chubbiest–of Maggie's bridesmaids, but she had the best dance moves.

"I love this song!" Aunt Maggie grabbed Sam's hands and swung around, Jessica McClintock bridal gown sailing out behind her like a puff-sleeved sail. As the crowded dance floor blurred and spun, Sam sucked in a deep breath and kept her smile plastered to her face. Her bridesmaid dress, carnation pink silk with a chocolate brown sash and a plastic cage to hold in her tummy and squish up her boobs, made her feel so grown up and pretty that she hadn't dared tell Maggie that she was so horribly uncomfortable wearing it.

Almost everyone in Blueberry Hill, Vermont, was at this wedding, which wasn't difficult to manage since literally everyone loved Maggie and Erik, and the entire population was like three hundred people and shrinking. The town common was strung with white Christmas lights from King's Diner to the Town Hall, and from the church to the bandstand, the paths were lined with white paper bag luminaries that Sam and her best friend, Marnie Burnham, had filled with sand and votive candles the weekend before.

Maggie Potter and Erik Dryer had been together since Sam was in sixth grade, and she only had one more year at Thornton Union High. Sam had plans to be one more subtraction from the shrinking population, even if she only got as far as somewhere else in New England. One of her two most secret dreams was to live somewhere where she could use the French she studied, like Montreal or New Orleans.

Maggie spun away and Sam took a moment to breathe. Looking around the dance floor, she recognized almost every face in the crowd, from her school friends to creepy Uncle Billy, who made a gross comment about her *bosoms* in front of Marnie's mom, then got mad when Mama Daphne muttered a hex under her breath.

The one person Sam didn't see was Will.

Will Dryer–a cousin of Erik's on his dad's side–was seventeen and a senior; captain of the hockey team and the second of Sam's two most secret dreams. He was tall, broad shouldered, and had the kind of smile Sam had only read about in the paperback romance novels her mother didn't let her check out of the library, but Marnie's mom left lying around their family room.

Rakish.

Maggie danced past, catching Erik around the waist to start a conga line, laughing as she passed. "Grab on, Sammy."

Unable to resist her favorite aunt, Sam skipped along the fast-forming line. The end kept getting further and further away, until an arm snaked out and yanked her into line. Looking back at her rescuer, she caught the full force of that rakish grin.

"Hey, Sam."

His hands put gentle pressure on her hips as the conga line circled the common, and for the life of her Sam couldn't have said how many songs played while they danced in a stupid line. She rested her hands on someone's shoulders, but it could have been creepy Uncle Billy for all she cared. Will had chosen her.

Some of the grown ups were breaking away to dance as couples, showing off moves that were frankly embarrassing for people their age, and the conga line fell apart. Sam shuffled away, turning to face Will.

"Thanks for the rescue," she said.

Will stuck his hands in his pockets. His smile went from rakish to shy. "No problem."

They'd been friends for years, ever since Maggie and Erik had gotten serious and their two families had merged into one huge complicated, small town pod. She supposed they were sort of related by marriage now, but if she couldn't quite figure out how she and Marnie and Maggie were actually related through their moms, then Will was definitely not a relative *like that.*

Which was good, because ever since the end of freshman year, when they'd stayed up at a Fourth of July bonfire together, Sam had wanted nothing more than for Will to kiss her. They went to the same high school, and when they saw each other in the hallways, her friends always embarrassed her by fawning over him like he was some kind of demigod. The only one who didn't was Marnie, who seemed to be impervious to Will's charms (another phrase from Mama Daphne's romance novels). Marnie and Will acted like guy friends did: they fought and insulted each other, they roughhoused, they always had each other's backs.

Sam wondered sometimes if it was easier for Marnie because she was still built more like a guy. Slim hips, flattish chest, strong legs from hours on skis–and lately snowboards. Sam was all flesh. Hips, butt, boobs. Her mom said it would even out at some point, but Sam had her doubts. They were both just about seventeen. How much evening-out time was left, really?

"Last dance, all you lovers," the band's frontman said, returning to the mic as the Gloria Estefan break ended. "This one's for the happy couple. Congratulations, Maggie and Erik." The band struck up a U2-inspired cover of *Unchained Melody.*

Sam could feel a blush stealing up her chest. She and Will were just standing there, in the middle of the dance floor. It was the last dance, and a slow song, and she wanted the town common to open up and swallow her whole.

"You wanna dance?" One corner of Will's mouth crooked up, like maybe he was a little embarrassed too.

Sam nodded, suddenly unsure of what to do with her hands.

"Do you trust me?" Will asked, sliding one hand around her waist and taking her right hand in his left.

"Uh-huh." She nodded like an idiot, but *two dances in one night!*

"You have swear you won't tell anyone, but Erik made me practice with him. I learned a bunch of moves, but then I had to practice in the mirror to figure out how to lead."

Sam would have followed Will off the edge of the Catmint Gap ravine if he'd asked. His hands were warm, and she could smell his soap and the wool from his rented tuxedo. He was wearing a little bit of aftershave or cologne, too.

He *had* learned some moves. He turned them and twirled her, and it was only as the song began to wind down that she realized she'd actually relaxed enough to be laughing with him. He ended with a little dip as the last chord faded, pulling her back up so that their noses nearly touched. She could feel his breath on her cheek.

If she turned her face...

"Dryer!"

"Hey, Will!"

He released her as some of his friends made their way across the dance floor to find him. Sam shuffled back, hoping Katy and Nikki Desrosiers wouldn't notice her. The twin sisters were the meanest girls in the graduating class, and Nikki in particular had a thing for Will.

Will was high-fiving the guys, sneaking a sip from Kurt Blake's flask, making plans for some after party at the Strickland's hunting cabin.

"Wanna come with us, Sam?" Will asked. "We're going out to Stricklands'. Just to chill."

"Yeah, so Will," Katy said, "I'm not supposed to invite any extras."

"You mean *losers*..." Nikki whispered, so low only Sam and Katy heard her.

The floor came rushing up, or Sam's heart went rushing down.

"Oh." Will couldn't quite look her in the eye. "I'm sorry, Sam."

"It's okay, see you guys later." She turned to flee, but was rescued again. This time by Marnie who appeared from out of nowhere. She was wearing a plaid miniskirt, black tank top, and combat boots, and while it wasn't Sam's look, or very romantic for a June wedding, Marnie looked completely at home in her skin, which made Sam sick with envy.

Marnie appraised the situation. "Nice one, Dryer. Skipping out on your own cousin's wedding for beers and skanks?"

"You are such a freak." Nikki rolled her eyes and hooked arms with her sister for a dramatic exit.

"Easy, Marn," Will said, a hint of laughter in his voice, "your claws are showing."

"Whatever." Marnie looped her arm through Sam's in an echo of Nikki's departure. "Come on, Sam. Let's go find some actually cool people."

"I'll see you around, Sam," Will said, looking back as he followed the party crowd. "You're a great dancer, by the way."

Sam squeezed her eyes closed, forcing back tears, holding her breath so hard she forgot to feel the boning digging into her chest. She stood there, Nikki's words rolling over one another in her head like a snowball, gathering in speed and volume until they drowned out the fading party, Marnie's chatter, and even Will's praise.

———

Chapter One

The key to Maggie and Erik's house was, as promised, under the mat, though the doors were unlocked. Sam slipped the key on her keychain and let herself into the kitchen, locking the door behind her. There was an unfamiliar car with out-of-state tags parked on the street in front of the house.

New habits die hard.

The Lacroixes never left a gate or a door unsecured on their Prytania Street property; Sam had learned quickly not to disobey Lilith Lacroix's instructions. Taking a deep breath, she reached back and deliberately turned the knob to release the lock.

She set her things down on the braided rug and pushed aside her yoga mat and towel, pulling out a can of Cafe du Monde coffee. Not *everything* about her years in New Orleans was worth forgetting.

She was a stranger in her aunt's kitchen, but it was simple enough to find the coffee maker and a measuring spoon, and a pan to steam some milk. She hummed to herself as she poured, so involved in her coffee ritual, she didn't hear the footsteps until a loose floorboard squeaked.

She turned with a start. The man filling up the archway between the kitchen and the front hall was older, leaner and a little weathered, but unmistakably himself. *Will.*

"Holy shit." That smile she'd adored as a kid–*still rakish*–crinkled the corners of his eyes. His smile was like a sunrise of recognition. He started toward her, but she shifted away to put the coffee pot back. "I can't believe it's you after all these years."

"What are you doing here?" *That's all you can say to him?*

"Erik told me I could crash in the rec room while I was in town. I got in late last night." Will scratched his scruffy cheeks and looked her over. "You look fantastic, Sam."

"Thanks. It's *Samantha* these days, but I suppose you're grandfathered in." Or was it? *Samantha* was someone she'd become. Maybe it was time to reclaim *Sam.* She fidgeted with the coffee pot to hide her shaking hands. "Why are you home?"

"Grandfathered? Come on." He yawned and stretched. Sam indulged in the view of his flat, muscled stomach. "We're not that old."

"I feel that old," she said, regretting it immediately. Will wasn't stupid, and who knows what the family had said. He would ask questions she didn't want to answer.

"That coffee smells amazing," Will remarked, crossing the kitchen. "Is there enough to share?"

"I made a full pot," Sam said. "Help yourself."

"Maggie said Gail was staying with the kids while they're away," he said, grabbing a mug from a hook under the cabinet. Damn him, he still smelled good, even first thing in the morning. "And K.B.'s getting married on Saturday night. I'm a groomsman."

She'd been in Blueberry Hill for almost a month, hiding out at Daphne Potter and Max Burnham's place, living in their loft apartment and licking her wounds since her divorce had gone through, not even taking Marnie's calls. Her parents told her she was crazy to go back to her hometown when she left their Tucson retirement village, but she'd felt a pull to the mountain hamlet she'd grown up in. Once upon a time, she'd trusted her instincts. She'd thought it was time to follow them again, but fear kept her hunkered down. No wonder she didn't know one of the few classmates still left in the area was getting married.

She wished them better luck than hers.

"Yeah, Gail was going to do it, but she's got classes to teach, and I'm around. No one told me you were coming home…" she trailed off, realizing that if they had, she'd never have agreed to stay here. "So Kurt Blake's getting married?"

Will looked so magnificently rumpled in the plaid flannel pajama pants and holey tee shirt, rubbing his long ago broken nose, wiping sleep from his eyes. She fought the urge to touch the tips of his hair as he reached past her for the sugar bowl.

"Yeah. He and Jen Miller are finally tying the knot. Didn't Marnie tell you?"

"Marnie doesn't exactly run with that crowd." *That was putting it mildly. And I haven't let my best friend in yet.* Redirecting uncomfortable questions was a relatively recent, but sharply honed survival skill.

Will chuckled. "Right. I was around when Nikki almost ruined everything with Micah. I forgot."

"Marnie didn't find it funny at the time."

"Look, Nikki's never going to change. She still likes all the things she liked in high school. She thought she'd give it a shot when I was home that time because she liked me back in high school." He paused there, leaning over her, watching her face. She couldn't look away. "For the record, I was never interested."

His voice dropped while he spoke, and Sam remembered the night Maggie and Erik got married. The way he asked her if she trusted him.

She had. Then. She didn't even know him anymore.

"So, what brought *you* all the way back to Vermont?" he asked, breaking the heavy silence. "Last time I heard, Marnie said you were the princess of New Orleans."

No one told him. Sam released a breath she hadn't realized she'd been holding.

Will started to pour the coffee, and she stopped him halfway up the mug. "Wait."

He stopped mid-pour, looking at her in alarm. "What?"

"It's just... the coffee's better *au lait*. Here," She picked up a Pyrex measuring cup of milk and topped off his coffee, "I have enough for you, too."

"Thanks," he said, meeting her eyes over the nearly empty Pyrex. He lifted the mug, took a sip. His whole face lit up with pleasure while he held the warm coffee in his mouth and swallowed.

"This is great," he said. "What is it?"

"Coffee and chicory. It's my favorite." She decided to change the subject while Will was distracted. "How's life in Montana?"

"Can't complain." He pulled out a chair and sat backwards, resting his arms on the back. "Room and board, no two days the same, and there's a youth hockey team to coach in the winters."

"That sounds perfect for you." She leaned against the counter, cradling the coffee cup in her hands. Watching the easy joy on his face when he spoke of his life in Montana, she wondered what he would think of her pathetic story, or of the fact that she couldn't honestly deny that–five minutes after seeing him again–she still had feelings for this man she'd once loved so desperately. So unrequitedly.

"Can you teach me how to make this? The coffee on the ranch is... not this good."

"Sure. You can order the coffee online." She laughed at the way he stared into the mug, as if it offered answers. "How'd you end up there in the first place?"

"Dumb luck, really," he said.

"Somehow I doubt your luck is dumb."

"No, really. I went out there with some guys on a dude ranch vacation a couple of years ago and got to talking with the owner. He was looking for someone who could work alongside the ranch hands, but also help him with the business. I did my degree in business administration–a lot of the athletes did. Next thing I know, I'm packing my stuff and flying out there to stay. I met some great people out there."

Will twisted to set the mug down on the table, but not before Sam caught a fleeting shadow in his eyes. "Haven't had a reason to leave. It's a boring story. I want to hear more about jazz and beignets and bayous."

She drained her coffee. There was no way she was going to tell him. "It's not all that interesting, really. I have a job interview later at a preschool in Thornton, and some errands to run before I pick the kids up at camp. I should shower and get ready for that."

Not breaking into a run on her way out of the kitchen counted as a major success.

Chapter Two

Hot damn. Samantha Ellis in his cousin's kitchen on a Monday morning after way too many years. Looking fine as hell.

Will Dryer had always relied on luck, or fate. Good fortune, whatever you called it. He'd stumbled into nearly everything good in his life.

When he'd come east for his old hockey buddy K.B.'s wedding, his cousin had offered up the rec room futon, since Erik and Maggie were taking a well-deserved trip to Jamaica and Erik's mother–his aunt Gail–was staying with the kids. Crashing in a rec room two floors down from his aunt was marginally more adult than sleeping in the twin bed he'd grown up in down the hall from his parents.

As his extraordinary luck would have it, he'd be sleeping two floors down from Sam. The one girl he'd never quite figured out. He'd known her forever. She'd grown up under his nose.

That's the problem, Dryer.

She was the girl who'd wandered in and out of his thoughts ever since, never quite releasing her hold on him.

Her heard the water turn on in the upstairs bathroom and his imagination took the wheel.

Some summer, early on in high school, they'd been the last ones around a family bonfire. She'd ruthlessly skewered their teachers with uncanny impressions. He'd never laughed so hard. Once he got her talking, she'd cracked jokes and offered insights into their classmates he knew he would ever share beyond that fire ring. They'd ended up talking about their futures, kind of, and she'd seen right to the heart of him.

"You just want to play hockey and live a good life, Will. There's nothing wrong with that."

He'd looked at her then. Really looked. Seen the gold tips of her eyelashes, and the amber glints in her dark brown hair where the firelight caught it. The way her lips bowed when she smiled. She wasn't skinny-hot like the girls who were always giving him their number, but he caught a glimpse of kicking curves under her baggy t-shirt and jeans. He'd gotten uncomfortably hard, sitting there at the bonfire with her. Like a jackass kid, he'd avoided her for a while after that, which probably hurt her feelings.

One day at school, he'd seen her at lunch, sitting with Marnie and some of their friends, and he'd just gone over to sit with her instead of with K.B., the Desrosiers twins, his usual hockey crowd and their hangers-on. It was completely out of character, but she'd smiled at him and he'd forgotten to feel awkward about the campfire. It was like she had a light inside her and he was a June bug. He'd just wanted to be near her. Marnie stuck her canned green beans in his chocolate pudding and called him a dork for abandoning his jock friends, but for that lunch period, he'd happily basked in Sam's smile.

After that, he'd made an effort to keep things friendly between them, but he could never quite get to the uncomplicated buddies level that he and Marnie had always existed on. Then Sam walked down the aisle at Maggie and Erik's wedding in the pink strapless dress, and the curves he'd suspected were definitely confirmed. And if she had few more curves than the Desrosiers twins and their crew, well, Will liked what he saw.

When the conga line formed, he'd noticed her looking a little lost, so he'd pulled her along. That was the first time Will felt the unique pleasure of satin sliding over a woman's skin. Then the band played a slow song and he didn't want to let her go right away. He knew she wouldn't tease him–or rat him out–for learning some steps with Erik to surprise Maggie on the big day, so he'd asked her to dance.

He heard the shower door close. She was naked up there, hot water running down a body that had *definitely* grown up. He got up from the chair, took his coffee cup to the sink, and waited there, hands braced on the stainless steel, until the moment passed.

His first year at UVM, he'd stayed away from Blueberry Hill as much as possible, preferring to pretend that forty-five minutes was too far to drive for visits home between breaks. He'd skated and studied. There were parties and girls and traveling with the hockey team while he was warming the bench.

That year had changed Sam. She'd taken up swimming and kick-boxing and cut her hair short. She and Marnie made plans and took trips to the beach and whispered secrets to one another. They barely saw one another before he started a summer internship at John Pease's law office in Thornton. She and Marnie didn't party out at the hunting camp or skinny dip at Arcadia Falls, and he was already back to Burlington when she left for UNH.

The water stopped with a thump in the pipes, and a moment later Will heard footsteps upstairs from the bathroom to the spare bedroom at the end of the hall.

Extended family gatherings brought them together at holidays while they were in college, but the last time Will saw her was a night he'd never forget, and one she'd likely never recall. The only people who knew about it were Marnie–and she didn't know the whole story, and his cousin Erik, because Will had spilled his guts when he found out Sam was getting married.

Two years ago now. He wondered what had ended her marriage so quickly.

He'd flown home that year for his mom's birthday at Marnie's request. She'd wanted him to get to know her new boyfriend.

Erik found him in his dad's den, holding the heavy, embossed cream envelope. "Will, they're bringing out the cake in a few."

When he hadn't answered, Erik had called his name again.

Will opened the flap and pulled the invitation out again, though he'd already read and replaced it twice. "Sam's getting married."

"So it would seem. Mags is bummed we can't make it, but who gets married on a Thursday morning? That's kind of a dick move."

He'd been unable to tear his eyes away from the gilded lettering–the fancy names, the cathedral, the white tie reception at a club–but the casual dismissal in Erik's voice pissed him off.

"You always liked Sam."

"So did you, I think." Erik didn't bullshit around. "But Sam literally hasn't been back to visit since Camille and Rich moved to Tucson. She's not the same girl anymore. What do you care?"

"I don't," Will tossed the invitation and envelope on his father's desk. He did care, though. Marnie had a bad feeling about Sam's fiancé. And he'd always figured there would be a chance to... "I don't care."

"Maggie and I are taking the kids to Londgren's farm after; there are lambs. You should come with us. Noah and Ava would be psyched." Erik pulled a matchbook out of his pocket and tapped it on his palm. "And it's time for cake."

Will picked up the invitation again. "Did you know I kissed her once?"

Erik stopped. Turned. "When?"

"Couple months before I graduated from college. We played down at UNH. She and Marnie came to the game." Will pushed the invitation around his dad's desk blotter. "When I saw her there with Marnie—"

"You acted like a jackass?"

Will laughed. "I showed off for her. I played like a gladiator, nearly got my head knocked in. After the game, Marnie dragged her down to the ice, and I invited them to come out with the team. We were going back to one of the UNH guys' parents' house. Some big old place on the coast in Rye. No parents. A lot of booze."

Erik winced. "This is my wife's niece we're talking about."

"Anyway, a bunch of us piled into Jay Briggs' big old Suburban and–"

"You partied with Jay Briggs?"

"I partied with a lot of guys, Erik."

"The Jay Briggs who plays for the 'Leafs?"

"Yeah," Will chuckled. "He owns center ice, but he can't hold his cheap beer."

Erik held up a hand. "Don't ruin him for me. He can fucking skate."

"Anyway, Marnie hooked up with some guy, and I found Sam alone in the kitchen. Some doofus was drooling all over her. She never realized how pretty she was. I got rid of the guy. We ended up grabbing a blanket, splitting a six pack, and talking out on the deck for most of the night."

"Do I really need to hear the rest of this?"

"Shut up." Will piled a stack of catalogs over the invitation to break its spell. "Our team manager had all the car keys, so I asked him to drive Sam back to her apartment. She asked me to come back with her." He could still see the hazy look in her eyes. The way she'd licked her lips before asking him to come home with her. The way her voice trembled. "Jesus, Erik, she was right there, making an offer like that, and I told her I needed to stay with the team. She didn't ask twice, just kind of touched my hand and said goodbye. I don't know what I was thinking, but it was freezing and there were about a million stars over the ocean and I just kind of kissed her."

Erik looked at him, eyes a little wide.

"It was really hot for about a minute." Will ignored his cousin's dark look. "She pulled away, turned around, and threw up on the team manager's shoes."

Erik laughed.

A smile tugged at Will's mouth. "She was all woozy after that. I ended up riding back with her, just to tuck her in on the sofa. I didn't know what else to do."

"Water. Advil?"

"Yeah, asshole, but I was a little drunk myself." Will heard someone outside calling them. "Marnie told me the next day that

Sam had no idea how she'd gotten home. She didn't remember anything after we took the beer outside."

"So you think she still doesn't know?"

"Nah. Marnie would've read me the riot act if she'd found out the rest. Now she never will." Will had followed his cousin out of the room toward the sounds of *Happy Birthday* being sung on the lawn, and he'd done his best to put thoughts of Sam out of his head.

Never was a long time. Will ran some warm water into the coffee cups to rinse them out, then washed them and set them on the drying rack. *And Sam wasn't married anymore.*

Chapter Three

Sam's phone rang as she was leaving her interview. The public preschool administrative position in Thornton wasn't her first choice, but she couldn't stay holed up in the loft at Daphne and Max's forever, and her teaching certification had expired. Her options were limited.

Just another thing Craig and Lilith had stripped away from her.

The name on the screen was unfamiliar. "Hello?"

"Hey, Sam."

Will's voice was warm and familiar in her ear. Would she ever not respond to it? And didn't she know now how devastating a hold like that could be on her heart? She inhaled through her nose, the way her yoga instructor instructed. "Hi, Will. What's up?"

"I have extra time today, want me to swing by the school and pick Noah and Ava up?"

"I'm in Thornton now," she said. Blueberry Hill was too small for a school of its own. Her younger cousins went to school in neighboring Catmint Gap. "I was planning to go by there on my way home anyway."

"You don't trust me to pick up the kids?" There was laughter in his voice.

"I'm the one the school's expecting." She sounded prim; not herself at all.

"I'll meet you there," Will said. "Surprise the munchkins."

"Fine. I'll see you in an hour." She was about to end the call when a tall, lean, dark-haired man turned the corner by the Thornton Credit Union. For a heartbeat, he looked like her ex-husband. She repeated her yoga breathing again, and made a mental note to mention it to Dr. Daley. "Will?"

"Yeah?"

"How did you get my cell number?"

"It's on the fridge." She heard the unspoken *duh* in his voice and blushed, though no one on the sidewalk could hear her heart pounding or feel the sweat that beaded up around her hairline.

"Right. Of course." She dropped her phone into her purse and wiped her clammy hands on her skirt. Dr. Daley's office was right around the corner.

When she parked Maggie's Subaru and walked towards the elementary school entrance at three o'clock, she could see the Mom Cluster from across the parking lot. Her stomach sank. Whether shaded from the wet bayou heat or soaking up mountain sunshine, there was always a group of them: casually gorgeous and smugly settled, coffee mugs and leashed dogs in hand, discussing homes, work, husbands, hair stylists...

This one sounded particularly animated today. Laughter sparkled across the grassy front yard of the school. An ostentation of peahens, preening, she thought, a random bit of vocabulary surfacing.

One of them knelt to tie her shoe, and Sam saw why.

Will stood in their midst; she hadn't noticed him because of a conveniently placed Japanese maple. The afternoon sun kissed his face and the breeze ruffled his hair. The peahens fluttered around him, subtly jostling one another to get close to him.

She caught the words *Erik* and *swim trunks* as she approached. She giggled in spite of herself. Will was telling them about the time Erik had lost his bathing suit jumping into Faye's Hollow over in

Catmint Gap when the stream was running high. Erik would be *thrilled*.

She'd heard the tale from Erik's point of view, but never Will's. She ached to join them, but she loitered where she was, unsure of her welcome.

Will finished the story with a flourish; Sam half expected the ostentation to applaud.

The front doors of the school opened. The attention of the flock turned to their offspring, but even as every other adult gravitated towards the children pouring from the building, Will walked towards her. His attention drew her forward like a tow-cable.

"Hi." She fidgeted with her ponytail on her way to meet him.

"Uncle Will! Sam!" Noah and Ava bolted out of the crowd of students.

Sam crouched to greet her cousins, grateful for the distraction.

A female voice interrupted Noah and Ava's after-school chatter. "You must be Samantha."

Sam looked up to find one of the peahens standing over her, and stood up. "Hi. Yes."

"Will mentioned you were meeting him." The woman shot a longing gaze in Will's direction. "Would you all like to join us at Wilson's for creemees? It's just about warm enough for ice cream, I think."

"Can we?" Ava bounced on her heels. Noah nodded, dancing around her in circles.

"Can we?" Will rocked on his heels in imitation of Ava. "Please? I haven't had a maple creemee in years, and Wilson's are the best."

He offered a hand, wiggling his fingers for her to accept.

Sam hadn't had a maple creemee in years, either. You didn't find maple soft serve cones outside of Vermont often, and even if she had found one in New Orleans, the Lacroix women skipped dessert unless it was for show. They had to watch their figures.

Will introduced her as Samantha, because she'd asked him to.

"That sounds perfect." She put her hand in Will's and smiled at the peahen. "Call me Sam."

Chapter Four

Will had no idea which kid belonged to the woman named Keely, but he owed that kid an extra ice cream.

Wilson's Creamery in Catmint Gap sat right on the state road, where it bent with the curve of the Catmint River. Prime real estate for catching skiers headed in and out of Singing Bowl Ski Area, leaf peepers coming through the Gap seeking fiery foliage, and pretty much anyone else whose mouth watered at the idea of a tall swirl of soft serve piled on a cake cone.

The sun was warm, the tables were sticky, and the river was high with winter runoff. Noah, Ava, and a gaggle of other second graders and Kindergarteners were braving the chilly pools that formed between rocks on the sandy river bank.

Not much had changed since he was that age. Except that he hadn't known Sam back then.

Will watched her anchor a stack of napkins with one elbow while she carefully licked her way around the edge of the cone, certain that image was going to linger on future lonely Montana nights. He wished he'd thought of coming here with her when they were in high school.

"How was your interview?"

She glanced over to where the kids were playing before answering. "Good, I think. I was there for a couple of hours, then I..." Her brow wrinkled. "I ran an errand before I met you at the school. What did you do all day?"

"Went for a run. Drove down to Rutland with K.B. to get our tuxes. Mowed the lawn."

Sam narrowed her eyes. Will wanted to kiss her nose where it turned up when she didn't believe him. "You mowed the lawn?"

"I earn my keep when my benevolent cousin keeps me out of a twin bed down the hall from William Dryer Senior's night time serenade."

Sam licked a melting drip of maple creemee off her cone. "Now's probably a bad time to tell you you're only two stories down from me, and I snore like a buzz saw, isn't it?"

"Such a beautiful woman could never snore like a buzz saw." Will polished off the last of his ice cream and took a bite of his cone. "Maybe a swarm of bees, or a gentle belt sander."

"You're awful." Sam giggled. She glanced at the kids again, and when she turned around, a hint of blush had risen behind the freckles on her cheeks. She wasn't trying to turn him on by laughing at his bad jokes and eating her ice cream, but damn, it was working.

"I know it's kind of last minute, but would you be my date for K.B. and Jen's wedding?"

"I can't," she said. Too quickly, he thought, like it was a knee-jerk reaction. "The kids. And I wasn't invited. It's terrible manners. They didn't count on an extra guest."

"Whoa." The way she'd escalated from practical to almost fearful sent a shiver down his back. "It's no big thing. My mom, or Erik's, would watch the kids for a few hours. And this isn't a society wedding. They rented the cider press barn at Strickland's Orchard in Thornton. It's a catered pig roast. And you'd be doing me a favor. If I don't have a date, I'm going to have to fend Nikki Desrosiers off with a sharp object."

"You'll have to do that even if you have a date," Sam muttered.

Will reached for her forearm, hating that he sensed a tiny flinch when he touched her. *What the hell was going on?* "So, is that a yes?"

Uncertainty played across her features for a moment. Will watched her look around the shady, riverside grove full of families and tourists enjoying the June afternoon, wishing he knew what was going on behind those moss-colored eyes.

"I'd really like to have you there with me."

She inhaled sharply, like she was choosing to jump from the tallest rock at Arcadia Falls. "Okay. I'll be your date. If someone can watch the kids."

"Sam, Sam!" Ava ran up from the riverbank. "Noah caught a frog!"

Like she'd been doing it all her life, Sam scooped up the napkins and rose from the picnic table. "Let's see." She turned back to him. "You coming?"

His luck was holding. Will popped the last bite of cone in his mouth and followed Sam and Ava down to the water where Noah was crouched barefoot in a pool of still water with his hands cupped around a shiny, quivering frog.

"I never catch them," Noah whispered.

"Nice work, pal. Whatcha gonna call him?" Will said. He got down on one knee to inspect the catch.

"Howl." Noah spoke reverently into his hands.

"Like a wolf?" Will said.

"Like the moving castle," Sam whispered, crouching down next to him. "Does he have a friend like Sophie to rescue?"

"Maybe," Noah said. "He's gonna beat the witch."

"I don't like the witch." Ava splashed past them and the frog leaped out of Noah's hands.

"Ava!" Noah's face screwed up in fury.

Sam looked at Will, her gaze shifting from Ava to Noah. She followed Ava, who'd crumpled into tears when her brother screamed at her.

"Hey, Noe. She didn't mean to–" Will put out a hand to balance himself on a nearby rock.

"Yes, she did. She ruins everything." His lip wobbled. "I never caught one before."

"And you'll catch about a million more, pal. Promise. I'll even help while I'm home this week." Wet feet and all, Will scooped his nephew up and carried him toward the picnic table.

"You will?"

"We'll go out tomorrow, see what we can catch at my parents creek."

Noah sniffled. "Aunt Lillian and Uncle Bill's?"

"Yep." Will ruffled Noah's hair. "Should we go see what Sam and Ava are up to?"

"We're right here." Sam, holding Ava's hand, came up behind him. She shuffled Ava forward.

"Sorry, Noah."

Noah buried his face in Will's shoulder. Will whispered so Sam and Ava wouldn't hear. "Listen, little man. She's your only sister and we both know she was just goofing off. She was pretty excited you caught Howl, too. Show her how to be cool and accept the apology."

Noah picked his head up, briefly. "S'ok."

Will caught Sam's smile over the kid's heads. *Crisis averted.* He wondered what she'd said to Ava.

"Keely–" Sam flagged the mom who'd invited them and started collecting their things. "Thanks for the invite. This has been great. We need to get these two home, though."

"Bye, you two!" Keely and all the mothers waved with their fingertips. "Bye, Noah. Bye, Ava!"

Will helped Sam get the kids buckled into Maggie's Subaru. They were still bickering, but it seemed the worst had passed. He walked Sam around to the driver's side. "We make a pretty good team, Ellis."

Sam put the keys in the ignition. "Let's not congratulate each other just yet. We haven't even done dinner."

Chapter Five

By Wednesday, it was clear to Sam they did make a pretty good pair, but that didn't mean she wasn't wiped out.

"Now I know why my mom always asked my dad to pour her a glass of cabernet after dinner," Sam twisted the corkscrew into the neck of the wine bottle.

Noah and Ava were tucked in upstairs, the dishwasher was running, and the kids' soccer uniforms were in the dryer for their practice the next afternoon.

Will's chuckle, rumbling in his chest, actually made her weak in the knees. Sam's fingers slipped a little on the plastic corkscrew handle. They'd coexisted for over forty-eight hours and she hadn't made a total ass of herself. There was no need to start now.

"Those two will wear you out, that's for sure." Will opened the fridge and eyed the contents.

"I missed so much of their lives." She offered him the wine bottle. "Do you want some?"

"No. Thanks, though," Will grabbed a beer and popped the tab. "You'll see more of them now that you're back."

Sam admired his silhouette in the refrigerator light. She tugged the cork out, poured the wine into a jelly jar, and toasted the air between them. "To long weeks and happy reunions."

"Long weeks, happy reunions," Will swallowed. "And old friends."

Sam watched him, fascinated by the lines of his neck and shoulders in the dim kitchen light. "Old friends." It was true, but the air never used to shimmer like a mirage between them. There had been moments over the years when she'd wondered if he felt something, but the last two days, Sam's skin had nearly crackled with electricity whenever Will was near. It was both exquisite and unbearable.

To save her sanity, Sam shattered the moment with small talk. Her laptop was on the counter. "Maggie emailed me a couple pictures of the resort. To show the kids. Do you want to see?"

"Sure." Will left his beer and joined her, leaning a hip against the countertop to look at her screen.

She'd miscalculated. Across the room, his eyes in shadow, she could at least breathe.

He'd been out with some of his friends earlier. They'd gone hiking, out to the Strickland's hunting cabin to relive some old times. He'd come home a little grubby, a little sweaty, and smelling of the woods.

Now, his proximity was more intoxicating than the wine.

Sam focused on opening her inbox and clicking on the photo files. Anything to stop thinking about the scent of Will's skin.

"They look relaxed," he said. "Now I get why they needed a break."

"Maggie's so lucky," Sam murmured.

Will shifted his body so he was looking over her shoulder. His breath was warm near her ear. "They're both lucky."

He moved a lock of her hair, tucking it behind her ear. Sam felt the contact run through her like an electrical current. She clicked the photos closed and ducked away, putting much needed distance between them. Forty-eight hours and she was a mess of longing, desire just the tip of an iceberg of fear, regret, and shame her sessions with Dr. Daley were only just beginning to untangle.

Will was watching her, concern evident in his eyes, which only made it worse.

"I have to be up early tomorrow. It's Ava's end-of-the-year party tomorrow, and Maggie said I should swing by the diner on the way to school and pick up some cupcakes Stu's wife baked."

Had she not wanted to crawl into bed and forget the entire exchange, she would have laughed at her own awkward exit. All it lacked was a puff of cartoon smoke.

She managed to avoid being alone with him the next day, and Will headed out in the evening with K.B.'s groomsmen for an early bachelor party. It was a half hour later than usual when she got the kids tucked in.

All week, she'd fought conflicting urges to burrow into Will's warmth or push him away. When he was there, she didn't know what to say or what to do with her hands, except in those moments when he broke the tension with humor. With him gone, the house was too quiet. The stillness too empty.

Dr. Daley had asked about her friendships. Had she given any thought to rebuilding the relationships that suffered during her marriage? Sam hadn't been able to answer. Marnie, despite the awful scenes before her wedding, had stuck by her. Hers was the only friendship Sam considered working on, until Will had come upstairs on Monday morning.

"And have you reached out to your friend since you've been living here again?" Dr. Daley had asked.

It was difficult to avoid Marnie, since she was living at Marnie's parents' place, but she hadn't made herself available. She certainly hadn't reached out. She'd kept Marnie's parents at as safe a distance as possible, too. She thought maybe Mama Daphne understood.

The longer Maggie and Erik's old house settled around her, the better the idea of reaching out sounded. She was about to pick up her phone when three knocks sounded on the kitchen door. She was so startled, she nearly knocked her phone to the floor.

Outside, standing in the porch light while a company of tiny insects buzzed around her hair, was Marnie herself.

Marnie spoke without preamble. "I'm sick of you avoiding me. I know Will's out with K.B. and the boys. You don't have to spill all your guts tonight, but we are going to have a good long talk."

Sam laughed. "I was just going to call you."

"Excellent." Marnie shoved past Sam and kicked off her shoes by the door. She noticed the jelly jar of red wine by Sam's laptop. "Where are those jars? I'll pour myself one, and we'll go out to the fire pit and pretend everything hasn't been super shitty for you since you got married and divorced."

"Make yourself at home," Sam said dryly, as Marnie did just that.

"Do you have any snacks? Micah's on this quinoa and micro greens kick. I'm going to eat my arm."

Sam knew Maggie's cupboards were full of lunchbox items for the kids, not the Cool Ranch Doritos she and Marnie had scarfed down in the loft as teens. "I'll make popcorn."

Marnie hugged her. "Extra butter."

Her friend's embrace cracked one of the too many walls she'd put up. Sam hugged her back, not bothering to hide her tears. "I'm sorry it took me this long to let you in."

Marnie giggled. "I was only outside for a minute."

Sam laughed, too, which only made her cry harder. "I hate you."

"Hey. Aw, Sam." Marnie squeezed her. "You're going to be okay. I promise."

Sam sniffled. "How do you know?"

"My mom says I'm magic, doesn't she?" Marnie picked up a kitchen towel from the table and mopped Sam's face.

Sam backed away, pushing the towel back at Marnie. "Gross."

"You love me," Marnie said, sitting down at the table. "So, how's living with Dryer working out? You two kids finally taking care of business?"

"Marnie!" Sam felt her whole face go as red as the wine. "We're just friends. I'm not sixteen anymore."

"Amen to that." Marnie raised her glass. "Look, seriously. I know your head's a mess, but as the *de facto* go between for the two of you since like, 1996, I can safely say there is *something* you two need to deal with, and if it were me, I'd at least like to get some good sex out of it."

"Good thing I'm not you," Sam muttered.

"Don't get all snippy with me, Sammy. I love you forever, but you two drive me nuts." Marnie refilled her jar. "*And* I saw Keely Bigelow at the Farmer's Market Committee meeting on Tuesday. She was telling me about meeting Maggie's niece and her adorable boyfriend at the school, and how cute they were with the kids at Wilson's."

"He's not my–"

Marnie leaned back in her chair, arms crossed. "But he is something."

All day Friday, Sam thought hard about her conversation with Marnie. Will was *something*. An old friend, in a lot of ways as comfortable as her favorite UNH sweatshirt. The one her mom had saved for her when she moved to Louisiana. But she hadn't spent over a decade hiding from her feelings for a sweatshirt.

By the time Will came back from the rehearsal dinner on Friday night, she'd put the kids to bed, cleaned the kitchen, changed the sheets on Maggie and Erik's bed, tidied the playroom, poured herself a glass of wine, and was trying–and failing–to find a job online. She'd heard nothing from the preschool, and Dr. Daley was pushing her to take more steps towards being a functional human.

Will took in the sparkling kitchen. "Well, I feel like a useless freeloader."

"Not at all," Sam said. "I don't know if I could have handled Noah and Ava on my own this week." She dropped her gaze and shifted her weight. "I'm glad you were here."

Will leaned against the counter. "You did fine last night while I was keeping Kurt from making every available mistake in the greater Burlington area."

It wasn't hard to picture K.B. stumbling around Burlington, wasted and trying to make poor bachelor party choices. The sarcastic remark on the tip of her tongue about Will being the wrong guy to keep him in line dried up. Maybe once upon a time, but she got the sense he'd grown out of that.

"The wrestle-Uncle-Will-until-everyone-is-ready-to-drop hour is essential, you know." Sam looked at him over the rim of her jar. "I'm not exactly the wrestle on the floor type."

He arched a brow. Her wine-warm skin tingled; she hadn't meant it like that, but now the image was there in the room with them. She could *feel* it.

"You'd have thought of something," Will said. His eyes lit up. "You could've danced them to exhaustion. I remember the way you danced at Erik and Maggie's wedding all those years ago. You always had moves."

"I loved it. Dancing." The Lacroix women only danced once at a party, with an appropriate partner to an appropriate song. "I don't anymore."

Will was incredulous. "You don't anymore?"

"Dance? Not so much."

Craig had come upon her dancing alone in the suite the Lacroixes had offered her, gleefully following Gram'ma Funk's instructions to shake that ass. He'd turned off her CD player mid-beat "If I want to see that, I'll go to Aubergine." The reference to the upscale gentlemen's club shamed her; she hadn't learned yet that Aubergine was the least of her humiliations.

"You want to?" Will asked, pushing away from the counter.

"Here?" she stammered, the memory still clinging to the backs of her eyelids.

"Too many mosquitos outside," he teased.

She looked at him, handsomely rumpled in the khakis and pale green button down he'd worn to K.B.'s rehearsal dinner. A rehearsal for the wedding tomorrow night. After which he was going back to Montana, and who knew when she might see him again.

Will. Oh, Will.

"Samantha. I'm asking you to dance."

As she stood there, unable to coherently form thoughts, he walked past her, into the living room.

There was a plastic snap and clack, a beat of silence, then Bono beckoned from the living room speakers, quietly enough so as not to wake the sleeping children upstairs.

Unchained Melody. He remembered.

Will reappeared in the archway, arms braced overhead. The playful teasing was gone from his eyes, replaced by a liquid warmth.

He held out his right hand. "Trust me."

His hand was warm. She could smell soap and a hint of something spicy. His shirt smelled faintly of charcoal and Deep Woods Off.

He still had moves, too, but they were a grown man's moves. He pulled her into the shelter of his body, threading their fingers together where their hands held. The hand at her waist fanned out to hold her hip. They swayed in time for a few beats, then Will twirled her away and back again, catching her with that rakish grin she'd always loved. His lips brushed her temple as he moved them into the middle of the room.

His left hand moved over her lower back, caressing the slope of her spine and the curve of her hip, while his right fingers remained laced with hers.

When he turned her again, he kept her near so their bodies brushed as she spun, before drawing her close and rocking them together in more of an embrace than a dance step. He ended with the same dip he'd done at Maggie and Erik's wedding as the last chord faded, lifting her slowly until his lips were a whisper from hers. Their breath mingled. Sam's heart pounded in her chest.

Déjà-vu washed over her. She'd wanted this kiss since she was fourteen years old. Of course Will's closeness felt familiar; she dreamed it so often it felt real.

The fuzzy daydream memory of Will blurred into actual memory of Craig's face, mottled with rage. Her mouth was wet and sore from the relentless, brutal sucking and licking Craig considered kissing. "Fucking hell, I don't know what my mother sees in you. You're as cold as a nun." She'd pushed him away that one time, earning a stinging slap. She'd thought it odd, afterwards, that he'd mentioned his mother.

The crack of the remembered blow snapped her out of her reverie and she shoved her way out of Will's arms with a gasp. "I'm sorry. I can't. Please, Will. Don't hate me, but I can't."

She ran up the stairs as lightly as she could, closing and locking the bedroom door. A few moments later she heard Will's soft steps outside her door.

She heard him sit, heard what sounded like his head leaning against her door.

"I couldn't hate you, Sam. I'll stay here, if that's okay. In case there's something besides me that scared you."

The tears she'd kept at bay for days finally spilled over. Sam muffled them with her pillow. She huddled, fully dressed, under the covers, for a long time before sleep came. When she woke, it was nearly ten in the morning, the house was silent, and there was nothing outside her door but a square of morning sunshine.

In the kitchen, she found a PostIt stuck to the fridge, reading, "Gone frog hunting at Lill & Bill's. Marnie says lunch at the Farmer's Market at noon. See you then. -W."

Chapter Six

Will piled the kids into Maggie's car a little before noon. He'd done his best to keep them busy while Sam slept. He'd dozed outside her door, heart aching while she cried, until after three, before finally shuffling downstairs to collapse in the rec room. "What are we getting at the market for lunch?"

"Grilled cheese!"

"Noodles!"

Marnie Burnham's vision for a year-round indoor local marketplace had not only survived, it was thriving. She and Micah worked their asses off traveling around the region to convince chefs, farmers, crafters, authors, beekeepers, brewers, cheesemakers, anyone who was making anything...to try out a booth. They'd hired people in town to oversee the weekly operations and administrative tasks, and Micah was talking about having to quit his job at Killington to take on a bigger role.

The payoff meant Will had to park a quarter mile out Old Quarry View Road and carry Ava on his shoulders through a lively crowd to find his friends.

Micah Reynolds, Blueberry Hill transplant and the only guy Will could imagine going toe-to-toe with Marnie, was waiting with Sam on the front steps of the Grange Hall. A steady stream of traffic moved in and out of the market, and a handful of vendors had carts and tents along the sidewalk, including Marnie's mother's pop-up soap trailer.

"Oh, Will Dryer, you rascal!" The soap-making mother in question ran down the sidewalk and hugged him, enveloping him–and Ava by extension–in an orange-vanilla scented cloud. "You're here for Sam. That's lovely. Her magic is dim, sweetie, but I think you can help her find it again."

Will kissed Daphne Potter's cheeks. Marnie's mother claimed to be a witch, through her mother's people before her. She despaired of her daughter's inherited abilities–Marnie was a brutally practical soul, but this was the first time he'd heard Daphne suggest Sam might have some of the Potter magic.

"I'm home for Kurt and Jen's wedding, Mama Daph, but making Sam smile is certainly a perk."

Ava squirmed, so he let her down. She and Noah ran to Sam and Micah.

Daphne took his face in her hands. "That girl saw terrible things. I can see their reflections in her eyes. I prayed at the Lake Pleiad spring for someone to help her heal, and here you are."

The way Sam had fled when he'd come so achingly close to kissing her again the night before came to mind.

"I'll do what I can, promise." He hugged Marnie's mom again for good measure. "Gotta go. Having lunch with Marnie and Micah."

"You're a good man, Will." Daphne floated away toward the soap trailer, greeting everyone she met by name.

Marnie exited the Grange Hall on Truman Bixby's arm. She was in the middle of an animated conversation between him and another older man Will didn't recognize. When she saw him, she waved.

Micah followed the direction of Will's gaze, and began shepherding Sam and the kids up the stairs through the crowd. They all met at the top of the stairs.

"Hey, guys." Marnie handled the introductions like a pro. "Everyone knows Mr. Bixby. Professor Corning, this is Samantha Ellis and Will Dryer. Sam, Will, Eustace Corning. Professor Corning teaches in the history department at Thornton College. He and Mr. Bixby are planning a civil union next month. I'm *trying* to convince them to have a huge blowout here at the Grange."

"You're exhausting, Ms. Burnham." Mr. Bixby kissed her cheek, despite his exasperated tone, and he and his partner excused themselves.

Marnie sighed. "They're so freaking sweet together. Fifty-eight and sixty-one, and about to tie as much of a knot as they can. Eustace says he's been asking since they passed the bill in 2000."

Micah wrapped an arm around Marnie's waist and nuzzled her neck. "Maybe by the time you say yes to me, we can have a double wedding."

"About the time they can have a legal wedding is when I'll have one, too." Marnie batted Micah away, then tugged him back for a kiss.

Will snuck a glance at Sam, whose eyes were shimmering. The topic of marriage was clearly a touchy one. He wondered if they were still on for the wedding later.

Marnie dropped into a squat to address Noah and Ava. "So, you two hooligans. What should I commandeer for your lunches?"

"Mac and cheese!"

"Peanut butter cookies!"

Sam laughed. "I'm pretty sure cookies don't qualify as lunch, Ava. Let's go inside and walk around. You two can pick out your lunches. Maybe Micah will find us a table outside?"

"Grab me a sandwich from the pulled pork guy?" Will asked, his stomach rumbling from the visual onslaught of food and the smell of cooking on the breeze. "I'll help Micah hold down the fort."

He followed Marnie's Viking–the dude *was* tall–around the side of the building to a small green space where the Market set up picnic tables appeared every spring. They watched as a family vacated one, then settled at it.

Micah gave him an opening. "What's going on?"

"How long has Sam been home?"

"A month or so. We really haven't seen much of her," Micah said. "It was driving Marnie crazy."

"I bet." Will picked at some loose paint on the table. "Marnie once told me she had a bad feeling about Sam's fiancé."

"That's putting it mildly. *Bad* upgraded to *terrible* when she married the guy. We were there. It was no good. Marnie flew down first. She wanted to take Sam out, do some best friend girls stuff, hear some jazz. Visit some markets." Micah rolled his eyes. "When I got down there a couple days later, Marnie was livid. Sam had met her for an hour for coffee the first day, then after that, excuses. Dress fittings, wedding commitments, dinners."

Will searched Micah's face for the joke. "That doesn't sound like Sam."

"No shit. Marnie marched up to their gated house in the Garden District, and they refused to let her in. Told her *Samantha was indisposed.* Like something out of a bad Gothic novel."

Will didn't like the way Micah paused. "What?"

"Later that night Sam actually snuck out of their house to meet Marnie at our hotel. I don't know a ton about makeup, but I'm pretty sure she was covering up a fresh shiner."

Will fought the urge to take Micah by the collar and shake him for not carrying Sam out of the bayou over his shoulder like the marauder Marnie always called him.

Micah must have seen the rage in his eyes. "Look, she didn't stay long enough for us to get through to her. And the next morning she walked down the aisle in that huge cathedral, looking like a fairytale. We went to the reception for as long as we could stand it, but it was pretty clear we weren't welcome."

"Fuck."

"That about sums it up. Broke Marnie's heart." Micah nodded in the direction of the Grange's front entrance. "They're on their way over. Listen, I guess all I'm saying is, her ex is a real piece of shit, but whatever went down, she's not talking about it yet."

Chapter Seven

The kids took off like a shot for the table where Will sat with Micah. Sam might have been their official guardian for the weekend, but Will was definitely the celebrity guest star.

She understood. Despite her best efforts, she was just as susceptible as ever to his charm, and there was real danger now. He appeared to be turning it on her intentionally.

"I'm glad you came out today," Marnie said, grinning as Noah scrambled up Micah's back. "My resolve is slipping. One of these days I'm gonna marry that guy and get knocked up."

"Remind me to start looking for the Hallmark card for that," Sam said.

"Shit, I'm sorry." Marnie slung an arm around her shoulders. "That was tactless. I know it's a touchy subject."

"Yeah." Sam shifted her grip on the cardboard flat that held the kids' lunches.

"So, you're going to K.B. and Jen's wedding with Will tonight?" Marnie changed the subject with the subtlety of an ocean liner.

"I said I would, but I don't know if it's a good idea anymore."

Marnie stepped out ahead of her and looked hard at her face. "There's a story there. Tell you what, let's scarf down our lunches, leave the kids with the men for a few hours, and go back to the loft. Mama Llama's got this goat's milk facial treatment... We'll be girly and you can tell me what the hell is brewing since I last checked in on Thursday."

Shame soured Sam's appetite. She avoided her best friend out of fear Marnie would judge her harshly, starting with her wedding. She'd pleaded with Lilith to invite Marnie. Family was unavoidable; appearances must be preserved, but friends were different. Lilith had seen the danger in friends. Marnie and Micah came to New Orleans for her wedding after Sam fought hard to put them on the guest list, and she'd let the Lacroixes treat them like garbage. One of the thousand awful manipulations that slowly eroded who she was.

"I don't deserve you."

"Who does?" Marnie hailed the table, where Noah and Ava were clearly holding court. "Shove over, beautiful humans. Sammy and I have a plan and we need sustenance."

The kids' kept them entertained with tales from the Dryer's stream. Micah and Marnie's banter was easy. Will was quiet, but Sam felt the weight of his gaze.

When they climbed into Marnie's Jeep, Will and Micah were debating between returning to Lillian and Bill Dryer's creek to hunt more frogs, or taking them over to the sheep farm to see this year's lambs.

"So," Marnie said, popping an old mix tap into her tape deck. Marnie's soft top Jeep was a technological relic, dating back to college. "What are you going to wear?"

"I have one dress I brought back from New Orleans. Other than that, I have yoga clothes and jeans."

"Note to self: take Sam shopping. STAT." Marnie glanced at her. "Are you cool wearing a dress from there?"

Tears stung Sam's eyes. Marnie just *got her* sometimes. Maybe Marnie had some of Mama Daph's magic, despite her protests. Sam took a deep breath and blinked away the urge to cry. "Craig bought it for me, but his mother never liked it. Let's give it a shot."

The dress was still in the boutique garment bag. Black with silver scrolling lettering: *Patrice's*. Lilith's favorite dressmaker kept a small collection of *prêt-à-porter* pieces that caught his eye–a curated trunk show that reflected his magpie fashion acumen. Sam had always liked the dressmaker, despite her fittings with him being one of Lilith's many ways of controlling and reimagining her. When she'd run her fingers over the pale pink knit and mermaid green sequins, Patrice had whispered in Craig's ear. Her fiancé had put the dress on his mother's account without even looking at it.

Lilith had called it trashy; Sam was never permitted to wear it.

Marnie put the Jeep in gear and honked at Will as she pulled out. "To the loft!"

The loft over Daphne Potter's soap workshop was nicer than it had been when the girls were in high school. Clean modern furniture and a new wood stove, a new bathroom, and a bedroom with a door replaced a dusty, exposed beam barn attic decorated with tapestries, Christmas lights and an old lava lamp.

"Not that I'm complaining, but when did they upgrade?"

Marnie's jaw dropped. "Five years ago. Mama Pajama hasn't pestered you with renovation details until your ears bleed?"

Five years before she was substitute teaching in New Haven. Not even that far away, but she hadn't come home all that often. She'd been so hell bent on getting out of Blueberry Hill and seeing the world. When she had come home, she and Marnie went out or spent their time at Marnie's apartment in the village.

"Your mom has basically let me be."

Marnie snorted. "She didn't tell me she wasn't feeling well."

Sam laughed. "She's given me space. I think she understood without my saying that I wasn't ready for a lot of conversation."

Marnie's eyes rolled and she groaned. "Which she'll tell me is because we're all part of some moon-sisterhood or something."

"I think it's just caring, Marn." Sam's rebuke was gentle. "She's always been like a second mother to me."

Her own parents had retired to Tucson. Sam had skipped family holidays to travel, moved to New Orleans for her Masters, and met Craig.

How had things with the Lacroixes spun out of control so quickly?

"The way they live, it's like a movie. Money and power. Everything looks beautiful and functions smoothly." The confession burst out of her as she stared out the picture window that looked over Marnie's parents' property. "I got sucked in. I fell for it, and I didn't notice they were remodeling me to fit some space they'd carved out."

"Not until that bastard hurt you." Marnie's tone was vicious.

Sam turned around. "Twice. I wasn't as far gone as I thought the second time." Her voice broke.

Marnie rushed her, wrapping her in a tight hug. "I'm so sorry, Sammy. I never should have left you there. We should have dragged you out of there kicking and screaming."

"I thought I loved him." Sam whispered against Marnie's shoulder. "I would have gone back."

Daphne Potter knocked and walked in, carrying a tray. "I brought the mask cream, and some treats for my girls."

"Hey, Mama Daphne." Sam took the tray from Daphne. Marnie's mother smelled of bergamot, lye, and comfort.

"Just Daphne, Sweet Sam." Daphne took Sam's face in her hands. Her gaze flicked briefly to her daughter. "We're all women now. Some of us more than others."

Marnie snorted.

"You were right to come home, Sam. She would have taken everything from you." Daphne's thumb stroked her cheek, then her hands floated away to unpack the contents of the tray.

Sam's pulse kicked over. "Who would have taken what?"

Daphne blinked. "I don't know her name. Platinum dye job. Rail thin. Chic clothes. Expression like she's sucking a lemon. I see her when I think about you. In the soap cauldron."

"Mom." Marnie's hands were on her hips. "Cut it out. Seriously."

"No, wait." Sam held up a hand to stop Marnie. "Daphne, that's my mother–*ex*-mother-in-law you just described."

"She's like me. Well, not like me." Daphne smiled. "Her aura is muddy and dark, like a bad eggplant."

Aubergine. Sam shuddered at the word association.

"Ugh." Marnie stomped across the room to unzip the garment bag holding Sam's dress.

"Are we trying on dresses?" Daphne asked. "What's the occasion?"

"Sam's going to Kurt Blake's wedding with Will tonight."

Daphne ran a hand over the sequins. Sam smiled. That was exactly how she'd reacted to the dress when she'd seen it in Patrice's shop. Marnie thrust the garment bag into Sam's arms.

"Go change, so we can see it. I can't deal with the witchy crap anymore."

Sam stripped down to her underwear in the bedroom. She'd put on a few pounds since coming home, despite her almost daily yoga practice. That was what happened when you ate like a person, she'd supposed.

She took a deep breath and stepped into the dress. It clung to her frame, and she had a brief moment of longing for the lingerie collection she'd left behind, followed by a wave of nausea and self-loathing as she recalled the night Craig's started the collection.

She'd had a suite of rooms in the Lacroix's home for a few weeks by then, decorated in cream and shell pink with dark walnut Antebellum-inspired furniture that didn't suit her at all, but gratitude kept her from complaining. Lilith had been grooming her for a social debut for some time. She was accompanying the family to their club for dinner with some of Louis Lacroix's business associates.

She knelt to fasten the slim ankle straps of her new black sandals into their tiny, sparkling buckles, and caught her reflection in the mirror. Her hair was elegantly *chignon*ed. Her steel-gray dress fit like a second skin on a body that was thinner than she'd ever imagined it should be. She barely recognized herself.

"Let me do that." Craig's voice from the doorway was low and intimate.

Desire fluttered in time with nerves as she rose to greet him. His eyes roamed the lean line of her leg, from the stiletto heel of her shoes to the swish of bias-cut silk just above her knee. Every hunger pang, every doubt about the need for extra sessions with Lilith's pilates instructor fled when she saw the raw hunger there.

He crossed to her, put his hands on her shoulders. He smoothed his palms over her breasts.

"Are you wearing it?" he whispered.

She nodded.

His hands traveled to her hips; his fingers dug into silk and flesh. "And here?"

She nodded. He'd conspicuously left an off-white La Perla bag on her bed earlier that day, next to her new dress and heels. The black lace inside wasn't anything Sam would have chosen for herself, but she'd put it on, understanding that the gift was also an instruction.

He nudged her, lowered her so she was perched on the edge of the bed. Briefly, she worried about wrinkling the dress, but then Craig dropped to one knee, picked her foot up and balanced it on his leg. The delicate satin strap looked even finer in his long, masculine fingers. He threaded it through the buckle slowly before running his hand up her calf, under her knee.

Sam remembered shivering as his fingers cruised up the inside of her thigh, fighting the impulse to fall back on the bed and open herself to him because his parents were waiting downstairs.

Then he squeezed her inner thigh. Hard.

"You'll want to watch what you have for dessert tonight, babe," he said casually, "Don't want people telling me my fiancée's let herself go."

She blinked back tears. As his hand slipped away, she focused on the slim bones of her ankles, the way the black satin straps shimmered against the glowing tan Lilith paid for.

Craig stood, straightening his tie. He took her hand and tugged her up, not noticing when she wobbled on the remaining unfastened shoe.

He checked his hair in the mirror and patted her ass as he walked away.

"The car's coming in ten, Samantha. You need to be ready," he reminded her before closing the door. "I'll be downstairs."

She stood there for a moment, only breathing, trying desperately not to cry. There was no time to fix her tastefully smokey eyes if the make-up ran, and she couldn't bear to see disappointment in their expressions.

A light tap at the door forced her to control herself.

"Come in."

Lilith Lacroix glided into the room. She assessed, plucked at Sam's bodice, smoothed a flyaway hair. Her shrewd gaze fell on the unfastened strap. Sam flushed uncomfortably, as though somehow Lilith could see in that unfastened buckle everything that had transpired with her son.

"Very nice, Samantha, but you'll want to put a compact in your bag. Your nose is looking a little pink," the older woman said. "Fix your shoe, and we'll join the men in the living room."

"Sammy?" Marnie's call snapped her out of her ugly memories. She was safe in Daphne Potter's guest loft, wearing her old Aerie underwear and the green sequined Betsey Johnson dress Lilith Lacroix had hated. "These facials aren't going to apply themselves. I wanna see the dress!"

She walked out of the bedroom in her bare feet.

"Hot shit, girl, look at you!" Marnie wolf-whistled.

Sam pointed a bare foot in Marnie's direction. "I'm going to need shoes."

"I've got the perfect ones!" Daphne jumped up and ran out of the loft, the screen door banging behind her.

"She doesn't know my shoe size," Sam said.

"I'm sure she'll just put a hex on them or whatever," Marnie muttered.

For a few moments, Sam squinted at her translucent reflection in the picture window. The woman who looked back at her loved the dress, knew she could pull it off. The woman who looked back at her remembered who she was before she hadn't let self-doubt or manipulation change her.

Sam kept her voice gentle. "Your mom's always been more in touch with things than anyone else I know."

"You're the one who used to call me when I was sad."

Used to. Sam heard the accusation, even if Marnie didn't mean it.

Daphne reappeared in the doorway, brandishing a pair of pearl pink vintage satin pumps with rosettes on the toes. "You both are Potters on your mother's sides. Magic does what it likes. And I think Sam's an eight. These were my mother's. They should fit."

"You always said you didn't like Gram's style," Marnie grumbled.

"And yet," Daphne said airily, "I've always felt compelled to save these shoes. Perhaps they have a destiny."

"Mama Drama," Marnie sighed, "Don't you have shampoo to bake, or something?"

Daphne winked at Sam. "Have fun tonight, Sweet Sam."

Marnie's eyes were rolling practically out of her head, but Sam smiled. When she said, "I'm going to try," she felt like it was a distinct possibility.

Chapter Eight

Will was in the shower when Marnie dropped Sam off at the house. He'd left Noah and Ava with Gail after an epic tromp through the sheep farm with Happy Londgren's three dogs. When he came up from the rec room, bow tie loose around his neck and tuxedo jacket over his arm, Sam was still upstairs.

He hung the jacket on a chair back and poured himself a glass of water. They'd need to leave shortly if they were going to make it to the Congregational Church in Thornton in time for Will to be where he needed to be.

He heard Sam's feet on the stairs and grabbed his jacket. "Hey, Sam, can you help me with the tie? I–"

The question dried up in his mouth, along with thoughts of anything but the woman who paused three steps from the bottom, uncertainty evident on her features. Her dress skimmed her thighs, hugged her hips and breasts, and crossed behind her neck with two delicate straps. It shimmered like mermaid scales, but on closer inspection it was actually pink with green sequins sewn into it. She was wearing a pair of shoes Marilyn Monroe would have envied, and her hair was loose and tousled around her shoulders.

She was perfect.

"Too much?" She finished the stairs and paused to check something about her face in the hall mirror.

"You're beautiful."

Her eyes fluttered closed for a moment, and Will wondered if K.B. would forgive him for skipping the wedding altogether. He wanted to take her someplace intimate and candlelit. Somewhere worthy of the dress and her luminous skin. Somewhere worthy of her, period. Preferably where he wouldn't have to share her.

"What were you going to ask me?"

What had he needed? Before rational thought fled... "Can you tie a bowtie?"

"I can." Her mouth tightened a little, and her fingers shook briefly when she reached for the tie. He turned his face away to give her some space, and her hands steadied.

"You're beautiful, too." Sam spoke softly, letting her fingers linger near the bowtie.

His pulse was pounding.

Will turned his head, just enough to meet her gaze. Once more, he found himself a breath away from her lips. He held himself still. Micah and Daphne's earlier words haunted him, and he was flying back to Montana tomorrow. A day ago, two days ago, he'd selfishly hoped to steal a few kisses, maybe get her out of his system.

Who was he kidding? He pressed a chaste kiss to her cheek, careful only to let his lips linger a heartbeat against the satin skin of her cheek. "Shall we go?"

"Let me grab my bag."

Will used the drive to Thornton to fill Sam in on the wedding party, largely comprised of people she'd known in school, and give her a rundown of the evening's schedule. While he knew she was a grown woman, and perfectly capable of handling herself while he executed his duties as a groomsman, he'd seen the haunted shadows in her eyes. He'd have walked on broken glass before he was the reason they appeared again.

He felt silly for worrying when she was immediately swept into the assembled crowd by a former classmate. He tried not to feel jealous of Niall Temple, who led Sam away, already talking about his younger sister's ambitious plans to open a pub in Thornton's downtown in a year or two.

After the ceremony, Sam drove his car to Strickland's Orchard, while Will spent an hour on and around the bridge that spanned downtown Thornton while the photographer put them through their paces. It wasn't until the cocktail hour was winding down and he'd escorted a far-too-clingy Nikki Desrosiers to the bridal table, that he found Sam again.

Careful not to sneak up on her, he slipped into a circle of her high school acquaintances and whispered in her ear. "Having fun?"

She didn't answer right away, but relaxed against him. The conversation lulled, and she leaned back. "Hi. I am. It's kind of a surprise."

Will put an arm around her. "Good."

They drifted through the room on a current of conversation. Word spread that Sam was there, and people who had known her in school sought her out to say hello. When he noticed her smile flagging, he suggested the buffet line. When her voice grew hoarse or her answers terse, he brought her sparkling water from the bar.

They toasted K.B. and Jen with terrible champagne and ate wedding cake, and they danced. No longer shy about the dance moves he'd picked up as a teenager, practiced in a PE class to impress college girls, and honed in Montana line dancing bars, he and Sam stole the floor on more than a few numbers.

She laughed when he spun her. Her eyes sparkled when he wasn't afraid to salsa. She twisted a mean Mia Wallace to his Vincent Vega while the summer stars floated over the orchard and the apple trees perfumed the night air.

When Etta James found her love at last, and the reception was coming to a close, Sam stretched her arm around his shoulders and laid her cheek on his chest. As he had the night before in Erik's living room, Will threaded their fingers together and held her close.

"Thank you," she whispered. "This was a perfect night."

"It's not over yet. There's something I want to show you before we head back." He'd heard about the meteor shower from the kids, who'd been begging his mom to wake them up to see it when he left them. Apparently, Noah's teacher was really into astronomy.

Sam picked her head up, a very kissable frown line forming between her eyes. "Don't you have an early flight?"

"Yeah, but I'll sleep on the plane." His eyes were already gritty from lack of sleep, but this was too good an opportunity to miss. "There's a meteor shower tonight, and the east orchard is a perfect viewing spot. I brought blankets."

"I heard something about that on the radio. Debris from something in the atmosphere?"

Etta James's last notes faded. Will shook his head. *When had she gotten so literal?* "Shooting stars, Sam."

Chapter Nine

Sam left Daphne's Marilyn Monroe shoes in Will's car. It felt wrong to hike through an orchard in borrowed vintage, pearl-pink satin pumps, and the dewy grass soothed her weary feet.

Will carried two thick blankets under one arm and held her hand with his free one. If he'd asked her to fly away with him, she would have. Just like that, her heart had declared itself for him again, scar tissue be damned. It wasn't her heart, though, that shied away from trust, from pain, that was her mind–she would hurt tomorrow when he was gone again.

They passed a marker for the Northern Spy grove. Will turned left and led them up a small rise of trees to the orchard's high point. The apple trees fanned out in rows for acres on the rolling hillside below. The sky was full of stars, so clear it almost hurt her eyes after years of soft New Orleans nights.

Sam didn't ask him how he knew where the best stargazing was, or how many girls he'd brought there in the past. Heaven knew, she didn't want to summon her own past to such a gentle moment.

He spread one blanket and sat, patting the space next to him. "C'mon."

The wool scratched her bare legs, just cutting the chill that rose from the ground–a reminder that June wasn't that far removed from the long, cold Vermont winter. Sam shivered.

Will shook out the second blanket and wrapped it around their shoulders, creating a cocoon of warmth. Sam snuggled close and let the vastness of the sky open up above her.

His hand stroked a slow, steady rhythm up and down her arm under the blanket, warming her skin and her blood. Desire warred with apprehension. She'd wanted to kiss him the night before, until she'd needed to run. There was nowhere to run to here, and no way to escape without telling him the awful truth.

I'm sorry, Will, I was weak, and I let money and comfort seduce me into a gaslit nightmare marriage. Tied myself to a monster I'm quite certain would have destroyed me if I hadn't run. If I hadn't snuck out of my room like a naughty kid and taken a bus to Arizona in the dead of night. I'm sorry I came back here to heal and got you mixed up in it.

"There's one," Will said, pointing to the South. "And another."

Sam let her worries go for a moment as a brief cascade of fiery debris streaked across the sky. When no more followed, Will lay back on the blanket, offering her the hollow of his shoulder. She hesitated, but only because she wanted to look at him. He'd been such a beautiful boy–dark-hair, laughter in his eyes and a quick smile, made human by a slight bump on his nose where he broke it playing hockey sophomore year. His ranch years had whittled away the boy; leaving a man whose embrace felt like home, and it scared her to death.

He got a haircut, she thought, noticing the fresh, blunt line at the nape of his neck where the sun hadn't deepened his tan.

She gave in to an impulse to touch his face, tentative and featherlight, tracing that long-ago imperfection where he'd hit the boards chasing the puck in his final game that season. She remembered the sound and the blood on the ice–and Will's ridiculous smile, because he'd managed to pass the puck to an upperclassman before he hit the Plexiglass, and they'd won the game.

The years, the distance, the longing, the ugliness, all of it burned away like the shooting stars, if only for a moment. Sam cradled his cheek in her palm, searched his eyes. Whisper soft, she touched her lips to his, and the whole world shifted.

She lingered, savoring the feel of his mouth, the unmistakable rightness of kissing him.

"I was hoping you'd decide to do that," he said.

Sam searched his face. There was nothing smug, nothing self-congratulatory. Only his eyes, intent on hers, and a wondering half-smile on his lips.

"I've been working up the courage for half my life."

Will shifted to gather her close. "I was an idiot kid. You know that, right?"

Sam fidgeted with the blanket to cover her bare legs. *I might be an idiot adult...*

Will's voice rumbled under her cheek. "Are you okay?"

"Just chilly."

"I can take you home."

"I don't want to go home yet," she said, settling against him to watch the sky. "Oh, there are more."

More was an understatement. Dozens of streaks of silver fire streaked across the sky. For more than a minute stars fell in a waterfall overhead while they held hands under the blanket.

The warmth of Will's body lulled her. His steady heartbeat and the slow rise and fall of his chest anchored her as the world spun underneath them. For the first time in a long while, she remembered what contentment felt like.

Chapter Ten

Over the years, Will had imagined more than once what it would be like to wake up with Sam in his arms. Her soft breathing, the smell of her sleep-warm skin, the tickle of her hair on his cheek...They slept like spoons, wrapped in stadium blankets now damp with dew on the outside and starting to soak through from the ground underneath them.

The sun was high overhead, dulled by a steely layer of haze. Will checked his watch.

Shit. My connector flight to O'Hare leaves in fifteen minutes.

Sam stretched as she woke, and the slide of her body against his sent a very different message than the one his watch did.

Maybe being stranded in Vermont for a few more hours wasn't so bad.

"Sam," he said softly. "It's morning. We've got to get going."

"Hm? What?" She turned in his arms, and he inched back to avoid anything awkward.

"We fell asleep." He kissed the tip of her nose. "It's eight."

She sat up so fast he had to dodge her or risk another broken nose. "Eight? Will, your flight."

"That ship has sailed," he said, letting his eyes drift closed, but

Sam was already getting up and dusting herself off. When he opened his eyes, she was wrapping her hair up in a messy knot and tugging her dress back into place. "How about we stop for breakfast, then I'll run us back to Maggie and Erik's so we can change."

"I'll get the kids at Gail's house so you can figure out another flight." Sam took the blanket that was still draped over his legs and folded it. Guilt was written all over her features, as though she thought she was to blame for one of the best mornings he'd had in a while. "I'm so sorry, Will."

Will hoisted himself to standing, taking the blanket with one hand and cupping her cheek with the other. "I'm not."

The innocence of their kiss the night before was fresh in his memory when he brushed her lips to hers, but when she responded, sliding her palms up his chest and around his neck, when that soft sound she made–somewhere between a sigh and a hum–teased his mouth, Will dropped the blanket and pulled her close.

Seven years before, when he'd kissed her behind a mansion on the New Hampshire seacoast, she'd tumbled headlong into the kiss in the same way. He still recalled the taste of cheap beer on their tongues, the fearless hunger she kept locked away from him until that moment. When he left her mouth to kiss her jaw and the soft skin beneath, she clutched his shoulders and pressed herself closer.

Lips parting in invitation, Sam sought him out and deepened the kiss. Will explored the trails of freckles on her arms, ran his hands over the sequined fabric at her hips. He would never be sorry he'd missed that flight; how many people actually experienced the fantasy kiss they'd imagined for almost as long as they'd dreamed of kisses?

Breathless, he pulled away. Fantasy or not, Erik's mom would want backup before long, and his stomach was calling in his mouth's breakfast debt. "I could demolish a diner breakfast right about now. What do you say to Rick's in Thornton?"

A slow smile spread across Sam's kiss-stung lips. *Damn, she's beautiful.* "Good call. We can't exactly walk into King's looking like this."

Will wondered, watching Sam walk to their booth at Rick's Diner a bit later, if there was something to Daphne Potter's claims that there was magic in her family. She'd always been different from the other girls he knew, in a way he couldn't describe. Now, seeing her walk through a crowded diner on a Sunday morning, wearing a mermaid sequined cocktail dress and some truly adorable party shoes, unfazed by the way people gawked, he thought she had to be part witch.

He'd ditched his jacket and untucked the tuxedo shirt, trying for a casual vibe, but it didn't matter. Everyone was looking at Sam, who made the walk of shame look pretty damned elegant. Once they were settled in the relative privacy of their booth, the diner's patrons forgot about them, and they ordered enough breakfast food between them for a small battalion.

Will was about to ask for the check when a guy in faded Carhartts and a hoodie bearing the seal of a well-known prep school crossed the diner. He took off a faded Bruins cap as he approached the table.

"Will Dryer?"

"Reed?" Will stood, hugging his former teammate with a sturdy clap on the shoulder. "Long time, man. How the hell have you been?"

"Too long," Reed replied. He turned to Sam. "Reed Gardner. I was–"

"Captain of the hockey team our sophomore year. I remember you, but I don't expect you to know who I am. Samantha Ellis." She offered a hand, which Reed lingered over shaking before he gave his attention to Will.

"Last I heard from the guys I still see, you were out west."

"Still am." Will glanced at Sam. "I'm home for Kurt Blake's wedding. It was last night."

"Damn. He was your year, right? Tried out with you."

"Made the team the next year," Will said. "Anyway, I'm headed home soon."

"Too bad," Reed said. "I came over here to say hello, but also, because I remember how you used to play, and I heard you were doing some coaching."

"Youth league. The local high school doesn't have a rink, so I got my boss to sponsor a travel team and cover practice fees on some ice a couple towns over."

"Sounds like a labor of love." Reed chuckled. "That's a shame."

The laugh surprised Will. "What do you mean?"

"I came over here to find out if you were back in Vermont and maybe interested in coaching full time. I run the hockey program at William Ford Hall Prep down in Brattleboro, and I'm looking for an assistant head coach to help me run the program, recruit some kids, maybe build up a JV team. I saw you walk in here with your beautiful friend, and thought maybe the answer was right in front of me."

"I'm flattered, Reed. Really."

"Flattered enough to let me buy you a beer before you head west? Let me sell it to you a little?" Reed reached into his wallet and pulled out a business card. "I can't actually hire anyone, but my recommendation to the administration carries a lot of weight. If you were a good fit, and the school could offer you something you liked, we'd be in business."

Will took the card, reading and re-reading Reed's name and titles: Varsity Hockey Coach, Hockey Program Director.

"I'm not sure how long I'll be in town, Reed. But I wouldn't say no to a beer and a conversation."

"Sounds like a plan." Reed turned back to Sam. "Nice to meet you, Samantha."

Sam must have said something funny; Reed laughed. Will was still staring at the card in his hand after Reed excused himself and left.

Sam was shaking her head. "I've found one place to apply for a job since I got here." She finished her coffee. "Granted, I just started looking, but still. You literally sleep through a flight out of town and get a soft job offer at breakfast."

"I haven't talked to Reed since he came back to play in an exhibition game senior year." He pushed the card into his shirt pocket and flagged their server for the check.

"Will you really call him?" Sam asked.

"I'm not going to pass up a chance to catch up, unless I get a flight out tonight," Will said. A flight that night was unlikely. He might get another connector to O'Hare, but the timing of the flight to Billings with a ride back to the ranch from Nat, the ranch foreman, was a little trickier. "And now that I've blown my itinerary–" He traced the veins on the back of Sam's hands, noting the way she curled her fingers in response "That means more time with you."

Chapter Eleven

True to his word, Will drove them back to Maggie and Erik's and let her have the first shower so she could go get the kids. The ride back to Blueberry Hill was quiet. The contained intimacy of Will's rental car left Sam unsure of what to say or where to put her limbs. The foolishness of what they'd done ballooned around her, taking up all the oxygen in the car.

Stargazing in an apple orchard was one thing, even that ever-so-tender kiss, but to have fallen asleep there in Strickland's Northern Spy grove...and that second kiss. That drowning, drugging, hot kiss, barefoot and wanton in the grass, left her feeling reckless and alive, like she had when she was first teaching in New Haven, or when she'd started her classes at Tulane. Like she used to feel when she was in a club or at a party, carried on the rhythm of a great song.

That kiss rushed through her body like wildfire, but like wildfire, its aftermath left her wrecked and exposed. The shivering, weak creature she'd become at the mercy of the Lacroixes had nowhere to hide from Will now. The longer he stayed, the harder it would be to keep her shame from him.

She heard him talking downstairs when she collected the Subaru keys and left for Gail Dryer's house to pick up the kids. Noah and Ava stalled, blissfully unaware of her distracted thoughts. Erik's mom welcomed her as she always had, part of the warp and weft of her son's extended family. She recounted a deeply abridged version of the previous evening's events, neglecting to report Will's continued presence in town, figuring Will's parents should hear from him first, not third-hand from his aunt.

She pulled in at Maggie and Erik's just as Maggie and Erik were climbing out of Erik's truck. Noah unbuckled himself and bolted for his mom. Ava wriggled and squirmed while Sam freed her from her booster seat, then streaked off after her brother.

Maggie hugged her hard, kids still bouncing around them, and whispered in her ear. "I hope the Will-surprise was okay."

"I could kill you," Sam whispered back. "But yes."

She watched as her aunt's family reunited, watched the kids morph from frantic with news about Will and Micah and frogs to teary over days-old disagreements Sam hadn't realized they even remembered having.

"I'm going to throw my stuff in a bag. Will you drive me to Daphne and Max's?" Sam said to Erik, while the kids were climbing all over Maggie.

"Sure. Speaking of cars, How come Will's is here?" Erik nodded at the rental. "He said he'd be gone by the time we got back."

"It's a long story," Sam said. "Short version is, he missed his flight."

"Figures. Knowing Will, he'll make the most of it." Erik slung an arm around her shoulders. "Thanks for the week off, Sam. We appreciate it."

She packed quickly, obeying an urge to get away from Maggie and Erik's observant eyes while Will wasn't around.

Erik met her in the driveway. "Looks like Will's making the most of a nap. Let's hit the road, kiddo."

Suddenly the idea of the empty loft wasn't so comforting, but Marnie would be at her office in the Grange Hall. "Can you drop me downtown instead?"

"Everything okay?" Erik's expression betrayed worry. "I don't mind running you out to Daphne and Max's."

"I'm okay. Promise," she said. "I'm going to check in with Marnie. She'll drive me home."

"Wear your seatbelt." Erik's dad-frown was strong. "That woman drives like a bat out of hell."

Sam laughed. It was true, but she'd never feared Marnie's handling of her Jeep.

Erik pulled over outside the Grange Hall, idling until she waved him off from the main entrance. She was about to push her way through the huge double doors when a platinum blonde climbed out of the backseat of a silver Mercedes parked nearby.

Lilith Lacroix ascended the stairs to the Blueberry Hill Grange Hall in her dove gray leather skirt and unwrinkled silk blouse, as though she owned not just the historic building, but the village it stood sentinel over as well.

Sam froze, unable to process the presence of her ex-husband's mother. Erik's truck vanished around the corner. Marnie's office was inside and down a long corridor; her friend was unaware Sam was there.

Lilith took off her sunglasses and tucked them in a small handbag Sam knew to be a bespoke piece of alligator skin, designed for her by Patrice a year ago, ostensibly a gift from Louis, but orchestrated entirely by her own hand.

"Samantha, how lovely to find you here." To a casual passerby, it sounded like a measured, polite greeting. Acknowledgment of a reasonable coincidence.

Sam's heart kicked over and her palms broke out in a clammy sweat. She gripped her crossbody bag strap and forced herself not to stammer. "Mrs. Lacroix."

"Call me Mother, dear. Always." Lilith's smile didn't touch her eyes. Her voice slithered across the space between them, wrapping itself around Sam.

"Why are you here?" Sam took a reflexive step back, bracing herself on the door.

"I missed my daughter, of course." There was a flinty gleam in Lilith's eyes to match her tone.

"Craig and I aren't together anymore," Sam said, digging deep for her yoga breath, for the sound of Noah's laughter when he caught his frog, for the joy of dancing with Will. For anything that might give her the strength not to crumble.

"I know you think that," Lilith said gently, as though she were addressing a child. "But you made promises to the family. Binding promises. You are bound to me in ways you couldn't possibly understand, and I need you to return home and fulfill your promises."

For a heartbeat, it all made sense. As though Lilith were speaking in her soul, instead of addressing her on a public street, in full hearing of the handful of people going about their business around her. Of course she had made promises, and Lilith had given her so much. It was only natural Lilith would want her to...

"Sam. What's up, girl?" Marnie strode around the corner of the building, accompanied by her mother, and the odd spell was broken.

Marnie stopped hard, staring open-mouthed at Lilith. "*You...*"

Lilith ignored Marnie completely. "Samantha, I've booked our return flights for tomorrow. I'll pick you up at six this evening at that hovel you're staying in. We'll have dinner in Woodstock and you can spend the night in my suite. The car will take us to Boston in the morning."

"Lady, you're out of your goddamn mind." Marnie stormed the steps, putting herself between Sam and Lilith. "She's not going as far as the ladies room with you. Unless I can come along and give you the swirly you so richly deserve."

"I see your friend is as classless as ever," Lilith said coolly. "More reason for you to come home right away. You are better than this. Craig needs his wife by his side, and I need my daughter."

Sam glanced at Daphne Potter, who'd approached Lilith from behind. At the word *daughter*, Daphne began to glow a little around the edges, as though she were backlit on a stage. "She is Camille Ellis's daughter, a Blueberry Hill Potter by birth, and you will never touch her again."

Marnie's head whipped around. She stared at her mother. "Mom?"

Sam had felt Daphne's words deep in her bones. They were both comforting and unsettling. What terrified her was the unhinged fury in Lilith Lacroix's expression when she whirled on Daphne.

"Who are you? I see you in my finger bowl, but you're not her mother."

"Daphne Ellen Potter, daughter of Ina Cleo Potter, and you are not welcome in Blueberry Hill."

The faint glow Sam sensed around Daphne flashed and faded. She was afraid to meet Marnie's eyes, though whether it was because she was afraid of confirmation or denial, she wasn't sure.

Lilith gathered the alligator bag close to her body and retreated toward the silver car. "We'll see whose daughter she is in the end, Daphne Potter."

Freed from her fear by adrenaline and the shock of Daphne's otherworldly display, Sam was able to look closely at Lilith. Her ex-mother-in-law had aged in the months since Sam fled New Orleans. Her cheeks were drawn and pinched, the skin around her eyes sunken and gray. She'd covered it expertly with a fortune in cosmetics, but Sam could see the truth. Lilith wasn't well.

Aside from a few sideways glances, no one around them seemed affected by the sheer strangeness of the whole encounter as Lilith climbed back into the Mercedes. The car purred down the road and around the bend that led toward Catmint Gap and eventually the route to I-89.

"Holy cats, Mama Drama," Marnie said. "What the ever-loving *heck* was that."

Sam stifled a giggle. Now was not the time for hysterics, but Daphne never used profanity, and Marnie's teasing somehow managed to make Daphne's gentle epithets sound filthy.

"That's your mother-in-law?" Daphne said, staring at the empty road where the car had been.

"Ex," Sam said quietly. "Lilith Lacroix."

"A finger bowl. Like a formal place setting has. How interesting…" Daphne murmured. "I suppose everyone sees in their own vessel…"

"Mom." Marnie said again. "Are we going to talk about you glowing on the sidewalk? Or like, incanting or whatever?"

"That's never happened to me before. Whoever she is, that Lilith woman has magic in her blood, too. And a lot of rage."

"Okay, this is just getting weird. I'm calling Micah and we are meeting up at the loft. There are things we need to talk about," Marnie said, pulling out her cell phone and pacing until she liked her location for a decent signal.

"Wait, Marn. No Micah. Not yet."

"That woman was threatening you. He'll want to help." Marnie pressed the keypad. "He can look pretty scary when he wants to."

"Please," Sam said. "Not yet."

Marnie sighed and pocketed her phone. "Fine. Mom?"

"You girls have a lot of talking to do. I'm going to go ahead now and take the truck home." Daphne pressed her key fob to unlock her Suburban, which was currently hitched to her soap truck. "Come down to the house when you're done. I want to research what just happened with my aura."

"Research how?" Marnie narrowed her eyes.

"I'm hardly planning a séance, Sweetie. I'm just going to get online and find out if anyone else has experience with illuminated auras."

"Online? There are witches on the internet?"

"It's not just for cats and porn, Marnie."

"MOM."

Sam watched the mother-daughter volley while she considered the implications of the last ten minutes. Lilith sometimes sounded strange or intense about family and duty, but Sam just assumed that was how people with money talked. And the Lacroixes were Southern to the bone; she'd chalked it up to cultural differences.

And buried it along with all the other things you denied were happening, her heart whispered.

Daphne seemed convinced Lilith was what? A witch?

Marnie jingled her keychain. "Let's get out of here."

"Before we head out, I should tell you I was dropping by because Will didn't leave this morning. We kissed twice and slept in the orchard. He missed his flight."

"You suck at girl talk since you came home." Marnie rolled her eyes, jumped in the open Jeep and turned the key. "Hop in. We've got a lot to get through."

Chapter Twelve

Will woke from Sunday's unscheduled nap to find a full house and dinner on the table, but no Sam. He was told she opted for a gab session with Marnie, so he left her to it. The wrestle-Uncle-Will-until-everyone-is-ready-to-drop hour wasn't nearly as much fun when he wasn't showing off for Sam. Maggie and Erik's house was brimming with happiness, and he just flat-out missed her.

Before his nap, he'd spent an hour on the phone, first to hunt down Nat Faucett, the ranch foreman at Left of Paradise.

Nat had–predictably–given him shit for missing a flight over a lady, but the old man had a string of girlfriends from Coeur d'Alene to Sioux Falls and a soft spot where Will was concerned.

"Get your ass out here on Thursday. I'm making a feed run and I can bring you back with me."

Will thought of the pastures, the grain silos, the massive hoppers of feed for the herd and flocks. "Who are you feeding that it isn't being trucked in?"

"Seems Trixie Hoult's Irish Wolfhound bitch had a litter a month or so back. The pups look a little like that mongrel that follows Sweet Joe around. Miss Trixie came around two nights ago, claiming we're responsible for the pups, on account of Sweet Joe never had the heart to have that beast snipped."

Will chuckled. "You're driving three hours round trip for puppy chow."

"Don't sass me, son, or I'll let you deliver that chow to Widow's Walk yourself."

Will meant to call the airline about rescheduling, but he found himself dialing Reed's number instead, which was how he found himself at the Denny's in Rutland at nine o'clock on Monday morning.

Reed met him wearing a WFHP polo and khakis. A clipboard lay on the table between their place settings.

Will raised a brow in question. "Soft sell?"

"I had a chat with the chairman of the board of directors last night." Reed flipped his menu open and set down again, folded back on the page featuring recurring breakfast specials. "I want to get a right hand man soon. If we hit the ground running, there's still time to be organized for the start of the season."

The *we* landed between them like a gauntlet. It sounded like opportunity.

Nat's easy laughter on the phone–even the threat of hauling puppy chow around the neighboring ranch–echoed in his ears. He loved the hard work and freedom of the ranch. Montana had been good to him, but what Reed was proposing could be a new challenge. Something lasting.

A waitress named Janet poured their coffee and promised to come back for their orders.

Will left the coffee black. No amount of sugar or half and half was going to improve it, not after a week of Sam's chicory coffee au lait. "Talk to me, buddy. Let's hear the pitch."

He waved goodbye to Reed two hours later. His old teammate headed south down Route 7, and Will contemplated the drive to the prep school's Brattleboro campus. Two hours wasn't far from Blueberry Hill, not when he'd lived two time zones away for years. The package Reed was offering–if Will decided to go for it, and got it, which was two big ifs–was generous. Two years of campus housing in a residence hall apartment, a combination of mentoring boarding students and helping Reed grow the hockey program, opportunities to teach where his expertise was useful.

Halfway back to Maggie and Erik's, just before the mountains would make it impossible, Will pulled out his phone and hit redial.

"Hey, Will." Reed's voice was tinny. "Sorry about the noise. I've got one of those earbud things that makes me look like a cyborg."

"Where should I send my resume?"

"Hell yes, brother. Email it to me. My address is on my card. I'll get the ball rolling."

Will disconnected the call after promises to brush up on the old playbook and get his suit cleaned. When he got to the four-way turn just before downtown, he turned right. Maggie and Erik's was to the left, but the person he wanted to share his good news with wasn't there. She was at Mama Daphne's.

Or at least he hoped she was. He pressed send when he got to her number in his phone and crossed his fingers on the steering wheel.

Chapter Thirteen

"She's leaving this morning," Sam insisted for the third time, while Daphne fussed over her in the workshop. Marnie had stayed the night before, confessing everything that happened between her and Will from Wednesday morning to when they woke up together in the Northern Spy grove.

Marnie had early vendor contract meetings, and was gone when Sam woke, but Daphne invited her to stay for breakfast and a tour of the soap workshop.

The tour, it turned out, was a ruse.

Sam's reflected face in the watery window glass bore a smear of red oil on her forehead to match the ones on her palms and just below her navel. "I'm not going anywhere with her. This really isn't necessary."

"Dragon's blood oil is harmless and full of potent magic." Daphne opened the unmarked cabinet above the one labeled *Essential Oils*. She pulled out a white linen jewelry bag, followed by a small gingham pouch, which she handed to Sam, before putting the Dragon's blood oil away. "It can't hurt.

Sam sniffed the pouch. The scent was sharp, sweet, astringent... and a little like the floral section at the grocery store. "What is this?"

"Yarrow." Daphne opened the mini-fridge under the counter and took out a glass jar. She shook a clove of garlic out of the jar and set it on a windowsill. "I prepared it myself. Keep the sachet in your pocket or under your pillow."

"Okay..." Sam tucked the pouch in her jacket pocket. "I don't have to sleep with the garlic, do I?"

"I'm cleansing it with sunlight," Daphne said seriously. "To recharge its protective properties. Just carry that with you today to ward her off."

Sam laughed. "She's not a vampire."

Daphne's eyes grew wide. "I never thought of that."

"What?"

"Just something I remembered," Daphne said. She picked up the white linen jewelry bag. "Now this."

She poured a necklace from the bag into Sam's palms. A black crystal pentagram the size of a sand dollar rested cool against her skin, its silver chain pooled around it. A shiver ran down her spine.

"This is beautiful, Daphne."

"It's black tourmaline, powerful on its own. The pendant was my grandmother's. The pentagram connects everything and protects what it contains. My mother put it on the silver chain. Silver is meaningful for healing and love, as well as emotional well-being. It strengthens the power in gems when they're worn together. I blessed it under a full moon before I put it away." Daphne took it from Sam's hands and clasped it around her neck. "That's five protections. More if you count the silver."

Marnie would lose her mind.

"I'll bring everything back tomorrow. I promise."

"No, Sweet Sam." Daphne collected the garlic clove and tucked it in Sam's other coat pocket. "You keep these things until you know you don't need them anymore."

"How–"

Daphne put a finger to Sam's lips. "You'll know. It's in your blood. And that's what that woman wants."

"Daphne." Sam cut Marnie's mother off.

"I don't mean literally. But when you said *vampire* before…I think she's been drawing on your power to feed hers."

Sam didn't have a reply. Lilith was definitely unstable, and Sam had always been willing to play along with Mama Daphne's magic stories, but this?

It must have gotten under her skin, though; when her phone rang, she startled and nearly knocked over a crate of liquid hand soap in Mason jars.

"Go ahead and take that, Sam. I've got to go over to the house for a few things. Be careful with yourself." Daphne breezed out of her workshop as though she hadn't only moments before been seriously discussing her ex-mother-in-law in terms of the occult.

The name on the screen banished thoughts of dark magic. "Hey."

"Where are you?" Even over the poor cell connection, Will's voice felt more like protection than any of Daphne's charms. "I've got something I really want to talk to you about."

Sam thought about the previous evening's scene and Daphne's bizarre behavior."Me, too. I'm at Daphne and Max's. Come rescue me, and we can swap stories."

Chapter Fourteen

Rescue her? From what?

He took the back roads a little faster than was prudent. She hadn't sounded alarmed, but a seed of worry had sprouted in his gut.

He found Daphne Potter and Max Burnham's property much as it always had been. Classic rambling New England farmhouse, complete with no fewer than four additions from varying periods, stretching what had probably originally been nothing more than a box with a roof. The barn had always housed Daphne's soap-making workshop, but a glance through the open barn door showed a decidedly more modern set up than he'd last seen.

Sam was waiting for him on the stairs to the loft. He knew from Marnie that the space once designated for the kids–rough hewn beams, old rugs over board floors, tapestries and bean bags–was now more of a modern crash pad.

He wondered if Sam's news had to do with her staying at the loft. "You okay?"

Sam slid to one side to make room for him. Will accepted the invitation.

"It's been a weird twenty-four hours." Sam rested her head on his shoulder.

Will leaned in, just enough to let her know he was there. "You left Maggie and Erik's in a hurry. What happened?"

Sam twisted her fingers together. "I had some things to think about. So I asked Erik to drop me off downtown. I was just about to go into the Grange Hall...Will, she was in a hired car waiting for me, I swear."

Will caught a tremor running through her. "Marnie?"

Sam shook her head against his shoulder. "My ex-husband's mother. Lilith Lacroix."

He didn't like the way her voice faltered and fell over the name. "What?"

"She came after me, to take me back to New Orleans. I've only been away a couple months, but I forgot what she's like. Hypnotic, like a snake...one you want to please."

"The hell you're going anywhere."

"I don't know how to explain that for a moment it made perfect sense, then Marnie and Daphne were there, and seriously Will...I think Daphne might be..."

"Might be what?"

If Sam heard the question, she ignored it. "Marnie and I stayed here last night, and this morning Daphne..." She picked her head up and reached inside the neckline of her t-shirt. "Don't tell Daphne, but I washed off the dragon's blood oil."

Will leaned forward, propping his elbows on his knees. "Dragon's Blood oil?"

Sam sighed. "You know how Daphne's always told Marnie she was a witch or whatever?"

Will chuckled. "Yeah."

"She thinks Lilith is, too, and me, and that I'm in danger." Sam giggled. "Oh, my god. It sounds ridiculous."

Will wrapped his hand around Sam's. "If that woman came up here to give you a hard time, that's not ridiculous."

Sam squeezed back. "Daphne covered me in magical protections. Made me promise to keep them all until I don't need them anymore, whatever that means. And now that I'm saying all of this out loud to you, it sounds insane."

"It sounds like we need to talk to the sheriff's office about hired cars in the area."

"Then you called," Sam said, laying her head back down on his shoulder. "And all I wanted was to see you. That scares me, too."

Will picked up Sam's hand and kissed her knuckles. "Here I am, though. Not so scary."

"And I didn't get the job at the preschool. They called while I was waiting." Her voice hitched as though she might cry.

Will let go of her hand and wrapped an arm around her. "You *have* had a weird twenty-four hours."

"What was your news?" Her wobbly smile steadied.

"I had breakfast with my buddy Reed this morning on his way out of Thornton." He took a deep breath. What he said next was going to matter. "I might have a job interview at William Ford Hall–"

"That's great!"

"–next week."

"Next week? Don't you have to go back to Montana?"

"They're expecting me Thursday. I'll have to make a quick trip back here to meet with Reed."

"Brattleboro..." Sam murmured.

"It's not a sure thing," Will said, knowing he was talking about more than the job. "But worth a shot."

"Will you stay down in Brattleboro, or..." Sam blushed.

Will turned to her. "I wouldn't miss a chance to see you again. I've done that too many times."

"Would you really leave the ranch?"

"It's just an interview, but Reed seems pretty serious."

"Montana must be so beautiful."

It was, and he would miss the ranch if he left, but there were memories he wouldn't mind leaving behind. Serendipity had always served him well. He could always visit; if he were lucky, someday bring Sam out there to see it.

Why wait for someday?

"Come with me. On Thursday. To the ranch. For a few days. We'll get away from your ex-mother-in-law and whatever bug Mama Daphne has in her ear. I'll show you around the ranch, and we'll fly back in time for my interview."

"I don't know..." She searched his face. "This isn't a hike through Strickland's Orchard. Where would I stay?" Her tone was light, but Will caught a flicker of unease in the depths of her eyes.

Will knew where he wanted her to stay, but that fear had no place there. "I have my own cabin. Small, but functional. I'll sleep on my couch and you can take the bed. No big thing." He took both her hands in his. "I've missed you for years. I want to show you where I've been. And you said you needed rescuing."

"From Daphne's...whatever it is." Sam stood and paced the distance to his car and back, coming to a stop in front of him. The morning light played with the highlights in her hair while she stood, right in front of him, but out of reach until she made a decision. "Are you sure?

"Come to Montana with me, Sam." He stood, bringing them toe to toe. "Please."

She chewed her lower lip for a moment, then smiled. Her deep exhale sealed their plans. "Okay."

Chapter Fifteen

Marnie insisted Sam and Will come for dinner at their rented house halfway between Blueberry Hill and Catmint Gap before Will's delayed departure. Will arrived to pick her up with a bouquet of lilacs.

"Where did you get fresh lilacs?" The sweet perfume filled the room, reminding her of Dr. Daley's office. Her therapist always had lilacs.

"There's a woman over in the Gap who grows them year round in a hothouse. Apparently her property is full of them, too. Marnie convinced her to sell at the Grange."

Sam fussed over the flowers, arranging them in a vase on the counter, then stretched up on her toes to kiss him.

Will slid a hand into her hair and drew out the kiss. "Worth every penny."

While he drove, he filled Sam in on the itinerary for their upcoming trip.

"How is your schedule so flexible?" Sam asked him, after learning he'd been to Marnie and Micah's a couple of times since they'd moved in the year before.

"The business stuff I do for Ed directly, as opposed to helping out the ranch hands, is structured like a corporate job. Paid time off, that kind of thing. But I never use it. Mostly I work the ranch with the seasonal help or I work with Nat when I'm done with Ed's business." Will swung the car into their driveway. "I have a lot of time off saved up. I don't spend a lot of money when I'm there, since I have room and board. Might as well use the time and money, you know? So, I come home for holidays and stuff."

Sam climbed out of the car. "You used to avoid trips home."

"In college," Will said. "After school, it didn't seem so claustrophobic."

That Sam understood. Her parents' move had put distance between her and Blueberry Hill, but her own hunger for adventure kept her away. Then she'd become entangled with the Lacroixes and Blueberry Hill might have been as far away as Antarctica.

Marnie, on the other hand, had always had firm roots in their mountain home. Taking in a rainbow of Adirondack chairs around a fire pit on the front lawn and the beginnings of a vegetable garden to the side, Sam felt a pang of envy for those roots. "Their house is so cute."

"Just like the two of them," Will said, rolling his eyes. Their gaze met over the hood of the car and they both laughed.

Marnie bolted out the door and hugged Sam. "You're late."

"I brought a bottle of Zinfandel," Will said.

Marnie snatched the bottle from him. "You're forgiven. Micah's around back around back, starting the grill."

Will touched her arm. "I'll go say hi."

Marnie caught her watching him walk away, She crossed her arms and struck a parental posture. "And why were we late?"

Sam started to mention the flowers before she caught the mischievous gleam in Marnie's eye and burst out laughing. "You're awful. It's not like that."

Marnie wasn't convinced. "Uh huh."

"Promise." Sam studied her toes. "I don't know if I can."

"Shit. I'm sorry." Marnie reached for the pentagram around Sam's neck. "Has my mom been bugging you?"

Sam took the pendant from Marnie's fingers and laid it against her skin again. Magic or not, the stone charm weighed comfortably against her breastbone. "She loaned me a few things. It's harmless."

"That whole thing with scary Lilith gave me the creeps," Marnie said. "But I still think she's bonkers."

"Something happened, Marn."

"Mass hallucination?" Marnie dropped into one of the lawn chairs. "Spontaneous phosphorescence?"

"At least Lilith left." Sam joined her. "The more I think about it, the creepy thing is that she was there, at the Grange, like she knew where to find me."

"Micah's been like a burr in my sock ever since."

Sam chucked at the image. Micah was too tall, broad, and blond to be mistaken for a burr. "I think we're fine. She's gone."

"I don't know, Sam. She gives me the willies."

"Keep Micah close, then." Sam took a deep breath. "I'm going to be out of town for a few days, anyway."

"What?" Marnie shot to her feet. "Where the hell are you going?"

"Left of Paradise, with Will for a long weekend. He's got to–"

"My mother addled your brains." Marnie shook her head. "It's the only excuse. You just sort of said you aren't ready to get physical with Will, but what the hell, you'll just up and fly across the continent with him?"

"He invited me to see the ranch. We bumped into Reed Gardner after the wedding. Do you remember him?"

Distracted by the question, Marnie squinted as though her memories were resting on Sam's shoulder. "Ahead of us in high school. Hockey player. Kind of hot if you're into tall Philip Seymour Hoffman impersonators."

Sam snorted. "So anyway, Reed comes over to say hi to Will, and now I guess Will's got a job interview at WFH Prep in Brattleboro."

"Oh my god, slow down." Marnie sat again. "A job interview?"

"I'll let him explain it," Sam said. "But he invited me to go back with him to the ranch for a few days, and I said yes."

"So, you two haven't seen each other in how many years, but six days babysitting for your aunt's stupidly adorable rugrats, and you're ready to jump in a plane and fly off with him?" Marnie was winding up. "You just got out of a colossally crappy marriage and your ex-mother-in-law is kind of stalking you, but okay, sure."

Sam's cheeks went hot. "Oh, so only Marnie Burnham is allowed to jump over the relationship cliff after a few days? Because I'm pretty sure I remember you calling me from a grocery store in Albany, all high on Micah, to tell me he was *relocating* to be with you."

Marnie pulled her feet up onto the chair, wrapping her arms around her knees. "I'm worried about you, for the love of Pete."

"Do I need to be worried about this Pete?" Micah asked, as he and Will came around the garage.

"Yes," Marnie snapped. "He's going to lure me away with promises of never being a bonehead."

Micah and Will shared a look that Sam interpreted as *the women have gone crazy again.*

"Sorry to interrupt." Micah gestured between her and Marnie. "I was going to throw some burgers on the grill. Hamburgers or lentil burgers?"

No one wanted the lentil burgers, which broke the tension until Sam and Will were getting ready to leave.

Marnie walked Sam to Will's car, whispering in Sam's ear when she hugged her goodbye. "Be careful. I love you both, but something about this trip feels wrong to me."

"You don't believe in that stuff," Sam reminded her.

Marnie shrugged. "Keep my mom's stupid stuff with you, at least."

Chapter Sixteen

"My imagination wasn't big enough." Sam whispered as she watched the scenery roll past. "There's so much space, so much sky."

As they bumped along in Nat's pickup, Will saw it all through Sam's eyes: the fir trees dividing the mud-tracked pastures from the mountains, the indigo and white peaks painted against the endless, cloudless pale blue of the Montana sky.

Nat gave Will a nod of conditional approval when he'd swung his truck into the pickup lane outside the airport. The foreman made some small talk, but mostly drove in silence, listening to the radio and the conversation. Sam didn't notice, but Nat's eyes crinkled with amusement at her wide-eyed wonder.

"Hits me every time I see it," Will replied, but he was watching her profile, lit by the late afternoon sunlight pouring in through the truck window.

The ends of her chestnut hair, pulled back in a low tail, twirled in the hot air from the dashboard vents. He reached out, caught a curl in his fingers. She was too riveted by the view to notice.

She peered out the window. "Is that a hawk?"

"Kestrel," Nat said.

"A kestrel. Daphne would love that." Sam pointed out the window.

In the distance, three figures on horseback rode a fence line in the foothills. "It's like another time. When do we get to Left of Paradise?"

"We're here," Nat said, negotiating the truck around a puddle the size of her Honda, "we've been on Ed's land for about five minutes now. Everything you see is the LP."

"Oh."

Will remembered feeling much the same way the first time he'd seen it.

A few minutes later they pulled up in front of a cluster of small log cabins.

"End of the line, Miss Samantha." Nat left the key in the ignition and climbed down from the cab. He'd already unloaded their things from the truck bed by the time he and Sam were out of the cab. "Will, we've got a paddock fence to repair in the morning if Ed doesn't need you. Miss Samantha, you're welcome to come if you ride. If not, I'm going to ask Will to take you out on his own time."

Sam looked at him; he could only shrug. Ed Atkinson might own the L.P., but Nat ran it.

"I don't ride," Sam said. "But if there's somewhere I can help, I'll keep myself busy until you get back."

"I hear from Will you make a mean pot of coffee," Nat said. "I won't insult you by asking you to fix it for us, but I'll admit I'm curious. Think you can teach some old ranchers how?"

"I'd be happy to."

"I'll have Daisy collect you in the morning. She can always use willing hands." Nat tipped his hat. The truck rumbled off down the road.

"Daisy? Sweet Joe? Foreman Nat?" She spun around, taking it all in. "Is this for real?"

Will caught her, brought her close. "Very real." He'd resisted the almost constant urge to touch her all day, but her obvious delight was irresistible. "Please tell me I can kiss you."

Her smile bordered on shy, but her answer wasn't. "Yes." She stretched up on her toes to press her lips to his. "Please."

Slowly, tempting himself with the feel of her body sliding along his, he lifted her off her feet and captured her mouth. She braced herself on his shoulders and met the kiss with abandon. He set her down without breaking the precious contact.

She stepped back in his arms, eyes shining. "I'm glad you invited me here."

He picked up her duffel and shouldered it. "I'm glad, too. Come on. We'll get you settled in the cabin, then I'll take you up to the big house to meet Ed."

Chapter Seventeen

Sam's quads were on fire and it was only Saturday.

They'd hiked for an hour, after leaving Will's cabin at first light. The only upshot so far to a dawn trek to the timberline forest was watching Will's easy stride through the tall grass and scrub.

She'd spent her first full day on the ranch with Daisy Quinn, officially Ed Atkinson's housekeeper, but as much of a foreman in her own way as Nat. Under Daisy's direction, Sam fed chickens, collected eggs, hauled water for the horses, learned to drive a tractor, pulled weeds in the kitchen garden, and helped check in a party of trout fishermen from Alabama, before meeting up with Will.

By way of welcome, Nat grilled steaks at his cabin for their dinner, and she'd fallen asleep before full dark fell on Left of Paradise.

"Are we still on the ranch?" she called out to him, regretting the idle question as the terrain sloped upward.

Her regular yoga practice had only given her the illusion of being in shape.

"We are." Will was unaffected by the elevation or the effort. Sam studied this new side of him, one that knew this land and felt responsible for it, in a way. At home, he skated by on hometown charm, comfortable among his extended family and a community that had always loved him.

Here he'd had to prove himself.

As they continued through the woods, the snap and brush of their steps and the steady whisper of the wind lulled Sam, despite her sore legs.

"Hold up." Will turned and stepped around a mountain laurel, into open air. They were on a ledge, high over a stretch of open grassland. What she's assumed was the wind was in fact a waterfall, pouring easily two hundred feet down into the stream bed below. He wrapped an arm around her as she came up beside him.

"Wow." Her words fell off the rock ledge and tumbled into the ravine, lost in the rush of water. She leaned her cheek against Will's arm.

He was quiet, and when she looked up, a single tear was tracking his cheek.

"What is it?"

"I lost two friends out here a while back."

Sam stepped back from the edge. The majestic view turned menacing.

"When the snow melts, the water comes through here pretty hard. We were tracking a big cat that was harassing the herd. Me, Nat, and Brady and Georgie from Hidden Hollow. That's the next ranch on the other side from Trixie Hoult's spread. The trail brought us in along the ravine near the bottom of the falls."

Will spoke easily enough, but his hand, clenched at her waist, betrayed tension.

"Brady was my age. He and Georgie were born here, worked these acres with their parents since they were kids. He knew how dangerous the water is when it's running hard. Georgie, too. She ran Hidden Hollow with her husband."

Past tense. Sam edged a little closer to him.

"Brady saw something across a narrow bend in the stream. He hopped the rocks to go check it out. Georgie always looked out for Brady. She was his babysitter when he was in footy pajamas, so she stayed with him. Nat and I hiked downstream a little farther; Brady and Georgie were going to come back across and meet us. It shouldn't have taken them more than ten minutes to find us."

Sam heard the thump and whoosh of her own pulse in her ears.

"Twenty minutes later, Brady and Georgie hadn't caught up, so we doubled back to find them. Brady was face down in a pool, fifteen feet from where he'd crossed. Nat and I pulled him out, but he was gone."

Sam watched the clouds of crashing water, the whorls foam that gathered under the rocky edge where the stream spilled over and down. She looked back at Will, whose eyes were fixed on the near-distant crest of the Rockies. "And Georgie?"

"We found her near the falls. She hit her head. It was too late."

When he spoke again, his voice was ragged.

"When I first came out here, as a guest, we hiked this trail. This spot took my breath away. When I came back here to work, I thought I was the luckiest guy in the world. Things just worked out for me." He sighed. "I know how that sounds. Losing Brady and Georgie stole its beauty, made it about loss, death... endings. Nat wouldn't let me avoid it." He walked them back a few steps and turned her to face him. "I had to do some growing up. I thought, maybe if I brought you here, showed you how beautiful it was, showed you what you mean to me, it could be about beginnings, too."

She reached for him, smoothing the tear track from his cheek and kissing him. It was a slow, sweet kiss, and Sam lost herself in feeling it. She'd been married, and she hadn't come to that marriage without knowing a few lovers, but everything about Will was new and right, from the layers of scent on his skin–sweat, soap, the forest air–to the familiar fit of his hands on her body. Even the way his body responded to hers was an invitation and a temptation. Her own echoing desire was something she thought Craig's cold words and rough treatment had destroyed.

Will's hand stilled over her jacket pocket. He reached into the pocket and pulled out Daphne's three-day-old sun-cleansed garlic clove. "Is this...?"

"Gah, yes." She took it from his palm, and reached into her pocket for the yarrow sachet and held it out for Will. "One of Daphne's charms. This is another."

Daphne asked her to carry them to protect her from Lilith, but she'd also said to carry them until she felt she didn't need to anymore. She wasn't the only one who needed protecting, and she was tired of feeling like a victim. Maybe it was a silly impulse, but she could leave behind something to watch over Will's lost friends.

Crouching down, she dug a small hole with her fingers and pushed the clove into the soil like a lily bulb, then patted the dirt back into place around it before pocketing the yarrow again.

"What was that for?"

"The garlic was one of Daphne's protections, but something told me I don't need it anymore. That felt like the thing to do. It'll grow, maybe. Wild garlic to guard their memories."

Will hugged her hard, burying his face in her hair. "Thank you."

Chapter Eighteen

"I can't believe you let me cook all last week." Sam was washing dishes after he'd made them dinner. He was no chef, but he'd learned quickly how to cook a few things well when his turn came up to make meals for the ranch staff.

"How could I resist you in an apron?" Will teased, dodging the wet towel Sam snapped at him. "Do you want another glass?"

Sam set the plate she'd been drying on the rack.

Through the window behind him, the black shadow of the mountains sprawled against the ink-stained sky. Will poured as she crossed to him.

He handed her the glass. A brush of fingertips. Heat and promise ghosted between them.

Will reached up to trace her jaw with his fingers. She flinched, no more than a tremor, when his fingertips grazed her face. "I'm sorry."

"It's nothing. Just sometimes…"

He kept his voice soft to disguise his anger at the man who'd vowed to care for her and hurt her instead. "Sometimes what?"

The Cabernet trembled in her glass and tears threatened behind her closed eyelids.

He reached for her again, cradling her against his chest. She buried her face in the warm curve of his shoulder.

"Tell me, please. What happened?"

"No. I can't."

"Whatever it is, Sam, this is me. What I said earlier, up at the falls, I meant that."

She stepped back and set her wine glass down, then ran her hands through her hair. "Okay, but you can't just stand there like that. It's...not easy."

She curled into the corner of his couch, pulling a pillow across her body like armor. Will sat at the other end of the sofa and waited.

"He's gorgeous." She spat it out, like her ex-husband's looks were something bitter under her tongue.

"Okay."

She heard the dismissal in his voice and frowned. "He is. It's important, because that was the first of his lies."

Will heard the sour way she spoke the word *lies*, and a hot wave of shame rolled over him. It was a small lie, but he'd lied to her, too. By omission.

"Thick, dark hair, emerald eyes. Tall, well-built. Everything about him is out of a magazine, but it's all lies."

She reached for her wine and took a generous sip.

"He was on the board of trustees of a school I was subbing at. He and his mother were at a family night. I was supervising a drinks table, and I spoke with his mother about some future event. The next thing I remember, she was introducing me to her son."

Sam hugged the pillow closer. Will wasn't sure he did want to hear the story.

"He called me to invite me to dinner the next night, and within the month he was buying me a new outfit, something ladylike, to wear to dinner with his family. To this day, I don't recall giving him my number, but he says I did."

"Guys like that will find a way." He'd seen it happen.

"The Lacroixes live in a beautiful home in the Garden District. Huge, sprawling Italianate mansion on a corner of Prytania Street.

When Lilith saw the crappy apartment I was sharing, she offered the guest suite."

"*She* did?"

Sam's brow wrinkled, as though the question confused her. "That's what my dad said, too. But it made perfect sense at the time. She came by to see...about something...and I moved in with them a week later."

Will didn't want to stop her; he got the feeling she was working through something, but the whole tale was giving him a weird vibe.

"They made it more comfortable for me to finish last semester. Took me under their wing, socially. Lilith bought me clothes and took me to lunches. Craig was always a perfect gentleman. I got my degree, and the school offered me a job. Craig told me he loved me, gave me his grandmother's ring. His mother started planning the wedding."

"I saw the invitation at Erik's," Will remarked quietly.

"There were whispers where Lilith couldn't hear them. At cafés, in the faculty lounge when they thought I wasn't listening. There was talk about a working girl ending up in the hospital. Craig's name kept coming up, but I ignored it. I loved him, or I believed I loved him."

Will's stomach turned at the thought of her alone with those people.

"The wedding was the first time anyone had come down to visit since I met the Lacroixes, and it never occurred to me to question that. My parents hadn't seen me in a year. Marnie and Micah came. Did you know that?" Her voice had taken on a faraway quality, as though she were reading aloud from a story about someone else.

He reached for her hand, just to let her know he was there, even as his gut clenched. *The bastard hit her.* "Micah told me his version of what happened."

"I felt terrible that I didn't have time for her, but Lilith said I was a bride and didn't have time for that kind of nostalgia." Sam shook her head. "Even talking about it, it's like there's the true version and the version I told myself."

"He hurt you." Will couldn't keep the growl entirely out of his reply.

"No," Sam shook her head again, her eyes filling with tears. "I mean, he did. But that time she did. Lilith hit me with a perfume bottle when I pushed back about Marnie. She was holding it in her hand when she lashed out at me."

"Why did you stay?"

"I don't know." Sam's voice broke. "Since I've been home, I've been seeing someone to talk about it, and...I think there was always a little part of me that never felt good enough, pretty enough, and that little part got too much control, even after I grew out of the awkward stages. It's like she–Lilith–preyed on it."

Tears were running down her cheeks now. He wanted to wipe them away, to stop the horrible story. To promise her that she was beautiful and kind and funny...that he loved her.

That he loved her.

"I snuck out," she continued. "I was terrified, but I still covered up the bruise. A twenty-seven year old woman, and I snuck out of my future in-laws house to meet my best friend and her boyfriend at a jazz bar."

Sam drained the class. Will took it from her with shaking hands.

"Marnie never mentioned my face. She just begged me to just give it all up and come home, but I defended them."

"You weren't yourself," Will said. He needed to get up, to pace or punch something, but Sam needed him to stay where he was.

"Craig was just a mean, spoiled child who grew up and stayed that way. Lilith was cruel. And controlling. As soon as we came back from our honeymoon, they assumed I would turn in my resignation, because I wouldn't need to work now that we were married."

Sam stopped for a breath, tears glittering in her eyes.

Will could barely form words. "What finally made you leave?"

"I told you Craig slapped me once. He got off on it. Hitting, but I didn't know that until...he didn't...like...the way I reacted. He always said I was cold, unresponsive. He told Lilith, and she tried to tell me how to...oh, my god, it's awful, isn't it?" She paused, her cheeks staining pink. "I'd been with guys before and no one ever complained, but when he said those things. I believed it."

No one ever complained? No wonder she'd shied away that night in the living room when he'd moved to kiss her. Fuck *that guy.*

But Sam wasn't finished.

"The whispered rumors never stopped, but then two dancers disappeared from a club Craig had a stake in, and another girl told the police Craig was with them before they vanished. That cracked some kind of shell of denial I'd built around myself. I asked Lilith about it, and she flew at me, clawing and scratching. Her husband pulled her off me and I locked myself in our bedroom. I didn't consider that, of course, Craig would have a key. I'd never seen him so enraged, and it wasn't even because I might have believed he hurt those girls. It was because I upset his mother."

"Sam." Will inched closer to her on the ratty sofa. *This was unbearable. How had she lived through it?*

"He shoved me up against a wall."

Will gave in and took her hand in his. It was like ice.

"He had a hand around my throat, squeezing, screaming at me. He'd given me everything, his parents had sacrificed their time, their money, their connections. I was ungrateful. I was nothing."

Her hand drifted to her neck. Will could see her pulse kicking over under the skin.

"It was Lilith who pulled him off me, as though she hadn't done nearly the same damage hours before. I slid down the wall, huddled there, whimpering. She sat her son down on our bed, glanced at me, and said: if you kill her, not even your father will be able to clean up after you."

She was breathing hard, working through the awful memories.

"It took me a week to plan how to escape."

"Sam."

"The missing dancers turned up a few months later. A woman from work sent me the article. They'd had extensive plastic surgery somewhere. I'm certain Craig was the reason."

"Come here." Will opened his arms, and when Sam crawled into his embrace and burrowed her face in the crook of his shoulder, he let out a breath he didn't realize he'd been holding.

Chapter Nineteen

Will held her while she cried through the shame and fear she'd carried. The tears hollowed her out. She knew the therapist she'd been seeing would be glad to hear she'd finally been able to release some of it. She'd dozed in his arms after that, thanks to the wine and the exhaustion. When she woke, Will was asleep, but his eyes fluttered open when she stirred.

"It's late," Will said. "You should go to bed."

She shivered at the slight chill in the room, despite the June weather. Will got up and moved across the room to stand at the kitchen sink. He stared out towards the Big House, where a second story window was illuminated against the dark.

Sam stepped softly on her way to the bathroom, unsure of the sudden change in him. He'd been so tender with her, but now he might as well have been back in Vermont. She changed her clothes and brushed her teeth, splashing cold water on her puffy eyes, then went back out to say goodnight.

He stood at the kitchen window, silhouetted in what pale light bled into the room. She'd said Craig was gorgeous; she'd told Will he was beautiful. Both were true, but so vastly different. Craig was nothing to the warm, decent man across the room whose beauty ran deep through him like a vein of precious ore.

Beauty she was tired of denying herself. "Will?"

He didn't turn around. "I thought you'd gone to bed."

"I was on my way," she said, going to him, "I'm taking a detour."

She pressed her cheek to his back and circled her arms around his waist, feeling his skin taut over muscle against her palm through one of the many holes in his shirt.

"You were wearing this that morning at Maggie and Erik's."

"Yeah." Will inhaled slowly, shivering at her touch. His voice was tight. "It's late. If you want to ride out with Nat and I tomorrow, you're going to need your sleep."

"I don't want to sleep."

Will whirled in her arms, catching her face between his hands. His sudden movement startled her and he dropped his hands. "I didn't fly you out here for sex."

The rejection stung. Anger welled up, hot, fast, and unexpected. There was no time to breathe through it, to respond like an adult. It just poured out of her, borne on shame and fear. "No? Then why the hell did you fly me out here?"

"Sam, I–"

"You were *worried* about me. You're *pissed* because my ex roughed me up, but you don't want to handle the damaged goods."

She turned away, bracing her arms on the counter, and sucked in a breath to hold back the tears.

"Shit, Sam. No. I mean, yes, but...I'm sorry." Will smoothed his palm over her shoulder. "I don't want to hurt you."

"I don't need some kind of big brother act from you, Will. That hurts. The way you kissed me Thursday afternoon, by the truck–"

"I *don't* want to be your big brother." He sighed. "I don't want to screw this up, either."

Sam turned back to him, let his words fill her up before she said the words she needed them both to hear. "You're not Craig."

The name crackled between them.

"I know." He was trembling, drawn tight like a bow. His emotions rolled off him in waves, colliding with her own like a thunderstorm.

"You're not Craig," she repeated, moving in close, "and I know that."

They came together greedily, drawing air from one another when desire burned up the oxygen in the room.

His hands roamed, exploring as far along the curves of her body as he could reach. Sam trailed her fingers over his stomach, flat and smooth from countless hours riding and working the ranch. She gathered up the ratty shirt and tugged it over his head.

Will pulled the band from her ponytail, letting her hair fall around her face. He slid the straps of her camisole off her shoulders, kissed the slope of her shoulder, skimmed her bare arms.

He held her hands still, let his pulse slow.

"You said you were taking a detour," he said, touching his lips to hers. "You're sure this is where you want to go?"

"Detours only take you where you were going all along," she reminded him, "the long, slow way."

Will groaned, pulling her tight against him. "I want you so badly." The words spilled out between kisses that feathered her jaw, her neck, the rise of her cheekbone. She could feel the truth of his words pressed between them and it lit a fuse she had no intention of snuffing out.

"It's your bed." It was hard to speak coherently when he was nudging her tank top away from her bra, his mouth hot and damp over the lace. She let her head fall back, gasping for air when his teeth scraped her nipple through the satin. "Come to bed. With me."

He didn't need to be asked twice. She laughed when he scooped her up and fireman-carried her to his bed, but he set her down as though she were a delicate thing, tracing her profile with a fingertip and then his lips as he laid down beside her.

"Is this okay?" He whispered, punctuating the question with deep, savoring kisses and long, slow strokes over her ribcage and hip.

"Yeah." She pushed him down into the mattress and rolled over to straddle him. "But I want more."

She pulled her top off over her head, rocking her hips and smiling when he hissed out a breath. His hands spanned her waist, holding her still, letting the friction of their clothed bodies torture them both for a moment. Sam unclasped her bra and tossed it aside.

Will took her breasts in his palms, tracing their shape, grazing her tight flesh with his calloused fingers. He pulled her down until he could take one nipple and then the other in his mouth. Bracing herself with one hand on his shoulder, Sam reached between them to stroke the hard length of him.

"Sam." He sounded desperate, needy.

She stroked him again, reveling in the way his body shamelessly asked for what it wanted; he kissed a map of her sighs from breast to collarbone. They fell into a languid, heavy rhythm of taste and touch, and the tender ache sharpened to need. She rolled her hips again in invitation.

Will rolled them over again, settling between her thighs. He touched the waistband of her cotton shorts, tugging it down enough to reveal her underwear. His face was still in concentration and wonder. "Is this still okay?"

"Yes." She heard her own breathy reply and laughed. "Yes."

"And this?" His smile turned wicked as he inched both pieces of clothing down. Sam arched off the bed to let him slide them over her hips. She reached for the fly button of his jeans, but he sat back to pull her shorts and underwear over her legs, leaving her spread naked beneath him on the bed.

Sam looked him in the eyes. "Yes."

Will swung his legs off the bed, hooked his hands under her knees and tugged her down so her legs draped over the bottom edge of the bed. Dropping to his knees on the floor, Will ran his tongue along the crease of her knee. "I want to taste you, Sam. Tell me I can." His eyes were hot with wanting as he gazed up her body.

He'd kissed his way up her thigh. She could feel his breath, cool where her core was wet and wanting. "Please."

With a chuckle of pleasure Sam felt in every nerve, he slipped away to repeat his path from her other knee back up her thigh. She lifted her hips, opening herself to him, offering herself to him, and crying his name when his tongue swept over her most sensitive flesh.

She felt rather than heard his sounds as he pleasured her. The hot knot of lust tightened in her until she bucked against his mouth. He stayed there, his kisses gentler, his hands smoothing over her electrified skin while she found her breath.

She let her eyes drift closed to the music of denim over skin and the slide of his bedside table drawer.

He was smiling when he crawled up the mattress to hold her against his now–nearly–naked body.

"I'm glad you're prepared." She kissed him, tasting herself on his lips. "Make love to me, Will."

He kissed her lips, her nose, then her forehead. "What do you think I've been doing?"

"I'm not sure." She blinked up at him. "Maybe you should show me again."

"I could learn to like detours." He laughed out loud when she wrapped her legs around his hips. Will took his time, letting her savor the way they fit together, but Sam was impatient.

"Now, Will. Please."

"Yes, ma'am." He moved inside her; she met him there and they rode their pleasure over the edge of a far more dangerous ravine than her reckless heart was ready for.

Chapter Twenty

Sam had been in his bedroom for an hour when she called him in. "Are you sure I won't be under-dressed?"

"It's dinner on a ranch, not black-tie." Humor softened Will's exasperation until he caught sight of her, scrutinizing her reflection in his bedroom window. *I don't have a mirror, except in the bathroom.* She wore a cherry red sundress that fit snugly over her breasts and floated over her hips to just above the knee.

"I've only got my sandals." She wagged a bare foot in his direction.

"No one's going to be looking at your feet." *Except maybe me.* The memory of the topography of her arches and ankles over his shoulders the night before was enough for him to seriously consider skipping dinner at the Big House.

"You said Nat told the boys to dress up."

"The boys would show up still dusty from work if he didn't." Will laughed. They'd been out together all day, Sam taking riding lessons from T.J., who always taught the inexperienced riders who stayed at the ranch. He was the third Joe to work for Nat, which accounted for the T in his nickname. The first two had moved on, but the name stuck, and every subsequent Joe to come through got his own moniker. "How're you feeling?"

She batted her lashes and bit her lip. "A little sore."

Will weighed his options. Ed would be disappointed if they skipped dinner, but not as disappointed as he'd be when Will told him about the interview in Vermont. "We could stay here. Best thing you can do is work through the soreness."

"Oh, no you don't. I want to go to the Big House barbecue."

He crossed the room slowly, holding her gaze. "Yes, ma'am."

She met him, arms outstretched, and Will slipped into her embrace. She stretched up to kiss him, then whispered in his ear. "I'll never hear those words the same way."

"Then I'll say them more often." He hitched her up and she wrapped her legs around his hips. Her lip gloss tasted like vanilla and coconut as he backed her up against the wall. "I can make time to say them right now."

"We'll be late..." She laughed, but there was a jangly warning in her laughter that gave him pause.

He shoved me up against a wall.

Will stepped back and she released him, sliding down to the floor.

"I'm sorry. I didn't think," he said.

Her smile fell. "I didn't want you to stop."

He held onto her hands. "I thought you sounded... You said he..."

"Oh." She dropped her forehead to his shoulder. "I didn't think you'd notice."

"I noticed." He tipped her chin up and kissed her. "Next time, I'll ask."

"Next time." She bit her lip again, but this time she wasn't flirting. A hint of a smile touched her eyes, but Will wasn't entirely convinced.

"Where are those sandals?" he said. "We should head over to the Big House."

She ducked out of his embrace, leaving a cold space in her wake. "I'll get them."

Will reached for her hand as they walked under the dusky sky, but Sam kept a safe distance. The summer nights were still growing longer, and the still-light evening was only beginning to show it's starry face. As the bright lights around the Big House came into view, Will reached for her again, as though Sam might somehow slip away from him.

She already is. Do something.

"Ed's asked for you two to join him at his table for dinner." Daisy Quinn met them at the edge of the gardens and pulled Will aside. "Will, honey," she glanced at Sam, "the prodigal's returned, so take care of your calf."

Will drew in a fortifying breath. "Thanks for the heads-up, Mrs. Q.," he said, kissing the housekeeper on the cheek.

"What was that about?" Sam asked.

"Just Mrs. Quinn letting me know Ed's daughter is here," he said, resting his hand at the small of her back and ushering her into the study.

"It's cute that you call her Mrs. Quinn when everyone else calls her Daisy."

"Almost everyone." *With one notable exception.* "Ed introduced us when I first came on, and it stuck."

They found Ed holding court around the grill of the massive stonework outdoor kitchen. Nat was grilling, and a whole pig cooked just off the terrace in the smoker. From the smell of things, dinner wasn't far off.

"Can I get a tour of the lodge?" Sam spoke low in Will's ear. "It's amazing."

"I'll ask Ed to show you around. He's proud of the place." Will stopped to appreciate the rustic luxury appeal of the Big House and its grounds. "But that's why people pay to come here and pretend to work at a ranch on vacation."

"William. Samantha." Ed Atkinson raised his glass to them.

Light from the café bulbs strung around the terrace caught the whiskey in his tumbler and cast a bar of light across Sam's cheek. Will struggled not to touch it.

Sam started towards Ed, but a cool voice from behind them brought her up short.

"I don't believe I've had the pleasure." Ed's daughter Lucy ran a hand over his shoulder and down his arm as she stepped into the circle. Her of-white sheath dress caressed endless tanned legs as she walked. Her smile was predatory. She offered a manicured hand to Sam. "Lucy Atkinson. You must be Will's friend from back east."

The way she said *friend* was cool and dismissive, a message to the room. When she greeted Will by kissing him full on the mouth, it sent another clear signal. One he'd thought was months out of date and mutually forgotten.

"You are mouth-watering as usual. Did Daddy tell you I'd be here? You know I love you in that shirt." Lucy ran a possessive finger under his collar, and whispered in his ear, "And out of it."

Never in all the years he'd known Sam, had Will ever seen fury in her eyes. His heart sank as he watched them turn shiny with unshed tears.

"Lucy, stop fussing over the boy and give your Daddy a hug," Ed said, breaking the awful tension for a moment.

Lucy did as her father asked, but the damage was done.

Mrs. Quinn materialized by their sides with a flute of champagne for Sam. She took it with trembling fingers; her eyes never left Lucy as Ed's daughter refreshed her father's bourbon and poured herself a finger.

"Sam," he said. "It isn't what you think."

"You have a past, Will," she said quietly. "I know that."

Her flat tone was like ice down his spine. "Lucy is part of it, but not an important one."

"Quinny?" Lucy trilled, "Can you put Will next to me for dinner? We have *so* much to catch up on."

Mrs. Quinn glanced at Ed, who nodded slightly. She glanced apologetically at Will as she passed him.

"So, Will." Lucy swirled the amber liquid around her glass as she made her way back to him. "Have you done anything about the awful wallpaper in your bedroom?"

Will felt the fierce flush rise up the back of his neck. *What the hell was Lucy thinking?* Sam's champagne sloshed and fizzed in her glass. She'd physically backed away from Lucy.

"No, Lucy." He tried to warn her off, but Lucy did what she liked. "I haven't."

Sam's knuckles were white around the stem of her glass. He glanced around, looking for some way to extract him and Sam without being overtly rude to his boss's daughter.

"Chow's up," Nat called from the smoker.

Ed grinned and rang a battered old chow bell. "Go on, boys. Enjoy."

The ranch staff made their way to the buffet while Ed led his inner circle to a table at the end of an event tent on the yard. A hired serving staff loaded Ed's table with family style platters, saving them the trip through the buffet line. It reminded Will of medieval halls in movies, with the king and his court seated above the villagers.

He'd been looking forward to this night since they arrived. He'd wanted Sam to experience the community that lived on the ranch, to see how it forged him in the years since they'd been close. He'd wanted to show her off to Ed, who'd been a good boss and something of a friend.

Sam lingered a moment, speaking quietly to Mrs. Quinn. The two women vanished into the Big House without a word. Left unguarded, Will had no choice but escort Lucy to dinner when she threaded her arm through his.

Mrs. Quinn appeared by his side ten minutes later; Lucy was distracted by a friend of her father's.

"Where's Sam?"

"I tried to warn you." Daisy Quinn's formidable face went stony. She shot a venomous look at Lucy before answering. "She asked for a light and to borrow a jacket. I tried to send her with some food, but she said she'd lost her appetite. Said she'd see you when you got back, but she set off in the wrong direction for your place, hon."

Jacket. She hadn't had her jacket, the one that held the charm. What if any of it was true? That left Sam out there in the dark, headed for the woods, unprotected. Memories of Georgie's blue lips and glazed eyes taunted him.

"Ed, excuse me. I need to check on Sam." Will shot out of his seat as quickly as was polite, before Lucy could get away from her conversation.

He squeezed Mrs. Quinn's hand on his way out of the tent. "Thanks."

Chapter Twenty-One

The chill Sam felt had little to do with the weather.

She shoved her hands deep into the barn coat Daisy lent her, surprised for a moment to be missing the yarrow sachet. The yarrow was in her jacket at the cabin.

Her everyday brown leather sandals weren't exactly walking shoes, but she could still cover ground in them, and that's what she'd needed to do.

She made it as far as the tree line, still in view of the Big House, before Will caught up with her.

"I hope you weren't going to be stupid enough to go into those woods alone."

The sunlight was gone, and a sliver of moon hung in the eastern sky, but they were still more than an hour from dark. She stared into the forest, as though answers would come out from the underbrush.

"It would just be one more stupid thing I've done." She sounded as petulant as she felt, but jealousy and uncertainty and desire for Will threatened to consume her, and it scared the hell out of her.

"I tried to talk you out of it. It takes everything I have not to touch you, then you said you wanted me."

He thought she meant sleeping with him. If he only knew how his tenderness had filled the dark corners of her soul with light, or how good it was to feel a man's hands on her body for the sheer joy of it.

Say it, then. Tell him how you feel. Tell him you love him. That you've loved him since you were fourteen. That you thought you'd forgotten him, but all it took was his smile on a Monday morning in June, and your heart wanted what you fear your soul can't handle yet.

Tell him the way Lucy touched him in front of everyone, like you weren't even there, is eating you alive, because he's yours.

She couldn't do it. Couldn't bear to see the pity in his eyes when he told her that hell, it had been amazing connecting with her again, and sure he wanted her, but love? Forever? Waiting for her to work through the pain and confusion that was the legacy of her brief, shocking disaster of a marriage?

"Say something, Sam. Talk to me."

She took a deep breath, enough to purge the awful, thick waves of envy for Lucy Atkinson's confidence and poise, for the uncomplicated history she and Will obviously shared, and when she turned around, her courage failed her.

"I think I should go home tomorrow. Daisy said she has to go to Billings for a doctor's appointment, and she'd drive me. I'll change my flight."

"What?" The betrayal in Will's reply destroyed her.

She needed Marnie, her family, Dr. Daley. Home. "I can't be here while that woman throws herself at you. I can't do it." The last words collapsed under a sob and she cried through the rest. "We'll talk when you come back for the interview."

She pushed past him, headed for the Big House. Daisy had said to come to her if she needed a friend on the ranch.

"Sam!" Will called after her, pleading as the darkness began to settle.

She broke into a run, but her personal demons were far more swift and sure footed than she was.

Chapter Twenty-Two

"Four shots of Wild Turkey and a couple'a High Lifes." Nat plunked down two twenties to cover the tab. Paradise boasted exactly one bar. Scotty's Lounge was a no-frills, hard drinking cowhand bar that catered to the folks whose livelihoods were closely woven with the LP, Hidden Hollow, and Widow's Walk.

"It's barely noon." Will eyed the line of glasses as the bartender set up the shots. "You expect me to drink that?"

"Son, I outrank you on the ranch, and I can outdrink you, too. So yes. I do."

Will winced as the liquor stung his throat. He was grateful for the cold beer chaser, though High Life wasn't his brew of choice.

"What's eating you?" Nat asked.

Will was grateful for Nat's lack of preamble. He knocked back the second shot, using the burn to buy him a moment. "Things didn't go well with Sam."

"No shit. I may be an old bachelor ranch hand, but I know women," Nat chuckled. "Screwed enough of 'em."

"Yeah, well, I screwed this one, and it went to hell." When Nat raised a brow at his candor, he realized what he'd said. "Crap."

"You fly a woman two thousand miles just to keep her close, and you don't screw her, I'm going to think you've gone all *Brokeback Mountain* on me."

Will almost laughed; he'd sought the older man's company for a reason. "You tired of sleeping alone, old man?"

Nat guffawed. "You're as pretty as half the girls in this place, but no thanks."

Will chafed his hands against the thighs of his jeans. The bourbon kindled a fire in his belly, but it did nothing to soothe the frantic blood in his veins since Sam's departure. "I love her, Nat."

"I know that." Nat signaled two fingers to the barman, who brought out the Wild Turkey bottle.

"I told you about her. I've known her forever. It's easy as anything, being with her, but this thing now is bigger. The stakes feel higher. Between the sex and Lucy's arrival like a fucking monkey wrench in the spokes, she left here thinking pretty poorly of me."

"You're a jackass, is why," Nat laughed and gestured to the full shot glasses.

Will swallowed the whiskey. "Fuck that," Will said, reaching for and pulling on the High Life. "I was a perfect gentleman."

"Which is why you're a jackass," Nat confirmed. "Son, a woman who's been hurt like that one has needs a fight."

Will gave him a baleful look. "Care to elaborate?"

Nat finished his beer and waved for another. "She's all messed up from that asshole who knocked her around. Course she's spoiling for a fight. You matter. Deep down she knows she's safe with you, but how the hell else is she going to be sure you'll fight *for* her?"

"Jesus, Nat, what century are you living in?"

"Calling it like I see it." Nat belched softly. "Know what else I see?"

Will accepted the beer the bartender put down along with Nat's. "Illuminate me."

"You know my Ma's people are Crow and Cheyenne. I don't know if I go for their Great Spirit any more than anyone else's gods, but I've seen the dances. I've seen people connect with something else. Your Sam, she's like them. She's connected to something and it sings to you. She's wearing that witch star on a silver chain. It's a powerful talisman, but she doesn't recognize it in herself just yet."

"You, too, Nat?"

"I ain't saying she's going to turns folks into frogs, but–"

"Who's turning folks into frogs?" Lucy bellied up to the bar on Will's other side.

"Miss Atkinson." Nat tipped an imaginary hat. "If you'll excuse me. The latrine's calling."

"Christ, Lucy. I'm sure you know. What was that, last night?"

Lucy ordered a double bourbon on the rocks. "I heard your little *friend* left this morning with Quinny."

"She's more than a friend, Luce, and we both know you were just being a bitch for sport. We were done months ago."

"I thought so, too," Lucy said, tapping her lacquered nails on the bar. "But it's awfully nice to see you again."

She ran a finger over the hollow of his throat.

Will flinched. "Cut the crap."

"It was the strangest thing." Lucy traded the bartender her platinum card for the tab. "I flew home to surprise Dad because Quinny told me he was going to throw a party for the staff."

"So you thought you'd just trash my life while you were at it."

"That's not fair, Will." Lucy knocked back half her bourbon in one swallow. "I don't think she's as innocent as you seem to."

Will squinted at her glass. "Are you drunk already?"

"I had a long layover in Las Vegas yesterday." Lucy ignored the jab and trailed her nail around the rim of the glass. "I was at a high stakes baccarat table with this woman, and we got to talking. She was on a hot streak. Older, classy."

Danger skittered along Will's arms.

"She said she recognized me from that feature *Vanity Fair* did a few years back. Said she was on her way to Billings to try to catch up with her daughter-in-law before the U.S. Marshals did. She knew who Daddy was. She even knew about you, Will. Your precious Sam is married to her son. I saw the pictures."

"*Was*, Lucy." He banged shoved the shot glasses out of the way. "You fell for that load of bull?"

Lucy's eyes went wide. "Lilith Lacroix told me her daughter-in-law was wanted in Louisiana for the murder of a stripper her husband was known to...associate with."

Will was halfway off his stool already. "And you swallowed this story whole?"

"She said Samantha was on the run and using her friendship with you to get lost in Montana." Lucy's confidence faltered a little. "I told her I'd confirm that Samantha was on the property. It was just convenient she turned tail and ran so quickly."

"You have no idea what you've done."

"Saved my father the embarrassment of having the Marshals on our land."

Nat returned from the men's room and picked up his beer. "Finish that, son. You're behind."

Will pushed his away. "I have to go. Sam's in trouble."

"Go on. I'll see Miss Atkinson gets home safe." Nat gave Lucy a hard look, then turned to Will. "Does she know you love her?"

"She has to."

The older man cuffed Will on the shoulder. "You're an idiot. Where women are concerned, you mean something, you say it. You let a woman stew in her own head, you're asking for a world of hurt."

Will checked his pockets for his wallet and phone. "I want to marry her."

"Will?" Lucy was watching the two of them in confusion. "Were you not listening to anything I said?"

"For the love of Christ, Miss Atkinson." Nat thunked his glass on the bar. "Shut your mouth."

Lucy gaped at them, her drink forgotten.

"Will." Nat raised his glass again. "Get your ass in gear. Get Sam out of trouble, and put a ring on her finger."

"I'm going." Will headed outside, pulling out his phone. He was going to need someone sober to drive him to the airport.

Outside, the daylight hit him like a slap after the dim light of the bar.

"Wait!" Lucy ran out after him–an impressive feat in her heeled boots. Her car keys dangled from her fingers. "I'll drive you. I've only had the one, and my platinum card will help get you on a flight."

"Ladies and gentleman, we're starting our final descent into Las Vegas." A pilot's voice recited the local time and temperature as Sam tried to blink away the heaviness that weighed on her.

Las Vegas? Her connection was supposed to be Chicago O'Hare. Wasn't it?

"You're awake. That will make changing planes easier."

Lilith? Her thoughts were slow like walking through deep water.

"–tell them my daughter had too much Dramamine…"

My daughter? Sam forced her eyes open to find herself in first class. She'd arrived, heartsick and weary, at the airport in Billings, ready to change her flight and go back to Vermont two days early. Daisy Quinn had dropped her off.

She'd gotten coffee after checking in, and set her things down to wait for her flight. The latte made her sleepy. She remembered someone helping her up, telling her her flight was being called, but it couldn't have been her…

Not her mother. Lilith. Her heart leaped into her throat. *What was in that coffee? How had Lilith managed it? Gate agents didn't just let people on planes with the wrong tickets.*

"By dinner we'll have you back on Prytania Street where you

belong. This time, I'll have to rely on myself to keep you there until you're ready to stay on your own. I hope this whole ordeal has shown you you're better off where we can look out for you."

The fog was clearing, but Sam didn't dare let on that she was more awake than she seemed. There was no way in hell she was going back to New Orleans with Lilith, never mind that the woman sounded downright deranged.

She concentrated on the pilot's voice and the flight attendants while the plane descended and landed, using Lilith's restless energy as a barometer for how close they were to disembarking. The grogginess was fading, but she used her yoga breathing to stay calm and focused on getting away from Lilith until her erstwhile mother-in-law nudged her.

"Time to disembark, Samantha." To an observer, Lilith likely sounded concerned. "Do you think you can manage?"

Sam heard the steel thread of threat that ran through the words and nodded, mumbling something that sounded affirmative. Summoning the same inner stillness that brought her through her asanas, Sam played at rising groggily from the generous first class seat and taking her bag from a solicitous flight attendant. She suppressed a shudder and leaned her weight on Lilith's slighter frame and shuffled down the gangway.

She was sweating hard with the effort of walking and her spiking anxiety. Lilith must have noticed. She put the back of her hand to Sam's forehead, as if to check her temperature, but there was a tiny snap of electricity, like Sam had picked up a static charge.

Lilith hissed in pain. The charged contact hadn't hurt Sam at all; she heard Daphne's voice in her ear: *Dragon's blood oil is harmless and full of potent magic.*

By the time they reached the first class lounge, Sam allowed herself to walk unassisted, if docilely. She didn't know the airport well enough to make a run for it, and she didn't know yet if she still had her original tickets or her ID.

What she did know was that dragon's blood oil hadn't done any harm, but it might just have repelled Lilith's touch.

Observing Craig's mother through downcast lashes, she was shocked by the change in Lilith since their brief, strange interaction in Blueberry Hill the week before. Lilith looked refreshed, younger and more vital. Like she had just before Sam's departure from New Orleans.

"I'll arrange for a porter to see us onto our next flight," Lilith was saying as she assisted Sam into a lounge chair. "You've put on weight since you left."

Sam waited until Lilith's back was turned to rummage through her bag. Her wallet was where she'd left it, and her ID inside. Her cell phone was turned off, but still in her bag. Her ticket, she saw, was visible in the document pocket of Lilith's carry-on.

And it still read Billings to Chicago to Boston to Burlington.

There was no time to wonder how Lilith had managed it. She needed to move. Now. She looped her hand through her bag strap and leaned over, snatching her ticket from Lilith's carry-on. The long entrance was maybe thirty feet away. Outside, the rest of the airport would provide cover while she found a security agent.

Taking a deep breath and holding tight to thoughts of her family, of Marnie and Daphne...and Will, Sam rose on her still shaky legs and lurched toward the entrance.

Chapter Twenty-Four

"You haven't heard from her at all?" Will paced the gate seating area, waiting for his flight. He was clenching his phone so hard the plastic was flexing at the seams. Lucy's lead foot and platinum card had booked him on a flight to Chicago, then on to Burlington; there was nothing to do but wait.

On the other end of the line, Marnie was muttering a string of profanities. Will could Micah asking questions in the background.

"She called me from the car on the way to the airport this morning." Marnie sounded winded. "Gave me a flight number and an arrival time, but...she texted me an hour later saying she'd changed her mind and she was staying in Montana with you."

"Fuck." Will scrubbed his face. No one he'd talked to at the airport had any recollection of Sam or Lilith Lacroix. Local law enforcement weren't interested in family drama, especially since there was no actual wrongdoing to point to, unless you counted a tall tale told to a gullible ranch heiress in a casino.

"What happened? She didn't say, but she sounded miserable."

"Long story short, I think I screwed up, and then my past arrived on the ranch to stir up trouble, and I'm sure that her ex-mother-in-law is part of it."

Marnie was quiet a moment. Will heard a muffled *whoosh*, then indistinguishable words from her side of the call. "I'm going to call my mom."

"This isn't the time for whatever homespun stuff Mama Daph is up to."

"You didn't see her when that woman was in town. You know I usually think she's full of it, but that was before Sam just up and vanished from an airport while that batshit hag is on the loose. And she's convinced Sam is connected to it, too."

Will heard Nat's words echo in his memory. *She's connected to something and it sings to you.*

The gate agent called Will's flight. "I gotta go. I'm flying through Chicago. I'm going to try to trace her steps. I'll call you when I'm on the ground again."

"I'm worried, Will." Marnie's voice shook.

"Me, too, Marnie. But I'm not letting her go this time." Will headed for the gate. "Not without a fight."

Chapter Twenty-Five

Sam barely made it out of the first class lounge before the vertigo overtook her. She stumbled, head swimming, and fell hard on her knees in front of a family in matching Walt Disney World tee shirts. In the ensuing chaos, Lilith stormed out of the lounge, crackling with rage. Sam blinked at the literal sparks she saw flying off the older woman.

"You okay, hon?" The woman into whose family Sam fell knelt to check on her.

"Stacey," the man said.

"Mom, that lady is all lightningy..." The smaller of the two kids, a little girl clutching a battered Eeyore was staring, wide-eyed, as Lilith bore down on them.

"Samantha, stop."

Sam felt more than heard Lilith's voice. It resonated in her chest. Against her skin, under her shirt, Daphne's pentagram warmed. The heat distracted Sam from the feeling of Lilith's command swelling inside her chest like a scream.

"You're such a liar, Sammy." The older boy was sticking his tongue out at his sister. "You always say stuff like that but I ain't seen it."

"Haven't," Stacey corrected robotically.

"Sammy?" Sam whispered to the little girl. "Is that your name?"

The little girl nodded mutely.

"That's my name, too. Hang on to Eeyore, okay?" Sam took the hand the kids' mom offered her.

Gathering her last reserves of steadiness, Sam let the warmth of the tourmaline pendant spread through her, the way she allowed the energy to flow through her during yoga practice. She drew a long, slow breath in through her nose, got to her feet, and met her ex-mother-in-law's gaze. "No, Lilith. I'm going home. And this is finished."

"Mom, that Sammy is glowing." Sam heard the little girl, but she was too focused on staying strong. On escaping. An adrenaline rush like nothing she'd ever felt before pulsed thick in her veins, cleaning her head.

"Hush, Sammy," the father said. "Stacey, we've got to catch the parking shuttle."

The boy was tugging his sister's toy and chanting *Liar, Liar,* but none of it touched her. Sam felt *powerful.*

"Justin, don't you see?" the woman's voice dropped to a whisper.

"Do you hear me, Lilith Lacroix? We are finished. Leave me and my family alone." The energy fizzing through her started to flag. "And if you come near me again, I promise you you'll regret it."

She lost her balance, but Sammy's mother steadied her.

Lilith seemed to age before her eyes. It was subtle, but her years wrote themselves on her face in an instant, leaving her looking weary and weak. Much as she had back in Blueberry Hill.

"Justin," the woman said, "Go find airport security. This poor girl needs a hand."

The man, looking rattled, nodded and left.

"Thank you," Sam said, allowing the woman to shepherd her towards a nearby lounge chair.

"I don't know what just happened, but I don't like leaving you here alone." She turned in Lilith's direction. "Where did she go? That woman..."

Sam followed her gaze. Lilith was gone. "Probably back to first class, where she belongs." Sam reached into her bag for her phone, pressing the power key. "I'll be okay. I'm going to call a friend and let whoever comes back with your husband help me get on my flight."

"If you're sure." The woman looked uncertain. Her son was fidgeting with a portable game system nearby. Little Sammy held her Eeyore, looking at Sam like she'd just met a Disney Princess.

"I am." She looked at the little girl. "If you ever see anyone like that lightningy lady, don't let them push you around, okay? I bet you glow, too."

Little Sammy grinned. The mother shook her head, but her husband was coming back with a security guard, and the incident was already being forgotten by the passersby who'd witnessed the exchange. Sam figured Las Vegas regularly saw more than its share of the unusual.

Sam reached into her jacket pocket for the yarrow sachet before remembering that she'd left it under Will's pillow when she and Daisy were packing her things. She couldn't be the one to do it, but she suspected Will might need protection from Lucy Atkinson.

"Excuse me, ma'am." The guard approached them with the kids' father. "This gentleman says you could use a hand?"

"Yes, thank you." Sam smiled at the family to include them in her gratitude, then turned her attention to the guard. "I need to get to Chicago."

Chapter Twenty-Six

Will dialed Marnie's number as soon as he was cleared to turn on his cell phone.

"Anything?"

Marnie laughed. It sounded tinny through the phone. "I've been calling you for an hour. She's okay!"

The relief was borderline painful. "She's okay? Where is she?"

"On her way home. One layover. I'm picking her up at the airport. You're going to have to get your own ride, Dryer. My girl needs some BFF time."

"Did she say that?" His heart sank.

"I just *know* things sometimes."

Will sighed. *Now Marnie decides to embrace the fabled family talents.* "Don't keep her from me, Marnie. There are...things I need to say to her."

"Damn straight you do." Marnie's parting words left Will feeling like he should never let Marnie meet Nat.

When he hung up, his phone showed a handful of missed calls, but only one saved his drowning heart.

He pressed the key to return Sam's call, but she didn't answer. Will hung up, unable to say anything into the void of voicemail. She was safe, and Marnie would have her home soon. He could wait until they were together in Blueberry Hill.

He caught a glimpse of brown waves caught back in a low tail as a woman vanished into the flow of traffic ahead and sighed. It was going to be a long flight home if he continued to see her everywhere.

Stepping to the side, Will dialed his father to ask for a ride home from the airport.

When he got to the gate, the woman he'd noticed earlier was standing at the glass, watching the plane. He rubbed his eyes with the heels of his hands; his worried mind was conjuring up visions of Sam. He hadn't slept well the night before, he'd hit a bar midday with his foreman, it was late afternoon and he was halfway across the country from where he'd woken up, and the woman he loved had vanished for a time, with a bizarre stranger in pursuit. No wonder he was seeing things.

A generic cell phone jingled and the woman at the glass pulled it out of her pocket. "Hi, Mom... Yes, I'm okay...It's a long story...I have a flight to catch, but I'll call when I'm back at Daphne's."

Will's heart squeezed in his chest. He waited, rooted to the utilitarian terminal floor carpeting, until the woman disconnected her call.

"Sam?"

Several other passengers waiting at the gate looked up. He knew he looked like a crazy person, staring longingly at this woman who'd yet to turn around, but he *knew*.

At the sound of her name, she turned around. He held his breath as confusion, uncertainty, and finally–*thank god*–relief played over her face.

"Will? What are you doing here?"

His name on her lips freed the breath he'd been holding and he rushed toward her, dodging suitcases and leaping over one set of extended legs in the aisle of seats between him and Sam. He pulled her close, burying his face in her hair and just holding her. Her hands gripped his shirt, and her tears dampened his shoulder.

"I came looking for you," he whispered. "I was so worried."

I love you. I'll always come looking for you.

She leaned back in his arms. "How did you know?"

"Lucy–" When Sam scowled, he combed his hands through her hair and kissed her softly. "It's a long story, and I'll tell you the whole thing. He drew his hands down her arms, threading their fingers together and drinking in the sight of her. "You're really okay?"

She let go of his hands and wrapped her arms around his waist. He felt her answer in his chest when she spoke. "I'm so far from okay, but I'm not hurt, and I'm really glad to see you."

Will reached into his jeans pocket and pulled out the fabric bag Sam had carried in Montana. Lucy found it while he was packing a bag for the trip east. She'd tried to make his bed, only succeeding at dislodging the sachet from its spot under the pillow.

"You left this behind. I'm sorry you didn't have it with you."

Sam touched his cheek. "I left it to take care of you."

Will glanced at his watch. "Let's see if we can get seats together for the flight. I don't want to let you go just yet."

Chapter Twenty-Seven

Two weeks later, Sam left Dr. Daley's office after a third emergency session since her return from Montana. Between extra yoga classes and extra therapy she was starting to get her bearings again. The only thing she hadn't been entirely open with Dr. Daley about was the strange exchange between her and Lilith in the Las Vegas airport.

For that, she'd turned to Daphne Potter.

They didn't have answers, but Daphne was more certain than ever that Sam had inherited the Potter magical talents. Daphne's working theory was that Lilith was like them, too, and had fed off Sam's insecurities and drawn from her power.

"I don't know if that's even possible, but I've got my online group working on it," Daphne had said. Sam wasn't sure it hadn't all been a hallucination brought on by whatever Lilith had put in her coffee, but it was oddly comforting to know that a group of strangers on the internet, all claiming magical ability of some kind, were banding together to help her.

Today, she and Dr. Daley had finally broached the subject of Will.

She and Will talked all through the flight home, speaking in hushed tones about the events of the past twenty-four hours, about the way they kept missing one another for the ten years before that.

Sam knew her feelings. She'd loved him since she was a girl, but boxing those feelings away had left her vulnerable, and she'd suffered for it.

The renewed connection between them was compelling; she wanted to trust it. To let herself love him.

The words were on the tip of her tongue, when Will had confessed the kiss they'd shared in college.

"You let me believe there was *nothing* between us but friendship for all those years?"

"It was a stupid call," he'd said. "I was an idiot kid."

A dam broke somewhere inside her. "An idiot kid who could have changed the entire future for both of us. I would have done anything to know you had feelings for me back then, but I was afraid you'd feel sorry for me. *Poor Sam, pining all these years.*"

"You know I didn't think of you like that."

"No, Will, I didn't know that. I knew we were friends, that we cared for one another, but I had no reason to think you wouldn't just laugh it off as a stupid crush if I told you how I felt."

"Please don't let this ruin what we've got now."

"It won't." The regret in his eyes was too much. "I'm just tired. I'm sorry."

Later, safely surrounded by Marnie and Daphne, with her parents visiting to check on her, she'd stewed over Will's confession. His texts and calls went unanswered, and while she stayed at Daphne and Max's, holed up like she had when she first arrived back in town, Will never came to find her.

The kiss she hadn't remembered took on a significance that frightened her. She couldn't stop herself from wondering if everything would have been different had she only known all those years before that his feelings weren't so different from her own.

It wasn't until this morning's talk with Dr. Daley that she'd been able to voice those awful thoughts. She made her way down Thornton's Main Street with her yoga mat in hand, feeling the sunshine on her shoulders. There was a class in an hour, which gave her some time to sit with Dr. Daley's suggestion that she absolve herself of any blame in terms of her marriage and the damage it wrought–before she decided whether or not she could forgive Will.

Thornton's town common was shaded by a ring of maples. The dappled sunlight invited forgiveness and second chances, Sam thought as she pulled her towel out of her bag to sit on the grass. A padded envelope tumbled out of the bag, her name written on it in Will's familiar block printing and Post-It from Marnie stuck to the back reading, "I snuck this in your bag for Will. Don't be mad."

Inside was Will's iPod Shuffle with its earbuds wrapped around it and a note on Maggie's kitchen notepad paper.

I CAN'T HONESTLY SAY I'D TAKE IT BACK, BUT I DO REGRET NEVER TELLING YOU. I THOUGHT THERE WOULD BE TIME. I THOUGHT I'D SEE YOU AGAIN, AND ONCE YOU WERE MARRIED TO SOMEONE ELSE, IT WAS TOO LATE. THERE ARE THINGS I WANT TO SAY WHEN YOU'RE READY TO HEAR THEM. UNTIL THEN, I'M LETTING THESE FOLKS SAY THEM FOR ME. ~W

Her hands shook as she put the earbuds in and activated the tiny music player. It began with *Unchained Melody*. All the naked longing she'd felt for him for so long came rushing in on Bono's tortured voice, only this time she read–and reread–his words: *I'm letting these folks say them for me.*

A dozen songs walked through her heart on lyrics Will had chosen to give her, each one a love story.

She had work to do to repair herself, that she knew, but she would be a fool to turn her back on Will–on them–over a long ago bad decision. In the silence that followed the last song he'd loaded into the player, Sam made her choice.

Yoga could wait. She had the rest of her life to start.

Chapter Twenty-Eight

Will followed his rumbling stomach upstairs, hoping the footsteps he heard in the kitchen were Maggie's. If she was making lunch for the kids, he could probably score some for himself. He'd heard them leave after breakfast, but he'd been too busy reading through Reed's plans for the fall hockey season at WFHP.

He'd still have to go back to Left of Paradise to pack up the cabin and say his goodbyes, but he'd given Ed and Nat the news that he was taking the prep school coaching position as soon as they could spare him.

Ed took the news in stride. His disappointment was obvious, but losing ranch hands happened all the time, and Will promised to keep in touch.

Nat cheered him on. "Good for you, son. I'm glad it's all working out according to plan."

Will didn't have the heart to tell Nat he'd gotten the job, but not the girl. Sam might as well have been in Tucson or New Orleans, though he'd caught sight of her around the village a few times in the weeks since their return.

He opened the basement door, announcing himself so as not to startle Maggie. "Any chance I can grab some lunch with Noah and Ava–" He stopped short, two steps into the hallway.

She stood where she had at the beginning of the month, near the coffee maker, a stack of drawings Ava had brought home from camp recently in her hands.

Will gripped the door jamb to keep his hands from shaking. "She needs to work on perspective, but her eye is pretty good."

Sam laughed and set the drawings carefully down on the counter. "I think she's got time."

In his head, he'd planned to be casual. Every daydream of seeing her again, of persuading her to give them a real chance began with her announcing that she was ready to talk.

"What about us, Sam. Do we have time?"

A tentative smile lit her eyes. "I hope so. That's why I'm here."

"Because you hope so?"

"Because I don't think I'll stop being afraid of my own feelings any time soon, but I'm working on it, and I miss you." She took a step forward, then stopped. "I miss you so much, and I don't know how your interview went–Marnie said I had to ask you myself. She wasn't going to play sixth-grade messenger."

Her hands fell to the sides as though she'd given up, and faced with the beautiful reality of her standing ten feet away, Will gave up every illusion of keeping it casual.

"I missed you too." He started toward her, but she was already coming into his arms. "And I got the job. I start as soon as they can arrange my living space, probably the end of next month."

"Congratulations." A hint of sadness crept into the smile he'd waited so long to see.

He stroked her cheek, running his thumb over her freckles. "Hey, it's happy news."

"I wasted two weeks," she said softly.

"Don't say that," he said. "Brattleboro is two hours from here. That's nothing."

Sam sighed. "But still..."

"Have these two weeks helped you?" He tucked her hair behind her ear. "Are you feeling stronger?"

"Yeah." She leaned into his palm, closing her eyes with a little hum of pleasure.

"Then they weren't wasted. And they brought you here today."

Her eyes opened and her smile widened. "Do you mean that?"

"Of course I do." He took her face in both hands. "I love you, and I almost lost you...more times than I deserve chances."

"Say it again."

He held her closer. "More times than I deserve chances?"

"The other thing."

He'd expected it to be difficult to say, but it wasn't. "I love you, Samantha Ellis, and I'm not taking any chances with that."

She put a hand over his heart. "I love you, too."

Chapter 29

BLUEBERRY HILL, JULY 4, ONE YEAR LATER

Will found Sam holding down a square of prime Blueberry Hill Town Common real estate with the same plaid blanket he'd used for stargazing the night of K.B.'s wedding.

"I love that dress. Almost as much as the mermaid one."

"Hey, stranger. Have a seat," Sam teased. "Stay awhile."

Sam was barefoot, her sundress straps revealing sun-burnished, freckle-kissed shoulders. She'd pulled her hair back, but a few stray locks teased her bare back. He filed the idea away as inspiration.

He dropped his backpack and leaned over to kiss her.

"Will!" Marnie was jumping up and down across the crowd, waving. Will laughed as Micah crept up behind Marnie and scooped her up at the knees, growling dramatically as he carried her through the crowd and dropped her, breathless and giggling, on the blanket.

Marnie grabbed Will in a bear hug. "I missed you!"

"I was in town two weeks ago."

Marnie plunked down next to Sam. "Tell this man it's been too long."

Sam nodded seriously, her eyes sparkling with mischief. "It's been too long."

Will dropped down next to Sam, gathering her close. A dark-haired reflection of Micah walked up and inserted himself between Micah and Marnie, earning a swift punch in the arm from Marnie.

The newcomer grinned and got out of Marnie's way. "You gonna introduce me?"

Micah slung an arm around the newcomer. "Sam, you already know my family's black sheep. Will, this is my little brother, Asher. He just landed at our place."

"It's Ash." Ash extended a hand. "Good to meet you."

Will shook Ash's hand. "Will Dryer."

"I used to run around Will's backyard naked when we were babies," Marnie added.

Ash shot Marnie a wry look. "Where *haven't* you run around naked?"

Sam and Marnie burst into giggles. "Fair point," Marnie said.

Ash was looking at Will as though trying to place him. The feeling was mutual, but Will couldn't figure out why.

"Wait a sec," Ash said. "Dryer. You played hockey for UVM back in the day."

"Guilty," Will said. "How did you know that?"

"I wrote for the UCONN *Daily Campus* sports section. I saw you play when I was a freshman."

"You remember the name of a college hockey player you've never met?" Marnie asked. "You can't remember where you left your glasses half the time."

Sam reached into her beach bag. She held a black leather case out for Ash. "Actually, you left them at practice last night."

Ash took the case from Sam.

"See?" Marnie rolled her eyes in Ash's direction before giving her attention back to Will. "So, how's your summer league going? Sam didn't say for sure whether you were going to make it up here for the big debut."

"Would I miss the two of you launching the Blueberry Hill Summer Concert Series?"

"Summer league?" Ash looked genuinely interested. "You still play?"

"I'm the assistant varsity hockey coach and part of the athletic development team at William Ford Hall Prep in Brattleboro," Will said. The title still gave him a little thrill, even a year later.

"That's awesome, man," Ash said.

"No ice talk. Gotta jet." Marnie shot Sam a sly look. "Gentlemen, this way please."

"What's Marnie being all squirrelly about?" Will asked when the trio disappeared into the crowd.

"It's a surprise," Sam said. "But don't worry. You won't miss it when it comes around."

Will nuzzled the soft spot behind her ear and traced the stray curling lock of hair on her back, grinning when she shivered. "You're not going to tell me?"

"Nope. But you can keep trying to get it out of me."

She was good at keeping a secret, but Will enjoyed the hell out of trying. When the sun dropped beyond the horizon, the evening breeze raised goosebumps on Sam's arms. She snuggled against him and Will unpacked the other blanket, grateful for the magic of a small town concert on a summer night.

He'd expected Marnie to welcome everyone to their first summer concert, so it was a surprise when Daphne walked up to the microphone on the bandstand to announce the start of the show.

"The Farmer's Market Committee–"

"Of one!" Someone who sounded a lot like Will's buddy K.B. hollered over the crowd.

"–more than that these days," Daphne continued. "Is pleased to welcome our first musician to the Blueberry Hill summer stage. Friends, let me present Ash Reynolds and guests!"

Ash Reynolds. In context, Will realized where he'd seen Micah's brother before. Micah's kid brother was an up and coming songwriter out west. He'd heard a few songs on the radio back in Montana, and Ed's tween granddaughters were playing his music in the barn.

Ash took the stage to enthusiastic, if unknowing applause. "Thanks for having me. I've had a great week here in town prepping for this show and catching up with my big brother, Micah."

The crowd reacted to Micah's name with applause.

"He's got to love that," Will whispered to Sam.

"Just wait," she replied.

Ash picked up his guitar. "So I hope you'll all give him another round of applause along with my favorite gal in Blueberry Hill, Miss Marnie Burnham."

Micah and Marnie joined Ash on the stage, along with Ash's band, as Ash struck the first chord. The assembled townsfolk cheered. Will couldn't help thinking of the first time he'd heard Micah's name on a visit to town. Neither Micah nor Marnie had been so popular with the town back then.

Micah took up another guitar; Marnie had a tambourine in hand, and then they both joined in on the vocals.

"They sound great," Will whispered.

"I know. I've been hanging out at the Grange Hall while they practice." Sam's hand strayed under his shirt. "It's been lonely at the loft lately."

Will kissed her. "It won't be tonight. How are things going with Mama Daph?"

"Pretty well. Half the time, I'm not sure exactly what I'm apprenticing at, but she says I might have a knack for love potions."

Will chuckled. "Doesn't surprise me at all."

"I wish you could stay longer," she whispered against his arm as the bass picked up and Marnie broke out the tambourine. Even after a year, just the sound of her voice was enough to make his pulse jump. He wondered if Marnie's growly vocals and the green smell of broken grass would forever conjure memories of Sam's breath on his skin.

"Me, too, but I'm glad I got to see this."

Sam tipped her head back and smiled at him. "Marnie's just amazing."

"She always has been." His mouth lingered over her skin.

"Sometimes I forget you know her as well as I do."

"Oh, I don't know about that. You and I know each other pretty well." He teased lazy circles on her palm with his thumb.

Onstage, Marnie took a bow and kissed Micah as their mini-set with Ash came to a close.

Will walked his fingers along her dress's strap. "You know all my favorite weaknesses." Will pressed his lips to hers and lowered his voice. "I know your laugh makes me think wicked thoughts."

He could see her pulse beating under her jaw. "I know how your mouth feels on mine."

Chapter 30

Sam closed her eyes. Will circled her wrists with his hands. His lips moved against the skin just behind her ear. A light nip of teeth lit her nerve-endings like neon.

"I know how you taste."

She hummed with pleasure.

"I know what that *mmm* of yours does to me."

He wrapped his arms around her, pulling her back against his chest, close enough that she could feel exactly what he was talking about.

"I know how your eyes half-close when I touch you." His hands drifted over her, brushing the tops of her thighs, fingertips just under the hem of her dress.

She wasn't sure if it was real or imagined, that her skin shimmered like a mirage on hot asphalt.

He tipped her chin up, catching her mouth in a long, wanting kiss. When he released her, his hand stayed on her cheek, holding her gaze. "I know that the way your hair fans out on your pillow will stay with me when I'm missing you tomorrow night."

He kissed her again as Ash played a ballad Will recognized from Scotty's jukebox.

"And I know Marnie well enough to know she won't care that I'm taking you home, now that she's had her surprise." He pulled them up to standing, hastily tossing the blanket over his shoulder. "Now."

They drove to Daphne Potter's barn in anticipatory quiet, hands entwined over the center console of Will's new secondhand car, but Sam's impatience got the better of her at the bottom of the stairs up to the loft.

They'd had a magical year, in more ways than one. She was delving into Daphne's version of magic, and the more she and Dr. Daley worked through the damage done by the Lacroixes, Sam found that her re-emerging intuition and inner strength was part of something much more potent. Will was setting down roots at the prep school, building something that meant a lot to him, and despite the distance, she felt more connected to him than ever.

"It's been a very good year," she said to him while he grabbed his backpack from the car. "And we get to start another one."

He must have heard the intent she'd put into the words, because he closed the distance and brought his lips down over hers. She leaned into him as his hands smoothed over her hair, resting at her hips. She drew her teeth over the softness of his lower lip. His fingers clenched in her dress's fabric.

There was no music, but he took her hand and spun her out. The familiar move, and the answering rush when he caught her, were all the music they needed.

"Sam—" he whispered against her mouth. "I want you."

Sam leaned away a little, feeling the tingle of what Daphne called her aura. "Come upstairs."

She knew when he saw it for the first time. Safety, clarity, desire… all rushing up from the depths of her. Magic wasn't spells and charms. It was this freedom that loving him unlocked in her.

She felt it in her fingertips when he finally understood the healing in her eyes.

He deepened the kiss, stealing her breath. "You really are a witch."

She gave him a coy smile. "Come upstairs and I'll show you."

Quick as the center-ice player he'd once been, he lifted her off her feet. She giggled as he staggered into her bedroom and they tumbled into her unmade bed. He braced himself over her on his elbows, and Sam stretched up to kiss him.

The planes and angles of his body were familiar under his Big Sky Youth Hockey tee-shirt. She wondered, as his mouth drifted from her lips to her shoulder to her breasts, if the feeling of his warm skin on hers would ever get old. He kissed a path from her lips to her breasts. The air grew thick; her heart raced as they peeled clothes away.

"Wait, there was something I wanted to ask you."

He rolled over, reaching for his discarded backpack. Sam turned towards him, unable to resist running her hand over the muscles of his back.

He sat up next to her, jeans unbuttoned, hair mused from her fingers. She felt like the most beautiful creature in the world when he looked at her the way he was now, taking in her half dressed body in the rumpled sheets.

He offered her a vintage ring box. "I love you, Sam. So much it hurts sometimes. I've been wanting to ask you to come to Brattleboro and live with me, but it turns out I'm an old fashioned guy."

She took the box from him and he dropped to one knee at the edge of the bed.

"Marry me, Sam. Come with me and make a life with me."

Inside was an antique diamond set in her grandmother's engagement band. Tears welled in her eyes. "Yes. Yes, I'll marry you."

He slipped the ring onto her finger and her body sang in response.

"I asked your mom and Marnie what you might like. I hope it's right."

She reached for him, her skin glowing faintly golden in the darkness, laughing when his eyes went wide. "I'm so happy, Will."

"I'm going to make you happy every day," he promised. Will laid down alongside her, taking her hand, where her ring was already warm from her skin. "I want that to be the last thing you say to me every night for the rest of our lives."

She brought their hands between their hearts. "In that case, you'd better get started."

Will's hoarse reply lit her up like the downtown fireworks just visible outside the window. "Yes, ma'am."

Familiar Heart

BOOK THREE

Chapter One

LATE SUMMER, 2009

It was a sad state of affairs when you had no one to accompany you to the funeral home to pick up your grandmother's ashes.

Worse still when your boss couldn't give you the morning off to do it.

It was a matter of adding insult to injury when the hearse-chasing real estate agent who'd also chased your skirt since ninth grade was the only body taking up oxygen at the counter.

"I was real sorry to hear about Miz Ada, Cat." Donny nudged his coffee cup in her direction. "There goin' to be a funeral?"

"Meemaw didn't want a fuss," Cat Brodey sighed and refilled his coffee. "So no. I'm going to pick up the urn after my shift."

"You shouldn't do that alone," Donny said, snaking a hand out to circle her wrist. "I don't have anything on my docket until four. Let me drive you over to Henderson's."

Cat tugged her arm away from the unwelcome contact, but it was too late. Donny's face swam out of focus, his voice went hollow like the echo in a well. A flickering filmstrip of images tore through her mind, even as she felt her body rush away: a little boy in a striped shirt catching frogs by the creek, the same little boy hiding something under a frilly pink coverlet, then his tear-stained face while his Ma paddled his butt.

She blinked away the images along with a swamping wave of nausea.

"Cat?" Donny's face hovering over hers wasn't improved by the blurriness. "Elmore, get out here. Cat's fainted."

Fainted? The word swirled around her brain. *Shit.*

The owner, who was also the chief cook, appeared over Donny's shoulder. "Let's get you up off the floor. Lucky thing you didn't hit your head on the way down."

Cat let the two men help her to her feet, pulling in a few long breaths to steady herself. She could feel a bruise starting on her hip, but otherwise, it was just another one of what Meemaw called her *spells*. She didn't have time to prepare for the sucker punch of grief that accompanied the thought of her grandmother, but she'd already embarrassed herself enough for the morning. "I'm fine. Really. It's been a long couple weeks."

"Elmore," Donny said. "I'm taking her home. She's in no condition to drive."

"Really, Donny. No." Cat gripped the countertop to halt the last of the spinning. "I'll just finish up here and see myself over to Henderson's when I'm feeling better."

"Nonsense. You're working too hard. We're leaving now." Donny puffed up his barrel chest and swept his hand across the expanse of the room. "It's dead in here. Elmore can call Clarice in. It won't kill her to miss an episode of whatever story she watches."

The thought of being trapped in Donny's car for the trip into town and back was less appealing than lying on the diner floor, clammy and disoriented, but Elmore seemed to respond to Donny's posturing, and before she could rally enough to fight them off, they'd gathered her sweater and purse and shuffled her out the door.

Cat closed her eyes to blot out the blurred motion of the road through the windshield, but there was nothing to be done about the aggressive smell of pine air freshener or Donny's incessant prattle about people who hadn't given a fig about her as a teenager and still didn't, if their willingness to help when Meemaw took her last turn for the worst was any indicator.

There was a hideous moment when the funeral director assumed Donny was *The Mister*, and a worse one when Donny offered to buy Cat an ornate brass urn to *upgrade* the hand-polished, burled hickory box she'd chosen. By the time Donny pulled up to the cottage she and Meemaw had lived in since Cat was nine, Cat was ready to vomit.

The car barely stopped before she shot out of the passenger seat, sucking in the clean air, fresh with the scents of forest soil and spring water. Clutching the hickory box under her arm, she dragged her free hand through her purse, trawling for her keys.

Donny sidled up, producing her keychain from his jeans' pocket. "I figured you might need a little help with everything."

Cat's stomach plummeted when she reached for the keys and Donny dangled them away from her fingertips. "I'm exhausted, Donny. Give me my keys."

"You need someone to look after you, Kitty Cat." His voice took on what he must have thought was a seductive tone. The result was oily; it curdled the already sour contents of her stomach.

"It's just Cat." She snatched the keys from him and gripped them tight. "Go home, Donald."

His eyes narrowed. His jaw worked. A frisson of true fear slithered up Cat's spine. She was saved from having to trust her instincts by the sweet music of wheels on the hardpack.

The pristine, twenty-five year-old pickup that growled to a halt next to Donny's sedan belonged to Meemaw's lawyer and closest confidante, Kelley Hart. All five-foot-ten, farm-muscled inches of Kelley's no-nonsense person descended from the car with quiet authority and not a little menace.

"Don Daniels, I already told you this house belongs to Cat." She took in the scene and advanced a step in Donny's direction. "There's no business for you here."

Donny's hackles went up. "Everybody knows it's just Cat up here alone, and she ain't got the means to keep it. If I don't sell it for her, the town's gonna collect on the back taxes and take everything she's got."

Kelley stared him down. Like a child who'd lost a toy, Donny slunk to his car. He made a show of adjusting his mirrors and fiddling with the radio before backing carefully around Kelley's truck.

"Cat, you look like a plucked chicken." She pulled a thick manilla envelope from the truck. "I won't take up time that ought to be spent being kind to yourself. This is from Ada. She instructed me quite specifically to deliver it a week after she died. Into your hands–and before you ask, I have no idea."

Cat took the packet from Kelley with trembling hands. She'd seen the will, she knew there was nothing but the property, Meemaw's silver charm bracelet, and a little money in a checking account–there'd be nothing left of that long before the end-of-life costs were settled.

"Go on inside, make yourself some food, then read whatever Ada had to say. Heaven knows you've been through the ringer without that fool sniffing around." Kelley looked around. "Where's your car, honey?"

Finally, noisily, Cat burst into tears.

Kelley rushed in, gathering Cat to her ample bosom. More than just Meemaw's lawyer, Kelley had been her grandmother's dearest friend for most of her life. Cat hadn't had a lot of friends, dearest or otherwise, but she'd had Kelley, sitting beside Meemaw on the deck to listen to her stories and hug away her tears. "I'm going to make you some of Ada's tea."

Cat took a moment to soak in the affection, Meemaw's ashes in their box hard between her body and Kelley's, before fitting the key in the front door's lock, only to find the door wide open.

A sandpaper drawl slithered out of the shadows. "'Bout time, Kitty Cat. Been waiting all day."

The tears Kelley soothed rose up her throat. "Momma?"

Kelley's reaction was harder. "What the hell are you doing here, Mona? Jesus."

Cat's mother stepped out of the dim corner of the sitting room. The only room besides the kitchen, bath, and two small bedrooms. Mona Brodey cocked a too-bony hip and swept an assessing gaze over Kelley's farm-grubby clothes. "Came to see Ma. See my baby girl. Ain't particularly interested in you, *Miz Hart*."

Cat still held Meemaw's ashes. Her voice hitched and broke. "She's gone, Momma. Week's ago."

Mona's hard features, so like Cat's own, but honed by hard living, went slack in a mockery of sympathy. "Oh, Ma. Oh, Kitty Cat."

Her mother started toward her, but Cat backed up, closer to Kelley. Mona had always had the knack for calling up convenient displays of emotion, and Cat feared what touching her mother might show her.

Cat's hesitation wiped the gentleness from her mother's expression. "What do you plan to do about this place? Ma leave anything for me?"

Cat had no words for her mother's shallowness, but Kelley made up for it. "You're a disgrace to your Ma's kind heart, Mona Brodey. Showing up like a good daughter now? You got a sixth sense for misery? This place–your childhood home–is Cat's now, and as Ada's attorney, I can safely say, you're the last creature'll ever get anything of what she left." Kelley paused for a deep breath. "Now, get back to whatever man's paying for whatever you're using and leave Cat alone."

Mona's lips worked around an O of shock for a beat, then she reached for a shabby hobo-style purse and shoved it over one shoulder. "I'm on a bus to New Orleans, anyway. Got a line on a job at one of them fancy social clubs." She paused to snatch a pad and pen from the phone table by the kitchen door. After scrawling what looked like a telephone number, Mona tossed the pad down and stomped across the room on her cheap mules. "That's my cell if you need me, baby girl."

For a moment after the door slammed shut behind Mona, Cat and Kelley stared at the door. Cat still clutched her bundle of grief to her chest.

Kelley's deep laugh cut the silence. "Christ on a bike, how Ada produced that she-devil is anyone's guess."

The absurdity of it, and Kelley's infectious dark humor released the last of Cat's tears in deep, hiccuping gasps. She set the box and the envelope on the coffee table and let Kelley settle her into the sofa.

When the final waves of crying receded, Kelley kissed her forehead and rose from the couch. When Kelley's fingers brushed the hickory box, Cat's heart squeezed.

"I'm going to see about that tea. You see about Ada's letter."

With a cup of Meemaw's jasmine flower tea, a box of tissues, and Kelley's steady presence, Cat found it easier to read the letter.

Sweet Cat, it began, *I'm sorry I left you. It must seem like everyone leaves you. Your mama is always going to ramble, and your daddy...well, I won't waste my last words on him. There were things I meant to tell you, but once I got sick, I got selfish. I didn't want you straining to be on your way out of Stag Creek.*

And once you know the truth, I imagine you will be.

It starts with your spells...

Cat looked up at Kelley, who watched her read with naked curiosity writ across her weathered features. "You really don't know what this is about?"

"Ada gave it to me about two months ago, when things got bad. She'd sealed it. That means something to me."

Cat nodded and read on.

You won't remember, but the first time you had one, we were visiting my Granny Fraser. This was when you and your momma both were living here. Seems to me your daddy was training with the reserves. I remember it clear as the stream. You kissed Granny's cheek, leaned back to look her square in the eye and said, "Mercy loved you."

People always talked about us, how Granny Fraser raised me because my own mother got in trouble young and died for it. How my mother was a wild thing. How I got married too young and my daughter was wild like my dead mother. That's why folks look at you the way they do, and I'm sorry for it.

Mercy rather famously died birthing me, and the old midwife heard her scream "I hate you!" to Granny Fraser on the verge of her last breath. What you said that day to Granny scared the stuffing out of her. She would ward off spirits after we left, as much as she loved to have you visit, right up until she passed.

Do you recall giving me that Ancestry.com membership so I could stay busy while I was stuck in bed? Well, I started climbing up my own family tree, and I poked a real wasp nest. Turns out, baby girl, that Mercy—my wild, long-dead mama—was adopted while Granny and Grampy Fraser lived up north for a while, and not only that. There are letters from Mercy's people back in Vermont to Grampy, answering to Grampy accusing them of passing off demon's spawn. Saying Mercy had the Sight and the devil in her heart. Those letters are in this packet for you to read, along with everything I've learned about Mercy and her Vermont people.

What this all comes to is, I believe there's a reason my teas are so good at doing what I hope they will, and a reason for the wild streak. I believe there's magic in our blood by way of Mercy.

Magic in you, Sweet Cat. Those spells, I think you see things people try to hide, secrets, memories, desires. Something in you is trying to tell their stories.

Here's where it gets tricky. I tried to find out more about Mercy's birth family, but there wasn't a lot to go on. I've got a name and a place, but it will be up to you to decide what to do with that.

Who you are isn't any different than it was before, but you get to decide how you want to be you. I can't give you much when I go, but I can give you this. I love you with my whole heart, and I'm sure we'll see each other again somehow or another. ~Meemaw

Cat folded the letter and reached into the packet for the rest of the documents. Her heart thumped hard against her chest when she read the words handwritten across the top of a printout of her family tree.

Daphne Potter.
Blueberry Hill, Vermont

Chapter Two

Ash Reynolds had been trying to talk his manager, Kylie, out of booking him in first class for years, but Kylie was an immovable object where Ash's budding rock star reputation was concerned. Last night's solo, acoustic show at a Raleigh club owned by a friend of Kylie's, was the final stop on a grueling tour, and Ash didn't care where in the plane he sat, as long as it took him into the sky and north.

"If you'd just do something crazy," Kylie said. He could hear the radio playing in her cab, tinny and distant. Kylie was running his musical career out of a sublet studio in Bed-Stuy. Ash hated New York, but the producer she'd locked in for his next studio album was a king-maker. "Fuck a starlet, throw a hotel rager, check in to rehab... I could lay off the preferred seating and stuff and let your actions speak for themselves."

"Not my scene."

"So you keep saying. It's annoying."

Ash glanced up at the flight board. RDU–>BVT: departing on time. His brother had texted with dire predictions of snow, but so far, so good.

"I gotta go, Ky. They'll be boarding soon."

"Get on that plane like a rock star," she said. "Swing your...*guitar* around."

"Not likely," Ash said. He hated the hungry look people got watching first class board early, hated the judgy faces as they passed him on the way to coach. Hated the way people simpered if they caught a whiff of his nascent fame. "I don't have my *guitar*, and I'm going to go see if there are any cute little old ladies I can escort to the gate."

"Ugh. Gross. You're too...nice." Kylie was laughing through her scorn.

"Love you too, boss. See you in a few weeks."

"Ash?" Kylie wasn't done with him yet.

"Yeah?"

"Seriously, you need to unwind. Get laid. Go fishing. I don't know. Do something crazy in your own way. You're no fun lately."

"Fishing?" He let her suggestion that he find an attractive woman who wasn't interested in the increase in both his net worth and his recognizability hang in the silence that followed.

"Fishing," she repeated firmly. For Kylie, that was almost like saying goodbye.

———

KELLEY DROVE Cat to the airport.

"Email me some pictures of the foliage. I wanna see why folks drive all the way to Vermont to see what we got here already."

Cat laughed to hide her anxious nerves. "Kelley, I–"

Kelley took her by the shoulders. "I know we aren't proper family, Cat honey, but Ada wouldn't want you dealing with things alone. She sent you on this quest to find your roots. She'd have wanted me to help you sort through the details."

Kelley didn't know the whole of it, but that much was true.

Cat thought of Donny's glee when she capitulated and listed the homestead with his office. That glee had dimmed somewhat when she'd announced she was leaving town. "You don't think she's heartbroken that I sold the house?"

"She loved that old place, but it had nothing to do with the walls or the stuff. The stash she set aside for you to travel with says that clearer than anything. She was squirreling that away despite her money troubles. She wouldn't take this, so it's yours now." Kelley reached into her coat pocket and produced a Hallmark card envelope.

Cat knew Kelley had wanted to help more, but Meemaw's pride only permitted so much. "Kelley, no."

"You let me decide what to do with my money." Kelley's tone was firm. "Ada never did. There's some extra cash for the trip, and a check, too, for expenses. It'll help until the closing. After the taxes are paid back, and Don gets his piece, there might be enough to get you on your feet, but I want you to embrace this trip. Live. Not a little. A lot."

Cat threw her arms around Kelley. "I love you."

"I love you, too, honey. Now skedaddle. You've got a flight to catch, and I'll see you in a month for the closing."

She checked in, left her bag with the agent and went in search of coffee, more to give her hands something to do than for the pleasure of it. In the end, she bought a bestseller from the shop next to the coffee shop instead and rolled her carry-on to the gate.

She couldn't get past the first page while she watched the minutes tick by. She hadn't been on a plane since her last flight home from Savannah. Grief led her mind through memories like portraits in a museum, curated by emotions rather than time. Art school had been an incredible extravagance, even with all the scholarships her portfolio earned her. She'd worked waiting tables and rented a room from an old lady in a house finer than anything Stag Creek had prepared her for.

Meemaw, so proud to send her off, always glad to have her home. Clucking because she was too skinny. Cat never mentioned the meals she skipped to stretch her paychecks.

Coming home with a degree–and a job offer–in hand, only to find Meemaw too sick to keep up with the housework, and Kelley fretting because Ada wouldn't see the doctor. By the end of that summer, she'd dragged Meemaw to every oncologist, every specialist, but the diagnosis refused to budge. Cat delayed her new job as long as she could, but the video game studio couldn't wait forever for the digital environment painter they'd hired.

Meemaw beat back every wave of cancer that came at her, but she never recovered fully, and ten years passed, punctuated by Donny's fumbling pursuits, Mona's infrequent appearances, and Meemaw's appointments.

Cat's dreams slipped out quietly, during the long nights, one by one until she found herself alone in the cabin, without even the dream of her beloved grandmother's recovery.

When the gate agent called her name, Cat gathered her things with trepidation. Boarding was underway, but her row was at the back of the line.

"We need to reseat a few passengers. Would you be willing to take a seat in First Class?"

"Oh." *Did that actually happen?* "I guess. Sure."

"I'll need your boarding pass."

Cat slid her ticket across the counter, sighing when the agent frowned. "Just Cat. It's not short for anything." She'd sung that song all her life. *Just Cat. It's not short for anything. I'm an only child. Just me. It's just Cat up here on her own. Just Cat.*

"I'm afraid we've already called priority boarding, but you're all set to go now."

The boarding line shuffled along until without warning, the teenage girls behind her freaked out, dissolving into a chorus of *ohmygod* and *isthatreallyhim?*

Cat craned her neck, but there was no one she recognized. Only a very broad pair of shoulders beneath dark, glossy, longish-but-not-ponytail-long hair.

"It's your turn." Giggling Girl A's nudge was laced with teen disdain and the same soft, North Carolina not-quite-twang Cat herself possessed. Girls B, C, and D giggled harder. One of the girls brushed her arm, just a touch, but reality shimmered just a little, and Cat saw clearly the girl and a boy sharing earbuds and watching a phone together.

With the vision came the swamping nausea, as if she were balanced on the edge of a black void.

Forcing back the vision and its aftermath, Cat hoisted her bag on her shoulder and handed over her ticket to be scanned. The girls behind her alternately whispered over their phones and leaned out to glance down the jetway.

It's happening too often...Ever since Meemaw's passing–ever since her letter, if Cat were being truthful–the spells had increased in both frequency and intensity.

The answers would be in Vermont; they had to be. Meemaw's papers only offered more questions, and the answers certainly weren't in the novel she'd picked up on a whim at Hudson News.

Cat shuffled into the plane, her gaze flicking to the seat printed on her new ticket.

A slightly roomy window seat at the front of the twin engine jet next to a long-legged, broad shouldered specimen who, but for the ratty jeans and broken in cotton button-down, could have walked out of an epic poem...or maybe that Leloir painting of Jacob and the angel. Cat glanced through her shaggy fringe at his profile and the way his black-coffee hair was artfully too-long around his collar. The same hair the Giggling Girls were fawning over in line.

At least the view is first class.

She almost laughed at herself. She hadn't seen a man that lovely since–well, probably since college. A lifetime ago. Or ten years. Who knew? Men like that didn't grow in Stag Creek.

Cat squeezed awkwardly past him to take her seat, choosing to press her butt into the seat back as she slid by, and regretting it instantly when his knees brushed her thighs as she passed.

He smelled like spices and citrus and the Smoky Mountain fir forests of home. Cat focused on stowing her carry-on and finding the book she'd bought.

"I just finished that," he said, touching the corner of her novel. "I like how he writes. Poetic, but rough around the edges, like Appalachian ballads."

Cat looked up from the book's cover to meet his eyes, clear blue and weary. She showed him the jacket blurb.

"I don't think Morgan Tate-Shaw of the Atlantic would approve of your assessment. The Orchard Gate is *transcendent prose*, and *a triumphant retelling of* King Lear *for the modern reader*."

He laughed; she liked the way it rippled through the air, like the wake around a stone tossed in deep water. Like the deep water, this stranger was restful...unless she counted the way awareness of him beat beneath her skin.

Thanks, Meemaw, she thought. It was just as likely as any other available explanation that her recently deceased grandmother had sent this literary-fiction-reading angel-wrestler to make this trip easier. *I should have known you'd find a way.*

"I should let you read, so you can tell me who's right."

Cat considered the first page, in which three sisters attend their dying father's birthday dinner, in a rambling old house overlooking the family's acres of Empire apple orchards.

"I don't know why I picked it up, really. I'm too anxious to read." *Why did I say that?* She closed the paperback to keep her hands busy. "I'm sorry."

"Why sorry?" The question was offered easily, an open door, as though he knew it wasn't just flying that plagued her.

"You don't need to hear my sad story."

His voice dropped to a conspiratorial whisper. "Sad stories are my business. Name's Ash."

"Cat." She replied automatically, and he answered with a puzzled expression. "It's my name. Just Cat."

"Pleased to meet you, Just Cat." Ash shot a look at the flight attendant making his way up their very short aisle. "Do you drink? I'm buying."

"Do they really serve champagne in first class?" Cat eyed the approaching attendant. "This is my first time."

Ash flagged the flight attendant. "For you, Just Cat, I'll see what I can do."

Chapter Three

The flight was halfway to Burlington before Ash let himself believe Just Cat truly didn't know who he was. Over two passable glasses of sparkling California rosé, they discussed Raleigh-Durham's nightlife, the New York City skyline, novelists beyond Ewan Lovatt, and his new iPhone.

The iPhone had come up because he'd texted Kylie–the rollout of in-flight wi-fi was a blessing and a curse–to ask if he'd flown into an alternate dimension where he wasn't at the tail end of *People Magazine*'s beautiful list.

Kylie: If flirting with this chick boosts you up that list, I'll buy her dinner

When Ash brought home a dark horse Grammy for his duet with 80s-arena-rock-queen turned singer-songwriter Moira Kennedy–a ballad they performed live on the awards show–the media had fixated on three things: their stage chemistry, the two-ish decade difference in their ages, and his looks.

If he'd have preferred they focus on the single, or his current record, or his tour schedule, well, Kylie told him to smile for the cameras and let the publicity do its job.

"So, what do you do with sad stories," Cat asked, "when you're not drinking champagne in what amounts to first class on a puddle jumper?"

The pilot interrupted his need to dodge the question; he wasn't ready for this pretty interlude to draw to a close.

"Hi, everyone, this is your captain. I'm sorry to let you know we've got a storm brewing along our flight plan and we're being redirected to Boston Logan. We'll be starting our descent shortly. Once again, our apologies for the inconvenience. I hope to have us in the air again before too long."

Cat squinted out the window. "Isn't it early for snow storms?"

"I hear it snows pretty much whenever it wants to in New England." Ash grinned when his half-assed attempt at a Smokey Mountain accent brought her away from the window.

"Don't tease. I'm a North Carolina mountain girl, born and bred. We get snow, but a storm before Halloween?"

Ash shrugged. "I haven't seen one in a long time, but I definitely remember bundling up under my Halloween costume growing up in northern New Jersey." He didn't add that he'd been living in Colorado and touring big bars and small clubs though the long, cold Wyoming and Montana winters before he broke onto the pop music charts.

That was snow.

"Do you live in Vermont?" she said.

They *were* supposed to be flying to Burlington. It was a reasonable assumption. "Nope. Just headed that way to see my family."

His soon to be sister-in-law probably wouldn't appreciate the casual dismissal of her wedding. Marnie was a force to be reckoned with, and Ash adored her.

"Me, too." Cat offered her plastic champagne flute for a toast. "To family and short layovers."

Ash clicked his glass against hers and glanced across the bubbles at her. "I'll drink to that–and to buying you another round while we wait in Boston?"

Just Cat's smile dawned over her face. Ash liked that about her. Maybe even more than her sunlight-on-creek-water eyes and hair that contained every shade of brown from honey to dark chocolate, with streaks of tawny port framing her face.

"To one more round," she said.

———

DESPITE THE CREW'S assurances that they were still Burlington-bound, Cat wasn't optimistic.

Through the long stretches of glass outside Logan's Terminal A, snow blew thick and hard, blustering around before piling up in the corners and against the buildings outside.

The seafood restaurant-slash-bar where she and Ash found seats was cozy, despite the airport around them. True to his word, Ash bought their drinks while she used the ladies room.

"I ordered steamed shrimp wontons with the drinks," he said. "Please tell me you're not allergic."

"Nope," Cat said. *How funny that he'd even think of something like that.* "But it's sweet of you to think about it."

"My sister Avery is allergic to shellfish. Our parents were super strict about us avoiding seafood at restaurants, just to be on the safe side." He swirled what looked like whiskey on the rocks. "My mom would be horrified I didn't ask you first."

"My grandmother would think you're a perfect gentleman for remembering," Cat said. As for her momma, Mona Brodey would've taken a good look at Ash's strong shoulders and flirted her way through the shellfish. *Even before Daddy died.* Better to leave that thought be. "Anything special about this family visit?"

"Wedding," Ash said. "My brother's getting married after seven years."

"Oh, that's wonderful." Cat tried her elderflower-gin martini and decided she'd made a good decision. She shot a sideways glance at Ash, whose slight smile didn't betray the overwhelming joy she associated with weddings. "Isn't it?"

He laughed. "It's great. Seriously, my future sister-in-law is a force of nature, and my brother is completely besotted."

"Besotted?" Cat loved the old fashioned word. "After seven years, that's impressive."

"Yeah."

"So why the long face?"

Ash swirled his glass again, and shifted on the stool to face her, cracking a grin. "No long face. Just thinking. What's your excuse?"

"For?" She sipped off the top of her drink, regarding him from under her lashes.

He laughed. "For traveling. You said family, too."

Cat busied herself tracing the rim of the martini glass with the lemon twist. Her purpose in Vermont sounded insane, even to her own ears. She glanced at him out of the corner of her eye. "Reunion."

Ash met her sideways gaze. "Are the rest of them as pretty?"

It was Cat's turn to laugh. "Does that line usually work?"

"You tell me."

She should have laughed. He switched on his smolder like Flynn Rider in *Rapunzel*.

The trouble was, his smolder set loose a flight of butterflies in her belly that had little to do with the wine and cocktails. A flight of butterflies whose delicious presence she hadn't felt in a good long time.

Cat had never taken care of small children, but she expected it wasn't all that different from elder care in terms of exhaustion and isolation.

In for a penny, in for a five gallon pickle barrel, Meemaw would have said. *Gal, you go on and have a flirtation.*

The bartender slid a plate of steamed dumplings, dipping sauce, and seaweed salad in front of them. Ash thanked her and pulled the food closer.

Cat pitched her voice low–a smolder of her own–and let her hand rest on his forearm. "It might just."

The contact was brief, but electric. As it had when the teenage girl brushed her arm, the room shimmered around Ash, but all she saw was light around him, hot, brilliant light.

His arm flexed under her touch, and she pulled her hand away.

He was too tempting. Her fingers itched to explore his skin. He was a gorgeous specimen–literally tall, dark, and handsome. She'd been on her own a long time, and there were moments she acknowledged that lonely was an improvement over her unremarkable dating history.

What was worse, he had secrets in his eyes.

"Tell me about North Carolina, Just Cat," he said.

"There's not much to tell," she said, busying herself with opening a paper-wrapped set of chopsticks. "When I was little, I lived near Asheville with my folks. My daddy joined the Army during Desert Storm, so Momma and I moved back to Stag Creek to live with my Meemaw. Daddy died over there. I was ten. Momma got remarried and left for Arizona when I was in middle school. Meemaw kept me. She said my step-daddy's soul stank like old shoes."

"That's one I've never heard," Ash said. "I'm sorry about your father." He skipped the chopsticks and plucked a wonton from the plate. He dunked it into the ramekin of sauce and bit half away.

It shouldn't have been sexy.

"Me, too. He was a good dad, but restless. Like Momma." Cat fidgeted with her water glass. *Where were all the closet skeletons coming from?*

Ash seemed to sense her distress; he changed the subject with more finesse than Cat expected.. "Where've you been since Stag Creek?"

"I went to school in Savannah," she said, pinching a wonton between her chopsticks and nearly sending it flying like the escargot in *Pretty Woman*. Her blush went hot all the way down her throat, but Ash didn't seem to notice. "But I stayed home to take care of Meemaw when she got sick."

Cat flushed. She hadn't meant to share so much. *Stupid martini.*

"I'm sorry. How long ago did you lose her?" Ash put a hand over hers. It was steady and warm, a capable hand; again she saw the lights around him, white-hot and flashing, and heard a thundering static.

"How did you know?" Cat's voice caught with the exertion of staying in the moment.

"I listen," Ash said. He was looking straight into her eyes, and Cat was certain he could see down to the bottom of her shattered self.

They'd drifted closer. Their breath mingled over their drinks. Awareness was like a drug in her veins. The storm whirled and snowflakes crashed against the glass outside, cocooning them until the loudspeaker beckoned.

"Attention please. Flight 462 to Burlington has been suspended due to weather. Passengers, please see the gate agent for more information."

"Damn," Ash said. Their little bubble of warmth and peace popped. "I guess we'd better settle up and finish these." He picked up a second wonton; it was unfair how attractive he was savoring his food.

With a sinking heart, Cat followed his lead and ate her second wonton with her fingers. "Do you want the seaweed?"

He wrinkled his nose delicately. "It's all yours."

Cat could already see people heading back to the gate. There would be a line and an uncertain rebooking in her future. She scooped the seaweed salad up with her chopsticks, enjoying the sweet vinegar tang. Who knew when she might get another snack?

Ash signaled the bartender and slid his card into the bill folio when it arrived.

While they waited for the check to come back, they both knocked back the rest of their drinks. Ash held her jacket for her. The warmth of his fingers brushing her neck chased the sparkle of intoxication through her bloodstream. This time the contact brought only echoes of what still sounded like static–and maybe the ghost of a melody. It was almost as if she were developing a tolerance for him.

Cat glanced at the check when he signed it. She nearly swooned when he left a thirty percent tip on their small check.

Meemaw's voice slipped into her head again, along with her throaty, belly-deep laugh. *A man who tips well is bound to be generous every which way.*

I'd give him a chance if we weren't about to say goodbye, Cat's heart replied.

Who says you have to say goodbye? Meemaw's remembered voice countered. *Marooned in Boston sounds like one of those saucy Harlequin books Mona used to read.*

They walked to the gate together, but Cat didn't say anything. She didn't know how to give words to the idea her imaginary grandmother kindled in her chest. Ash was texting someone, his thumbs flying over the keyboard on his fancy new iPhone.

The line to speak to the gate agents was long, but it gave Cat time to think about what she was about to propose. Visions be damned.

Ash graciously let her step up to the desk first, where she was informed that the flight was being cancelled, that she could rebook for a flight in two days, and that the airline would be issuing vouchers for a hotel a few miles north of the airport.

"I'm afraid we're down to junior suites, though," the agent said. He sounded either genuinely sorry or thoroughly exhausted. Cat figured it had to be the latter. His expression dared her to pick a fight. "Yours wasn't the only flight grounded tonight. I am sorry about the extra expense."

Here was the five-gallon pickle barrel moment. Being stingy wouldn't bring Meemaw back. "I'll take it." She turned to Ash, who looked up from his phone, and steeled herself. She was on an adventure, after all, and Kelley's generosity weighed heavy. *Live. Not a little. A lot.*

"Wanna share?"

Ash blinked. Had Just Cat of the sad eyes and pretty smile just offered to share her hotel room?

While he and Cat were sharing dumplings, Kylie had booked him a room at the Fairmont Copley and arranged for a car to pick him up, but this changed everything.

He swallowed and played it cool. "Why, Just Cat. I'm flattered."

"You should be," she said. Her tongue darted out and she licked her lips, scraping the bottom one with her teeth before her smiled dawned again. "I'm not ready to say goodbye just yet."

He swept his fingers over the keyboard, telling Kylie to cancel the Fairmont, then answered her in a husky stage whisper. "Only if you let me handle the transportation."

"Ma'am?" The gate agent was waiting for Cat's information.

Ash took a step back to give her space to finish her reservation, smiling when she declined a seat on the hotel shuttle.

"Good evening, Sir," the gate agent said as Cat sidled out of line.

"Seems I'm all set," Ash said, following her. He stopped, fished a twenty out of his wallet, and slid the bill over the desk. "Thanks for putting up with us."

"Thanks," the agent said. He blinked at Ash. "Hey, are you?"

"Nah," Ash said quickly while Cat was still looking ahead. "But I get it all the time."

"Get what?" Cat said.

"He thought I looked like a Skarsgård." While that was a white lie, Kylie often teased him about his tall, somewhat Nordic good looks. In truth, his brother Micah had more of that going on, especially with his blond surfer hair. He ignored the twinge of guilt at the dishonesty. The fiction preserved what felt like a more important honesty: Cat liked him for him, not for his Grammy or his newfound solvency, or the chance to ride his coattails to a record contract or a b-list reality show.

When Cat's eyes roamed the length of him, sparkling with approval, the lie mattered even less. "He's not wrong." Cat checked the arrivals board, now updated with their flight's luggage carousel. "I have a checked bag. You?"

Ash adjusted the backpack he'd been carrying since they disembarked. He spent enough time in Blueberry Hill that he kept clean clothes in Micah and Marnie's spare room, and his guitar was en route to Brooklyn with Jericho, the one roady who'd stayed for the Raleigh gig. "Nope. Traveling light. Let's get your bag, Just Cat. I'll tell the car where to meet us."

It was completely surreal, the ease with which they moved through the airport together. They'd known one another for a matter of hours, shared a couple of drinks and navigated a cancelled flight. She'd propositioned him rather outrageously–unless he'd really misread her intent–and still, he felt like he was spending time with an old friend.

You don't want to get naked with your old friends, his conscience argued.

When they stepped outside into the bluster and cold, the driver got out of the black car and took Cat's suitcase. She looked at him with impressed, but questioning eyes. "A private car?"

He shrugged. "I travel a lot. It's a perk." Truthfully, he preferred the tour bus, but this had its advantages.

Cat gave the driver the hotel information, and they settled into the leather seats.

When Cat peered out the window at the slow-moving traffic; Ash felt suddenly shy. "Are you hungry? We could order food, have it delivered to your room."

She turned to him and grinned, then leaned forward to talk to the driver. "Where should we get take-out?"

They ended up detouring through Boston's North End and collecting a moveable feast of Italian food from a little place a block off Hanover that the driver promised offered the best baked gnocchi in Boston. At their driver's insistence, they stopped down the block at a modest all-night pastry shop for to-go cups of tiramisu. By the time they checked in at the Sheraton, Ash was legitimately hungry, but the air was thick with anticipation.

Ash dropped his backpack near the door. Cat prowled the junior suite. He noted the king-size bed beyond a dividing wall, and the pull-out sofa in the meeting area. *Always good to have a backup plan.*

"Listen, Ash," Cat said, coming around the partition, "I–"

"I know." *Speaking of plan B.* Maybe the moment had passed for her; the car trip took the spontaneity out of the crazy gesture. "It's okay. I'll sleep on the couch."

Chapter Five

Oh, hell no he wouldn't.

She'd been about to suggest they eat, treat it like a date. Break the ice again. Get their toes wet. Any number of ridiculous cliches if it ended with her finding out how those lips tasted. The intensity of her want, and the speed at which it burned through her, shocked her.

She wanted to be ravaged; she wanted to hear her name ground out of him like a desperate prayer.

She wanted to be more than Just Cat, caregiver and local waitress only the wrong guy thought was worth a second notice.

Cat stopped, tilted her head and examined him from the tips of his wavy mahogany hair to to the soles of his cowboy boots–she'd return to the cowboy boots later. When she met his gaze, she let him see she liked what she saw. "I was going to suggest we have a little Italian picnic here on the coffee table."

He caught the look in her eyes; she could feel it. He rocked back on his heels and shoved his hands in his pockets. "Were you?"

"Now, I'm thinking we might be skipping the appetizer." She took a few steps toward him, giving him room to stop her.

He didn't. He leaned against the door and crossed his ankles.

"A little something to whet the appetite?" His smile turned wolfish and a shiver of lust traveled along her skin.

Cat closed the remaining feet between them, bracketing his feet with her own–clad in more sensible riding-style boots. She trapped him between her hands; the steel door was cool–and free of visions–against her palms. The broad expanse of his chest pressed warmly into hers; her heartbeat was steady, echoed in the pulse she could see dancing at his throat.

"I've wanted to kiss you since you compared Ewan Lovatt to a bluegrass poet."

Once again, their breath mingled. Cat could almost feel the rasp of the day's stubble on his chin.

"I can't think of anything I'd like more right now," Ash said, his voice a husky whisper.

Embracing whatever this strange magic between them was, Cat touched her lips to his. Her palms were still pressed to the door on either side of his body; his hands were still in his pockets. She melted against him when he whispered what sounded like *perfect* against her lips.

If the faint strains of a song she didn't know echoed in her ears, she could live with that.

He angled his mouth and deepened the kiss, coaxing a sigh from her. His hands came out of his pockets, and he buried them in her hair. His tongue brushed hers, just a sample, really, and a thrill zipped through her like lightning. Those forearms she'd admired banded around her body and he unlocked his knees, sliding them both down the door and drawing her into his lap on the floor.

Ash traced a path of feather-light touches and kisses along her jaw and down her neck. She arched against him to feel his body heat, ran her hands over the muscles of his arms and shoulders, twined her legs over his.

He slid his palms up her back, bunching her shirt up at his wrists. The rough warmth of his fingertips left fiery trails on her skin. His lips quested over hers; their greedy kisses gave and took, and left Cat breathless, boneless and electrified with wanting.

"Ash." She was panting–*sweet lord*. "Wait."

He rested his cheek against hers. She could hear his pulse thud in his chest. "You okay?"

She pushed herself away from him and stood. The concern in his expression touched her.

"I'm fine. I was just..." She leaned over to unzip her boots. "Thinking..." She toed them off one at a time. "There's a perfectly..." She unbuttoned the top two buttons on her gray dress shirt, enough to let her lacy, pale pink bra peek out. "Comfortable..."

She didn't get to finish her teasing. With a growl and more grace than a man that big deserved to have, Ash leaped up and gathered her in his arms. She let her head fall back, looped her arms around his neck, and laughed all the way to the bed.

———

AS ASH TUMBLED into the bed with Cat, he sent up a little prayer to whatever higher power seated them together on this unexpectedly wintry October night.

Propping himself up on one elbow, he slipped her blouse's remaining buttons from their holes and smoothed the shirt away. Her skin was pale and smooth, her belly shivered when he breathed in the scent of her just where her bra met her breastbone. From there, he let his lips and her sounds guide him.

She threaded her hands through his hair, touched his cheek, scraped her trim nails over his back...she writhed under him, pressing their bodies ever closer. She pushed his shirt up over his head and undid his belt buckle while he explored the dip of her clavicle.

Under the pink lace and satin, Ash found more soft, pale skin. His thumbs brushed her nipples and she rocked her hips against him with a groan that brought him up short.

"Just Cat–" He nuzzled her ear. "Before we let this thing get out of hand."

She put her hands on his shoulders and rolled them so they lay on their sides fading one another and blew a lock of hair out of her face. Her cheeks were flushed; her eyes sparkled.

Ash tucked the wayward strands behind her ear.

"I'm on the pill," she said. "But I didn't expect any trysts on this trip–" Her blush deepened. "I'll go across the street to that drug store right now, but I really hope you're carrying something…"

"I am." He sighed in relief. "I don't make a habit of this kind of thing, I swear, but I *was* a Boy Scout."

"Be prepared," she said with a laugh.

"Hold that thought," he said, rolling to the edge of the bed. His backpack was ten long steps away.

Cat ran a bold hand down the front of his jeans, his body responded appropriately. "I'd rather hold this one."

At least the Boy Scout thing was true. He'd dropped out in high school; chicks were more into guitar players than Eagle Scouts–and anyway, Micah had his, which fulfilled the suburban family quota. The condoms were in his bag because despite his own reservations and the ever-deepening well of disappointment it brought, he didn't completely live like a monk on the road, and kids were for a lifetime.

He brought the whole box back with him, tossing it on the nightstand. Cat had made use of his back being turned. Her jeans and shirt were puddled on the floor next to the probably questionable hotel bedspread. All that remained was that pink bra and a pair of oddly appealing white cotton bikini briefs.

"You're overdressed," she said, leaning back on her elbows.

He was already pulling his Seldom Scene tour shirt over his head. If he saw those guys out of the road, he'd have to thank them for the lucky shirt. "Give me a minute to fix that."

She's just so damn pretty.

Every cell in his body was straining, but Ash was resolved to make this crazy one-night-stand worth it for her. For both of them. He crawled over the blanket to her, and when he kissed her, the sweet tangle of lips and tongues was the only contact. It only made him hungrier.

Cat put her hands on his hips and guided him down to her, until they were pressed together, toes to navels. She wrapped her legs around him and held him deliciously captive while she led the kiss, showing him what she liked.

She drew her teeth gently over his lower lip; he answered by nipping at her jaw and kissing his way from the sweet thrum of blood under her skin to the edge of her bra. She arched up and–bless women for this unique dexterity–reached behind her to undo the clasp.

Ash slipped the straps from her shoulders, smoothing reverent fingertips over the skin left bare until he cupped her breasts. Cat hummed with pleasure; Ash chased that sound over her body, lingering when he found it, until he reached the demure white cotton.

For a moment, he only breathed. His heart was racing.

"You smell amazing." He nuzzled the cotton, just where it met the juncture of her pelvis and thigh.

Cat hooked her thumbs in the waistband and wriggled, but Ash stilled her hands.

"Let me." He inched the cotton down, trailing his lips after it. Down the length of her leg, coaxing her underwear away with patient hands.

She pressed her toes against his shoulder. "Ash," she said. "Come here."

Ash treated himself to the view. She was glorious. "I'll be there just as soon as I can."

She tasted every bit like he'd imagined; that *hmm* he liked so much turned to an *ohh* he liked even better. He pursued that *ohh* until her thighs shook and she clutched his hair.

He slid up her body, watching her eyes as she returned to the world. "God, Cat." He was barely capable of coherent syllables.

She smiled, a feline-in-the-cream curve of the lips that nearly undid him without a touch. "That's exactly what I was thinking."

Ash leaned toward the nightstand, but it was Cat's turn to still his hands. "Let me."

So he did.

Chapter Six

Cat was an early riser. She woke at dawn, despite spending more hours awake with Ash than sleeping. They'd warmed up the half-forgotten take-out at some point between the far-less-awkward-than-it-should-have-been first time and the unfairly memorable second time, during which Ash had made further excellent, enthusiastic use of his clever mouth to drive her over the edge at least twice.

The third time was sleepy and tender. Ash had tucked her body into the protective curve of his and fallen into a deep sleep, his face almost boyish in dreams. In the aftermath, she heard it again, the faint hint of music that twined with his breathing in time with the pulse in his chest.

She'd dozed there for a while, but sunrise called her.

Daylight revealed all kinds of ugly truths about people. Bad breath, uncomfortable opinions. Meanness. Disillusionment. Worse, guilt and hindsight.

She didn't even know what he did for a living, with his good looks and his fancy car service. Caught up in a kind of purgatory between grief and adventure, she hadn't even asked.

Truthfully, it hadn't mattered. She'd wanted him, not whatever paid his bills.

She gathered her clothes and took a hasty shower before wheeling her suitcase out of the room and out of Ash's life as unexpectedly as she'd arrived in both.

This is for the best.

The airline was willing to cancel her flight; the hotel concierge helped her rent a car. By the time the sun was fully up over Boston Harbor, the city was in her rearview mirror. Despite the wild storm the night before, the highways were clear. The world beyond them glittered white under a diamond sky.

If she didn't stop, she could be in Blueberry Hill, Vermont, before lunchtime.

As she drove, Cat tried to put the scratch of Ash's five-o-clock shadow and the scent that clung to his skin out of her head. She'd never in her life done anything so impulsive, but being with Ash hadn't felt like an impulse. Those hours together felt real.

She picked up a college radio station out of Cambridge and stuck with it until New Hampshire, where the signal grew increasingly patchy. One of the last, choppy tracks was a banjo-heavy bluegrass song that crept into her heart. She caught herself humming along as it moved into the second verse.

Just as she was about to surrender to static, the DJ mentioned The Seldom Scene. A vision of Ash's worn t-shirt just before he'd taken it off flitted through her memory, and warmth kindled in her belly. He had good taste in music to go with that flat-out beautiful chest and eyes that saw almost to the bottom of your secrets.

"Sticking with bluegrass ballads," the DJ went on, broken up by bursts of hissing static and silence, "here's one from Grammy-winners Moira Kennedy and–"

The static cut off the rest of the announcement, but there was a name she knew. She'd been too young to go to a Mikki Vixen show back then, but Momma had the cassettes in the car. Cat heard that Moira Kennedy made a comeback, but she'd stopped following music about the time Meemaw got sick.

As the car devoured the miles along I-93 and I-89, the magic of the lackluster hotel room and the man in it began to lose its hold. In its place, a fresh crop of worry sprouted. The time-yellowed letters and smeared, left-handed journal in Meemaw's shoebox told a story so old folks in Blueberry Hill had likely long forgotten it.

Despite her determination, there was a very real possibility that these people would want nothing to with her. After all, she'd grown up in Stag Creek and they still didn't embrace her.

The rolling hills and dramatic skylines along the winding interstate through New Hampshire and Vermont were no Blue Ridge Parkway, but they spoke a natural language that soothed Cat. It took the better part of four hours, but she passed the Village of Blueberry Hill marker sign with the midday sun high in the sky.

She pulled over to calm her galloping heart. Somewhere in this town was a woman named Daphne Potter, and Cat was going to find her. First, however, she was going to find the cabin she'd rented, take a long hot shower, and sleep.

Following the directions the concierge printed for her, she continued through the village and drove deeper into the mountains before emerging on a state highway that boasted signs for Thornton College to the east and Singing Bowl Ski Area to the east. The cabin wasn't far from the ski area. Some clever entrepreneur had refurbished a roadside motor court as seasonal rentals. According to her booking email, she was in a cabin called Thimbleweed. Others she passed bore plaques naming them Angelica, Bearberry, Jack in the Pulpit, Horsemint, and Ladyfern.

She parked at the sixth cabin, where an envelope with her name on it peeked out from a miniature mailbox on the tiny front porch. Cat found the key and a note from the owner with instructions for the laundry and vending facilities which were housed in the office building–open 24 hours with a lock box code.

While the exteriors were all straight out of a mid-century American fairy tale, complete with picket fences and potted flowers, the interior of Thimbleweed Cottage was a tastefully neutral oasis featuring a series of woodcut prints and textiles in the same palette.

The bed, piled high with quilts and comforters, beckoned, but Cat could almost feel the road grime on her skin. To her delight, the bathroom was clean and the hot water plentiful. She tumbled into the bed in an oversized t-shirt with her hair still turbaned in a towel.

If she were very lucky, she wouldn't dream of Ash's eyes, or the melody that clung to her memories.

———

ASH SWAM into consciousness with the faint sweetness of strawberries in his nose, but Cat's pillow was cool next to his head.

"Mornin', Just Cat," he called softly into the artificial gloom induced by hotel blackout curtains. When she didn't answer, Ash swung his legs out of the bed and pulled his jeans up over his naked hips. "Cat?"

No sound of a shower, no lights under the bathroom door.

No suitcase.

No Cat.

Oh, hell. He'd been so pleased she hadn't recognized him, he hadn't asked her last name. Hadn't gotten her number. He'd fallen for her outrageous invitation and tumbled into bed with a stranger. Worse, he'd slept like a child. She could have robbed him blind.

For three betrayed heartbeats, he dug around his backpack until he found his wallet. His untouched wallet.

He pulled out his phone and texted Kylie about his flight to Burlington, setting his jaw against the urge to ask her to find out for him who Cat was.

It turned out waiting for a commuter flight to Burlington would take longer than driving, so Ash took the rental Kylie arranged and set out for Blueberry Hill, promising her that someone would drive with him over to Montpelier to return it.

"Maybe you should trash it," she laughed. "Just don't damage yourself."

"You have the worst one-track mind I've ever known."

Despite his resolutions to the contrary, Ash thought about Cat as he drove. Snippets of thought chased each other through his contemplations, and as so often happened when something—or someone—got under his skin, those snippets coalesced into bits of lyric.

Just Cat, strawberry hair, dawn smile, you knew my heart before you knew my name...

A pretty interlude in a night of solitude and snow#

A ballad then. He half-sang, half-chanted the silly, overly romantic words to himself, trying out their cadence, feeling for motif or melody. It would stew in the back corners of his consciousness for however long it took. It would be real when he could sit down with a guitar.

The vintage 1964 Gibson acoustic in his room at Marnie and Micah's place would need tuning before he could make use of it; he hadn't been to Blueberry Hill in six months.

The extravagant gift from the Potter-Burnham clan was their way of welcoming him to the mountain village. He'd first arrived, on the verge of burnout, after his first big tour. Micah and his then girlfriend took him in for six weeks without a sideways glance. He'd fallen in love with the crazy, tangled family as much as the cozy, slightly shabby town nestled against mountains so lovely they took your breath away.

He hadn't had even the trace of fame he claimed now, not back then. He'd only been Micah Reynolds' kid brother, the one who sang at Fourth of July concerts and sometimes played a set in the Thirsty Catamount for string money.

No one in Blueberry Hill gave a hoot about the interviews on Pitchfork.com or the A.V. Club. He predicted approximately no one would give a crap about his Grammy. He adored them, even the rougher characters in town, for letting him be himself when he was around, and so he found himself heading there whenever he had enough downtime to justify it.

Thought I'd find solace in my mountain home
Your sad eyes, your breathless sighs,
They follow me as I roam...

Jesus, that was terrible. It was a good thing he had some time before the band was reconvening in Brooklyn to test out new material.

When he pulled into the driveway at Marnie and Micah's rambling cottage outside of town, he was greeted by barking. *That was new.*

Marnie appeared around the side of the house, on the far end of a leash. On the close end, ears and muzzle flapping, was a huge puppy of indiscriminate parentage.

"Henry, sit!" Marnie called. Like she'd flipped a switch, the dog skidded to a halt and plopped his butt down on the snow. His haunches quivered, but he sat. Brindle coat, but soft like a lab instead of sleek like a hound or wiry like a terrier. Floppy ears. Long, feathered tail. Gentle eyes and about a yard of lolling tongue.

"Henry?" Ash said, climbing out of the car with his backpack on his shoulder. "Pretty sure, Killer or Fang works just as well."

"Say hi, Henry," Marnie said, her laughter banked in her eyes.

Henry padded over and sniffed the hand Ash offered, then promptly collapsed on his back for belly rubs.

"He's such a good dog." Marnie beamed as Ash scratched the fuzzy belly. "He's only seven months old, but he's a quick learner. He didn't have any training when we picked him up at the shelter last month."

Ash dropped to his knees and ruffled Henry's ears, letting the puppy get a good long, get-to-know-you sniff.

"A month before your wedding, and you adopt a puppy the size of a miniature pony." Ash rose, keeping a hand on Henry's vast head to continue the ear scratches. Henry leaned heavily into his leg. The dog's warmth was welcome.

"The family magic," Marnie wiggled her fingers in front of his face and rolled her eyes dramatically, "told me to."

"The family magic you don't believe in."

Marnie laughed. "I saw him at the county adoption fair and told Micah I'd marry Stu instead if he didn't let me have Henry."

The idea of Marnie marrying the grizzled old bartender at the Thirsty Catamount was highly entertaining. Almost song-worthy. He was going to need some time with the leather-bound journal he kept in his backpack before the ideas escaped.

"The timing is perfect," Marnie went on. "You were already going to stay here and keep an eye on the plumbing while we're in Barbados. Now you can take care of Henry, too."

Ash stroked Henry's silky ears. "If you insist."

"Come on in. Your room's ready. Your brother is–get this," Marnie snapped her fingers and Henry rose and trotted along next to her toward the door, "presenting at a marketing conference in Montreal today. He's talking about how community marketplaces, sustainability, and shopping local are going to be successful business narratives in the coming decade."

"Well, shit." Ash held the door for Marnie and Henry. "Puts my sorry existence in perspective."

Marnie rolled her eyes and unclipped the puppy's leash. "Yes, of course. It's humbling to be you, Mr. 'Troubadour Heart of the Rockies.'"

Pride and embarrassment warred for the flush that rose up Ash's neck. Rolling Stone gave him the moniker in an interview about his *bluegrass-influenced, country-ish, storytelling songwriting that always managed to stay rooted in alt rock.*

Ash just wrote and played what he wanted to listen to. He brushed off comparisons to a young Springsteen. Their Jersey upbringings and rough-and-tumble vocal styles were about all they had in common, not that it wasn't flattering as hell.

"You're never going to let me live that down, are you?"

"Nope." Marnie tossed the puppy a long knotted rope. Henry bounded down the hall after it. "It's my right and privilege as your soon-to-be sister-in-law to keep you humble when you're bigger than Beyoncé."

"Unlikely." Ash crouched to collect Henry's rope and give it a tug. "But if she decides Jay-Z is wrong for her, I'd step up."

"Asher Knowles," Marnie mused. "I like it."

Her expression turned serious and Ash knew what was coming.

Marnie took it easy on him most of the time, at least with regard to his love life, but when she hit, she hit hard.

"It has a better ring than Ash Reynolds, Secret Moper and Closet Romantic Pining for True Love."

Ash didn't look away from Henry's soulful gaze over the hemp knot. "Shut up, Marnie."

"You know I'm right, and you're never going to meet someone hiding here when you're not on the road. Everyone knows you have to bring fresh blood into a town like this."

"What about Sam?" It was a cheap shot, Ash knew. Marnie's life-long best friend was married to her childhood sweetheart, also a hometown boy.

"Gross." Marnie pulled a face, but her eyes told a different story. "They're the exception that proves the rule. And they don't live here anymore."

"I'm going to go shower, and maybe," he tossed her Henry's rope and picked up his backpack as he rose, "just maybe I'll tell you about a girl I met on a plane yesterday."

He dashed for the stairs and locked himself in the bathroom while Marnie hollered from the hallway.

"You stinker! I'll make Micah make you pay for that. Or Henry. Or someone. Ugh!"

Ash chuckled as he started the shower. It was good to be back in Blueberry Hill.

Chapter Seven

King's Diner smelled just like Elmore's greasy spoon in Stag Creek.

Cat took a seat at the counter and turned over the laminated menu. The chatter between the waitress and the cook was far more cheerful than the banter between Elmore and Clarice, but Cat knew the cadence just the same. It sounded like they were trading old-school short-order slang. When the waitress made her way over with a mug and a pot of steaming coffee, Cat was ready.

"Hey, hon. I'm Nikki. Coffee?"

Cat grinned. "Draw it in the dark."

"I know that one," Nikki said, filling her mug with black coffee. "Heinrich's been teaching me. It passes the time."

"I wonder if Heinrich can do a Jack Benny with a side of Frog Sticks."

"*Ja*," came a lightly-accented voice from the kitchen. "Comin' right up."

His American impression was spot-on; she and Nikki shared a laugh that settled the butterflies in her gut. These were a different sort, rooted in nerves and uncertainty. She preferred the delicate, desirous flight Ash set loose in her, but Ash was somewhere else in Vermont by now, celebrating his brother and new sister-in-law.

When Cat finished her bacon grilled cheese with fries, she tidied her dishes into a stack. "Nikki?"

"Yeah, hon. What can I get you?"

"Actually," Cat swallowed the butterflies. "I'm looking for someone. Daphne Potter?"

A shadow crossed Nikki's face and Cat's stomach fell. *Was this Daphne a dragon-lady? Crazy? A criminal? A horrible bitch?*

Nikki's expression cleared. "You're in luck. She's just down the block. That's her truck." Nikki pointed at a refurbished pop-up trailer with a jaunty awning parked outside the fanciest Grange Hall Cat had ever seen.

"Oh." It was almost too easy. "Does she sell something?"

Nikki leaned on the counter. "Mostly soaps and stuff, all organic and handmade. Rumor has it, you can get *other* things from her, too..."

Nikki's words took on something edgy, maybe almost mean. A thrill ran down Cat's spine. *Other* was exactly what she'd hoped for.

Cat lowered her voice and pulled out her wallet to pay the check. "Like..."

She left the question open, hoping Nikki would bite. She'd known a hundred Nikkis over the years, there was a good chance she'd get what she was looking for.

"Love potions, fortunes, that kind of thing." Nikki glanced back over her shoulder. "The Kings are friends of hers, so I won't get into it, but folks around here think she might be a witch."

It was Cat's turn to glance over her shoulder, out the door at the cheerful little camper parked on the sunny side of the street. "I'll keep that in mind." She left cash with a twenty-five percent tip for Nikki. "Thanks a lot."

Nikki counted her take with her eyes and offered Cat a warm smile. "No problem. Figured it was only fair to warn you, being new here and all."

How small is this town?

Cat grabbed her bag and made her way around the town common to where the soap truck was parked. In addition to the awning, Daphne Potter had set out buckets of potted mums in front of her camper and a rolling cart full of samples. Cat couldn't see the woman inside the pop-up, but she could hear the conversation she was having with the customer at the window.

"Molly, I can't thank you enough for introducing me to the Goat Goddess ladies. Eleanor and Joanie are supplying all my goat milk now, and they hooked me up with an essential oil distiller over near Ticonderoga. Her prices are incredible and the product is potent."

The woman named Molly had a gracious laugh. "It's a pleasure. We gals need to stick together if we're going to build the kind of businesses that feed the community."

"How's your boy? Still in New York? If he ever comes home, I want to commission some pieces for the soap truck and the workshop. His work is so *connected* to the forest..."

"Actually, Joss is home now. Staying with us, butting heads with Walt. Boy's got a thorn in his paw, but he doesn't want to talk about it yet." Molly sighed. "I dearly love having him home, but he needs space of his own if he's not going to take the farm."

"Walt's friendly with Russ Warren, isn't he?"

Cat chose a lemony hand cream to sample. The ladies' conversation surrounded her like a quilt. She could almost see the young man, her age maybe? Stewing over something personal, frustrated with farm life. She took her time smoothing the lotion into her skin.

"He is. Why do you ask?" Molly said.

"Russ's brother-in-law is looking to rent that old hunting camp they keep in Catmint Gap. It's solid, but it needs work. It has plumbing and heat, which is more than you can say for some places. Maybe Joss could take it on, trade rent for renovations."

"That's up off Bobolink Road, right?"

"Near Susie Daley's lilac spread," Daphne said.

"That might work, " Molly said. "I'll have Walt give Russ a call. Thanks, Daph."

Molly turned abruptly, change and a small paper bag in hand, and crashed directly into Cat. "Oh, honey, I'm sorry."

"No, I was daydreaming. Excuse me." Cat shook her head. Molly's steadying touch on her arm conjured a vision of a simple farmhouse, a long red dairy barn, and a seemingly endless view of rolling pastures and evergreen woods. Nothing that couldn't be explained by the eavesdropping, but it felt so *real*.

"You all right? You look like you've seen a ghost."

"I'm fine, thank you."

"Take care, honey. And get some of that hand cream. It's divine." Molly released Cat's arm and waved to Daphne Potter. "See you!"

"Bye, Molly," Daphne called, before leaning out the camper's modified window. "Good morning. Anything I can help you with?"

"I'd like this." Cat placed a jar of the lotion on the window ledge. "And I'd like to buy you a cup of coffee when you're free."

Daphne blinked; the furrows between her eyes deepened. "Do we know each other?"

Shivers coasted over Cat's skin. "No, ma'am, but I have every reason to believe we're kin."

———

EVEN AFTER SEVEN YEARS, sometimes his brother's life still caught Ash by surprise.

Micah was the good son: recruited out of Thornton College to work for a big commercial real estate developer in Albany; his own studio apartment; responsible pickup truck; promising American dream boxes, all checked. Their older sister Avery was tracking similarly back then, with the addition of a successful, good-looking boyfriend who was probably going to propose.

Ash was already out west, busking and playing open mics to sell CDs he'd recorded and produced in a friend's parents' basement on a laptop computer he'd had no business springing for. He'd had the family-black-sheep thing covered.

Then Micah tossed out his corporate career to help Marnie build what was now the most prominent community market in the state, and suddenly *aspiring professional musician* didn't seem so rebellious.

Standing amidst the happy confusion of the Blueberry Hill

Farmer's Market, Ash figured his brother's rebellion was the way to do it. Even with the snow outside, vendors and shoppers alike spilled down the outside stairs and onto the sidewalk. Hemp jewelry, organic squash, local honey, a nature poet who printed her own books on an antique press and hand-bound them using secondhand leather... Micah made his way through it all dropping names and greetings along the way. Here Micah was the celebrity, and Ash was happy to fade into the background.

Ash paused at a vendor selling venison curry and bought himself a cup for lunch.When he looked up, Micah was hip-deep in conversation with a group of fiber artists up from Connecticut to see what was for sale.

Deciding a sunny October afternoon was too nice to spend inside the market, Ash made his way outside and down to the sidewalk. Marnie's mom's soap company was set up down the street, as was usual for a Saturday. Ash figured traditions were traditions and took his curried venison to say hello to Daphne Potter. If he were lucky, she'd have the lemon balm and Fraser fir soap he liked; if he were extra lucky, she'd slip a love charm in with his order, along with a knowing wink.

The unused crystal charms filled a bowl in his room at Micah and Marnie's place, but Ash liked that Daphne was looking out for him in her way.

Marnie hadn't fallen far from that tree, even if she denied there was actual magic in their blood.

The crowd parted as he was walking and for just a moment, Ash was sure the woman at the soap truck's purchase window was Just Cat. Much to his chagrin, she hadn't been far from his thoughts since their night together, but imagining her here was a fresh hell.

"Ash!" He had just enough time to turn towards the voice, when the very pregnant woman attached to it threw her arms around him. "Will and I were wondering when you'd get here."

Ash hugged Samantha Dryer as hard as he dared, murmuring into her hair. "It's so good to see you."

Sam pulled back and looked him over. "What's wrong?"

"Nothing a week in your company can't fix." Ash returned her inspection. "You're *huge*."

"Will says he's going to be a cattle rustler." Sam cradled her belly. "I'm convinced *she's* got her Aunty Daphne's magic."

Ash glanced over Sam's head towards the soap truck, but the woman he'd seen was gone.

"Ash?" Sam was looking at him again. If Marnie ignored the magic in her family tree, Sam–who was Marnie's cousin somehow through their mothers–embraced it. She and Will lived down in Brattleboro, but Samantha was often found in Blueberry Hill, learning folklore and soap-making in Daphne Potter's workshop.

In Ash's experience, Sam had the kind of energy that fed the soul and a connection to certain people that gave her insight into their deepest selves, but the jury was still out as far as actual *hocus pocus* stuff was concerned.

"Who was she?"

"What?"

"You were looking for someone–a woman–just then." Sam blushed. "I'm sorry. I promise I'm not snooping, it was just a feeling I had."

"No one. Nothing," he said. "It doesn't matter."

Sam decided to let the matter go. "So, when did you get in?"

"Yesterday. Flew up after a show in Raleigh-Durham. I've got three weeks before I have to meet the band in the studio."

Sam patted her baby bump. "Maybe you'll still be here when this little one arrives."

"I'd better look into baby's first ukulele," he said, putting an arm around Sam. "Let's go find the happy couple."

"And Will. He was looking for Micah, and probably falafel, when I lost track of him."

Wishing losing track of Cat could be that simple, Ash took Sam's arm and walked them both toward the market.

Chapter Eight

Daphne Potter closed the truck without hesitation. She led Cat across the common towards the library. "They serve coffee in the basement. The coffee's terrible, but it's private."

Blueberry Hill's library was a large salt-box style farmhouse with a historical plaque on it that read "Dodd Homestead, est. 1697." Cat reached out to touch the clapboards and blinked as the modern world shimmered around the library, revealing a woman in a belted coat and cloche hat carrying a very little girl–a toddler, really–toward a horse-drawn cart at twilight. Driving the cart was a man in a heavy suit and brimmed hat.

The little girl was crying, arms reaching back to whatever was beyond the cart.

Inanimate objects triggering her spells was a new development.

"It's your eyes," Daphne Potter said, once they'd settled into a cozy sofa in the back of the library's downstairs reading room and coffee shop. "You've got my mother's eyes. How do you have my mother's eyes?"

Cat reached into her bag and pulled out the plastic folio that contained the letter Meemaw left her in her will, and a paper-clipped stack of printed pages. She pushed them across the table to Daphne.

Their fingers brushed, ever so slightly, but power coursed through Cat's fingers. There was no other way to describe it. Not a vision, but a burst of heat and energy that crackled.

Daphne's eyes widened; her nostrils flared, but she didn't comment. She chose the printed pages first, pausing to fish a pair of cheaters from the pocket of her oversized cardigan. Cat squeezed her fingers together as Daphne read.

"Is this true?" Daphne's eyes were wide. The air around them nearly *swished* gently on her exhale.

"I believe it to be," Cat replied. "Meemaw loved internet research, and I got her an Ancestry.com subscription for Christmas a couple years back. She said there wasn't much there when I asked, but..." Cat gestured to the papers. "She wasn't telling me the whole truth."

"These printouts suggest your grandmother's grandparents left Stag Creek, North Carolina, in 1925, and returned in 1927 with their two-year-old daughter Mercy in tow." Daphne looked up. "There was no Mercy in our family tree."

"Which," Cat gave Daphne a pointed look, "given your family's *peculiar* history, has probably been carefully kept–especially the maternal lines."

Cat would have sworn the light around Daphne Potter flashed a deep violet, but no one else in the snug basement room so much as blinked in their direction. She wanted desperately to ask Daphne about the visions, but not here. Not yet.

"You're correct on both counts, young lady." Daphne squared her shoulders and took off her cheaters. "I think this conversation needs to continue at my workshop. Are you willing to visit me tomorrow morning?"

"Ma'am," Cat said gently, "if I have kin in this place, I'll do whatever I need to to learn who I am."

"I'm an early riser," Daphne Potter said. "And no more *ma'am*. You can call me Daphne, I think it's safe to say we're *sisters*, kin or not."

Chapter Nine

"Tell me you've written at least three new songs," Kylie said.

"I've been here less than forty-eight hours." Ash had to laugh. He was bundled up in sweats and flannel, drinking coffee on his brother's deck while the puppy chased dry leaves in the yard. "And it's supposed to be a vacation."

Kylie laughed. "So only one?"

Ash could hear the New York City traffic behind her. "I've written down some lyric stuff, but I haven't done anything more than tune up the '64 Gibson."

"The higher-ups would really like a pop-ballad on the new record. Something upbeat and lovey-dovey they can market by leveraging the Moira Kennedy shippers."

"Shippers?" Ash's heart sunk. "Tell me there is no Mulder-and-Scully-thing going on on the internet."

"I can lie–1633 Broadway." Traffic sounds gave way to fuzzy radio behind her. Kylie didn't bother muffling the phone while she directed her cab. "Or I can tell you you're well on your way to becoming a household name."

"Shea Gallagher is a good guy..."

"Sweet summer child. Shippers gonna ship–has nothing to do with Moira's actual husband or your actual left hand."

"Kylie."

She ignored his embarrassment. "What stuff are you writing down? Can there be banjos *and* a kick drum? There's this bluegrass rock outfit brewing in the UK right now. They're gonna be huge in like a year, and I want to be favorably positioned for that wave."

Ash sighed. "I'll email you some lines."

"Have you found some wholesome small town girl to debauch yet? Preferably someone you can pine over a little while you're hiding out in the loft I just rented for you guys to share while you're in the studio."

Ash drained the last of his coffee and rattled a treat pouch to get Henry's attention. "You thrive on my misery."

"I thrive on your commercial success. And I've got a call coming in. Talk soon."

The call disconnected. Ash tossed a treat for Henry, who snapped it out of the air, tail whipping back and forth.

Kylie would definitely qualify Cat as a wholesome small town girl, but Ash wasn't sure who debauched who. She'd propositioned him. She'd led the dance. She'd left him alone in the bed they'd shared without so much as a forwarding phone number.

She'd slipped into his thoughts and followed him to Blueberry Hill.

"Where'd she go, Henry?" Ash asked the dog.

Henry didn't have an answer.

Chapter Ten

Cat pulled into 972 Old Quarry View Road at ten to seven the following morning. She'd been up for almost two hours already, rereading Meemaw's journal and the papers she'd left along with it.

After leaving Daphne the day before, she'd driven to Burlington to return the rental, but not before stopping to deposit Kelley's check in a NexBank ATM she found in a shopping center not far from the airport.

Her next stop was a car dealership. Kelley's money was too much, but refusing was pointless. The 1997 Toyota was in decent shape, despite the hundred-plus-thousand miles on it, and the deal she got for paying cash made the twelve-year-old sedan more economical than renting.

She cut the headlights in Daphne's driveway and let the car idle while she waited.

Daphne told her she liked to start working around seven; Cat took the woman at her word. Sure enough, at three minutes past the hour, Daphne Potter emerged from the house in overalls and clogs, wearing the same chunky-knit oversized cardigan and a brightly patterned scarf wrapped around her gray and bronze streaked curls. Daphne waved with one hand; she carried a pottery mug in the other.

In the burgeoning light, Cat could make out the steam from the mug and Daphne's breath on the morning air. The mountains curved around a bowl of land that made up the Potter homestead; lawn gave way to long grass, and then to woods before the mountains swept up into the clouds.

It reminded her of home.

Cat climbed out of the car. "Morning."

"I'm told," Daphne said around a sip from her mug, "that the modern witches say, 'bright blessings,' or something like that, but I came to this through my mother, and let's just say, there wasn't an internet to make the craft acceptable cocktail party chitchat when she was a girl."

Laughing dissipated some of the tension Cat was carrying. "I appreciate you taking the time to do this."

"The women in this family take care of our own, and while I might not know *how* you're family, I do know it. I knew it the moment I saw my mother's eyes looking out from your face." Daphne reached out and Cat took her hand. "Let's get to the bottom of this."

At once, Cat saw, like an overlay against Daphne's skin, the face of a young woman, her delicate features made-up like June Cleaver, leaning over a soup pot on a vintage stove. Cat saw through her own eyes the reflected face of a pigtailed girl, warped by the curve of the pot.

She gasped. She'd never felt as though she was inside the visions before, only there as an observer.

"Cat, honey. That took me by surprise." Daphne's expression was firm, but kind. Maternal. "You can't just walk around in someone's memories like that."

"I..." Cat stammered. "Is that what I did? Sometimes I see..things, but–"

"But you've never done that before?" Daphne was gentle. "I think you should meet my daughter's friend Samantha. She has more experience with heightened intuition than I do, and you're going to need self-protection and etiquette practice." Daphne closed the door behind them. "Starting today."

Daphne's workshop inside the barn was a blend of modern industrial kitchen and something out of a living history museum. The rafters were hung with drying herbs and plants–only a handful of which Cat could name by sight. A huge greenhouse addition stuck out from the back wall, full of living flowers and plants. A turkey fryer propane ring held court in the center of the dirt floor, and a series of clean, stainless steel frying kettles lay on their sides on a large stainless steel counter. There was a commercial kitchen sink and an apothecary's chest that looked about two hundred years old. Mismatched twentieth century kitchen cabinets lined the walls, neatly labeled with one of those handheld label makers.

"At the library," Cat said, "when our hands brushed, I didn't have a vision. Why this morning?"

"My guard was up, I suppose," Daphne replied, as though protecting her thoughts from idle interlopers was an everyday occurrence.

An old utility desk with a blotter and stacks of papers occupied one corner. A laptop computer slept on an adjacent filing cabinet. Daphne took a small key from her keyring and unlocked the top drawer of the filing cabinet. From there, she pulled out an archival box.

Inside the archival box, Cat saw what looked like an old Bible inside a polyethylene sleeve. Daphne removed the book and laid it on a bookstand that stood on an old wooden lectern in the corner of the room.

"This was a Proctor family Bible," Daphne said, beckoning Cat over as she gently eased the book open and retrieved her reading glasses from her sweater pocket. "It was re-bound sometime after my ancestors fled Salem and changed their name to Potter."

Salem. A shiver ran down Cat's spine. Her fingers itched to touch the pages. It was a compelling, sensual pull, not unlike the memory of her desire to touch Ash.

Daphne used a ribbon bookmark to turn over a large chunk of pages. At the back of the book, the pages were no longer printed, but handwritten in faded, spidery script.

"Is that a *grimoire*?" The word felt foreign on Cat's tongue. She'd only discovered it when she'd begun to explore the strange possibilities in her heritage.

"It's a cookbook, a diary, a manual, a genealogy, and yes, a spell book. Hidden in plain sight behind the Book of Revelations." Daphne's eyes twinkled at the joke.

"But there's no mention of someone who could be my great-grandmother?"

"I looked at it last night," Daphne said. "Let me show you."

This time, when Daphne turned the pages, Cat noticed that her fingers only brushed the thin paper. The pages turned almost responsively, like a cat rubbing against a friendly hand. Another chill coasted over her skin.

Meemaw's remembered voice whispered in her ear. *It ain't my grave you're walking over, goose.*

She read the lines of births, deaths, and marriages, noting that once the name Proctor changed to Potter, many of the women kept their surname. As the lines marched down the pages, the hand-writing grew smoother and darker, until she saw Daphne's name, followed by the name Marnie Helene Potter–and a childish printed addition to the surname: -Burnham.

Daphne noticed her observation. "My daughter. She's not inter-ested in her legacy, but she's not without her own kind of magic."

"Who are these other lines?" Other columns of names marched down the opposite page.

"Siblings of my direct line," Daphne said. She let her finger hover over *Camille Ellis*. "This is my cousin. Sam is her daughter, and an apprentice of mine, so to speak."

Cat tracked the names back from *Marnie Helene*. "I think if Mercy belongs here, she's closest to your mother. In age, anyway."

"How did my name end up in your grandmother's papers?" Daphne asked, peering at Cat over her frames.

Cat took a deep breath. This is where she had to accept a leap of faith, and hope that Daphne Potter would join her.

Daphne's tea smelled of bergamot and jasmine. Cat closed her eyes, letting the fragrant steam conjure up Meemaw's face and voice, but the eyes that looked back at her through the billows of moisture weren't Meemaw's. Or Daphne's. They were cruel, glittering eyes, full of madness and malice. Lit up with an unholy glee.

Cat stumbled back.

"Cat? What happened?"

""I swear...eyes...in the steam. Looking right at me." She was stuttering, thrown entirely off guard by what she'd seen.

Daphne touched her palm to Cat's cheek, a pair of small creases deepening between her eyes.. "We need to get your protections up."

"Yes, but..." *Who did I just see?*

Daphne shook off whatever she'd been about to say. "Now, where were we?"

Cat blinked. She knew she hadn't imagined Daphne's distress, or the spectral eyes she'd seen in the steam. *Where had they been? Just about to explain about the letters and Granny.*

"Meemaw's mother died in childbirth at sixteen. Her Granny Fraser raised her. She told me once that she'd heard her Granny talk about traveling down from Vermont in the spring on a horse cart, leaving just as the sap was flowing and the maple sugar houses were boiling. Granny Fraser was still alive when I was a little girl. I thought she was a thousand years old. If you look at Meemaw's notes, she was almost a hundred when she died."

Cat pulled out the diary Meemaw left her, and opened it to a purple Post-It-flagged page. She turned the book around to show Daphne. "Here: *The more I think on it, the more I think Granny Fraser was telling me something when she talked about traveling to Vermont back in the 20s.*

"She used to say how my dead mama, Mercy, was a
wicked creature, and how I should always be a
good girl. Even as a little thing, I knew that meant
to keep things to myself. Things like my imaginary
friends. One time she caught me and Bessie
MacAllister playing at witches, cooking up mud

and grass in an old washtub like a potion and
Grampy took a strap to my bottom.
 Cat's momma is like that, restless and a magnet for
trouble, but after growing up like I did, I didn't
curb her. That was a mistake, but I didn't know
what I do now. What I learned from the letters."

When Daphne looked up from the page, Cat reached into her folder and drew out the packet of letters, worn thin with time, faded and yellowed. The air crackled between Daphne's reaching fingers and the letters. Cat saw a faint sparkle of energy; a tickle chased that energy from her neck to her fingertips.

For a few moments, Cat watched Daphne read the old letters. The older woman's lips moved faintly over certain passages, almost like an incantation. When Daphne finished the letter she tucked it into the pages of Meemaw's journal, which still lay open on the table between them.

"That letter is from Abram Clutch."

"Yes, it is." Cat knew that much, but it had taken a glance at the Potter women's grimoire to confirm his relationship to Daphne. "He was your great-grandfather."

Tears brimmed and fell from Daphne's eyes. "And your great-great...great? Grandfather."

"That's what Meemaw believed," Cat said.

She'd read the letters herself. Enough time to know the contents by heart. There were four letters from Abram Clutch. Each answering questions posed by Meemaw's grandfather, Arthur Fraser. The first reply began, *"With regard to the child Mercy, your description of her strangeness is not foreign to me.*

I saw the same in my own daughter Philomena until she gave birth. The experience settled her. She is biddable and quiet now. It is my opinion that the women in this family believe themselves to be something more than human, a flaw which must be disciplined out of their spirit or they run mad and wild. I had hoped by removing the child from any closeness to her maternal relations, I might spare her a future of the same fate, but it seems to be something in the blood. I recommend a strong hand and an early marriage to a man of stern character."

"My mother told me she was terrified of him–her own grandfather," Daphne said softly. "Philomena was never *biddable*. Not from what I've heard, or from what I knew of her. My granddad was a pastor, a gentle man with a deep voice and big shoulders, but not a *stern character*. He knew what his daughter and her mother were, what I am, and it never bothered him. If that's what Abram believed, his daughter had him fooled."

"And no one ever let slip that Philomena had a daughter at sixteen?"

"If my mother knew, she'd have told me. Marnie got her bluntness somewhere." Daphne laughed, but her eyes were far away and serious.

The mention of Daphne's daughter sent a strange thrill through Cat's bones. She had a cousin. Cousins plural; Daphne had mentioned her apprentice, Samantha.

"Keep reading the journal. Once Meemaw had an idea of what to look for, she got started."

Just for fun, and because Cat showed me how, I
Googled 'witches in Vermont,' and 'Vermont witch
coven.' Turns out, witches are right out in the open
on the internet these days. It took some clicking
around, but what else have I got besides time. I
found Daphne Potter in Blueberry Hill and I got a
funny swooping feeling in my belly like I did when
I met Howard, or like when I saw baby Cat for the
first time. I never was anything more than a wife to
Howard and a mother to Mona until Cat came to
stay. The witches call me a Crone, and it's powerful
stuff, getting old and being alive..."

Cat pulled the journal back, tears welling at Meemaw's words despite the number of times she'd read them. "She knew, just like you knew when you saw me."

"I wish we'd known one another. Camille, the cousin I knew, wasn't interested in practicing. She didn't feel the pull of it. It would've been nice to have someone to learn with back then." Daphne's eyes overflowed too; they stood rooted in the lost years for a moment.

A light tap on the workroom door disturbed the tears, and a bald man with a graying goatee pushed open the door.

"I brought tea," he said. He paused to take in Cat's blotchy face. His eyes widened, but he said nothing except, "You must be Cat. I'm Max."

Daphne smiled. "You see it too."

Max grinned at Cat. "You've got Ida's eyes."

Daphne took the tea tray and dismissed her husband. "We'll figure out the genealogy later. For now, we need to start with how not to march into someone's memories." She handed Cat a mug and poured more tea from the pot into her own. "And how to protect yourself from unwanted visions."

Cat wasn't sure what she expected, but it wasn't Daphne opening her laptop and setting it on the work table.

Daphne caught Cat's puzzled expression. "I need to ask around in the forums. You really can learn anything on the internet."

Chapter Eleven

"What exactly does this have to do with your wedding?" Ash asked his brother over a pile of cordwood and a splitting maul.

"Nothing." Micah handed him a pair of work gloves and maneuvered a chunk of stump into place between them. "You just look like someone who needs a few hours of sweaty, mindless labor."

Ash eyed the cut lengths of tree limb. "I've never split firewood in my life. What makes you think it's a good idea?"

Micah picked up a log, stood it on the stump. "Hand me the maul."

"The what now?"

Micah pointed to what Ash would have called an axe. *Shows you what you know.* Ash handed it across the log, then stepped back a reasonable amount. Micah placed the maul's blade on the log's upright end, tested its weight, and in a motion so sudden and smooth Ash barely saw it, raised the maul overhead and swung it down, burying the blade halfway into the log. With a second swing, Micah drove the blade through. The split pieces tumbled into the dirt next to the driveway.

His brother split firewood.

"It takes a little practice," Micah said. "I'm pretty sure I looked like an idiot until I got the hang of it, but…" And here Micah grinned. "You can learn anything on YouTube."

A laugh burst out of Ash. "You learned to split firewood on YouTube."

Micah handed the maul to Ash and stepped back. "Now you don't have to."

Hefting the handle a little to get a feel for it, Ash realized he could use a physical outlet. Not that Cat had been far from his thoughts since the hotel in Revere, but since he'd thought he'd seen her at the market, he'd been turning their brief time together over in his mind until it shone like an amber bead.

Propping the splitting maul against the heap of firewood, he pulled the miniature moleskin he kept in his back pocket out and jotted that thought down. When he put it away, Micah was looking at him like a museum curiosity.

"What?"

Micah crooked a brow. "You're keeping a diary?"

Ash shrugged. "Grammy-winning songs don't write themselves."

"This cordwood isn't going to split itself, either."

Ash picked up the splitting maul again. "Fair enough."

He settled his grip on the hand and mimicked Micah's movements, feeling the shock of the impact through to his shoulder, and whooping when the log split into an awkward sixty-forty pair.

"Satisfying, isn't it?" Micah said. "I'm going to stack the stuff I split yesterday while you work on the cordwood. Maybe it'll help you banish the girl that broke your heart."

"She didn't break–" Ash looked up to find his big brother grinning. "Asshole. How did you know?"

"Remember when Caitlyn Murray told you 'anyone can play guitar,' and she was only going to date frontmen?"

Ash swung the maul again, this time getting closer to the split he was aiming for. "Yeah. She thought she was being real clever, quoting Radiohead to me while she was destroying my ego."

"Same face," Micah said. "If you want to get it off your chest, let me know."

Ash didn't answer, he just queued up another log. It took a while, but he fell into a halting rhythm, one with no room for wayward thoughts. His arms and back were aching by the time Marnie called him from the front porch. "Supper's in ten, gentlemen. Time to finish up your feats of strength or whatever."

They tidied up the woodpile and Micah left to put the maul back in the shed. Ash was greeted at the front door by Marnie and Henry. She handed Ash the leash.

"Can you walk him down as far as the end of the driveway and get his business done?"

Wordlessly, Ash took the leash and looped it around his wrist. Henry dashed ahead of him, pulling the line taut. "Henry," Ash called, "come here, you meatball."

The dog stopped at the sound of his name and trotted back to Ash. Ash took up a little of the leash's slack and crouched to look the dog in the eye. "Let's walk like the men we are, okay?"

Henry's canine eyes appeared to agree, and by some small miracle the puppy trotted along close to Ash as they made their way to the mailbox and back. There were some brief stops for *business*, as Marnie put it, but on the whole it was uneventful. When they got back to the porch, Ash sat on the stairs to contemplate the falling dark. October was on the verge of giving way to November; sunset was long past this time of year, but the light lingered near the horizon.

Henry plopped his butt down next to Ash and leaned his big, warm body against him. The dog set one of his admirably large paws on Ash's leg, which Ash took for a request for scratches.

"So, what's your story?" He asked the dog. "Some woman break your heart, too?"

Henry licked his face.

"Sucks, man. I didn't really even know her, but there was...something, anyway."

The puppy's tail thumped on the boards; he cocked his head, ears lifting.

"See?" Ash said. "You get it."

Marnie opened the front door. "Supper, you two."

Henry leapt to his feet and nearly flew inside, nails scrabbling on the worn hardwood between him and his bowl, leash dragging behind him. Ash pushed to his feet with a sigh.

"What gives, brother-to-be?" Marnie asked.

Enough. It wasn't worth stewing on. He hadn't told Marnie anything about Cat in the end. The wedding dominated all their conversations.

Ash arranged his face into a bland expression, and wrapped an arm around Marnie's shoulder. "Absolutely nothing, sister-to-be."

Cat liked the look of Samantha Dryer from the moment Daphne's apprentice hoisted her very pregnant body from a sporty hatchback and glided into the workshop like a madonna in yoga pants and an oversized hoodie.

Samantha and Daphne hugged for a long moment, before Daphne held Samantha out at arms' length. "Motherhood agrees with you."

"I'm gestating like a pro," Samantha said, patting her baby bump. She looked past Daphne to Cat and smiled. "You must be Cat. Daphne mentioned you'd be here today. Samantha Dryer. Call me Sam."

"Hi. It's nice to meet you, Sam." Cat said. She wasn't sure what to do with her hands except squeeze them together. She and Daphne had worked on her third eye for hours the previous day, but Cat wasn't sure she'd be able to keep her newly acquired defenses up. Everything about Samantha radiated openness.

Sam walked around Daphne and drew Cat into a gentle hug. "You're doing great," she said softly.

"Am I?" Cat said, stepping back.

Sam looked back at Daphne. "I'm not getting much. You could

coach this." She turned back to Cat. "Daphne says you have visions? I'm a little jealous," Sam went on. "I only get *feelings*. Like an emotional barometer. And I'm garbage with everything but the love potion."

"Don't be jealous. It's awful. I get sick...Sometimes I pass out if I'm tired or hungry, and it happens whether I want to or not." It felt so good to talk about the visions with someone who wouldn't think she was crazy, or *touched*, or frightening. Everything about Sam felt safe.

Sam laughed. "It's so hard when it's new and you don't know how to manage it. I've had mine since I hit puberty, more or less, but it was kind of running in the background when I was a teen. I didn't realize what was really happening to me, until..." Her expression darkened. "Let's just say someone who knew better took advantage." She shook her head slightly. "Anyway. It's taken forever to focus, and to use my own energy with intent. I still get a little ahead of myself sometimes when someone's really emotional."

Sam's matter of fact acceptance and honestly about her own experience set Cat at ease.

"Well, girls," Daphne said. "Tea and some third-eye opening, then we get to work. It's a beautiful day for personal care products. The Halloween celebration is at the end of the week, and I'm low on #9 body oil and Max's soap."

Sam grinned and rolled her eyes at Cat, "Magic-schmagic. She's just using us as free labor."

"I heard that," Daphne said, rolling open the barn doors.

The scent that wafted out of the workshop hit her like a wave. Evergreen and lemon, clean and sharp, and as it dissipated into the air around, the memory of Ash's sleeping body beside hers in the hotel bed was so strong she almost felt it physically.

"You okay?" Sam said.

"Yeah," Cat replied. "Just thinking about...someone."

"Someone you lost?"

"Am I that transparent?" Cat sighed. "I didn't lose him. I walked away from him." Sam nodded in sympathy, and Cat felt the need to explain. "Not like a boyfriend or anything. We'd just met, but the timing was wrong, and I..."

I laughed. We made love all night while the snow fell. He trusted me, and I vanished.

"Whatever you just didn't say, you kept it to yourself." Sam nudged Cat's arm with her own and gave her a knowing look. "You really are doing great."

Hours of mixing and pouring soaps and bottling body oil and about a gallon of Daphne's tea forced Cat into the main house to find the bathroom. On her return, she paused at the door to the workshop when realized Daphne was talking about Cat's awful vision.

"...don't know what she saw, but I felt it in the room with us. Nothing good, Sweet Sam."

Samanthan's voice. "She said she saw eyes? Maybe it's to do with our ancestors?"

"I don't want to rule anything out," Daphne said, "but there's only one other time I've felt darkness like that, and it wasn't about the Potters."

Cat was sure she heard Sam gasp. "That's not possible. I told you what happened in Las Vegas. That's over now."

"I'm sure you're right, but be careful, honey."

Cat made a show of opening the door to give the two women a moment to pretend they hadn't been talking about her.

"So, what did I miss?"

Chapter Thirteen

The snow was gone by October 31, with a long stretch of unseason-
ably warm weather in the forecast, which was perfect as far as Ash
was concerned. He'd been waiting a long time for a Blueberry Hill
Halloween.

Blueberry Hill was a rural village, with a handful of what a
suburban kid might call neighborhoods, but generally, folks were
pretty far flung. Instead of trick-or-treating, kids in Blueberry Hill
congregated on the town common and went candy-begging around
the center of the village, hitting up the shops and town offices, as well
as the few homes that clustered around the downtown. Folks drove in
and handed out candy from lawn chairs on the common. The diner
and the Thirsty Catamount sold food and drink.

At the last minute, Marnie decided they were all dressing up,
including Henry, which was how Ash found himself as the Tin Man
to Marnie and Micah's Dorothy and the Scarecrow. Henry, obviously
too big to be Toto, was wearing a shaggy brown yarn "mane" with a
red bow and playing the part of the Cowardly Lion.

"It's a week before my wedding. Consider the costumes part of an
early and unconventional Jack-and-Jill stag party," Marnie had said.

Ash figured there were worse impromptu costumes. He was wearing a gray sweater, gray sweatpants, and an old galvanized funnel on his head, and carrying the splitting maul with it's leather protector over the blade for safety. Marnie had driven down to Rutland to the seasonal Halloween Store to get generic masks for all of them, so his face was obscured by a scrap of shiny silver plastic.

There was nothing obscure about Henry, who strained at his leash to kiss every stranger they passed. He was so excited to be among his next few hundred best friends, he didn't even notice that Ash had rigged up a candy bucket on his walking harness.

Ash bought a hot spiced cider from King's Diner's table and wandered through the crowd, occasionally catching sight of Marnie and Micah. He kept an eye out for Sam and Will, who were reportedly attending as Harry Potter and the Golden Snitch.

The Snitch found him first. Sam was dressed all in black, save for the golden ball of the Snitch painted over her belly, with golden wings flying out from either side of her abdomen.

She went to Henry first. The pretty girls always did. Sam scratched his tremendous ears while Henry gazed into her eyes. "You're not cowardly, you gorgeous boy."

If you excused the string of drool forming on Henry's lower lip, the picture was positively picturesque.

Sam pushed herself to standing, placing a palm on his chest. "If you only had a heart..."

"You'd open at the close?" He squeezed Sam's hand, then reached for Will's. "Hey, Will–er, Harry. Good to see you."

Will had gone for the Quidditch robe look, right down to the racing broom. The two of them took cute to a whole new level.

"Is Marnie around?" Sam asked. "I need to talk to her about Daphne's new apprentice. I'm curious what she thinks of the whole thing, and Daph's got the new girl working the candy cauldron tonight."

"New apprentice?" Ash asked. "Did you get fired?"

Sam laughed. "No. I'm still trying to prove I'm competent enough at salves and tisanes to give something besides love potions a try." She leaned in close. "It's not the intent, I'm just a terrible cook. But this woman turned up on her doorstep a few days ago claiming to be some long-lost relative. Daphne says she's got the Sight; she's definitely got something."

You don't need to hear my sad story... family business... Reunion...

His heart kicked over and raced away like a dirt bike motor. "What's her name?"

"Cat," Sam said. "Just Cat. It's not short for anything. How adorable is that?"

His chest heaved as though he'd careened over a cliff into open air. He'd thought of nothing but her–despite his promise to himself–and she'd been in Blueberry Hill all week? And working closely with his brother's future mother-in-law?

"Excuse me," he said. "I've got to go."

"Ash?" Sam called after him, but he was already weaving through the crowd in search of Daphne Potter's soap truck.

———

CAT HADN'T WANTED to be a part of the village's Halloween, but Daphne insisted. Now that she was in the thick of it, she couldn't recall why.

Each day she'd met Daphne on Old Quarry View Road for a few hours, but with her daughter's wedding coming up fast, the subject of Mercy Fraser, or Potter, or whoever she was, never came up again. Nor did her confusing visions or Daphne's unspoken concerns about them.

The daughter in question was a thorn in Cat's side. She had no idea what Marnie Burnham's problem was, but every time their path's might have crossed, Marnie simply narrowed her eyes and avoided the workshop in favor of her parents' house.

If looks could kill, Cat would've died a dozen times before Halloween.

What came up was meditation. Soap and lotion. Lip balm and cleaning products. Long hours alone over the steaming industrial stock pots. Suspiciously yoga-like meditation and mantra recitation to close her mind to unwanted input. Drying plants for ingredients with Samantha.

Cat learned that Max was semi-retired from the pro-shop, or whatever you called it, and that he was an excellent maker of sandwiches.

A whole lot of *not magic.* Very few answers.

She hadn't been willing to press the issue, or Daphne's hospitality, by insisting she get another look at the family Bible.

Between customers and trick-or-treaters, Cat adjusted the brim of her black witch's hat and the elastic holding on a fake nose with the hideous wart. Daphne had offered her the use of a huge trunk full of costume pieces–a surprising number of which were witch themed– and given her the run of the walk-in cedar closet in the main house's guest room to create her own magical costume.

For a woman approaching sixty, Daphne Potter's closet was brimming with sex appeal. The hat and nose were paired with a late-Sixties black mod minidress, a pair of orange and black striped tights, a vintage peacoat, and her own black buckled ankle boots. If it weren't for the warty nose, Cat figured she might just have pulled off Sexy Witch–clichéd though it was.

Daphne had gone a little more sinister with her magical outfit. She was wearing a Victorian-inspired mourning dress and shawl, and a Gibson Girl pompadour with her witch's hat perched atop. A hearth broom leaned against the back of the truck.

"Does this happen every year?" Cat was in love with the jack o'lanterns lining the sidewalks, the café lights strung between buildings, and the gazebo in the center of a common strewn with fake cobwebs, spiders, and bats.

"For as long as Marnie's been alive, at least," Daphne said. "When most folks' nearest neighbors are a half mile away, trick or treating is less fun."

"I wish every town did this. It's so...welcoming."

Of course, she said that, but she'd been hiding out from the town itself, keeping to the cabin she'd rented or Daphne's workshop.

"Trick or treat!" A chorus of small ghosts, ghouls, and super heroes approached the truck. Cat crouched down with a huge plastic cauldron of candy.

A shy little girl with long, nearly black braids pulled her hand out of the cauldron just in time. Before Cat could stand up, she was knocked to the ground by two massive paws. Held there by breath that could fell a lion and the threat of drool.

"Henry, no! Sit!"

That voice. It couldn't be.

It was, though. At the word *no*, the dog, and it was a dog, backed off and sat. Behind him, at the other end of a leash, was Ash. The whole gorgeous package, despite a funnel on his head. Her breath was trapped in her chest, crushing her heart, which bashed against her ribs in time with the swishing pulse in her ears.

Daphne popped out of the truck with an apple crate full of bar soaps and lip salve tins and stopped short at the scene, before blowing out a long breath and setting down her burden.

"I see Marnie decided to bring my grand-puppy to the party." Daphne turned her attention on the dog and fixed him with a stern expression. "Lie down, Henry. Paws to yourself."

The dog–puppy?–dropped from sitting to lying down without hesitation, crossing his paws and looking up at Daphne Potter, utterly captivated. In turn, Daphne snatched a homemade dog cookie from the bowl by the checkout window and tossed it. The puppy caught it in the air, swallowed it whole, and grinned, tail thumping.

Did dogs smile?

The entire exchange took about a minute, during which Ash barely moved. Cat hoisted herself up and faced him, heart still thrashing around in her chest, unsure of what to say.

Ash's lips compressed; Cat watched him banish all sense of recognition from his expression. "Sorry about this oaf. He belongs to my future sister-in-law."

Cat knew how it felt to wish the ground would swallow you whole. This was a thousand times worse.

Samantha's heightened intuition proved to be inconveniently accurate at exactly that moment. She stopped breathlessly, just behind Ash. "Hey, Ash, what–oh." Her head swiveled almost comically between Cat and Ash. "You two know each other."

Chapter Fourteen

Ash squeezed Henry's leash, letting the bite of nylon against his palm root him in the truth. Just Cat was right in front of him, dressed like a cartoon witch–right down to the lean lines of her legs encased in striped stockings that ought to have looked ridiculous. His imagination's memory of those legs hadn't done them justice.

He mustered every ounce of self control he had, looked Sam directly in the eyes and said, "We met on the plane last weekend. I didn't know if Cat would remember me."

Samantha's eyes narrowed, her gaze continued to volley between them for a beat before she offered the growing crowd a tight smile. "Of course. I'm just going to go..." She grabbed Will's hand–he'd come up quietly behind her–and glanced around the common for an escape route. "...go see if they need help at the donut-on-a-string station."

The donuts on a string appealed to more than a few witnesses to their terse exchange. Ash exhaled slowly as folks moved on to the next distraction. Folks, all save Daphne Potter, whose inquisitive gaze missed nothing.

"Daphne," Ash said. "Might I borrow your assistant for a moment?"

Cat's plea overlapped. "Ash, I–"

Daphne nodded, focusing on straightening the displays while Ash marched away from the soap truck, trusting–ironically, someone were to ask–that Cat would follow. Henry, attuned to the tension, trotted quietly along at the end of his leash.

He didn't stop until he'd cornered the Grange Hall. The outdoor seating was closed for the season, tables covered with tarps and waiting for winter. Ash looped Henry's leash around the abandoned bike racks.

When he turned around, Cat waited two tables away. Her tawny hair and expressive eyes were the same ones he'd last seen glazed over with desire that mirrored his own. Her body was strung tight; anxious energy rolled off her.

"Family reunion, hmm?" He clung to his anger, because his raw heart demanded armor.

"It's complicated. Oh…" She inhaled as understanding filled her expression. "Marnie's your amazing future sister-in-law."

"The one and only." He leaned his weight on one table. "And I've been hanging around Blueberry Hill for *seven* years." He leaned his weight on the word seven, one he knew she'd recall from their chat on the plane. "I know most of the families in this town. It's that small."

"I might be Marnie's cousin. Sort of. It's complicated." She blurted it out, and like an unseen latch released the coiled spring inside her, she flung her arms out and shouted. "I don't know, Ash. I didn't know on the plane, and I didn't know in the hotel when I woke up next to you. There are so many questions and not enough time for answers."

He had no idea what she was talking about, and it was getting increasingly more difficult to not reach for her. "Why did you leave without saying goodbye?"

He hadn't meant to ask it like that, to sound vulnerable. They barely knew one another. *What was it about this woman?*

The tears shining in her eyes spilled over. "I was scared. I mean, what would have happened? Awkward teeth brushing and soulless continental brunch in the lobby?"

Damn his traitorous imagination, he could see exactly that, and he *liked* it.

"And I'd never done anything like that before," Cat went on. "How was I to know we'd end up in the same small town?"

That's not the point...

Ash was saved from embarrassing himself and comforting her by Marnie, who came around the corner of the Grange Hall, Dorothy pigtails and gingham flying.

Marnie stopped short, unsure of what to make of them.

Henry pulled at his leash, trying to get to Marnie. Ash leaned over and loosened the leash from the bike rack.

"Henry, no," Marnie said as the huge puppy barreled toward her. Henry veered out of his direct trajectory and collapsed at her feet, tongue lolling. Ash suppressed a laugh at the doggy antics.

Marnie took up the leash, keeping her eyes on Ash. "Your brother is looking for you."

Ash saw the unspoken *scram* in her eyes; he looked over at Cat. If she was truly connected to the Potter-Burnhams, there would be no keeping Marnie out of this. "We're not done talking."

He couldn't help sneaking one last look at Cat as he walked away.

Chapter Fifteen

Cat and Marnie looked like amateur actors in a rehearsal: Dorothy and the Wicked Witch of the West facing off over the ruby slippers. Henry embraced his cowardly character, sitting behind Marnie's legs.

Cat steeled herself. This conversation had steeped too long; it was bound to be bitter, though Cat still didn't understand Marnie's vitriol.

Marnie planted her hands on her pinafored hips. "Who are you? Really."

"I'm sure you know already, but I'll indulge you. Exactly who I told your mother I was. Cat Brodey, from Stag Creek, North Carolina. My grandmother passed recently and left me family papers that suggest I'm descended from your..." Cat paused to tick off the generations on her hand. "...great-grandmother, Philomena. I came here looking for answers. Your mother has been kind."

Marnie's eyes narrowed. "There aren't any Brodeys in the book."

Cat knew Marnie meant the family Bible Daphne showed her. "I'm not sure yet, but I think your grandmother had a sister she didn't know. A secret."

"Bullshit," Marnie said softly. "This is worse than the damn magic. I suppose you think you're some kind of witch, too?"

"Your mother does," Cat said.

"My mother thinks she can make people fall in love using soap and tea." Marnie countered. "She's always been batty, but she's my mom, and I'm not letting some–"

"Whatever the insult is, save it." Cat clenched her jaw to hold back words she wouldn't be able to take back.

"No? Then what's the deal with you and Ash? Because getting with him isn't your ticket to Practical Magic on HGTV or some shit. He's a good man, not your basic cable meal-ticket."

"What are you talking about?" Cat's hands were shaking.

"You appear out of nowhere with some supposed connection to my family and your claws in Ash. He's been moping around the house for days."

Cat shook her head, even as her heart lurched. *Moping?* "No, what do you mean meal-ticket?"

"You expect me to believe you cozied up to Ash Reynolds for any other reason than every other little groupie? Follow the musician, get your picture on the tabloid sites, maybe be his arm candy for some red carpet and start working the connections until you get yourself a nice contract for some stupid reality show or a fitness video or whatever your *brand* is..."

Marnie's voice dripped with derision.

Follow the musician? The giggling girls in line at the airport... Ohmygod, isthatreallyhim? *The hot lights and melody she experienced when they'd touched the first few times...*

Henry lifted his head from where he'd laid down behind Marnie, as though he had things to add about Ash, but not the words to add them.

"I have no idea who he is," she told Marnie. "I've been nursing my dying grandmother, working crappy shifts, waiting tables, and trying to keep my head above water in a town that makes this one look like a metropolis. I don't have time for top-forty lists."

"You're good," Marnie said. "I'll give you that. The big eyes, the startled doe look? But you picked the wrong Potter for the whole earnest, witches-can't-lie-to-one-another thing. I think it's a whole lot of hogwash."

"Marnie, I–"

"No. We're done here. I don't want you hanging around my mother, I don't want you making nice to Sam or sniffing around Ash. I'm getting married next weekend, and I need you out of this town before I walk down the aisle, or I'll run you out myself." Marnie snapped her fingers, and Henry rose and stretched. "Come on, Henry."

The shaking in Cat's hands spread out over her body. For a moment, she could only stand in the shadow of the Grange Hall with her frantic thoughts tumbling over one another. *Ash was a well-known musician? Someone who walked red-carpets? She'd rented the cabin for a month, there was no way she was leaving. What did Marnie think she was?*

"Wait!" Cat lunged after Marnie, grabbing her arm. Marnie yanked herself free but not before Cat saw–as clear as the walls of the Grange Hall beside her–Daphne standing in front of the same building, her aura glowing strong and palest violet; Cat couldn't catch the words, but she felt the intent. The warning. She saw Marnie turn to her mother, and Sam, energy flickering around her like fireflies, staring at a woman Cat had never seen before. A woman whose aura pulsed sickly green, her eyes dark and shining with hatred.

Dark eyes Cat knew from that morning in Daphne's workshop.

Daphne's magic was real, and Marnie knows it–even if she doesn't believe.

"You'll have to run me out of town," Cat whispered to Marnie's retreating back.

———

ASH WATCHED Marnie and Henry round the Grange Hall a few moments later, Marnie's face stormy, but Cat didn't follow.

He felt a little lost without Henry. Marnie's ridiculous puppy had glued himself to Ash's side over the past few days. It was possible the dog was more his tether than the other way around. At the very least, holding the leash would give his loitering some purpose. Ash melted into the crowd as much as a tall man in a silver funnel hat could, and kept a lookout for Cat. He didn't really think Marnie was capable of violence...

He spotted the Scarecrow leading Dorothy and the Lion to the music playing on speakers near the bandstand. Harry and the Snitch were sharing the swing bench outside the diner. Sam's head rested on Will's shoulder. Max and Daphne snuck a kiss beside the soap truck.

So much for Halloween. In Blueberry Hill, folks were celebrating like it was Valentine's Day in October.

Ash pulled his miniature notebook out and jotted *Valentine's Day in October* down on a page with other such incomplete thoughts.

He was about ready to tell Marnie and his brother to bum a ride with some of their friends, when he saw Cat slip out of the shadows gathering around the Grange Hall. She'd ditched the witch's hat and ridiculous fake nose; in the mini-dress and striped tights, she looked overdressed, but not costumed.

Ash watched her stick to the sidewalks on the quiet side of the common until the soap truck was directly across the street from her. She crossed the street and paused to rap on the door of Daphne's pop-up trailer. He didn't make a conscious decision to follow her, but before he'd given it any thought he was weaving through the crowd.

As he drew closer to Daphne's camper, he caught the tail end of what Cat was saying.

"...are you sure? I'm sorry to–"

Daphne's voice was gentle when she replied. "Get some rest, hon. I'll see you tomorrow."

Cat appeared again, making a beeline for a car parked outside King's Diner. Ash jogged after her. "Cat, please wait."

She stopped without turning to acknowledge him.

"I'm sorry," he said. "Seeing you again–here–was a gut-punch, and I reacted badly."

She turned slowly, raising her head to meet his eyes. "Who exactly are you?"

Ash pushed his hands into the pockets of his brother's gray sweats. "Ash Reynolds, a guy with a guitar who until recently had enough of a following to keep a roof over his head and more records coming."

He saw when it clicked. Her lips parted, she tilted her head and narrowed her gaze. "Moira Kennedy. You did that pretty duet with Moira Kennedy. Everyone was sharing the video on social media, but I didn't really look at it. That was *you*?"

Ash liked it when she forgot to be angry at him, since he was finding it increasingly hard to be angry with her. Not with those eyes still looking at him like he was Ash, not like he was a marginally famous guy.

"The lights, the static..." This she murmured to herself before tilting her head the other way like a curious sparrow; Ash had no idea what she was talking about. "A stage, applause. And the melody...of course."

"You lost me," he said, trying to keep the moment light.

She blinked. "Oh, nothing. Just something about the video."

She was lying. He'd bet his favorite guitar.

"Listen, I really am sorry about that scene back there. I hope Marnie wasn't too hard on you. She can be...protective."

Cat's answering laugh was bitter. "That's a word."

He groaned. *What had Marnie said?* "I'm here with her and my brother tonight, but can we talk tomorrow? Just us."

"Just us." She pursed her lips, then smiled–just a little. "Just talking."

Ash nodded. He *wanted* to take her in his arms and hold her until he was sure she wouldn't run again. "Can I put my number in your phone? You can text me where to meet you."

She reached into the bodice of the minidress and drew out a slim flip phone. It was still warm from her skin when she handed it into his palm. Ash flipped it open and dialed his own number, then hit call. His pocked vibrated in response.

He'd never related more to a mobile phone.

Chapter Sixteen

When Cat arrived at Daphne's workshop the next morning, a Jeep was parked in front of the barn. She didn't have to wonder long at who was visiting. Marnie's voice rang out across the driveway.

"I told her to beat it."

"Marnie Helene." Daphne's voice took on an edge Cat hadn't yet experienced. It reminded her of Meemaw when her dander was up. "*I told her to come on out so we can take another look at her letters. If you'd calm down for five minutes, you might find this interesting.*"

"What's *interesting* is how she's using you and your–" Marnie waved her hands around. "*Woowoo* to worm her way into Ash's life."

Daphne took her daughter's face between her palms. "I love you more than anything or anyone in the world, but you're being a horrible brat. Go home. I'll meet you at the seamstress's shop in Thornton around two." She kissed Marnie's forehead, which required her to stand on her toes.

The look Marnie gave Cat was lethal, but she stalked across the driveway and peeled out, spinning gravel under the Jeep's wheels.

"My daughter has a strong will, and wedding stress sometimes brings out the worst in people," Daphne said mildly. "She also has her doubts about her legacy."

Cat was about to force herself to say something nice about Marnie when Daphne gasped and covered her mouth with both hands. "What?"

Daphne's eyes went huge. "Doubts!" She hurried into the barn. Cat was more than a few steps behind her, and Daphne was already unpacking the Bible when Cat caught up.

Once more, Cat watched as the pages of the old book responded to Daphne's touch. It was hard to describe. Like a cat, they arched against Daphne's fingers. If you weren't looking for it, you might miss it. Daphne was murmuring something under her breath as she paged through the end of the book.

"Aha!" Daphne dropped the pages, her smile luminous. "Look!"

Cat peered down at the cramped, spidery notes. A journal entry, from the looks of it, but with what could be spells or perhaps just elaborate mnemonics written in the margins. "What am I looking at?"

Daphne underlined a section with her finger. "This was written by my Great Grammy Sarah. I have fuzzy memories of her from when I was a girl. It says, *When Mercy's line is restored, a doubting daughter's eye will open. Sisters three unite to usher a new spirit safely home,* then *Pma 26.*"

A chill coasted down Cat's spine. *Mercy, a doubting daughter...*

"My grandmother Philomena was like Sam," Daphne said. "She had a way about her people flocked to, and a sense of them that others didn't. Occasionally, she'd go funny around the eyes and say things like this. Great Grammy Sarah recorded them all in the Book. The *Pma* is for Philomena. I must've asked my mother a hundred times what they all meant, but all she would say is, 'These things reveal themselves in their own time.'"

"If Mercy is Philomena's daughter she wasn't allowed to keep..." Cat's words faded as the realization sunk in.

Daphne drew her into an embrace. "You, sweetheart, are Mercy's line restored to Blueberry Hill. You've come home."

The hug certainly felt like home in a way Cat missed so much she ached for it, but she pulled away. "I'm not sure about the doubting daughter, Daphne. Her eyes seem wide open to me."

"No, that's just it," Daphne said. "Not *eyes*, eye. Her third eye. Her witch's eye."

"I don't follow," Cat said. She was wading in deep now, but it felt too right to turn back.

"Marnie's never practiced anything to do with magic. Her witch's eye is completely closed. Most of the time." Daphne harrumphed. "When it peeks open at all, she's magnificent."

"So, if Marnie doesn't believe in...magic...now, she will, because I've arrived?"

Daphne chuckled. "It's never that simple. But yes, that's what I think Philomena saw."

"What about the rest? Sisters three?"

Daphne started putting the Bible away. "No idea. Like my mother said..."

These things reveal themselves in their own time.

Cat decided to change the topic. "So, we have until sometime after one?"

Daphne tucked the Book and it's packaging into the archival box. "Yes, why?"

"I'm meeting someone later, and I need to text–"

"Tell that young man from me he had no business surprising you like that at the Halloween celebration."

"I didn't...I'm not..." Cat stammered. "He didn't."

"You're not meeting Ash?" Daphne asked, all innocence. "It certainly seemed like you two had things to talk about."

Cat could only sigh and press the key for Ash's number in her phone.

Once the text was sent, Cat gave her attention back to Daphne, who was measuring dried something into a mortar. "Can I ask you a question?"

"Sure, hon."

"What happened with Sam a few years ago?"

Daphne's hand stilled on the pestle. "I'm sorry, Cat. That's not my story to tell."

"I'll tell you what I saw. Maybe you can make sense of it where I can't."

Daphne turned and retrieved a baggie full of crushed dried leaves. Cat didn't need Samantha's intuition to see Daphne was rattled. "Portion these out by tablespoons while you talk."

"One of the first couple times I was here with you, I told you I saw a pair of eyes in the steam coming off your tea mug," Cat began. "Black tea?" When Daphne nodded, Cat continued. "Those eyes were human, but they scared the crap out of me. Then, on Halloween, when Marnie was angry with me, I touched her arm, and I saw the three of you–you, Marnie, and Samantha–outside the Grange Hall with a woman whose eyes were the same ones I saw in the steam. You made a spell of some kind, and auras were lit up like Christmas."

Daphne sighed heavily.

Cat pressed on. "I could feel how much Marnie hated that woman, and how much the woman hated Marnie, but everything led back to Samantha."

"That woman you saw, she's got a heart full of darkness and some powerful magic," Daphne said. "I think those eyes you saw had some-thing to do with her, too. I felt something I haven't felt since...I hesi-tate to name something I don't understand, but where Lilith is concerned, I know it's dangerous."

"Lilith?"

"Samantha's mother-in-law. *Ex mother-in-law*." Daphne frowned. "Sam suffered terribly at her hands and came here to recover. There was a confrontation with Lilith a few years ago that unlocked Sam's abilities, and Lilith vanished back to New Orleans. I'm worried about how you're connected to that."

Unease trickled down Cat's spine at the mention of New Orleans. Mona had mentioned that as her next stop. "I promise, Daphne. I'm not here to harm Samantha."

"I know that, Cat. As sure as I know you're one of us."

"Do we need to warn Sam?"

"I did, but after the wedding, Sam can tell you her story, and we'll get to the bottom of all the mysteries,"

Chapter Seventeen

Ash drove into Catmint Gap with a low hum of anticipation running under his skin. Cat's text was little more than a time and an address, but she'd texted at all, which felt like a victory.

He knew the location. A touristy, refurbished motor court just off the main drag east of what passed for the center of the town, on the way up to Singing Bowl. There were cars parked outside a couple of the one-room vacation cottages.

It was easy to find Thimbleweed; Cat herself sat on the front porch steps with a mug cradled in her hands. With the afternoon sunlight pouring through the pine forest beyond the motor court and the cheerful pots of mums and cabbages all around her, she would have looked at home in the brochure.

She stood when he climbed out of Micah's pickup.

He closed the truck's door and stood with his hand on the window for a moment, letting her decide to make the first overture.

"I like your music," she said. "I downloaded some earlier."

"Thanks." Ash released the truck and took a tentative step toward her. "I'm glad."

"Why didn't you tell me who you were?"

"The truth? Ever since the Grammy performance, all the attention has been on my face, or tabloid speculation that Moira and I are some kind of May-December hookup." He leaned a hip against the truck's front grill. "It had been a while since a beautiful woman talked to me without an agenda. I was selfish."

"That's fair," she said.

If they were asking blunt questions, it was his turn. "Really, why did you leave?"

"Take a walk with me?" Cat set the mug down on the porch. "There's a pretty foot path that runs from here to the ski area. I've been walking it every day."

The path was broad, its packed soil level enough to suggest regular maintenance. In the summer, it would be canopied by birch and ash leaves. Now, those leaves crunched underfoot as they set out. Cat put a safe distance between them. Ash stuffed his hands in his pockets.

The motor court disappeared behind them before Cat spoke.

"Do you believe Daphne's a witch?"

Not the question he'd been expecting. "Daphne believes it. That's enough for me."

"So you don't think she's crazy?"

"We're practically family." Ash smiled. "I know she's crazy, but not unstable, if that's what you're getting at."

"The first time you and I touched I saw...no, *experienced* being surrounded by hot, white light and a massive wall of static."

Ash stopped. She'd just described what it had been like the first time he'd taken the stage at a huge outdoor arena. The heat and the glare, the disconnected knowledge that the starry sky was out there somewhere. The wild applause like the static at the low end of the radio dial gone supernova.

"By the time we were in that hotel room together, I could touch you and only hear a faraway melody. Like someone was listening to the radio across the street from me. Daphne says my third eye has the Sight." Cat stopped when she realized Ash was no longer walking alongside her. She faced him from a few feet away. "My grandmother died three weeks ago."

"I'm so sorry." The words came out of Ash's mouth automatically, but they were true nonetheless. He thought of his own grandparents, one set still living two towns over from his parents in New Jersey, the other in a pet-friendly retirement condo in Fort Lauderdale.

"She was all the blood family I had left to turn to," Cat said. "Or so I thought until I got a letter she left with her lawyer."

They'd nearly reached the Singing Bowl base lodge. A small, seemingly man made pond surrounded by benches occupied the clearing beyond the path. Cat made her way toward the nearest bench.

Ash wasn't sure what, if anything, to say. She was talking to him, but he got the feeling she was talking to herself just as much. Cat sat on the bench and waited for him to catch up. He didn't want to crowd her, so he sat on the ground nearby.

"The letter led me here, put me on that plane from Raleigh. Sat me next to you. You were a happy accident. An adventure. I couldn't bear the idea that we might wake up and discover we didn't like each other."

"I don't go to bed with women I don't like," Ash said.

"And I don't go to bed with strangers," she countered. "We all do things that are out of character sometimes."

"Out of character doesn't mean wrong, Just Cat." Ash leaned toward her. "I wish you'd stayed. Even if you had dragon breath."

She laughed, briefly dispelling the somber light in her eyes. "Maybe *you* had dragon breath."

"I'd have brushed my teeth for another kiss." He was teasing, but there was an urgency building under the conversation that unnerved him. He took a deep breath. "Tell me more about the letter?"

Cat pulled her knees up, wrapping her arms around them. She gazed out over the pond. "There were things she told me in that letter that might explain why I see things like what happened with you and the lights. They go back to her mother, who was adopted. Her mother was very likely Daphne's great-aunt." She looked back at him; he saw her plea to believe written across her expression. "I came here to find out."

Ash rose and closed the distance between them. He crouched in front of her, bracing himself on the bench. "I'm glad you're here, even if I didn't do a very good job of conveying that last night. I do like you, Cat, and I'd like to get to know you better."

She didn't say anything, merely closed her eyes briefly.

"I'd like to take you on a date. A proper one. Dinner together somewhere with lighting that plays in your hair and a dessert menu that's almost as sweet as your mouth."

The corner of her lip twitched in an almost smile. "Does that line actually work?"

He refrained from touching her, afraid to scare her away. "You tell me."

She drew her lower lip under her front teeth. He shifted away to give her space.

"I'd like dinner," she said. "But I have to tell you, Marnie warned me off you."

Ash chuckled. Marnie would be Marnie. "I'll deal with her. Unless you want to?"

"Not really," Cat said ruefully. "I'm going to have to, though. She warned me off her mother, too."

"She'll come around," Ash said. He'd make sure she did.

The first call he made, once he left Cat, wasn't to Marnie. It was to Kylie.

"Can you get me a table at Tamarack in Catmint Gap, Vermont?"

"I can get you anything, especially if you tell me you're going to show up looking fine and let tourists take your picture. Who's the date?"

"None of your business. Make the reservation under Brodey."

"Whoa, whoa, whoa," Kylie said. "Like, One Night in Boston Brodey?"

Shit. He'd forgotten Kylie was tenacious to the point of terror. He hadn't geven her anything to go on, and she'd still dug up his dirt. Best to just let it go.

"Thanks." He deliberately didn't acknowledge her taunt. "You're the best."

"You bet your ass I am. See you in two weeks."

Chapter Eighteen

Samantha was already at Daphne's workshop when Cat arrived the next morning.

"I didn't know you'd still be here," Cat said, feeling badly for interrupting Samantha at what looked like their third-eye meditation.

"Please, don't worry," Sam said, awkwardly hefting herself to her knees. "Will and I are staying upstairs until after the wedding. I've been feeling a little off, kind of drained and sad, so I was trying to settle myself a little."

Cat remembered Daphne's request that they wait until after the wedding to discuss what she'd seen. She reached to help Samantha up, but instead of feeling Sam's slightly chapped skin, she felt the soft, plump hands of a child's take hers.

"Auntie Cat," a dark-haired toddler grinned up at her from under a mop of curls. Their gray eyes sparkled with mischief. From out of the mist behind the child, a pale, slim young woman in a serviceable calico dress, with long, honey-hued braids appeared and placed her hands on the child's shoulders. Cat knew somehow that this woman was the child she'd seen outside the library the day she'd met Daphne.

"Mercy," Cat whispered.

The young woman glanced over her shoulder and her eyes flashed a warning. She wrapped a protective arm around the child. Cat reached into the mist to see the threat, but all she felt was a steady, clacking rhythm, like high heels on tile, and a deep malevolence.

The vision faded as quickly as it had come on, and Cat blinked to find Samantha staring at her in concern. "Are you okay? You were wide open just then."

"Yeah." Cat wasn't sure what to say. *I think I just met your unborn child? And my great-grandmother.* Her heart was pounding. "Another vision. I need to be better about protecting myself, I guess."

Daphne's entrance gave Cat a moment to regroup. "Morning, Sweet Sam. Morning, Cat. Did I hear we need to do a little practicing?"

Daphne was carrying a tea tray, and Cat was grateful for her mothering nature, even as she missed Meemaw.

"Marnie's coming out after lunch to set up the ceremony site in the garden, so we'll focus on Cat's protections to start, and then I want to dig out my mother's photo albums and see what we can find. Maybe something will get us closer to Philomena's prophecy."

"Prophecy?" Sam said. "What's that about?"

Daphne clapped. "Oh, I forgot to tell you what Cat and I discovered!"

As Daphne launched into the prophecy and their theory about Marnie The Doubting Daughter–a title which made Samantha laugh–Cat let her thoughts drift into the memory of what she'd seen when she touched Samantha's hand, but like a dream, the harder she tried to save the details, the more elusive they became.

The three women meditated, Daphne leading them through her third eye mantras from the internet. Cat had to admit, focusing on that part of her that was different always left her feeling stronger and better centered. The vision of Mercy and Sam's unborn baby faded enough to let her concentrate on the tasks at hand.

Daphne led them through the house and up to the attic, where her mother's photo albums were carefully arranged on a bookshelf. Cat wasn't sure what she'd expected, but the tidy, mismatched midcentury vinyl albums wasn't it. Under cellophane gone brittle with age, were hundreds of photos of Daphne's childhood, interspersed with much older, more severe images of the Potter women before her.

Cat paused over a candid shot of a kind, stern matron in a tweed skirt suit and blouse. From her sepia washed world, she appeared to gaze serenely into forever. "Who's this?"

Daphne removed the photograph from the page and turned it over. "Philomena in 1969. She never did take to being photographed, but my father always took her picture, anyway."

"She looks like my Meemaw."

"I remember her," Sam said. "Philomena. Great Grandma Phil."

"That's right, hon," Daphne said. "She passed when you and Marnie were little, but you both knew her a little."

"She was Mercy's mother, right?" Cat asked, though she knew the answer. She'd memorized Meemaw's lineage the same morning she'd learned of it.

"Poor woman," Sam whispered, touching Philomena's heart in the photo. "To have her child stolen from her by her own father, and never know what happened to her daughter."

Cat laid her hand over Sam's. "Her great-granddaughter is here now."

Daphne didn't add her hand, but she pressed a palm to Sam and Cat's faces. "So she is."

Chapter Nineteen

Ash returned from his visit to Cat full of song ideas. Marnie and Micah were out for the evening, Henry along with them, so he'd retired to his room with the Gibson and Kylie's voice in his ear pushing him for a pop ballad.

Henry woke him in the morning, with wet paws and a cold nose, but Marnie was conspicuously absent from the house.

After a few errands using Marnie's car, Ash spent several hours on the couch with his guitar and the dog, but he hadn't lost sight of his promise to Cat. He'd make sure Marnie came around; he was planning on starting with borrowing her car again to take Cat out.

"I know, Hank," he said to the dog. "It's a tall order."

"Don't call my dog *Hank*," Marnie's voice commanded from the front hall.

"You leave a coupla' guys alone for a while, we're gonna make up silly names for each other."

Marnie appeared in the doorway to the den. "And what does Henry call you?"

"Boss." Ash patted the cushion next to him, and Henry hopped up, turned in a circle and plopped down next to Ash.

"Great," Marnie said.

"Where's everyone today?"

"Your sister and Lane and the kids drove up this morning. We went down to see the house they rented in Stockbridge."

"Avery's here? Nobody thought to mention that to me?"

"We were having dinner with the misters Bixby last night. Truman's officiating. You were off chasing that woman last night when we made plans."

"Don't, Marnie."

"Don't what? You asked."

Henry slunk off the couch, cowed by the brewing argument. Ash felt bad, but he needed to get this out in the open.

"I met Cat on a plane. It was an accident. She got relocated to the seat next to mine. We talked about books and the weather in Vermont and a whole lot of nothing about my being the *Troubadour Heart* of anywhere. Not a word about Moira or what other musicians I know or whether it's true that Taylor Swift wrote *Love Story* about an affair we had before anyone knew who were were, never mind that she's not even *twenty years old*, and for chrissakes Marnie–" He jumped up from the couch and set the Gibson on the coffee table. "I like her."

"Taylor Swift?" Marnie's mouth went a little crooked and Ash backed down.

"Cat, Marnie. I like Cat. A lot. And I'm going to spend some time with her while we're both here. I want to know if it's worth us trying to figure out spending time together when we're not both here. Whether you like it or not."

"Ugh. Fine." Marnie plunked down in an armchair of decidedly questionable provenance. "But don't come crying to me when you find out she's nothing all that special. I'm going to be busy consoling my mother."

"You really don't believe she could be your cousin? Why would she lie about that?"

"Why does anyone lie about anything?" Marnie pushed up from the chair, prowling restlessly. "Why *now*? Why the week of my damn wedding?"

"She didn't know, and I think she's trying to stay out of the way, but your mom does love a project."

"I'm going to give Mom and Dad to Daphne, if she's looking for a project." Micah came down the hall, and Henry promptly sat on his feet. "Off, you oaf."

Micah scratched Henry's ears.

"She's got my mystery magic cousin to keep her busy," Marnie grumbled. "Even Sam likes her."

"Ah," Micah said. "This is about Cat."

"I'm taking her to dinner tomorrow," Ash said. "Kylie got us a table at Tamarack."

"Whoa," Micah said. "Kylie's good."

"She is." Ash turned to his soon-to-be sister-in-law. "I took my sports jacket down to Thornton to get it cleaned. Now all I need is a car."

"Oh, no," Marnie said.

"Please, Marn?" Ash grabbed Marnie in a bear hug. "You'll be my favorite sister ever. I'll even say that to Avery's face."

"Fine. Take the car, but do not get up to any funny business in it."

Micah snickered when Ash let her go like she might be venomous.

"Did I say favorite sister?" Ash said, feeling a hot flush up the back of his neck.

Marnie snuggled into Micah's side. "You did, and I *will* make you say it to Avery's face. And you know what? Kylie can get *us* a table at Tamarack for after our honeymoon. Your treat."

Ash put the request in to Kylie right away. *Worth it.*

Chapter Twenty

Cat fussed with her outfit far longer than she was comfortable with. The mirror on the back of the cabin's bathroom door showed her a silly young woman who didn't have the sense to save her own skin. She hadn't brought date clothes with her from Stag Creek, but like a fairy godmother Daphne had produced a dress from the depths of her closet. The midnight blue silk sheath, with its single silver embroidered vine that twined from one hip, across her back, over one shoulder, and traced her curves down to the hem, somehow fit like it had been made for her.. Daphne offered shoes, too, but Cat needed to stand on her own feet, even symbolically, and so she wore her own red leather flats and Meemaw's charm bracelet dangled from her wrist.

She had no business dating someone on the verge of stardom. And he was. Her laptop wasn't top-of-the-line, but it was capable of a Google search. She'd had no business coming on to him at all, but this had to be her most colossal work of self-sabotage.

Too late. She heard tires on the crushed stone followed by heavy treads on the dainty front porch steps and a confident knock.

"Just a sec," she called. One last exasperated look at her reflection in the cheap glass and it was time to face the music.

Literally.

She grabbed her scarf–almost two yards of wholly impractical, finely-knit vintage softness that once belonged to Granny Fraser–and opened the door to the cool, silky darkness of a November night. To Ash under the warm gold glow of the porch light. *Good lord.* He was tall and well-built, his dark hair caught the light and turned fair at the ends, like a halo.

"Hi."

The look in his eyes belied any angelic comparisons. She already knew how good it could be between them; so, it seemed, did he.

"Hi." He cleared his throat. "You look incredible."

"Thank you." She let herself appreciate Ash. He wore dark-wash jeans that fit like a glove, a button down shirt that matched his deep blue eyes, and a gray wool sport coat. "We look a little like we tried to coordinate."

"Kismet," he said with a smile. "Shall we?"

Cat pulled the cabin door closed behind her and turned her key in the lock. "Let's."

Ash opened the passenger door of a well-loved Subaru wagon. "It's not exactly a chariot."

"What happened to the truck?" Cat recalled it from the day before.

"That's my brother's. He's using it to haul about a ton of hay bales out to the homestead for the wedding." He closed her door, walked around behind the car and got in. "This is Marnie's car."

Cat blinked. "She let you take me out in her car?"

"Let's just say, we had a heart-to-heart." Ash's low rumbling laugh filled the car. "I might have to tell my sister that I love Marnie more. And I promised to play a third song at the wedding."

Cat laughed. "If she hadn't threatened me, I think I'd like her."

"If she'd stop being hardheaded, she'd like you."

Ash pulled out, headed toward Catmint Gap, but instead of continuing through the village, he pulled into a driveway that ran alongside and around a large field.

The sign at the end of the driveway read, *Tamarack House.* On the other side of the field, a large, cedar-shingled, Mansard-roofed building waited adjacent to a huge red barn.

Ash led her from the car, around the main building to a garden hidden from the road by a rambling hedge of lilac and tall grasses. She imagined it would smell divine in May. Beyond it was a scene from a modern fairy-tale.

Crystal, silver, and candles adorned white linen clad tables. Roses in bud vases dotted the table-scapes. Cafe bulbs strung overhead, waving in a breeze Cat couldn't feel due to the outdoor heaters that stood like sentinels against the cool November night. A half dozen of maybe nine tables were occupied with diners who could have been film extras.

"What is this place?" Cat fought the urge to whisper. The place felt like a secret fairy grotto–or something out of Jareth's palace in *Labyrinth.*

A host materialized from behind a pair of lavish ferns. "Welcome to Tamarack House. Do you have a reservation?"

Ash nodded. "Brodey, party of two."

The host led them toward a table for two. "Right this way."

Cat took the arm Ash gallantly offered. "Brodey, hmm?"

Ash leaned down, his voice soft. "Saves me worrying about my name matching my face."

Cat squeezed his arm. "I'll defend you from the hordes."

Once again, without an invitation, familiarity settled in. Never in her life had Cat felt so easy with someone. Even with Meemaw, one of them had always been the caregiver. With Ash, it was as if they were equals, though on so many levels, they were nothing of the kind.

Feeding the illusion might be foolhardy, but it buoyed her.

A server arrived to collect their drink orders and explain the *prix fixe* menu. Cat marveled at the coincidence of another elderflower drink as she ordered the Elderflower Lemon Drop. When he left again, Cat toyed with her water glass.

"Why do you believe me? About the visions, and Daphne."

Ash reached across the table to touch her fingertips. "Besides you telling me?"

"Yes. Besides that." She sipped the water. "It all sounds insane, even to me. The day you came out to the cabin to talk, I was at Daphne's in the morning, and she showed me a prophecy made by her grandmother. It involved my Meemaw's mother, legacies and Marnie's third eye. If we're interpreting it correctly."

She had to give him credit, he didn't so much as flinch. The server arrived with their cocktails, giving her a moment to study him.

He stirred his Gibson with the three onions on their stainless pick. "And here I was thinking you liked me for more than my pretty face."

"It is a pretty face," Cat said, enjoying the hint of a blush that rose on Ash's cheeks. "But more, I don't understand why you aren't freaked out."

"By what?"Ash slipped one of the onions from the pick, then sipped his drink. "If you and Marnie are family, then you and Sam are family, and Sam is absolutely magic, by any definition. It's not a leap for me."

"I never had a best friend like Marnie and Sam are." Cat's voice turned wistful. "Like a sister, almost."

Ash traced along her fingers from knuckle to knuckle. "I have Avery, and I love her, but Sam is exactly how I always thought a sister should be."

Sisters three in spirit...

Cat flexed her hand under Ash's. "Do you know how Marnie and Sam are related?"

He turned his hand to hold hers across the table. The warmth of his skin spread out along hers, more effective than the heat lamps. "I think Sam's mother is Daphne's cousin. Camille is her name, but I haven't met her. Yet. She's coming up from Arizona or New Mexico with Sam's dad for Marnie's wedding."

"And neither Marnie nor Sam has any sisters?"

"Nope. Only children, both of them."

Cat closed her eyes, picturing the thin pages of Daphne's grimoire, where the family lines were recorded, and the extra column that recorded siblings.

"Where did you go just then?" Ash asked.

Cat's reply was delayed by the arrival of an *amuse bouche* from the kitchen. The grilled pattypan squash "on the half shell" had been hollowed out like a clam, and stuffed with shredded squash, a mild chèvre and chives, all sprinkled with toasted filberts. It was almost too pretty to eat.

Almost.

"Sorry." She smiled at her own distraction. "Magic can wait."

Ash watched her savor her food. "Doesn't look like it's waiting to me."

Cat stifled a laugh, hiding her smile behind her napkin. "Does *that* line work?"

Ash laughed, but there was heat behind the laughter, the kind that sent a tingle of awareness from her scalp to her toes. "Tell me later?"

They hadn't made plans for later, but that didn't stop Cat's imagination.

———

SHE'S THINKING ABOUT US. *Together.* It was sexy as hell, watching the idea catch and burn in her expression for a moment, before she remembered his earlier question.

"I was thinking about Daphne and Camille and my Meemaw. Three women in their generation, but they didn't know it. And before that, Mercy, then Ida and her sister Helene, but Mercy was lost to secrets."

"Is that significant?" Ash wasn't sure where she was going with this, but he found he really wanted to go along.

"Technically, even though she's a lot older, my mother and Marnie and Samantha are in the same generation, but my mom rejected everything about her family a long time ago."

Ash heard her unspoken words. *My mom rejected me.* Sorrow welled up in his chest, but Cat's voice lost its brief flatness when she reached her conclusion.

"I think I'm meant to take her place and complete the *sisters three in spirit*." Her smile took a wicked turn. "Marnie doesn't have to like me. She might be stuck with me."

Ash laughed. "I'm missing something, but I'm really enjoying this."

Again, any explanation she might have offered was interrupted by the arrival of their appetizers, medallions of seared swordfish topped with a spicy pesto-like sauce the server called *chermoula*.

"I want to hear about doing a duet with Moira Kennedy," Cat said. Ash noticed she pitched her voice low, and was grateful for it.

"My sister Avery was super into Mikki Vixen when she was in high school, so it was honestly a little surreal. My mom dug up old video of me lip-synching to *Mine, Baby* in my Ninja Turtles jammies."

Cat giggled. "Sounds like destiny to me."

"Moira's great. She's got this ultra-cool, rock queen vibe, but like, friendly. Zero tolerance for bullshit and not a lot of filter." He scraped the last of his swordfish with his fork. "I guess I'm a little bit of a fanboy."

"I get it," Cat said. "I could see how much fun the two of you were having in the YouTube footage."

He grinned. "It's not even my favorite duet with her, if I'm being honest."

Her lip and brow quirked up in concert. "Wait, there's more?"

"Actually," he said, pulling out his phone, "I can send you a link. This is from an after party hosted by her old bandmates, Fitz and Shandy. We did a cover of a song off her first album; I'm actually thinking about asking her if she'd do it with me and my band on our next album."

"When is that?" Cat asked the question idly, the same way she might ask when a library book was due.

"Soon," he said. "I'm supposed to be in Brooklyn as soon as Marnie and Micah get back from their honeymoon. Kylie, my manager, is already there getting things set up."

"We're on the same timeline." There was a note of sadness in her voice again, but different than her earlier reference to her absent mother.

"What do you mean?"

"That's when I need to be back in Stag Creek."

It should have been a splash of cold water, a reminder that they had no future, but her words had the opposite effect. Ash felt a greedy flicker of need rise up in his chest. *I want her again. Every day until I have to let her go.*

"Tell me more about it. Where you're from."

She concentrated on her food for a moment. "It's beautiful. In the woods, and the hills, like Blueberry Hill, but different. Softer, hazier. Wilder. Meemaw's place isn't much to look at, but it's tucked into the foothills, surrounded by the woods and a stream. I work in a diner that's a lot like King's."

"You're a waitress?" He blurted it out in surprise, regretting it instantly when her expression shuttered.

Cats eyes narrowed. "I nursed Meemaw through the last awful years of her illness. I took the only work I could get without having to leave town and be too far from her if she needed me, or not able to get away because the people didn't know her, or me."

Ash reached again for her hand. "I'm sorry. That was stupid, and not how I meant it."

She pulled her hand away, but not too far. "How did you mean it?"

"You surprised me. The way you talked about the book on the plane, the way you propositioned me that night," He couldn't help grinning at the memory. "I made up a whole backstory for you that didn't involve a diner.. And I completely forgot about your grandmother. I'm sorry if I hurt you just then."

She didn't move her hand any further away. Ash took that as the beginning of forgiveness.

"I went to art school."

"But things didn't go according to plan," he said. Plans be damned. Circumstance brought them together. He couldn't shake it, the rightness of being near her.

"When Donny is finished, at least I'll have the money from the cottage to start over."

Her mouth snapped shut, and Ash knew she hadn't meant to reveal so much.

"Who's Donny?" Ash took a page from her playbook and kept the question light.

Cat sighed. "No one. A guy I went to highschool with. Thinks he's god's gift to real estate sales. And me…He selling Meemaw's place for me, but he wants…more."

Their dinners arrived in a riot of colorful vegetables and rosemary and black peppercorn seared lamb sirloin tips.

"Is that what you want?" Ash was careful to occupy himself with carving a bite of lamb. He didn't want Cat to see the concern her words prompted. "More?"

"No," she said, pushing a roasted carrot through the soy-balsamic glaze.

Ash raised his eyes and saw that she wasn't sad. She was angry, though she was working hard to contain it. "I didn't want to sell, but I don't know how not to. The money's just not there, and I promised myself I'd see this thought for Meemaw."

"I'd like to help you figure it out," Ash said. "I have no idea how, but…"

Cat tilted her head like a curious bird. "You mean that."

"Of course I do. I like you, Just Cat."

"I guess it's been a while since a man liked me instead of just wanting to get into my pants."

There was an image. Ash cleared his throat. "I never said I didn't want to get into your pants. Trust me, that's an experience I'd love to repeat some time, if time and your preference allow."

Cat sipped her drink and blinked slowly, letting her lashes rest briefly on her cheeks. "I guess it's down to time, then?"

Ash wondered if it would be wrong to drop his credit card on the table, scoop her up, and make a run straight for her miniature cottage.

Chapter Twenty-One

Never in her life had Cat wanted to rush through dessert, but she'd tossed a gauntlet she knew Ash would pick up. She'd failed at forgetting the way their bodies fit together for a week; now she let herself remember, much to the detriment of the lemon-thyme shortcakes, lemon curd, and saffron chantilly cream.

She'd ponder the decadent meal–like no other she'd eaten–another time.

Ash settled the check while they talked about his affection for Blueberry Hill. She had to admit, his description of busking in the local pub the first few times he'd come to stay with his brother made her laugh. She hadn't experienced the town the way Ash had. Yet.

Another thing to consider once she'd had her fill of Ash himself.

They drove back to her motor court cottage under a dark sky gone dramatic with low-floating clouds and a crescent moon that danced in and out of view. Their fingers twined over the console while Ash maneuvered the mountain roads, and conversation seemed trivial.

Ash parked Marnie's Subaru next to her rental car and walked around to open her door for her. He stepped back to let her out of the car, and gave her space to gather her bag and close the door.

They stood beneath the patchy moonlight while she fished her key from her bag. The bedside lamp she'd left on glowed a warm welcome within.

"Ash, I–"

"Cat–"

Their colliding uncertainty made them laugh.

Cat reached for Ash's hand. "Come inside."

Ash's fingers closed warm around hers, and she led him inside, aware that the music of his touch was no more than a whisper of comfort around her.

She turned the lock behind him and set her purse on the cafe table under the front window. She unwound the scarf from her shoulders and a shiver coasted down her arms at the cool air as she laid it over the back of the room's small sofa. The cottage's efficiency kitchen had been cleaned during the day, leaving only a box of Frosted Mini Wheats and a bag of Green Mountain Coffee as the only evidence she'd used it at all.

"Do you need anything?" she asked, "Water? Or…"

"I'm good. Thanks." Ash filled the small space, tall and broad, dark hair running over his fingers as he pushed them through it. "What are you thinking about?"

"How the only evidence of my existence is a box of cereal and a bag of ground coffee."

How did a man his size move with that swift, silent grace? He held her upper arms gently, leaning in to press his nose behind her ear. "Not the only evidence. This whole room smells like you. It's perfect."

His mouth replaced his nose, she braced her hands on his shoulders, kneading the muscles there. He dropped her arms, hands splayed on her back and drew her close. She tipped her head back to see his face and their lips met.

It was a slow-burning kiss, unhurried and dreamy. His fingers threaded through her hair to cradle her head while the other hand strummed a languid rhythm along her spine. She explored the column of his throat and the pulse that beat where the top button of his dress shirt was undone. They swayed and turned together, though no music played except the ghost of a melody only she could hear.

She ran her palms over his jacket lapels, smoothing them over his chest and underneath the soft wool and satiny lining. He threw heat like a furnace, and for a moment she burrowed against his chest just to feel the spicy, woodsy warmth of him against her cheek.

"You're cold." His voice rumbled in his chest.

Cat pushed the jacket over his shoulders and down his arms, catching it and tossing it over the back of the couch with her wrap. "You're not. And there are blankets on the bed." She turned in his arms and offered him her back, and the zipper which ran from her neck to the small of her back. "Help a lady with her zipper."

"Dear god, yes." His fingers drew the zipper down, while his mouth cruised over her neck and bared shoulders.

She led him to bed in her underthings, flats, and Meemaw's bracelet, which jingled playfully. *Pretty sure he's worth at least a five gallon pickle barrel.* Meemaw's cackling laugh echoed in her ears, and Cat laughed.

She turned, and Ash was unbuttoning his shirt.

"What's so funny?"

Hearing her grandmother's voice cheering her on just before she got naked with a guy didn't strike her as something Ash should hear in the moment. "I'll tell you later." She pushed her shoes off and climbed onto the bed. Kneeling, she tugged Ash close by his belt loops.

"I can live with that." He shucked his shirt and kissed her again. She undid his belt and fly and dipped a hand past the elastic at the waist of his boxer briefs to cup his ass. "That too."

He slid a knee between her thighs and the mattress bowed beneath them. He flicked open the clasp of her bra and her nipples chafed against his chest hair as it fell away. He caught her gasped *oh* with his mouth and they sank into the bedclothes together.

They were so good together, so easy together. Cat stretched her body against Ash as they moved together, letting her touch stray to the divot at his hip, the sinews behind his knees, the knobs of his spine. They took their time removing the last of their clothes, drawing out the pleasure with sampling kisses and questing touches until Cat once again sought the soft curve of his butt beneath his underwear, this time taking the fabric with her. Ash finished peeling it away, then traced a slow path from her collarbone to her navel, pausing to hook a finger under the lace waistband of her panties.

"May I?"

"Mmm, yes," Cat murmured, raising her hips to his touch as he stripped her, entranced by the way he was looking at her, hot and wanting.

Naked and aching with desire, she reached for him. He rolled his body under her so she straddled him, held her there with his wide palms over the swell of her hips.

"What are you thinking?" Cat echoed his earlier question.

"Just you, Just Cat." Bracing himself on one hand, he leaned up to kiss her, sliding the other hand between their bodies to where she was already wet and needy.

She rocked against his hand until the first orgasm came. Opening her eyes, she met his hazy gaze. Shifting, she took him in her hand, stroking slowly. "Ash?"

"Jacket pocket. Inside." He was breathless, sweat beading on his brow as she traced the length of him, stroked, traced...She climbed over him and off the bed to hunt in his suit jacket pocket for the condom.

When she found not one, but two, she grinned. "An optimist, are we?"

"Like I said before," he said.

"You were a Boy Scout, but only until you discovered girls." She let her breasts brush against his chest as she stretched along him to kiss his jaw.

She tossed the spare on the nightstand and got to work, but Ash took over. "I won't last if you keep touching me."

"Oh?" Cat swung her leg over his body, rising up over him, hands planted on either side of his waist.

When he could only nod, she lowered her body, taking him in.

He groaned when she rocked over him. "Just you, Cat."

———

ASH WOKE to the strawberry scent of Cat's shampoo, but this time his arm rested in the valley of her waist and her rather lovely backside was nestled against evidence that he was more than inclined to find a third condom anywhere he could.

He nuzzled behind her ear. "Morning, Just Cat."

"Mmm." Cat stirred in his arms. "I've never liked the sound of that before."

Her words were adorably muffled by the pillow, but Ash liked the sound of them. He shifted away from her, leaving the warm cocoon of her queen-size bed, pulled on his suit pants and let himself outside to go to Marnie's car, where he'd left his ever-present notebook. It wasn't much past dawn, which didn't mean much in terms of being early, not this late in the year, and the still slumbering sun painted the gaps in the trees in glowing gold and violet light.

Kylie may just get her ballad. He grabbed a pen from Marnie's console and jotted Cat's words and a few notes about the sunrise.

When he got back inside, Cat was sitting up in the middle of the bed, the sheet pulled up over her breasts and pooling in her lap.

Ash unbuttoned his pants and shook them off one leg at a time on the way back to her. "I have to get the car back to Blueberry Hill." He crawled across the mattress, wrapping his arms around Cat and lowering them back down into the covers. "But I think I can spare five more minutes."

Cat laughed. "And what are we going to do with those five minutes?"

Ash flashed her a naughty grin, and kissed a path between her nipples and down her belly. "Let's just say, it won't matter if I have dragon breath."

He continued kissing his way south until her giggles went breathy, then dissolved into the low, incoherent sounds he was fondest of.

He left her flushed and sated, and cleaned up enough to drive the car back before Marnie had the locks changed.

Cat was wearing an oversized Carolina Panthers tee shirt and making coffee when he came out of her bathroom.

"What are you up to today?"

Cat pushed the brew button. "Daphne's busy with wedding stuff, and Sam and Will are spending a hooky day with their niece and nephew, so I'm on my own. I thought I might drive over to the cemetery. It feels like what Meemaw would want."

"Do you want company? I'm free until tonight. My sister Avery and her family are taking us to dinner. She found this farm-to-table place that seats family style by the open kitchen." He drifted closer to Cat, twisting the ends of her hair between his fingers. "I'd rather get a pizza and spend the evening holed up here."

Cat's coffee maker burbled on the counter in concert with her laugh. "Didn't you tell me Avery had kids? They must be looking forward to Uncle Ash."

Avery and Lane's two boys *would* be looking forward to Uncle Ash. "They probably are. I'm only famous in their house for my ability to rhyme with 'fart' while strumming in major keys."

Cat's shoulders shook. "I can only imagine."

Ash dropped a kiss on her cheek, letting his lips linger. "No, you really can't."

"I could pick you up at Marnie and Micah's house in an hour if you still want to come with me." She sounded almost shy about asking.

"That sounds perfect." Ash grabbed the motor court notepad and pan from the kitchenette counter and wrote down the address.

Chapter Twenty-Two

Cat decided, as she pulled into Marnie and Micah's driveway, that Marnie might not allow herself to believe in the family magic, but she sure as hell was able to wield it in her own backyard. The farmhouse she and Micah rented was set back from the road just enough to be private without being isolated. A tangle of rhododendrons worthy of an enchanted castle protected the gently sloping front yard's privacy.

The house itself was modest. White clapboards, a small covered front porch. A one car garage.

One side of the yard boasted apple trees. Cat could see the last of the harvest, quietly spoiling at the top of the mostly bare limbs. The mountain forest crept right up to peer into the back windows of the house. It reminded Cat of Meemaw's place in that regard.

She got out of the car to go fetch Ash, but he opened the front door, and instead of warm, solid man, she got an armful of warm, solid dog.

Henry licked her face before she had a chance to say *down* in her sternest voice.

The big puppy dropped down instantly.

"Sit," Cat said.

Henry's butt plopped into the grass; his tongue lolled magnif-icently.

She wasn't much of a dog person, but Henry might just win her over. She scratched behind his ears, earning a contented noise some-where between a groan and burp from the dog, who promptly collapsed, rolled over and showed her his belly.

"Some guard dog," Ash said.

Cat leaned down to rub the hollow beneath Henry's deep chest. "He stopped me from getting to the house, didn't he?"

"Good boy, Hank." Ash clipped a leash to Henry's collar while the dog was still squirming in the grass. "Let me take this clown back inside before we go."

The Blueberry Hill Burial Ground wasn't far from the center of the village. It occupied a grassy knoll above a bend in one of the rivers. Cat couldn't be sure if it was the Catmint, Gooseneck Creek, or some other local waterway. More than a century's occupation gave the place a peaceful gravitas Cat found soothing.

"Do you know where you're looking?" Ash climbed out of Cat's car and looked around.

"I don't, but it's not that big..." It was haphazard in the way of country graveyards, not tidy and gleaming with marble, or dramatic with statuary and Spanish moss like the ones in Savannah.

Instinct–or something else–drew her eye to the far corner of the cemetery, where a massive maple tree shaded a dip in the landscape that overlooked a spot where the river got excited and tumbled over a miniature spillway.

"Let's start out there and work our way back."

"Desrosier, Hill, Ellis, Dryer and Blake," Ash said, weaving between the stones. "I know these families."

"Dryer is Will's family, right?"

"Yeah," Ash said, pushing his hands into his pockets, "but no Potters."

Cat hadn't lingered over the names Ash read from the stones; she reached the shady corner and called back. "They're all here."

And so they were. Three hundred years of Potter women and

their men under stones ranging from slim, barely legible curved markers to more modern stones. The newest of which was only a few years old, and read *Ida Cleo Potter, 1932-2007, "Those who don't believe in magic will never find it." Roald Dahl.*

"That's Marnie's Grandma Potter," Ash said. "She died two years ago."

"She wasn't too old," Cat said softly, suddenly wishing she had some of Meemaw's ashes to leave behind here with the mothers and sisters she'd never known.

At first, she thought it was Ash who lifted her hair from her shoulders, but he'd moved deeper into the Potter family plot. A breeze swirled around her hair, but Cat saw no evidence of the grass or leaves around her blowing. She looked up and the woman from her vision of Sam's child stood with Ida's headstone between them.

"Mercy," Cat whispered. The ghost–*vision?*– wore a fierce expression beneath a brow as familiar to her as her own. Her dress was a simple one, belted at the waist with short, slightly gathered sleeves. Her hair was shoulder length and worn in loose rolled curls. Cat managed the math, despite her heart slamming in her ears. Mercy had died in childbirth in 1941, delivering her Meemaw. At all of sixteen.

"Cat?"

She heard Ash's voice, but she didn't dare look away from her great-grandmother.

The breeze lifted her hair again, and this time Cat was almost sure she heard, "Keep them safe so I can rest."

"Cat."

Ash was there beside her, concern evident in his eyes. Cat blinked and Mercy was gone.

"What just happened?"

"I saw her. Again. Mercy, my great-grandmother."

Ash stepped in front of her. "Again?"

Cat edged back from Ida's grave. The stone bench at the edge of the clearing was a far better place to have this conversation. Ash followed.

"I've seen her twice before," Cat said. "The first time, I didn't realize it. I told you when I touch people, sometimes I see things. This time, it was touching the library in the village. I think I saw my great-grandmother being taken away by her adoptive parents. I saw an older couple, the people I grew up calling ancestors, and a child. That's how we ended up in North Carolina. Mercy's grandfather gave her away because she was born out of wedlock."

"Jesus, that's grim." He took a deep breath. "And you saw her just now?"

"Yeah. The second time was," Cat hesitated. *Would he tell Marnie about this? Would he tell Samantha?* Cat knew they were close.

"Was what?"

Cat laid a hand on Ash's knee. "Promise me you'll let me tell Samantha in my own time?"

His eyes narrowed–just a touch–but he promised.

"The second time was in Daphne's workshop a couple days ago. I was helping Sam get up off the floor after meditating..."

Ash chuckled. "She's so pregnant. It's awesome."

"And I saw...I saw her child. And then Mercy appeared behind the child, like she was protecting them from something."

"You. Saw. Sam's. Kid? Her unborn child?"

Cat's stomach dropped. This was the moment she was going to lose him. It sounded flat-out bonkers. She nodded.

"That's awesome," Ash said, grinning wide. "Boy, girl? What are they like?"

"I don't know, I couldn't tell. Curly hair, pretty eyes, I saw a toddler."

Ash's smile faded. "You said Mercy was protective? Is Sam in trouble?"

"I don't know. I wish I did." Cat buried her face in her hands for a moment to regroup. "I didn't know what to say in the moment, then Daphne was there, and she wanted to do guided mediation. We ended up in her attic looking at old photos trying to figure out what the prophecy might mean."

"Whoa. Whoa. *Prophecy?*" Ash's eyes were huge.

"The thing I didn't explain at dinner. *Sisters three...* Daphne says her grandmother–Mercy's biological mother, Philomena–made prophecies. Philomena's mother, Sarah, wrote them down. Daphne thinks one of them is about me and Mercy." Cat took a deep breath and plunged into the choice to trust Ash, hoping the water wasn't as icy as it looked. "Just now, I saw Mercy at around the age she was when she died giving birth to my Meemaw. I heard words. *Keep them safe so I can rest.* I think it's about Sam and her baby, too, and I'm worried."

———

ASH RODE BACK TO TOWN, head swimming with questions. What Cat was describing was a lot more than Sam's extra-perceptive nature, or Daphne's bottles of *love potion #9* body oil. This was ghosts and warnings and *seeing visions of someone's unborn child.*

Cat chewed her lip as she drove. She was well and truly freaked out, but Ash got the feeling it was less about seeing the apparition of the great-grandmother she never knew, and more worry over Samantha. When they reached Marnie and Micah's house, he leaned across the front seat to kiss her.

"Are you going to be okay?"

She squeezed the steering wheel. "I think so. I need to talk to Daphne. And Samantha."

"Can I help?"

"Do you have Samantha's number? I'm sure she's up to her chin in maid-of-honor stuff, but maybe she'd see me for a few minutes."

Ash pulled up her contact info in his phone and let Cat type the number into hers.

"Thanks." Cat looked at her lap for a moment. "For the number. For not running screaming for the hills when I saw an actual ghost."

"I won't say it didn't give me some serious goosebumps, but what a cool thing to be able to do." Ash rubbed his arms. "Imagine the stories you could tell with a gift like that."

"Aren't you the storyteller here, Mr. *Troubadour Heart*?"

Ash groaned. "I hate the internet. And Rolling Stone."

"I think it's beautiful. The idea of you traveling around, telling stories with your songs."

Ash touched her cheek. "That's how I see you. Beautiful. Freeing all these stories from the shadows."

Cat leaned into his touch. "It doesn't seem creepy to you?"

Ash stretched over the console and kissed her. Cat melted into the kiss. Her soft sigh flowed through his veins like warm honey. When their lips parted, they stayed close, noses tip to tip.

"Like I said, I've been around Sam and Daphne long enough to keep an open mind."

"But not Marnie," Cat said softly.

"Actually, yeah Marnie. Her denial is a little bit *the lady doth protest too much* sometimes."

Cat laughed, but it was a weak echo of humor, and Ash knew it.

"Call me later?" Ash said. "If you wanted, I could borrow my brother's truck and come out after dinner."

"Ash," Cat said. "Go enjoy your family. I'll be okay. Promise."

He watched her drive away, Henry at his side on the porch, and wasn't so sure about that. There wasn't time to dwell on it, though, since Kylie's name lit up his phone.

"How's the fling?" Wherever Kylie was, there was shouting, honking, and laughter in the background.

"Could you be more crass?"

"You know I could."

"Where are you?"

"Food truck. Gyros. There's a fucking *spit of meat* in this truck. It's awesome. How's the song coming?"

Ash let Henry into the house and headed for his room, and the Gibson. "Two days ago, I'd have said so-so, but I've got some ideas I'm going to record for you this afternoon."

"That's seriously hot."

"You're a weirdo."

"I'm a weirdo who's getting you *paiiiiiiiid*. Gotta go, spit-roasted meat time for me."

Ash, as promised, picked up the guitar to get his thoughts together. He pressed the spine of his notebook flat on the desk and read back.

> Just Cat, strawberry hair, dawn smile,
> you knew my heart before you knew my name...
> A pretty interlude in a night of solitude and snow
> Thought I'd find solace in my mountain home
> Your sad eyes, your breathless sighs,
> They follow me as I roam...
> I've never liked the sound of that before

It wasn't much, but he'd started with less.

Cat's phone started ringing while she was showering the next morning, and it didn't quit until she answered it, dripping all over the floor by the bed. The name on the display put a hitch in her pulse.

"Kelley? What's wrong?"

"Honey, we got a right shit storm brewing down here."

"Hang on." Cat wrung out her wet hair and wrapped the towel tighter around herself. No sense dripping into the already cheap electronics of her aging flip phone. "What happened?"

"Mona's back in town, sweetie. Making noises about how the will's invalid on account of her being Ada's next of kin. How you don't have the right to sell."

The room closed in around her; she could feel her pulse in her thumbs. Maybe that's what Shakespeare meant about the pricking of thumbs. Her mother was something wicked, anyway. "What?"

"She turned up a couple of days ago." Kelley huffed. "Played the wailing, grieving daughter around town. I hoped she'd just pack up and move on, but–"

"But what?"

"She's been cozying up to Don Daniels a bit, talking a little too loud about how her baby girl's selling her birthright out from under her. A lot of *oh, Ma always said I should have that wild ol' place* kinda shit. She paid the back taxes in cash, but I told Don to keep moving ahead with the closing unless a judge says otherwise." Kelley paused for a breath. "God only knows where she got that kind of money. I don't want to, but Mona always could cling like a burr if there was gain to be had."

Cat groaned. "Lord only knows what she promised Donny if it were hers."

"That's about the long and short of it," Kelley said. "It would help to have you here, to remind folks that Mona has never been the victim."

"I'll leave today. I can be home by..." Cat glanced at the clock and counted on her fingers. She winced at the expense of putting gas in the Toyota, but figuring out the logistics of flying would eat up precious time. "If I leave now, get lucky with traffic around New York and Washington, and don't stop too many times, maybe a little after midnight? Before, if I'm *really* lucky."

"Why don't you come out to my place when you get here? Mona's holed up at Ada's house. I don't want you dealing with that."

"Thanks, Kelley."

"Don't thank me yet, Cat."

Cat set the phone down on the nightstand and took a minute to gather her spinning thoughts before indulging in one deep, growling scream. She slammed her fist into the mattress and forced back her tears.

Her mother hadn't sent so much as a postcard since she married the nomadic biker-slash-mechanic who'd drifted into town that year. They'd walked into town hall together, said *I do*, and hit the open road on a honeymoon that lasted five years. When Ray split, Mona drifted, showing up on Meemaw's doorstep with chaos in her wake. She never stayed more than a week or two before blowing out the door again on an ill wind.

Meemaw's love and a harried, but kind school counselor had gotten Cat through the worst of it, but she had to acknowledge, even now, that the wound left by Mona's abandonment healed crooked, leaving a raw, puckered scar on her heart.

She pulled on the jeans and sweater she'd laid out before her shower and swept the rest of her things into her suitcase. Her finger was on the call button to check out with the motor court's owner, but she stopped.

Ash. She couldn't just disappear–not twice–but she didn't want to drag him any further into her personal drama. There was Daphne to think about. And Sam and the baby.

Cat wasn't her mother; she wasn't going to abandon them now. She'd hold on to the reservation as a promise to herself, and to them.

Chapter Twenty-Four

The day before his brother's wedding, Ash woke up with the full-blown song in his head, and no time to practice. He settled for scratching down the complete lyrics in his notebook along with some chords before putting that away. He had a bachelor day to plan and a rehearsal dinner to help out with.

His first stop, however, was to snag the bride for a quick conversation before she left to spend the day getting pampered with her mom and Sam.

"Don't know why you're going to the spa. You're gorgeous already," Ash said, offering her a cup of coffee with so much milk and sugar in it, it was barely recognizable.

"You're a really bad suck-up," Marnie said, downing half the mug in one go. "What do you want?"

"I know it's a lot, Marn, but–"

Marnie's shoulders slumped even as she cut him off. She rolled her eyes. "Ugh. Fine. But I don't have to be nice to her."

"How did you know?" *And are you sure you don't believe in the family magic?*

"First you give me the 'I like her a lot,' speech, then you stay there the night before last, and you've been upstairs writing a song since yesterday." Marnie slugged down the rest of her coffee. "Wild guess, you want to bring her to the wedding."

Ash leaned down and kissed her forehead. "Thanks, Sis."

"God, you're as much of a bonehead as your brother," Marnie said, hugging him hard around the waist. "But I love you."

Ash hugged her back. "Love you, too."

Marnie let him go and grabbed her bag. "See you tomorrow. I'll be the one in white."

He had about an hour before he and Micah planned to leave for their hike with Will. He called Cat, but the signal wasn't great, and she didn't pick up anyway.

Ash looked at Henry, who was nosing around in his empty food dish. "Wanna take a ride in the truck? Let's go see Just Cat. Invite her to the wedding like the gentlemen we are."

Henry loved the words *truck* and *ride*. He had his leash in his mouth and was waiting by the door before Ash was done brushing his teeth.

With the big puppy by his side and Cat's song in his head, Ash drove out to the motor court singing through his lyrics. Maybe he could add it to the set he'd planned to surprise Micah and Marnie with at the reception.

His phone jangled once during the drive to let him know he had a voicemail. Probably Kylie with more nudging to behave like a real rock star.

He hoped she'd forgive him, driving out to ask a pretty girl on a date in a truck with a faithful dog by your side was definitely a little more country than rock 'n roll.

When he pulled up in front of the Thimbleweed cottage, he was met by a cleaning crew of two leaving.

He waved toward Cat's cabin. "Is she out? The woman who's staying here?"

The older woman smoothed back her ponytail. "She didn't check out, but her stuff's all gone."

"And you didn't talk to her at all?"

Ponytail woman's eyes narrowed. "None of my business. Is it?"

"No, you're right. Sorry," he backed off. "I'm just a friend, making sure she's all right."

"Heard that one a time or two," the younger woman said.

"I'll leave her a message with the owner. Thanks." Ash headed for the office door, feeling two pairs of eyes on his back the whole way.

He left the promised note with the owner, who wasn't saying what he might or might not know, and Ash climbed back into the truck's cab, where Henry waited, tongue lolling out the open window. The two women were still outside, this time watching him more speculatively. He wondered if they recognized him.

"Good lookin' dog you got there," the younger cleaning woman said before she followed the ponytail into another of the cabins.

"Thanks," Ash muttered, turning the key in the ignition.

He was about to pull out when he remembered the voicemail. Cat's number popped up on his screen and he released a breath he hadn't been aware he was holding.

"I'm sorry to leave this on your voicemail, but something came up at home. I have to go back to Stag Creek for a few days. I'll be back after the wedding. I promise. I'll see you again before you go to Brooklyn."

Disappointment sank like a stone in his gut, worry sprouted there. *What kind of something pulled her away?* He knew she didn't text a ton, but he had to at least let her know he was thinking about her.

Hope you're okay. Call if you can

Ash tossed his phone into a cup holder and put the truck in gear. "Well, Hank. Looks like I'm flying solo for this wedding after all."

Chapter Twenty-Five

Cat drove through Stag Creek's one traffic light just after eleven that night. She'd stopped three times: once north of Albany, for coffee and sugar in the form of doughnuts, just south of Philadelphia for food and a bathroom, and one last time somewhere in Virginia for a soda and another bathroom trip. Her butt was numb and her hands were stiff and sore from clenching the wheel.

Ash's lone text, checked in the parking lot of the Stewart's in Clifton Park Center, was her lodestar, pointing her back north to where he was, but Kelley was right. She needed to confront her mother on her own terms.

The smart thing to do would be taking a left and heading out to Kelley's farm. A warm bed waited there, and Kelley would see she was at least fed before facing her long-estranged mother.

Cat didn't feel smart. She felt reckless. Angry beyond words, exhausted and wound up to the point of collapse was more like it.

She pushed the accelerator down and took the mountain road as fast as she dared, wondering if Mona would see her coming.

An unfamiliar car with Louisiana tags was parked off to the side, as though it were making way for her. Cat cut the engine, plunging the dooryard into darkness. The house was quiet. If her mother was there, she was asleep.

Cat used her key to open the front door, stopping in her tracks. The house was empty except for Meemaw's sturdy-but-dated furniture and a few of the window treatments. The photographs, the knick knacks, the refrigerator magnets, all gone.

Kelley said she'd stage the place, but Cat never imagined how empty it would feel without Meemaw's trinkets.

The house was sparkling clean, save for a box of cheap Cabernet on the counter and an amber drinking glass next to the sink with a red ring around the bottom on the inside.

"Momma, you in here?"

Cat laid a tentative hand on the glass, but it was only a glass, not a conduit for visions.

Of all the times for this curse to fail me.

"Momma!"

Meemaw's bedroom door opened and her mother shuffled into the open doorway, tightening the belt on a cheap silk-knockoff robe.

"Kitty Cat?"

"Just *Cat*, Momma. You oughta know. You gave me the name."

Just you, Cat. Ash was so far away, but the memory of his voice, broken with desire while they moved together, bolstered her.

Her mother finger-combed her hair and pasted on a welcoming smile. "I found some of Ma's tea. I'll put on water."

Cat blocked her path to the kitchen. "How did you even get into the house?"

Her mother's expression went from welcoming to calculating in a heartbeat. "Ada never changed the locks in all those years. And the key's still under the old birdbath out back."

Cat struggled with the quiver of rage creeping into her voice. "This house isn't yours to just let yourself into."

"Well, now, I don't know about that, Kitty Cat. Your boyfriend thinks I might have a claim," Mona's nose wrinkled as she glanced around the room.

"I don't have a boyfriend, Momma," Cat said. "Whatever Donny said. And that's beside the point. I'm selling. If you cared so much about your birthright, maybe you should've stayed around to look after it."

"That's what that old Hart dyke said, too."

"I swear, if I hear you talk like that about Kelley again, I'll put you out of this house now, middle of the night or not. She's more family to me than you ever were."

"You always did have a mouth on you. That's why we left you here. Ray never could put up with sass."

"Where's Ray now?" Cat lost her battle with manners. "Too much sass from you? Or did he just figure out you're mean as a snake and about as warm?"

Quick as the snake Cat compared her to, Mona's hand whipped out, catching Cat's cheek just under her eye.

"I don't care what that rich bitch in New Orleans is paying. I ain't gonna be insulted by my own flesh and blood."

Cat grabbed her mother by the shoulders, but she didn't *see* anything. "What are you talking about?"

"Oh, no." Her mother shrugged out of Cat's grasp and backed off. "Already said too much. This is my Ma's house, and I should be the one to decide what's done with it.."

"No, Momma." Something about the way her mother's face had gone pale and clammy sent skitters of alarm down Cat's arms. She forced herself to sound calm and stared into her mother's twitchy gaze. "You have no claim here, Momma."

Mona recoiled, backing up against the wall. "What? Now you got that voodoo, hoodoo whatever, too?"

Something is very wrong here. "Momma, you're not making sense."

"Don't you start. I did what I was supposed to."

"Supposed to?" Cat wished hard that Daphne would forgive her for what she was about to try, but her mother was acting strangely, and if there was one thing her time in Blueberry Hill had shown her, it was to trust the strangeness to be real. She closed in on her mother, gripping her hands hard and looking straight into her eyes. "Tell me what's going on, Mona Brodey."

Her mother moaned, eyes rolling back in her head as a wave of disjointed images flooded Cat's head. A bus station in the rain, a cheap hotel, the tinkle of crystal and silver, polite laughter and a bussing station, an elegant, aging hand sliding a twenty-dollar-bill under an empty saucer. An empty, clean kitchen with dingy windows, the same fingers, skin loose like crepe paper, writing a check. A garden, plush with bougainvillea and a burbling fountain, plates of finger food and coffee in fine china cups, her mother's work-worn hands, fingertips resting in a shallow glass dish.

With every flickering picture, Cat felt herself slipping into her mother's head. She strained to catch the words. *A little favor, your daughter, my daughter, the baby...we're sisters now, distraction, Blueberry Hill...*

Cat gasped when the voice and visions coalesced to form a face. Those soulless eyes looking into her mother's were the same ones she'd seen in her visions.

There was a burst of power like a physical blow to her chest, and just before everything went black, Cat heard the door bang open, the rack of a shotgun, and Kelley's booming voice filling everything.

"Back off, Mona, before I put you down like the rabid bitch you always were."

When Cat woke, her head was pounding. She was lying on Meemaw's old sofa, with a heavy barn coat laid over her like a blanket.

Kelly sat in a nearby chair. The shotgun she'd heard lay on the coffee table like a deadly conversation piece. "Hey, hon."

"What happened? Where's Momma?"

"She took off. Back to whatever hole she crawled out of." Kelley patted the shotgun's stock. "Packed her things in an awful hurry."

Cat sat up, blinking away the nausea that followed. "How long have I been out?"

"An hour, maybe. You didn't miss much, but what the hell possessed you to come here. I told you to crash at my place."

"I don't know. I had to." Just like she knew she needed to warn Sam. That woman–Daphne called her Lilith–had known Cat was watching. *Would be watching?* She didn't know how it worked. "I have to go, Kelley. I have to get back there. Vermont. It's hard to explain, I don't actually understand everything that's happening, but I think my friend–my cousin–might be in trouble."

"Cat, it's pushing two-o'clock in the morning."

Car groaned. "I won't make it there, but I can call from the road."

Kelley stood. "You're not getting in a car right now."

Cat pleaded with her grandmother's friend. "I have to."

"Then I'm going with you." Kelley offered Cat a hand. "We'll take my truck."

"My car's a rental…" Cat's head was swimming, but Kelly's hand was firm and warm in hers.

"I'll get someone to drive it back to wherever. What's the point of having clout in this town if I don't flex it a little." Kelly hugged her. "Let's go, hon. I haven't had an adventure like this in years. You can tell me the story to pass the time."

Chapter Twenty-Six

Ash woke surprisingly clear-headed, given the long night at Will's parents' fire pit. He wasn't interested in a seven-year wait beforehand, but he hoped when it was his turn, he approached marriage with the same joyful enthusiasm Micah displayed.

Micah welcomed half the town to the elder Dryer's back yard, accepting claps on the shoulder, hugs, and arm punches equally.

His brother-in-law Lane, one of the straightest arrows Ash knew, drank them all under the table and shocked the hell out of everyone with a soulful rendition of The Cure's *Love Song* on Ash's Gibson.

It was a good night, but he missed Cat. A one night stand, a date, and a second night of incredible sex did not a meaningful relationship make–she'd ghosted him before–but he'd bet the Gibson they had a real shot at something, under the right circumstances.

Rolling over and wincing, clear-headed wasn't the same as hangover-free, Ash reached for his phone. He was rewarded with a text notification with Cat's name on it.

This will sound nuts, but please tell Samantha to be careful today. I'm on my way back but I might not get there in time. I don't know what exactly, but I'm sure something is wrong and it involves Lilith. You have to tell her that

I miss you

Ash reread the message twice. The first time, all he'd seen was the warning for Sam. She'd be with Marnie and Daphne all day because of the wedding, but he'd call and tell her what Cat texted him. The second time, he lingered over *I'm on my way back*, and *I miss you*.

The third time, he noticed the timestamp. She'd texted him at three in the morning.

Ash reached for his notebook and scribbled down his thoughts. He'd found the bridge that was missing from the recording he'd sent to Kylie, he just needed time to work out the music. Time he didn't have, because his brother was getting married in about seven hours.

First things, first, he called Sam. Whatever spooked Cat, he'd told her he trusted her.

"Morning, Ash." Sam didn't sound at all sleepy. "What's up?"

"I'm not sure," he said.

"That doesn't sound good." The sound of muffling the phone filled his ear before Sam's voice returned. "Please tell me Micah doesn't have cold feet. Marnie's approaching bridezilla here, mostly because of nerves."

"Marnie doesn't have nerves."

"Today she does."

"Micah's not going anywhere but to the homestead in a suit, and I've got the rings," Ash said. "Sam, Cat left town at some point in the last two days. She said it was a family emergency or something, but then she texted me in the middle of the night to tell me she was coming back."

"Okay, Ash." A touch of annoyance bled through Sam's voice through the phone. "But this is–"

"Marnie's day. I know. The other thing Cat said was to warn you."

"Me?"

"Her test said, 'please tell Samantha to be careful today,' she was worried she wouldn't make it here in time, and she said it's about someone called Lilith."

Sam's voice went wary. "She said *Lilith*?"

She believes me. He opened his texts to read Cat's message aloud. "Who's Lilith?"

"Too long a story for right now. I'll stay with Daphne or Will all day, and Ash?" Sam's voice shook a little on his name. "Text her back and tell her to be careful, too."

———

CAT TALKED until her throat was dry, explaining everything to Kelley, from her *spells* to Meemaw's letter, Ash and Daphne and Marnie and Samantha and Mercy, all the way to the crazy things she'd seen in her mother's head.

"I just wish the two of you had told me." Kelley didn't bat an eyelash, though her voice was sad. "I've seen weird shit in my day, hon. This is just a new variation on the theme, and you've never been a liar."

Kelley's profile in the darkness reassured her, and Cat drifted off.

When she woke enough to take in their surroundings, the sun was high and they were somewhere near the Maryland-Pennsylvania border.

"Your phone rattled around in the glove box a while back," Kelley said. "Have a look at it while I pull over for gas."

Two messages from Ash waited on her phone.

Sam says be careful too. She's going to stay close to Daphne and Will today

Trouble or not, I'm glad you're coming back. There are things I want to say to you

Kelley returned to the truck with a couple of hot coffees and huge, sticky doughnuts. "Sustenance. You feel up to driving, or should I keep going? I've got another hour or two once the caffeine and sugar kick in."

"I'll take the next leg. We're doing okay for time, but I'm still worried about that woman I saw. It was like...like she saw me see her. Like she could see right through Momma into me for a second and it scared me."

Kelley switched seats with her, arranging the coffees in the cupholders. "You told me Mona said something about Voodoo? She'd be the type not to pay too much attention to the finer points of spiritual practice. D'you suppose she got herself in with some bad folks practicing a dark kind of magic down in New Orleans?"

Cat considered that for a moment. "If Momma is like Meemaw and me, like Daphne or Sam, maybe?"

"Could be. It would stand to reason she is like you, but she'd have no way of knowing. I figure there's more mystery than not in the world, and what I don't know is about as big as the universe. If you're some kinda good witch, then I have to accept that there's folks who channel the dark stuff, too. Folks who'd prey on an impulsive, ignorant fool like Mona."

Cat laid a hand on Kelley's arm as they drove. "I'm a little freaked out at how not freaked out you are."

"I'm plenty freaked out, as you say, but I'm not letting it stop me from trusting you." Kelley halved her doughnut and bit off a chunk. She washed it down with a sip from the styrofoam cup. "That's terrible coffee. So, let's just work with the idea that your Momma somehow fell in with some folks who are up to no magical good."

Cat reached for her doughnut. "That still doesn't explain what this has to do with Momma stirring up trouble in Stag Creek. Momma said she did what she was supposed to do."

Kelley fell silent as the interstate rolled away beneath the truck.

Cat tried to recall the snippets of conversation she'd pulled from her mother, but it was something Samantha *hadn't* said that hit her like another slap.

"Samantha told me *someone who knew better took advantage.* Of her abilities, or whatever. And I know from Daphne that Samantha lived in New Orleans for a while before she ended up back in Vermont and married to her husband, but I didn't put it together until now."

Kelley sat up straighter. "Someone who takes advantage of folks who don't know better would find a goldmine in your momma."

"If Samantha and I are connected through the Potter family, then Momma is too. Lilith might have stumbled on Momma by accident, but maybe she found a connection to Samantha through us?" Cat banged on the wheel. "I wish I understood how all this works."

"You warned your friend, and she's going to stay with this Daphne of yours. All we can do now is get you back there to figure out the rest." Kelley picked up Cat's coffee, swished it to stir the sugar and hand it to Cat. "Drink this."

All we can do now is get you back there...

"Oh no. Kelley," Cat gave her friend a stricken look. "This was all just a distraction."

———

ASH CAUGHT up with Sam later in the day at Daphne's loft. She was paler than he liked, and he wasn't sure, but he thought she might be concealing dark circles under her eyes.

The sun was warm on his back; the temperatures so mild they might not need to heat the tent for the reception. *Did modern witches adjust the weather to suits their daughter's wedding?*

Marnie was managing to star in and direct the event; Ash wondered if Cat was predicting Sam finally wringing Marnie's neck. With an hour left before the ceremony, the catering staff, DJ, string quartet, and florist moved like ants across the property, setting everything up and doing last minute checks.

"Ash, get out of here," Marnie said. "This is bride central. Aren't you supposed to be keeping your brother from running off?"

Ash kissed Marnie's cheek, sharing a glance with Sam. There was a tacit agreement in place to not mention Cat or the family magic in front of the bride. "We both know he's not going anywhere. Will asked me to check up on Sam, that's all."

"Which you've done. Scram." Marnie waved a hand to shoo him out. "I have to finish getting gorgeous."

Ash appraised her current look–bare feet, a robe, hair in curlers. "You're always gorgeous."

Marnie pulled a face. "Yeah, sure, sweet talker."

"It's okay, Ash." Sam said. "I'm good."

"What's his deal?"

He didn't hear Sam's answer to Marnie's question as he let himself out, but he almost crashed into Daphne on her way up the stairs.

"I'm sorry, Daphne. My head was somewhere else."

Marnie's mom stopped him. "Thank you for believing Cat. And for telling Sammy to be careful. I'd never say it in front of Marnie, not today, but I had a terrible nightmare last night. I can't remember it, but I woke up screaming. Max was scared to death. The woman Cat warned us about, Lilith, is no one to be trifled with."

A shiver ran down Ash's spine. "You'd tell me if you knew what all this was about, wouldn't you?"

"I wouldn't have before Cat came to town," Daphne said. "There's only so eccentric I can get away with being out there. But she trusts you."

"I care about her," Ash said, shocked at how easily that truth came out of his mouth around his brother's about-to-be mother-in-law. "Almost since the moment we met. I want to get to know her better. I want to be around when she figures all this—" He waved his hands over Daphne and the homestead. "–out."

Daphne's smile dimmed. "I suspect we're going to find out very soon exactly how much she's figured out. I only hope that hag doesn't somehow spoil the wedding."

Ash thought of Marnie upstairs in her robe, willfully oblivious to the vein of worry running under the day's surface. "Me, too. Speaking of which, I should go find my guitar. I need to get tuned and warmed up."

He'd left the guitar in Will's car, having hitched a ride to Max and Daphne's. Micah and Henry were due any minute. Will hadn't said anything to him about Cat's text, which made him wonder if Sam had shared the information, but Ash hadn't quite known how to bring it up.

Guitar in hand, Ash headed for the meadow where a temporary pergola and chairs were set up, waiting for the ceremony. He'd hoped to find Will there, but Sam's husband was nowhere to be found. The only other person in the meadow was a frail old woman in a fussy floral dress who'd moved her chair into the shade of a huge maple tree.

"Can I get you anything?" Ash asked. When she shook her head, he pulled out a chair and sat down with the guitar.

"You play beautifully, young man," the old woman said.

"Thank you, ma'am." Marnie had given him specific instructions to play Marc Cohn's *True Companion* while she walked down the aisle. After that, she and Micah had given him free reign. He'd chosen a few well-loved songs from his own catalog, but he hardly needed to practice those. They came as easily as breathing after years touring. It was the new song, Cat's song, that begged him to play it.

When he looked up from his guitar midway through his freshly inspired bridge, the old woman was gone.

The sun began to sink in the sky, and wedding guests began to arrive while he noodled around with Cat's song. When Truman Bixby arrived to perform the ceremony, Ash left the Gibson on his guitar stand and joined him near the pergola.

"Good to see you, Ash," he said.

"You, too, Mr. B. How's the Professor?"

Truman Bixby's entire countenance lightened at the mention of his husband. "He's well. He'll be along in time for the ceremony. Do you know where to find the bride? I stopped to look in on her, but no one was in the loft. I assumed I'd find them here."

"No...." Ash looked at his watch. "I expect Micah any minute. Will should already be here, but I haven't seen him since we got here earlier."

A ball of fear solidified in his gut. Will's absence wasn't right, and he'd been a fool not to notice it. He pulled his phone out and texted Micah.

Micah replied. Just pulled in. Everything ready?

Ash typed back. *Will with you?*

Thought he was with you

Shit.

He was spinning his wheels trying to figure out what was

happening when Daphne charged down the garden path, her skirts swirling around her legs.

"Ash, is Sam with you?"

His chest clenched. "No, Daph. I thought she was with you and Marnie."

"She was going to get you. Will wasn't answering his phone." Daphne stopped and drew in a few heaving breaths. "She was hoping it was a signal issue, and maybe he was with you or Micah."

Ash hardly recognized his own strangled voice. "He's not with me or Micah."

Daphne's eyes went wide. She turned around, taking in the crowd of event workers and guests. "Has anyone seen Sam Dryer?" When no one said anything, she tried again. "Dark-haired pregnant woman? Harvest gold silk dress?"

A murmur of alarm was building among the assembled guests, but it was the viola player who spoke up.

"I saw her. About twenty minutes ago, helping an old woman get to the...um...mobile restroom."

Fear washed over Ash like ice water. "In a flowery dress?"

"Yes, exactly," said the violist.

One of the catering servers approached from the garden where the heated reception tent was set up. "Ma'am, my boss said you were looking for one of the groomsmen. I saw him about a half hour ago, escorting someone's granny to the port-a-potty."

"I saw the woman a bit ago, under the big tree," Ash said. "She...I swear she vanished into thin air."

"Ash." Daphne's lips barely moved. "Go."

He took off without looking back toward the secluded spot at the edge of the meadow where Max had mowed the tall grass to make a path for mobile restrooms. The units themselves had been trucked in and set up behind a huge laurel hedge near where the Stricklands' off-road trails ended at the Potter-Burnhams' land.

"Sam? Will?" He was shouting like a fool, hoping against all evidence to the contrary they'd snuck off for a little pre-wedding nookie, inappropriate as it would have been, but there was no sign of either of them. His phone signal, never exactly robust, got worse with every inch he put between himself and the homestead.

Banging from one of the mobile restrooms caught Ash's attention. He jogged up the three steps and let himself in, only to have Will stumble out of the stall, clutching his head, ankles bound with zip ties. "What the–"

"Fuck." Will sank to the floor, rubbing his head, focusing on Ash. "*What the fuck* is what you're looking for. That little old lady was stronger than she looked. I don't even know who she was."

Ash reached into his suit pocket for the engraved Swiss Army knife Micah had given him the night before. He cut the ties and pocketed the knife. "Oh, hell. Will...I think her name is Lilith, and Sam hasn't been seen since she walked away with her."

"No. Tell me you didn't say *Lilith*." At Ash's silent nod, Will's gaze cleared; he rubbed his ankles and hoisted himself to standing. "We have to find her. Now."

Chapter Twenty-Seven

A heaviness settled over Cat as they sped north. More than once, she intentionally reached into the heaviness, but she didn't know what exactly she was seeking or how to find it.

Half a dozen times, she brought up Ash's number on her phone, but it was Marnie and Micah's wedding day. He'd be busy, and Marnie wouldn't appreciate her butting in. She had to trust that Samantha got the warning, and hope she was overreacting to her confused visions.

Kelley turned the driving over to her at a gas station in Glens Falls, NY. Cat fought the temptation to take the rural roads too fast, but as signs began to advertise Thornton College and its surrounding attractions, she couldn't help nudging the pedal.

"Slow down, hon." Kelley yawned from the passenger seat. "Last thing you want is getting pulled over."

Hope was losing to the seasick feeling of foreboding lodged in her chest. Darkness had fallen over Thornton by the time they drove through and headed into the mountains. Her phone stayed suspiciously silent, and Cat wished she'd asked Ash to call her after the ceremony to check in.

"I know, but we're only about twenty-five minutes away."

Some kind of luck was on her side, and they hit Old Quarry View Road without law enforcement hauling her over for speeding. Cat slowed the truck as they approached number 972. Cars and trucks were parked along both sides of the road, and the homestead was lit up like Christmas.

"Cat!" Kelley grabbed her arm.

Cat stomped on the brakes and stopped the truck. She'd looked away from the road, and nearly run down a teenage girl in an old-fashioned party dress standing in the middle of the road.

A teenage girl who'd been dead for more than sixty years.

Cat's heart slammed against her ribs. "You can see her?"

"Plain as day," Kelley said, breathing hard. "Friend of yours?"

"Something like that." Cat laughed, but it was a thin, hysterical sound. Mercy's form didn't move as they regarded her through the windshield. "Kelley, meet Meemaw's mother, Mercy."

"Hot shit," Kelley whispered. "Go on."

Cat climbed down from the cab, shaking hard, and started toward Mercy, but the ghost only turned and walked into the woods. Cat hesitated, but Mercy remained visible, waiting for her just beyond the shoulder of the road.

"Kelley, go over to the house and explain who you are. Find Daphne Potter and tell her what you saw just now." Cat glanced at the sky and the silhouette of the mountains. "Tell her I'm headed more or less east into the woods. With Mercy."

Kelley didn't hesitate. She grabbed the keys and rushed in the direction of the driveway, and Cat gave her full attention to the apparition leading her into the woods.

They walked for more than a half hour, Cat trailing Mercy. The forest went silent around them as they walked, even the night noises hushed where Mercy's ghost walked. Somewhere, they'd picked up an ATV trail, which gave Cat a moment to concentrate. She wished she knew the area well-enough to know where they were going.

Marnie would have known. Daphne or even Samantha would have known.

Thoughts of her new cousins squeezed her heart hard enough to dispel the epic weirdness of following her great-grandmother's ghost through the woods on a cold, November night.

After a steep incline, Cat had to scrabble over a crumbling stone wall to stay with Mercy. The ghost stopped; Cat stopped as well.

The remnants of a foundation and a stone chimney stood in an overgrown clearing. Voices emerged from the quiet, drowning the pounding in Cat's ears. She crept closer, listening hard.

"Leaving was a mistake, but I think you know that now. The damage is done, but you can still make it up to me. This baby will have everything you tossed away, and I'll have my youth again."

Cat stopped, frozen in place at the sight of Samantha, zip-tied and gagged, leaning against one half-broken wall. From her vantage point, Cat could see Sam was pale, forehead beaded with sweat and breath coming hard.

A gray and haggard woman in a filthy, torn floral dress crouched over her, hands on Samantha's distended belly. The clouds overhead shifted, and in the moonlight Cat's heart skipped. Lilith.

She must have gasped audibly, or perhaps the force of her emotions crossed the space between them, because Samantha glanced in her direction. Her eyes were wide with fear, but Cat saw a flicker of hope there.

The old woman didn't look exactly robust, but she'd managed to subdue and drag a healthy pregnant woman through the forest. Cat suspected there was something sinister assisting.

Not exactly reassuring.

In a movie version of the moment, Cat would have harnessed some previously untapped telekinesis and shoved the old woman off Samantha, but this wasn't the movies, and she'd only just begun to explore the idea of magic, never mind Hollywood-style power. She glanced around, hoping for some hint from Mercy, but the ghost was gone.

Ash and Will, flashlights in hand, had trekked the perimeter of the homestead without finding anything. Max, the professor, and some of the other locals had split into parties to search along the road and knock on their neighbors' doors. The trouble was, nearly everyone was already at the homestead.

Will's face was a mask of worry; Ash felt sick to his stomach when they looped back to the loft and found Marnie and Micah in Daphne workshop. Marnie's veil was gone, the hem of her wedding dress was mud-stained. Her face was wild and tear-tracked.

"Will?" Marnie's voice was hoarse from calling for her friend. "Tell me you found her."

Ash shook his head. Will seemed beyond coherent words.

A knock on the door started all of them. The woman who stood in the bleached out light of the driveway floods was unfamiliar.

Ash put himself between the stranger and his people. "Can I help you?"

"Name's Kelley Hart, I come from Stag Creek, North Carolina. I've known Cat since she was born."

Ash knew the name. Relief washed over him at the same time anxiety grabbed hold. "I'm Ash. Is Cat with you?"

"We drove together," Kelley said, noticing Marnie in her dirty wedding dress. "You're Marnie. You and Cat have the same nose."

Kelley's observation broke Marnie's silence. "Where is Cat now?"

Kelley looked to Ash. "Promise me you'll let me explain."

Micah answered. "Do you know where our friend is?"

"We arrived down the road about ten minutes ago, and I swear on everything I hold dear, we were stopped by the ghost of my best friend's mother."

Ash's mind turned hard, putting together what Cat had shared with him. "Cat, too?"

Kelley nodded. "I don't half believe myself when I say it, but Cat followed that ghost into the woods and told me to come here and find Daphne. Tell her Cat went east."

"East from where. Exactly where?" Daphne came up behind Kelley.

"Mama," Marnie's voice was shaking. "Did you find Sam?"

"No, baby, but...I'm sorry," Daphne said to Kelley, "what's your name?"

"Kelley Hart. You're Daphne?" When Daphne nodded, Kelley continued. "Not far. Ten car lengths down the road, headed back toward town. It took me a few minutes to find someone who knew where you folks were."

Daphne acknowledged the information with a grim nod. "I think I know where Cat is headed. Boys–" Daphne turned to Ash, Micah, and Will. "Get your flashlights, your Swiss Army knives, and there's a .22 in the locked cabinet behind the desk. I don't want to use it, but I'd feel better having it. Will?"

"Yeah?" Will was wound tight. Ash could feel waves of fear and rage coming off him.

"The woman who hit you, what did she sound like?"

"Southern." Will shook his head as if the recollection was an effort. "Elegant. Ash said...But that can't be right..."

"Four years," Daphne murmured. "Let's go. We've got ground to cover, and I need to find Max."

———

CAT WAS IMMOBILIZED by fear and uncertainty until Samantha screamed around the gag, her body going rigid.

The baby!

She charged out of hiding, hoping like hell she could take the old witch by surprise, but the woman looked up in time, catching Cat in a predatory gaze.

"Stop."

Cat nearly tripped over her own feet as they halted nearly of their own volition. The command was powerful; she grabbed at a sapling to steady herself.

"You're Mona's girl," Lilith. "I thought maybe Mona was the answer. She wasn't, but she is quite a conduit. She told me all about her mother and her child, but what she didn't know was most useful in the end. I thought maybe I could use you. I sought you out in my finger bowl." The witch's eyes narrowed. "Imagine my delight when I realized your connection to my *daughter* and her baby."

Samantha moaned and struggled.

"You're not her mother." Cat knew that much. In the distance, she thought she saw a flicker of light. Maybe Kelley found Daphne? *If she could keep the witch talking...* "Use me for what?"

"Look at me," she said. "A Lacroix doesn't let herself decline in such a fashion. Samantha has a gift, you know. A rare compassion, and with it, an aura that the right practitioner can use as a veritable fountain of youth."

The woman is utterly mad.

"And you're that kind of," Cat swallowed, "practitioner?"

Samantha rolled onto her side, breathing hard.

"I made sure she married my son," the witch said. "Kept her close, kept her *dependent*. And how did she repay that? Leaving us, defying me, and spoiling the spells that kept my youth intact."

"Can't imagine why she'd want to leave," Cat said. "Sounds awesome."

"Your sarcasm is vulgar, just like your bloodline."

Cat thought of her Meemaw, regal as a backwoods queen, making up sachets of headache tea, tending her gardens, bringing up a granddaughter when she might have been free to do so much more. Cat thought of Kelley, steady, affectionate, ever present.

Had she really been so blind she couldn't see the bond they'd shared? Anger flooded her veins and broke the hold the witch had on her.

Cat advanced on the old woman.

"Stop," the witch said, louder than before, but with just a hint of a tremor.

"No," Cat said, free from whatever bindings Lilith controlled. "Whatever this is, it ends now."

"Damn straight it does, Lilith."

Cat was never so glad to hear Marnie Burnham's voice. She turned to see Marnie, leaves and twigs in her limp bridal updo, dirt smeared on her white satin dress, with Micah, Will, Daphne, and Ash in her wake.

Will broke off from the group and rushed to Samantha.

Lilith shrunk back from Marnie. Cat swore Marnie was lit from within with a shining, pale green energy. Her own pulse skittered. The light in Marnie's eyes was terrifying.

Marnie stepped in close to Cat. "I owe you an apology, but it's going to have to wait. I'm going to kill this bitch first."

Cat took Marnie's hand, whether to stop her or join her she didn't know, and was nearly knocked down by the feeling of power flowing between them.

Lilith, meanwhile, pressed herself back against the foundation. She seemed to diminish by the moment. "I'm just an old woman. I don't know what came over me…"

"Shut up." Will had cut Sam's bonds and was rubbing her wrists and checking her for damage. "I need to get her to a doctor. I think she's having contractions."

"Wait," Samantha leaned heavily on Will and rose to her feet. Wincing, she limped toward Marnie, who took her outstretched hand.

Like a completed circuit, Cat felt a current flow through the three of them. She fixed her gaze on the crumpled creature in front of them. Beyond the remains of the house, Mercy's ghost appeared, but Cat knew she was the only one who could see.

Clinging to Marnie, she reached across the clearing to her great-grandmother's ghost with all the hope and love for Meemaw she had in her heart.

Cat knew from the gasps and sharp breaths around her when Mercy's form solidified enough for everyone to see her.

"This ends tonight," Mercy said to Lilith, who'd gone corpse-pale and shuddering. "You are powerless here. *Mercy's line is restored and a doubting daughter's eye opens.*"

Marnie squeezed Cat's hand. Hard.

"*Sisters three unite to usher a new spirit safely home.*"

Samantha cradled her belly.

Lilith sobbed as Micah closed in on her. Cat had enough time to notice Max Burnham and Kelley move to help Micah restrain the witch before once again the world went black around her. Her last thought was a wish that Ash's were the arms that caught her as she fell.

Chapter Twenty-Nine

Ash answered his phone reluctantly. Kylie had called no fewer than a dozen times since he'd left her a voicemail saying he'd be a few days late getting to Brooklyn. He rolled out of bed and reached for a pair of flannel pants.

"I can explain," He kept his voice low so as to avoid waking Cat, and let himself out of Thimbleweed cottage, pausing for a moment to clip Henry's leash to his collar.

Every day since the night of Micah and Marnie's wedding had passed in a sweet fog of privacy. They'd brought Sam, Cat, and Lilith out of the woods, and handed the old witch off to the sheriff's department. Mr. Bixby had, despite the filthy, bedraggled bride and conspicuous lack of guests and maid of honor, performed the wedding ceremony in the small hours of the morning, one law enforcement finished with everyone. Micah and Marnie boarded their plane for Barbados at Will's insistence. Ash packed Henry's things and installed himself at the motor court with Cat.

"I hope so," Kylie said. "The fees are eating into our production budget in a big way."

Ash sighed. "I know, Ky. I wish I could explain, but it's too long a story for a phone call."

"It's not entirely a waste," Kylie conceded. "I've got the guys in the studio working on supporting tracks for that demo you sent me last week. Whoever she is, I'm tempted to hire her on as your muse permanently."

Ash chuckled. "Trust me, I'm working toward a long-term commitment in that regard."

Kylie wailed into the phone. "No, no, no. Long-term is so boring. Ugh. You're literally the only rock star alive who wants to settle down."

"I think that's a little bit of an exaggeration."

"Three days, Reynolds," Kylie said. "Your ass needs to be in this studio in three days."

She didn't give him the opportunity to argue before she hung up.

"Was that your manager?" Cat joined him on the porch steps, sitting with Henry between them.

"Sorry," Ash said, reaching for her hand over the dog's back. "I didn't mean to wake you."

"It's okay. " Cat twined her fingers with his. "I've spent a lot of time in bed."

Ash nudged Henry enough to lean in and kiss Cat. "Not sleeping as much as you should."

Cat laughed. "And whose fault is that?"

Ash kissed her again, a little longer, a little slower. "I hate that I have to go."

"You'll come back, or I'll come down to New York." She slid her hand up his thigh. "There are hotel rooms in New York, from what I hear."

Henry's warm, solid body was definitely in the way. "I just hate leaving you alone, after everything."

Cat leaned over, picked up a pinecone, and tossed it into the grass next to the cottage. When Henry gave chase, she scooted into the space the dog vacated. "I'm hardly alone."

"What about here?"

"Well," Cat said, "I can't stay at the motor court forever, and Daphne offered me the loft..."

"That'll be great for you." He wondered at the memory of Cat, glowing silver in the moonlight, hand in hand with Marnie and Sam, their own auras illuminating the night. He'd be laughed out of any room he tried to tell it to, but he knew what he'd seen in those woods. "Any big plans?"

"Well," Cat ran her hands through his hair. "Aside from enticing you back to bed with my witchy wiles, Marnie asked me to drive down to Brattleboro with her to visit Sam and baby Georgiana when she and Micah get back from Barbados."

"Marnie did?" *Would wonders never cease?* "I knew you two would get along."

"We have a lot to talk about anyway, now that Marnie is grudgingly admitting to possessing some kind of magical ability." Cat laid her head on his shoulder. "We're going to learn together. All three of us. And teach little Georgie when she's bigger."

"I can't wait to see it," Ash said, standing up and pulling Cat to her feet with him. "But first, those witchy wiles you mentioned."

———

CAT HELD on tight when Ash scooped her up and carried her inside the motor court cabin. She laughed when he held the door open for Henry, who plopped down on his dog bed near the door and ignored them.

Ash set her down and lowered his lips to hers. His kiss was everything Cat wanted, hungry, gentle...him.

"Kylie wants to hire you, you know." He unzipped the hoodie she'd thrown on to join him outside, revealing the bare skin beneath. "I'm glad I didn't know you were naked under this. We'd have been arrested for public indecency."

"The only one watching was Henry. Poor pup."

"He'll get over it when I drive him back to Micah and Marnie's house in the truck later."

Cat slipped the hoodie off her shoulders and let it fall to the floor. She reached for the waistband of her leggings, but Ash stilled her hands. He smoothed his palms up her belly to cup her breasts, rolling her tight nipples between his fingertips and stealing the gasp of pleasure from her lips with a kiss.

He lowered them both to the bed, drawing his tongue from one breast to the other, then down, until, with sure fingers, he slid the leggings down himself, covering her skin with kisses as he went.

"Nothing on under these either? You're going to kill me."

When he got to her ankles, he stripped the leggings off and began another trail of kisses up the inside of her thigh.

Cat sighed as the hot anticipation of his mouth wound her up. "You never said why Kylie wants to hire me."

She felt his answering laughter on his tongue when he dipped it between her folds. Her hips arched off the mattress to meet him and pleasure ripped through her.

Ash looked up, the landscape of her body between them.

"You inspire me. That's why."

She laughed. "Far be it from me to interrupt your creative process."

Cat dropped her head back as he hooked her legs over his shoulders with a growl.

When, some while later, she snuggled into his side, he said, "How long are you thinking about staying with Daphne and Max?"

"As long as it takes to work out what I can do, and what I want to be when I grow up."

"I'd like to see that."

"What?" She laughed. "Me growing up?"

"More like what you decide to be with what you have." He kissed her temple. "Discovering the story of Cat and sharing it with the world."

Happiness was threatening to spill over in the form of tears, so Cat focused on the way the soft hair on his forearms felt under her palms. "You should definitely stick around for that."

Ash was quiet a moment. "Have you given any thought to the house in Stag Creek?"

"Well, since Momma paid cash for the back taxes with Lilith's money, I backed out of the sale. Kelley was doing some research and there's a company online that lets people rent their homes like vacation houses. She thinks, because there's hunting and fishing and winter sports nearby, that I could make some money renting it while I'm in Vermont. At least enough to keep Donny away."

"I've never truly wanted to punch someone I've never met before."

"Don't waste your energy on him." She peered up at him from under her lashes. "I've got better ideas."

"Mmm?" Ash's lips lingered around her ear. "Such as?"

"Telling me what new song Kylie's all fired up about."

His laugh rumbled in his chest. "You heard that?"

"The whole mountain heard it. That woman is loud."

He rolled onto his side and tucked his arm around her. "She's not the only one."

Cat squirmed, giggling. "Seriously, what's the song about?"

Ash's expression turned tender. He kissed her, softly. "Just you, Cat."

———

Also by Cameron D Garriepy

Thornton Vermont

Damselfly Inn

Sweet Pease

Family Practice

Sugaring Season: Stories from Thornton & Beyond

Bread & Promises (Yuletide)

The Best Laid Plans: A Socially Distanced Thornton Vermont Romance

Green Mountain Hearts

Ambitious Heart

Unbound Heart

Familiar Heart

Standalone Romance

Buck's Landing

Short Fiction in Anthologies

Valentine (Metaphysical Gravity)

Requiring of Care (Echoes in Darkness)

———

Christmas Mini-Romances

Bread & Promises (Yuletide)

Cinnamon Girl (Wish)

The Soloist (Joy)

Star of Wonder (Merry Little Christmas)

Santa's Photographer (Secret Santas)

Merry's Christmas (Atlantic to Pacific)

Twelve Days 'til Christmas

———

Children of the Parallels
Speculative Middle Grade Short Fiction

Parallel Jump

Parallel Hunt

———

Writing As Isla Brighton
Speculative Serial Fiction on Kindle Vella

Silvertongue: Crowbourne Series, Part One

Excerpt from The Best Laid Plans

"I know, I know," Poppy said to Mathilda, the plump Golden Laced Wyandotte hen who liked belly rubs and was occupying the picnic table near the run, "I'm wearing mascara. But it's because I like it, not because that woman thought I was the housekeeper."

Mathilda regarded her with aviary nonchalance before hopping down to scratch at an ants' nest she found in the grass.

The sun was out and the breeze was blowing fluffy clouds across the sky, so Poppy was free ranging with the chickens while she worked. The picnic table caught the last vestiges of the household internet connection, allowing Poppy to bring her laptop out and monitor Professor Bixby's classes.

The mascara was a whole lot of too little too late, but she did enjoy the effect. The thin veneer of professionalism she'd cultivated working for Thornton College's History Department had entirely faded since the lockdown started. She favored unstructured skirts with pockets and stretchy tees and tanks in her free time. Her freshly washed curls would look decidedly untamed after air drying without any product, but it didn't really matter. The chickens didn't care, her laptop's camera–like the mic–was off.

With the exception of snooty Elisha, Poppy hadn't seen anyone but the cashier at the Thornton Co-op in days.

Professor Bixby finished his video lecture, and Poppy watched as the individual tiles of his forty-two students closed. She emailed the attendance list, a summary of the lecture, and a transcript of the student questions from the chat to the professor's inbox. *If only he would learn to look at some of those things for himself...*

She was closing her computer when a lost Hemsworth wandered out of the woods.

Or, upon closer inspection, a previously undiscovered, Forty-Something Hemsworth? At least six rangy feet, soulful eyes and a generous mouth, with a twig in his hair, just where a few silver strands shot through the rich brown.

The laptop nearly slipped as Poppy shot to her feet, heart hammering.

"Oh, hey. Sorry," he said, coming to a stop as The Orpington Twins, Lavender and Buffy, flapped over to him. *Shameless hussies.* Forty-Something Hemsworth took in the ever-so-charming coop and run, the profusion of lilacs, even Poppy herself in a swift, unnerving gaze. "Did I stumble into some kind of fairy tale quest?"

Definitely not an actual Hemsworth...that accent was pure prep school with a touch of New York. Having spent her entire life in close proximity to a NESCAC college gave her an ear for it. Still criminally good looking.

Her pulse slowed. The Twins kept him at the edge of the clearing, conducting a thorough examination of his feet and ankles. If he was a criminal, their prey-animal instincts failed them. The two hens, sisters by choice, might have walked straight out of a Disney animation. Both broad and a little swaybacked with smooth feathers, one palest blue-gray, the other the color of a summer wheat field in an over-exposed Ridley Scott dream sequence, they circled the stranger's feet, clucking softly and picking at his shoelaces.

He'd better keep his distance; her masks were all in the house. How could she have anticipated company appearing from out of the woods in the form of a ridiculously attractive hiker?

"You're off the Horizon Trail, if that's where you were walking. This is private property."

He picked a dandelion and offered it to Lavender, who snatched the treat and hopped away, Buffy in her wake. "Lilac Lane?"

Poppy narrowed her eyes at him. Not a totally lost hiker, then.

"Nick Cooper." He started to offer his hand, then remembered and pushed it back into his pocket with an adorably awkward laugh. "I'm renting the Fullers' cabin for...well, for now."

Nicky didn't mention... So that was where Professor McNair was on her way to in that enviable car.

Poppy sighed. Of course *available, age-appropriate* Hemsworth lookalikes didn't wander into her parents' backyard. Mathilda flapped back onto the picnic table, greeting them both with the whirring chirp Poppy thought of as purring. "Poppy Daley. My mother cultivates the lilacs."

Nick grinned, charmed by Mathilda. "And you keep the hens?"

Stung, Poppy snatched up her laptop. "Yes. I keep the hens." She gestured to a nearby hemlock stand. "You can pick up the Horizon Trail about 40 yards that way."

Mustering the small dignity afforded to her by Maybelline Lash Sensational, Poppy spun on her heel and made for the barn, hoping Nick Cooper didn't notice the chicken poop on her flip-flop heel.

———

"You owe me," Nick said into the phone. "You didn't tell me she was pretty. And not retired. I swallowed not only my foot, but my ankle and most of my shin."

Elisha laughed. "I mistook her for your housekeeper. What makes you think I'm going to be any help?"

"You let me think my retired neighbors were down there, not a woman my age who's probably their daughter."

"I didn't know." She laughed again, musical and unrepentant. "And what can you do? This whole lockdown scenario is less than ideal for romantic gestures."

"Whoa." Nick pulled the phone away from his face for a second, as though Elisha could see his expression. "Who said *romantic*?"

"You called me asking what you could do for your pretty, not-retired neighbor..."

Elisha was often right. Infuriatingly so. She also often had the answers. Infuriatingly.

"Did you make it into the pastry shop in town before all this?" Nick imagined her hand waving in the direction of the window of her airy loft, one of three upscale condos carved out of a barn on a hillside north of the college. *All this...* The unobstructed view of the valley priceless. Nick wondered if her self-quarantine was made easier by the gilded sunsets she watched every night.

She would worry about her grandparents. She would worry about Ben. But he didn't mention them. "I didn't. Probably should have, huh?"

"Call them and order the lilac woman some chocolate croissants. The owner is delivering orders until she can reopen."

"Let me guess," Nick said. "You two got pedicures together before the salons closed?"

"No. Frankly, she drives me crazy, but her chocolate croissants are a decent alternative to sex."

Nick wasn't sure anything made of flour and butter was quite that good. "Why does the Princess of Pomfret even have a list of alternatives to sex?"

"I hate that nickname." She paused for a long moment. "And I'm not interested in sex right now. Too many complications. Croissants, however, can be forgiven by sufficient running and lifting."

Nick heard her unspoken closing of the topic. "So, I should order a chocolate croissant delivery from that bakery to say I'm sorry to my neighbor." *My very pretty, very much not-retired-matron neighbor who makes keeping chickens very appealing.*

"I'll text you the link. If your lilac girl's the irresponsible type, she'll turn up at your door in sexy lingerie to say thank you."

"She's not my lilac girl—"

But Elisha ended the call. Nick peered out over the forest canopy in the direction of Lilac Lane, unable to unsee the image of Poppy Daley, all those nearly blue-black curls tumbling over soft shoulders, smoldering up at him from beneath long, sooty lashes.

Fantasy Poppy wasn't wearing scraps of satin and lace. Nick found everyday underthings far sexier than delicate, complicated straps and netting. Easier to slide hands under, easier to discard en route to sweet curves and warm flesh.

When Elisha's text disturbed his runaway imagination, Nick clicked the link and called the bakery straightaway. Whether she thanked him or not, he owed Poppy an apology, and he was too practical to leave an imaginary girl outside in the woods in her underwear. She'd get eaten alive.

If this was his fantasy, that was *his* privilege.

———

About the Author

Cameron D. Garriepy attended a small Vermont college in a town very like Thornton. She's missed it since the day she packed up her Subaru and drove off into the real world. Some might say she created the fictional village as wish fulfillment, and they would be correct.

She is the author of the Thornton Vermont series, and the founder of Bannerwing Books, a co-op of independent authors. Prior to Bannerwing, Cameron was an editor at Write on Edge, where she curated three volumes of the online writing group's literary anthology, Precipice. Cameron appeared in the inaugural cast of Listen to Your Mother – Boston, and irregularly contributed flash fiction to the Word Count Podcast.

Since her time at Middlebury College, Cameron has worked as a camp counselor, nanny, pastry cook, an event ticket resale specialist, and an office manager. Cameron's ghost-writing and editing hides in the tech and finance sectors. In her spare time, she is an archer, a baker, a gardener, a knitter, and a reader of a lot of romance novels.

Cameron writes from the greater Boston area, where she lives with her husband, son, a very silly pug, and four naughty hens.

Connect with Cameron online at www.camerondgarriepy.com
Hear first about sales and new releases via Cameron's newsletter—
subscribe at
bit.ly/smartsexynewsletter
Join the conversation in Cameron's Facebook group at
bit.ly/thorntonfbgroup

amazon.com/author/camerondgarriepy

facebook.com/camerondgarriepy

twitter.com/camerongarriepy

goodreads.com/camerondgarriepy

bookbub.com/authors/cameron-d-garriepy

instagram.com/camerongarriepy

pinterest.com/camerongarriepy

From the Earth to the Moon, a short story set in the small town of Thornton, Vermont, just after the Korean War.

"Wake up, son. This is your stop."

George Cartwright blinked at the elderly woman across the aisle of the coach car. Her wrinkled hand rested on his wrist.

"Port Henry, dear." She pointed out the window.

George peered at the slowing landscape. Six long years since he'd seen the particular color of the Adirondack sky. Six years since he'd smelled the wind off Lake Champlain. Six years of tracing the ridge line of the Green Mountains in his memory, letting his mind's eye drop just there—soaring into downtown Thornton and coming to rest on the front porch of the Gingerbread Victorian on Chapel Street that was his boyhood home.

When George was a child, he dreamed of spaceships as often as he dreamed of anything. In the summer of 1939, when his little brother reverently smoothed the edges of new *Superman* comics, ten-year-old George nudged them aside on the nightstand to make room for his grandfather's copy of Jules Verne's *From the Earth to the Moon*. Stars and infinite blue sang him a siren song. His red Elgin Robin became a sleek ship, his pumping legs rockets, flying out County Road to help his Uncle Jed on his farm.

For years George dreamed of shedding Thornton, Vermont. He dreamed of adventure and foreign worlds. He pedaled his imagination-fueled starship long after dreams of softer, sweeter adventures crowded the thoughts of the boys he knew from school.

George's father Oscar Cartwright owned Cartwright's Mercantile, which sold everything from hunting rifles to three-piece suits, from household appliances to party dresses, and always had the current Montgomery-Ward catalog available for orders. His mother Eolia, a Boston Adams on her mother's side, dreamed of an elder son who took up the family business and the political mantle of his imagined forebears, but the wide sky called to George in a way that commerce or legislation never could.

Eolia was devastated when George enlisted in the Navy the day after he graduated from Thornton High School, eager to see the world, if not the impossible universe, aboard ship.

He assured her the war was over; and surely the world was ready for peace?

Six years later, his grandfather's copy of *From the Earth to the Moon* lay wrapped in brown paper at the bottom of his Navy-issue duffel, and his elderly seat-mate woke him from dreams of the deadly, churning Sea of Japan off the coast of Korea.

"Thank you, ma'am." George nodded solemnly, gathered his duffel, and made his way off the train.

He scanned the sparse crowd waiting at the station. His brother had been a scrawny fifteen-year-old kid with thick glasses and comic book ink on his fingers, but there was no one waiting who looked he might be a twenty-one-year-old Charlie Cartwright.

George sat himself down in the shade and watched the cars pulling into the station.

The Chevy Bel-Air cruised into the dusty lot like something out of the movies. Two shades of green; one the color of the fir forests he'd missed so badly, the other the color of the sea along Waikiki

Beach. The car's sparkling paint was nothing, though, to the pair of legs that swung out of the driver-side door.

Those legs drew his eye over a curving hip and slim waist. Her cap-sleeved dress revealed slender arms and a smooth neck. Her hair was a raven reflection of Marilyn Monroe's, but even Marilyn couldn't hold a candle to this girl's glossy red pout.

She held a hand over her eyes to block the light and looked over the station yard. When her gaze stopped on him, his heart turned over in his chest.

"George?" She called out to him as she walked to him. Her voice was low and warm, a smoky-bar saxophone. "George Cartwright? I'm Ginny Fletcher. Charlie sent me to get you. He had something come up at the store."

George stood, dusting off his khaki trousers and taking the outstretched hand she met him with. She smiled up at him and George's fate was sealed. "The pleasure is all mine, Ginny Fletcher. How is it my brother has such a pretty secretary?"

"Oh, I'm not Charlie's secretary, George." Her laugh, like her voice, was musical. She slipped her arm through his and steered him back towards the waiting Chevy. "I'm his fiancée."

Read on...

———

Revisit modern-day Thornton in *Damselfly Inn*:

Over the southwestern end of Lake Champlain, on the New York side, the storm was stirring up the lake water, whipping itself into a frenzied spiral between the high wall of the Adirondacks in New York and the rolling Green Mountains of Vermont. Electricity flashed and crackled between the clouds, dancing down over the water, licking at the shoreline as the storm approached.

Thunderheads cast the Adirondack Suite into shadow. Nan Grady closed the windows and took a long look at the room around her.

When the storm hit, at least the jewel of the Damselfly Inn's six guest rooms would stay dry.

A low roll of thunder growled. Nan trailed her hand along the natural cherry-wood sleigh bed as she passed, caught her reflection in the repainted Victorian mirror in the en suite bathroom. She let out a breath of self-approval; everything was exactly as she'd imagined it. Admiring the freesias she'd arranged in a milk glass vase, she straightened the hand-embroidered dresser scarf she'd bought at a church bazaar the weekend after she'd closed on the house.

The third story of the house was smaller than the two main levels, and there was already a full bathroom tucked into the gable. Nan had known the first time she'd seen the house that it would take minimal effort to transform the two small rooms into a bedroom and sitting room.

She'd poured her heart into the third floor, creating a haven for fairytale romance. Splurging on satiny cotton linens for the bed and oversized, lush towels in the bath, searching antique shops and flea markets for the chaise and love seat in the sitting room, spinning her dreams of romance and luxury and her inherent practicality into a snug retreat.

Her Gran had always told her she had an old soul. She supposed it must be true. At 31, her most devoted relationship was with a century old house.

In the deepening shadows, she imagined newlyweds at the window, flushed with joy and anticipation. She could almost hear the sigh of the bride as the man she loved loosened the stays on her gown, the two of them bathed in the rose light of a late summer Vermont sunset.

She closed and locked the suite's door, stopping to rub a smudge on the door's pewter nameplate with her sleeve. The fragrance of the freesias followed her as she headed downstairs.

Downstairs, she tidied up her office and took the opportunity to go over the instructions delivered with the next day's pastries. She'd need to put the tray of croissant and Danish in the fridge in the morning, so they could defrost throughout the day, before going into the warming tray overnight to proof. Her best friend—and pastry chef—insisted that a slow final rise was essential if she wanted the pastries to be perfect for Sunday breakfast.

Nan had to laugh. She and Kate had studied the basics of pastry together, put in the same early hours at the school's patisserie together, but Kate wasn't likely to leave anything to chance when it concerned her finished product.

The darkening clouds blotted out the setting sun. The storm was looking like a sure thing. She decided to batten down the hatches and retreat upstairs to her private apartment over the garage. She could make phone calls and check e-mail from the comfort of her snug sitting room.

While the storm grew in intensity and barreled across the lake and valley, Nan gathered up her laptop and phone, closed and locked the door to her office. On the way through, she snagged the day's mail from where she'd dropped it on the kitchen table earlier and headed upstairs.

With visions of a busy inn dancing in her head, she sorted through the pile of catalogs and bills, dropping the junk mail into a recycling pile on the floor. The postcard stood out from the rest of the post, with its too-bright, beachy vista and a bikini-clad model on a towel splashed across it. She turned it over, scanning the back. It was addressed to a Danny Beaudette. Nan couldn't help reading the broad, looping penmanship on the back. Hey Danny, miss you. The beach doesn't really look like this at all. It kinda sucks. Wish you could come visit. Ellie.

Nan set the card with the bills, making a mental note as the storm threw itself down on the farmland to drop it at the post office on Monday. There weren't any Beaudettes in the neighborhood, but the postmaster was likely to know who the card was meant for. The storm blew into the valley, kicking against the trees and homes like an angry child. The wind howled and rain railed against the windows. Whoever Danny was, Nan hoped he got to visit Ellie at the beach someday.

She smiled to herself as she opened her bookkeeping software, determined to stay focused on the inn. Her spirits flagged a little at the low numbers in the black columns. She wasn't in serious debt, but she would need every reservation she could get to keep it that way, between the mortgage and the business loan.

The local bank had taken a chance on her, and loaned her the start up money in addition to her mortgage. She'd been lucky to have a nest-egg large enough to make the down payment and cushion the loan, and she knew it.

She looked at the collection of photographs on her painted pine bookshelf. Her grandfather had built it for her when she was born, and now his careworn face and that of her grandmother graced its shelves.

Her grandparents had been frugal New Englanders, living a productive and restrained life. Growing up with them, Nan had never wanted for the necessities, but her Gran and Grandpa had never felt the need for extravagances. They had been stern, but loving, and when they had passed away, Nan found they had left her with enough to put a down payment on this house, on her dream.

Despite the personal sacrifices she knew were ahead, she was certain she could make the inn a success. For her grandparents.

For herself.

The storm continued its tantrum as it drove eastward, rushing up to and over the Green Mountains like water over a spillway. Rain pelted down, blown nearly horizontal, and the huge maple tree behind the inn groaned in protest.

Nan was pulled out of her thoughts by a vivid flash of lightening. A sickening crack echoed against the back of the house; a crash shook the whole house, followed by a growl of thunder.

Nan sat frozen for a heartbeat, then she was on her feet and running down from her apartment, through the kitchen and into the foyer. She scrambled into her office and grabbed a hefty flashlight. A cold wind tumbled down from the third floor.

With a hard knot of dread already forming in her stomach, she raced up to the third floor landing. She yanked open the door to the Adirondack Suite with her heart pounding.

She cried out as if she'd been struck. Rain was pouring in through the remains of the gabled roof, lumber and insulation hanging down like broken bones and torn flesh. The hot smell of ozone was fresh in the air. Shingles and debris littered the floor. The silk drapes whipped and snapped at the sills. A limb from the ancient maple tree that grew next to the house lay across the sleigh bed, its raw end sizzling.

"Oh, god. No," she said aloud to the empty room, her voice swallowed by the noise of the storm. "No."

She forced herself to loosen the death grip in which she held the doorknob. She forced herself to inhale and exhale. If she let herself cry now, she would fall to pieces. She jumped when a man's voice called her name from downstairs.

"Miss Grady? Hello! Is anyone up there? Hello?"

She thought of her phone, waiting for her back in her apartment. The man calling knew her name, but she had no idea who she was facing, alone in the house in a storm. She gripped the flashlight tightly and started slowly down the stairs.

They all reached the second story landing at the same time. Nan stopped short in relief. Walt Fuller, the dairy farmer from down the road, stood in the second floor hallway in a dripping slicker and muddy boots, with a similarly dressed younger man at his side.

"Miss Grady? Are you all right?" Walt asked, catching his breath.

Nan almost laughed at the absurdity of the question. She was far from all right. There was a tree branch in her bridal suite. There were muddy boot tracks on the hallway runner. She could feel panic welling up again. Then she saw Walt's expression, and realized they must have heard the lightning strike, seen her roof, and come running to find out if she'd been underneath it.

She was all right. The suite was another story.

"I'm fine, Mr. Fuller. The room upstairs—" she began.

She started to shake and pressed her hand against her mouth, fearing she might be having hysterics.

"Come on down to the kitchen, now, Miss Grady. Molly's making tea for you, and Joss here's going to go take a look at your damage," said Walt, gesturing to his companion.

As Walt Fuller put a hand on her shoulder and steered her towards the stairs, she looked back at the younger man. He gave off an impression of quiet competence that momentarily quelled the panic brewing in her belly, and his eyes were the same shade as the thunderheads outside.

In the kitchen, Molly Fuller was boiling water and getting out the tea and teapot.

"I went ahead and poked around your kitchen, hon. I hope that's ok," she said to Nan, before turning to her eyes to her husband. "How bad is it?"

"Joss'll tell us in a minute. I sent him on up," Walt replied. He joined his wife at the counter.

"Mr. and Mrs. Fuller, thank you—" Nan started.

"None of that, now," Molly interrupted. "We've barged into your house; we're past formalities. I'm Molly, he's Walt, and we're all neighbors. We take care of our own. Now, I put a fair amount of sugar in this one. It'll help with the shock." She handed Nan a mug.

The mug was solid and warm, the tea sweet and strong. She felt the panic begin to dissipate, the knot of dread loosen. She took a deep breath, and remembered her manners.

"I hope you'll call me Nan, then," she said to the two of them. She almost blushed to note that Walt was holding his wife's hand. "There are cookies from Sweet Pease on a plate under that pie dome, if you'd like."

Molly smiled, "Your mother raised you well."

"My Gran, actually," Nan found herself smiling in response. "My grandparents raised me. My mother passed away when I was small, and my father was never what you could call present." She flushed, feeling she'd revealed too much to these kind people. "Joss...is your son?" she asked, hoping to shift the topic of conversation away from her rootless past.

"He is," answered Molly. "Joss is short for Josiah. Contractor and carpenter, so you're in good hands. He'll get things buttoned up for you tonight, and I'm sure he'll come back in the morning to do a proper estimate, if you'd like."

The man himself walked into the kitchen, wiping a hand on his jeans; he carried his slicker in the other. Rain clung to his hair, leaving damp streaks on his shirt as it beaded and rolled off. His presence filled the kitchen.

"Mom, my ears are burning," he said, a smile in his voice.

Something like envy kindled in her heart. The Fullers had that intangible ease that came with love and familiarity. They were family.

Molly introduced them, "Josiah, this is Nan Grady. Nan, our son, Josiah Fuller."

"A pleasure, Nan, circumstances notwithstanding," he said, reaching for her hand. "And please," he said with a wry look at his mother, "Call me Joss."

"I will. It's nice to meet you, too." Or it would be, she thought, if my livelihood wasn't in serious trouble.

She put her hand in his. Their eyes met over the handshake. A current flared between them. She was sure she must be blushing. His hands were calloused, warm, pleasantly rough. She wondered how they would feel sliding up her back, running through her hair.

"Well, son, what needs to be done tonight?" Walt asked, interrupting her wayward thoughts. She almost laughed; she was more in shock than she'd realized.

Nan pulled her hand away, but she wasn't sure what to do with it. It took her a moment to realize that Joss was speaking to her.

"Miss Grady, have you got tarps and rope? Tie-downs? I'm going to get up on the roof and cover the hole until morning. The rain's clearing off, but I don't want to leave that hole exposed. You're lucky." He said. "There's no wiring or plumbing in that section of ceiling."

Maybe she'd imagined the heat, the spark between them. Joss didn't seem affected by it at all. Maybe it had been so long since she'd looked up from her goals that the first good looking man she'd seen had set her skin humming.

"I've got some tie-downs in my car, but no tarps," she said, wishing she'd thought to buy them on one of her many trips up to Burlington for supplies.

"That's no trouble at all," he replied, turning away from her. "But Dad, I'll need to borrow some from you, and come back."

"I'll help you get some from the barn," Walt said. "Let's not keep the poor girl up all night."

"I think I'll be up anyway," Nan sighed.

"Nonsense, Nan," Molly said. "I'll stay to help you clean up."

Flustered by her neighbors generosity, Nan started to tidy the tea tin and sugar bowl.

"Please, Molly, Walt," she turned to them, embarrassed but resolute, "I can handle it tonight."

Molly met her eyes before getting up and clearing the mugs. Nan hoped the older woman understood what she saw there. She needed to fall apart and pull herself back together again in peace.

Molly rinsed out the tea pot, and dried her hands. She took a key from her pocket and set it on the island. "I can be over first thing in the morning, if you like, and you're going to want to put that key back under the mat," she said with a wink.

Nan stared at the key as Molly bustled out the kitchen door, followed by her men. In all the panic and confusion, she hadn't given a thought to how the Fullers had gotten into the house. She was grateful Molly Fuller had figured out where her spare key was; she supposed it wasn't a very original hiding place.

"Molly, wait!" she called. "Take the key. If I ever need it, I'll know where to look."

Joss, who'd been the last to go through the kitchen door, turned and took the key from her outstretched hand.

Pack a towel and a picnic and spend the summer at *Buck's Landing*:

Whoever was pounding on the door had better have their affairs in order, Sofia thought as she pushed herself up off the sofa, because she was going to murder them with her bare hands. With a grimace at the empty bottle of pinot noir on the coffee table, she cursed herself for drinking too much the night before, pressing her knuckles against her sleep-crusted eyes. Hadn't she fled this coastal New England beach town to escape her father's drinking? She scraped her mane of dark brown curls into a hasty knot, wondering what the hell else a lone woman was expected to do in Hampton Beach when she wasn't one of the vacationing hordes.

A glance at the clock told her she'd overslept. The mini-golf course at Buck's Landing would be open by now, and she should be getting the Snack Bar ready.

She opened the door to Amy, her assistant manager. The coed's perky ponytail and crisp uniform polo shirt practically sparkled in the July sun.

"I'm sorry, Sofia." Amy glanced down from Sofia's third story landing at the Astroturf greens, where a small crowd had gathered around the cement "tree" on the twelfth hole. "There's a kitten stuck up the tree, and I can't get him down."

"Of course." With a sigh, Sofia slid her feet into the sensible sport sandals she wore to work, and followed Amy down the stairs to the waiting cat. She praised herself for falling asleep in a tank top and soft cotton pants. At least she was decent enough to rescue stray kittens from fake cement trees.

The sun glittered off the crushed stone paths that wound through the course, sparkled on the blue-gray sea washing ashore across the street at the state beach. Heat was already pooling on the sidewalk, the boardwalk, and the road between. Sofia squinted, wishing for sunglasses, and did her best to ignore the faint throbbing at her temple.

A six-foot ladder proved enough to get her into the tree, and the little scrap of fur came to her easily. Sofia had never had a cat, but as this kitten's body went soft in her hands, she wondered briefly why not.

"Aren't you a pretty...well, now what are you?" She raised the tiny cat up and inspected its underside. "A pretty boy." He cocked his head to one side, and Sofia chuckled. She tucked the purring feline under her arm and backed down the ladder. "Amy, can you stash the ladder on your way back to the window? I'm going to find a place for this guy to stay until I find his owner."

"Sure."

Sofia envied the college girl's boundless energy. She hadn't remembered having that much buoyant charm at twenty-two. All she remembered about being a college kid was planning her summers off from UNH so that she could be home as little as possible. The summer she was twenty-two, she'd worked her third consecutive summer at a girls' camp in the White Mountains, blessing them for providing room and board. She'd stashed her paychecks away, saving for the precious future, intent on escaping her father's grief and its companion, Canadian whiskey. She had planned to get out of New England, alone.

She carried the kitten up to the landing outside her apartment. Below her, Hampton's Ocean Boulevard was already awake and bustling. Salt and sand seasoned the breeze blowing in off the water. Motels, restaurants, food counters, and seaside souvenir shops lined the sidewalk of the boulevard as far as she could see before the coastline curved eastward at Rocky Bend. She smoothed out the cat's long tail while her eye traced the farthest point where the year-round colony sat on the bluff.

Buck's Landing sat amongst all the tourist traps, three stories high and half a block wide in every direction. Her grandfather had designed the mini-golf course on a parcel of land acquired after a fire, turning the charred remains of a boarding house into his personal dream of summer vacation family fun. Her father had run the course as a young man, bringing his new wife to live in the apartment on the third floor, turning the ground floor into an ice-cream and soda counter. It had been her mother who suggested, after Grampa Buck passed away, that they convert his second floor dwelling to apartments: weekly rentals for summer vacationers, monthly rentals for UNH students in the off-season.

While Sofia watched, the beach filled in with umbrellas and tents. Half a dozen kites flew over the boardwalk. Vacationing families were using the new bathhouse at the State Park—far better than the old one, she thought with a shudder. Kids and gulls shrieked from the high tide line, and the scent of Coppertone drifted over the piped-in music on the course. The kitten rested contentedly in the crook of her arm.

"You like it here, don't you?" She stroked one silky, steel gray ear. "You don't know that there's a whole world beyond this tacky town, a whole universe outside of New England."

The kitten's pleasant rumble was disturbed by the buzzing in her pocket. With her free hand, she fished out her phone. "Sofia Buck."

The tenants in 2B had clogged the toilet again. "I'll be right down."

Pocketing her phone, she shifted the small bundle on her arm. He blinked sleepily, stretching his skinny legs and flexing his fuzzy, half-dollar coin-sized paws.

"You're going to have to stay here alone for a few minutes. Can you do that?" Her companion yawned.

Sofia took him inside and carried him down the short hall, past the tiny bathroom and her parents' bedroom, to her childhood sanctuary. She focused on finding a pair of khaki shorts and a Buck's Landing polo, her glance coasting over the photos her father had set on the dresser sometime in the years between her departure and his death. There was a kind of madness in nostalgia, and Hampton Beach was not going to be her asylum.

Her guest began to knead the bedspread, and Sofia scooped him up. The kitten squeaked in protest. "No way, little man. This is the people bed, not the cat bed." She shut the bedroom door firmly behind her.

Plopping him down on the sofa, she headed for the utility closet. She grabbed a pair of long rubber gloves, a bucket, mop, and plunger. Giving the kitten a stern look, she said, "Be good."

She jogged down the stairs to the second of the two rental apartments that made up the second floor. This week, a family from upstate New York had 2B. During their brief exchange on Saturday afternoon, the mother had fretted over her.

"I'm so sorry to hear about your Dad, honey. He was such a nice man. Nick and I have been renting this place since before we got married. He was part of our vacation tradition."

Sofia had murmured the correct responses before showing them a few of the updates she'd arranged for over the past few weeks, including wireless internet. If she was going to be trapped in this place, she was at least going to be able to access the rest of the world from her laptop.

Pinning on her brightest smile, she knocked on the door. The mother opened the door. Her small child, a kindergartener named after a character from a movie—Trinity?—peered out from behind her legs.

"Hey, Sophie." The mother pushed a mop of sweaty curls from her forehead. "We're just heading across to the beach. Thanks for taking care of this."

Sofia swallowed the name correction that surfaced on her tongue. "Have fun. The waves are up this morning."

Thankfully, the toilet was only clogged with an abundance of quilted toilet paper. As she worked the plunger, she wondered what the fascination was with little kids and toilet paper rolls. Sofia cleaned up behind herself and locked the unit. She stowed the supplies back in her apartment, washed her hands, and poured herself a cup of coffee. Leaning on the counter to write up a to-do list, she ticked off her duties for the day.

The water in the fountain shared by the fourth and fifteenth holes was looking brackish, and she was running low on paper goods. Buck's Landing wasn't enough in the black to warrant a delivery service, which meant she'd be trucking over to Manchester for provisions and to stop at the pool supply place. And, at some point, she was going to have to call someone about the kitten.

She stood upright so quickly she nearly rapped her head on the upper cabinets. The kitten!

Her gaze flicked to the sofa, where a slight depression in her mother's once-favorite throw pillow was the only evidence of the feline adventurer's existence. She clicked her tongue and kissed the air in her apartment, willing the gray ball of fluff to appear from beneath some piece of furniture.

For twenty minutes she scoured her apartment for him, but the kitten was nowhere to be found. She was impressed. It was essentially a four room home. Her bedroom, the cramped-but-functional bathroom, her parents' bedroom, and the living space, with a single line of counter-tops and cabinets along one wall to hold the kitchen appliances. The dining table served as a visual separator for the room. When her efforts proved fruitless, she upped the ante. But a saucer of half-and-half and a bowl of chunk light tuna didn't coax the little monster out either. It wasn't until she went to the outside landing that she realized where he was.

The ghost of a smile played over her lips at the sight. Her furry friend had scaled another miniature landmark on the course. Not just any landmark, but the twelve-foot replica Easter Island head at the seventeenth hole.

Down again, out onto the course she went, grabbing the ladder from the utility room.

Amy spotted her coming. "He's awfully cute. Will you keep him?"

"I'm sure the little beast belongs to someone." Sofia propped the ladder against the statue and spoke to the three parties queued up at the tee. "Play through, folks. Amy will comp you all a soft-serve in the snack bar for your trouble." Amy herded everyone through while Sofia surveyed the head, looking for the best path to get to her little pal, who batted a passing white butterfly and mewed at her from his perch.

"Well, I know what I'm going to call you when I find you." Silas Wilde pushed up to standing, brushing a fine dusting of beach sand from his knees. He gave up hope that the little thing had only gone to ground under the sofa; he was fairly certain he was talking to an empty room. So far, the kitten his sister had given him at the beginning of the summer—a housewarming gift, or so Mallory claimed—

had escaped his apartment no less than ten times, this last time managing, Silas feared, to get out of the building altogether.

He made a cursory examination of the bathroom and efficiency kitchen before taking the back stairway down to the Atlantis Market, the convenience store and gift shop that was his new livelihood, half-hoping the kitten was playing with the mops and brooms in the hall-way. When his search disappointed him, he headed into the Market. His older sister's oldest son, Theo, looked up from the register. He was ringing up a big sale: two beach chairs, a soft-sided cooler, and a picnic's worth of bottled water, soda, and junk food.

Silas had developed a great affection for impulse beachgoers.

"Cat got out again," he said.

Theo laughed. "I've got everything taken care of."

Silas let himself out through the store's front door, leaving Theo to handle the morning beachcombers in search of a snow globe of the Casino Ballroom, a new pair of flip-flops, or aloe gel. "Hopefully, I won't be gone more than a half hour. I've got my phone."

Silas had traced the New England coast north from New York City six months earlier, abandoning Interstate 95 in Boston to weave a northbound route along route 1 and 1A, in a Jeep Wrangler he'd bought from the Want Ads. A thousand times, his breath was stolen by the pewter sea and the rocky shoreline, peppered with stretches of coarse sand beaches and faded boardwalks, but something about Hampton Beach called to him. Following the tug, he'd checked into a motel a block inland, one of the few open in the frigid winter months, and fallen asleep to the north wind wailing over the snowy beach.

He'd thought Ocean Boulevard had stolen his heart in January, abandoned and near silent, save for some hardy year-round dwellers and a handful of businesses that defied the off-season. As he looked out over the summer expanse of state beach, pristine and already baking under a ninety-degree sun, the music of tourism and the magic of vacation coursed through him like the first swallow of a cold beer.

Had he still been in New York, sweltering in his Brooklyn walkup or hunched over his desk in the maze of cubicles on the litigation floor at Stern & Lowe, he might never have known the heady mix of kitsch and tradition that was Hampton. Owning a convenience store in a summer town was a good, long way from the document review sweatshop of corporate law.

Not even ten in the morning, and his worn R.E.M. tour tee-shirt was stuck to the small of his back. A bead of sweat rolled down his face, and he wiped it with the hem of the shirt. A gaggle of teenage girls wandered by in bikinis, and one of them turned to give him a sassy grin, her eyes lingering over the flat expanse of his stomach. Silas watched them pass, doing his best not to appreciate the view too much.

He walked the perimeter of his building, examining a patch of newer cedar shingles, not yet weathered silver, while he looked for the cat. The previous owner had taken care of the Atlantis, even if his taste in interior decorating was a blend of seventies aesthetic and thrift store pragmatism. Silas called to the kitten with the whistle and click combination he'd found seemed to attract the small adventurer.

It wasn't long before he heard the meow from over the fence. The kitten was small, but he had lungs and feet worth watching. Following the cries, he arrived at the gate of Buck's Landing. His next door neighbor's building was taller, casting his apartment into welcome shade for most of the day. The owner, Jimmy Buck, had passed away about a month ago, leaving the whole property to his estranged daughter.

The jury was still out on the new Buck at the Landing, as far as Silas was concerned. She'd breezed into town in a slick BMW sedan, holed up in her late father's apartment, and kept mostly to herself. He'd only seen her once in the three weeks she'd been in residence; she'd been hauling a huge suitcase out of the trunk of that Beamer. She had refused his friendly offer of help, called down over the railing from the porch roof that served as his deck. He'd watched Jimmy's daughter drag that luggage up the two flights of narrow exterior stairs to the apartment with equal parts amusement and distaste.

Silas recognized the young woman working the register at Buck's. Amy had pounded pavement before the last frost looking for a summer job, even coming into the Atlantis Market to see if he was hiring. Turning her down had been tough, so he'd been glad to hear Jimmy had hired her on for the summer. Later in the spring when he'd run the numbers and knew he could afford a part-timer, he'd hired his nephew Theo at his sister's insistence. Mallory was a persistent woman.

"Amy." He smiled. She was reading one of those creased and worn steamy beach novels that passed from rental to rental. He imagined this one had been up and down the strip. Amy stashed the novel under the counter.

"Mr. Wilde. Can I help you?"

"I'm wondering if you've seen a kitten around the place this morning."

Amy lit up like the Funarama on a Saturday night. "Seventeenth hole. He's a troublemaker, huh?"

"You could say that. Thinking of calling him Houdini." He peered around the building towards the course. "Seventeen, you said?"

"Go on through, Mr. Wilde."

Silas couldn't help inspecting Jimmy Buck's Astroturf and the gravel paths that wound between the holes as he walked. Jimmy had been a good neighbor in the few months they'd known one another. The older man had introduced himself immediately following the first evening Silas spent in the apartment over the Atlantis; Jimmy had turned up on the welcome mat with a pair of to-go coffees and a half-dozen box of donuts. They'd grown close before his passing. Jimmy had told him stories about his family, mainly centered on his daughter's childhood, and had often confided in Silas that he wished he had more time and resources to put into the endless maintenance the property required.

There were changes at Buck's Landing, Silas noted. He had to admit, they were for the better. The paths were weeded, their gravel leveled. The turf and obstacles had been cleaned, and the greens patched in the worn spots. The music Jimmy had favored leaned toward classic country and western, so much so that Silas considered loaning the man his collection of Police and U2 CDs. Today he appreciated the thump of bass and electronic warble of Auto-Tune. The younger Buck knew what the kids listened to, anyway.

He heard Jimmy's daughter before she came into view. Unlike the overproduced pop-princess voice on the sound system, hers was a smoky voice that belonged in a speakeasy.

He rounded the corner at the sixteenth hole and burst out laughing. There was Houdini, surveying his kingdom from the top of the Easter Island head, his posture comically regal. The cat watched his would-be rescuer hoist herself from a short ladder by using the statue's left shoulder as a foothold.

"Come on, sweetheart," she cajoled, that bourbon voice pitched low. With an arm wrapped around the statue's head, she swung her leg over it, braced her other foot against its chest, and reached up for his cat.

Silas closed the distance between them and pushed his hair back with his sunglasses, the better to get an eye full of Jimmy Buck's mini-golf heiress. Silas took in the khaki shorts stretched across a toned rear and the strong, tanned legs, and briefly envied the statue, with his cement face pressed against that body.

"That's one lucky statue," he said with a chuckle. "I see you found my cat."

———

Arrogant bastard. Sofia's cheeks went hot at the thought of how she looked, clinging to the impassive face of the golf course obstacle. There was a click and whistle from the man, and the kitten flicked its ears. With a flash of gray fur and a scrabble of little nails, he streaked down from the monolith.

"I think his name is Houdini," the man laughed.

Sofia couldn't tell if he was laughing at his own joke, at the cat's name, or at her predicament.

She swung her leg towards the ladder. When she'd taken a leave from her position as the event planner for the DeVarona hotel in Washington, DC to return to Hampton Beach and sort out her father's property, she'd expected a hot, miserable summer of tourists in cheap tee-shirts spilling ice cream all over the run-down course. She hadn't been prepared for the changes to the old boulevard and the changes to Buck's Landing. She hadn't been prepared to get caught halfway up a Polynesian deity's face by her surfer-boy next door neighbor, but she was accustomed to damage control. She could face some local guy who'd lost his cat. When her foot missed and kicked the ladder instead of landing on a rung, she swore roundly and hung on to the cement.

To her horror, a pair of male hands steadied her, holding the backs of her thighs. The cheery conversations from the parties playing the course were gone, replaced by giggles and whispering.

"Easy now. I've got you." Her rescuer grasped her waist and lowered her to the turf. She sucked in a breath. It wouldn't do to fly off the handle in front of paying customers. Spinning around, she got a good look at her next door neighbor.

"You must be Jimmy's daughter," he said. The little gray cat sat on his broad shoulder like a pirate's parrot, delicately grooming one of his white-stockinged paws. "Thanks for helping out this little trouble-maker. I'm Silas Wilde, your—"

"Next door neighbor, yes." She leveled him with her coolest managerial look and held out a hand. "Sofia Buck." His hands were big, she thought, watching hers disappear into his grip. And warm. His smile wrinkled his eyes, but she judged him to be near her age. From his shoulder, the kitten offered her his freshly groomed foot. His serious, whiskered expression charmed. "And you're Houdini."

Silas reached up and plucked the cat off his shoulder. "He's new, still getting the hang of being neighborly."

"I'd suggest locking your door, but he got out of my locked apartment earlier." She flicked an eyebrow at the pair. The gray kitten fit in his hand like a toy. "He's already been up the tree at hole twelve this morning."

Silas laughed, taking the measure of the so-called tree. Turning the kitten around to face him, he went nose-to-nose with his feline.

"No more causing trouble for Ms. Buck. Though she does look fantastic stretched out on the moai."

Sofia snorted. "I am standing right here."

Silas turned his gaze on her. His eyes were the exact cool blue-gray of the Atlantic and his messy, honey-colored waves, pushed away from his face by a pair of sport sunglasses, were streaked summery blond. She felt his appraisal sweep over her. "So you are."

"Excuse me?" A barrel-chested man in a Red Sox tee-shirt was tapping his putter on the gravel. "Can we play?"

Sofia suppressed a grin as the sunburnt woman at his side smacked his upper arm and shushed him under her breath. "Please. I was just clearing up a hazard on the hole." She turned to Silas. "Mr. Wilde?"

"Silas." He stepped off the turf, Houdini settled in the crook of his arm. "And I've got to get back to the store."

Sofia flashed a smile at the golfers. "Enjoy your game."

She followed Silas's retreating form toward the gate, indulging in the fantastic view of his ass in hibiscus patterned surf shorts. When he stopped short, she very nearly crashed into him.

"Sofia," he said. "Let Houdini and I buy you a drink tonight."

She blinked. "No." Her manners surfaced. "Thank you, but no."

He scratched the cat's chin. "You've made the lady angry, you monster." His gaze was warm when he turned to her. "Another time, then."

A note and thanks

Ambitious Heart first appeared in the Love Kissed Books anthology, *Love In A Small Town*. Many thanks to Nicole Andrews Moore and the Love Kissed Coachables for the opportunity and the push to get it done.

Thanks to Mandy Dawson and Angela Amman for not slapping me silly (from a safe social distance) when I decided to write both AH and its sequel, *Unbound Heart*, over two months during the long autumn of 2020. They were inevitably dragged along for the ride, and handled it like only sisters-of-the-heart could.

Familiar Heart followed at a less rigorous pace, but that doesn't mean it was easier to get right. Thank you, friends and readers, for spending your time in Blueberry Hill.

If you enjoyed your visit, reviews on Goodreads, Amazon, Bookbub, or anywhere else you talk up your favorite books, are always appreciated. Reviews are to authors as applause is to Tinker Bell.

About the Publisher

Bannerwing Books is a writers' co-op founded in 2012 by Cameron D. Garriepy, and completed by Angela Amman and Mandy Dawson. Currently residing on Slack, somewhere in the ether between Boston, Detroit, and Paso Robles, Bannerwing also presents works by Stephanie Ayers, Ericka Clay, and Liz Zimmers, as well as collections featuring Andra Watkins, Kate Shrewsday, and Kameko Murakami.

www.bannerwingbooks.com

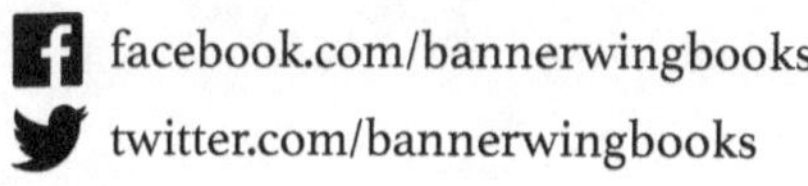

facebook.com/bannerwingbooks

twitter.com/bannerwingbooks